Emylia Hall was born in 1978 and grew up in the Devon countryside, the daughter of an English artist and a Hungarian quiltmaker. After studying English and Related Literature at the universities of York and Lausanne, she spent five years working in a London ad agency, before moving to the French Alps. It was there that she began to write. Emylia now lives in Bristol with her husband, the comic-book writer and children's author Robin Etherington, and young son. She is the author of *The Book of Summers*, which was a Richard & Judy Summer Book club pick in 2012, *A Heart Bent Out of Shape* and *The Sea Between Us*.

Praise for Emylia Hall:

'*The Sea Between Us* is that rare beast – a beautifully written, intricately observed love story that's both lyrical and enchanting. The story ebbs and flows like the Cornish coast as love is gained, lost and gained again. This is a novel that deserves to be savoured' Hannah Beckerman, author of *The Dead Wife's Handbook*

'A perfect summer read. A book as magical as its Rockabilly Cove, as Jago and Robyn's tantalising, teasing journey' Tiffany Murray, author of *Diamond Star Halo* and *Sugar Hall*

'Luscious tastes of Cornwall wrapped in yearning, loss, regret and love . . . wonderful' Liz Fenwick

'A compelling coming-of-age story with a superb twist' *Easy Living*

'A delicate, atmospheric, regretful tale, but full of redemption too. I absolutely loved it' Richard Madeley

'A novel that glints with passion, loss and doubt' *Marie Claire*

'Highly evocative and a joy to read' *Sunday Express*

'As tender and insightful as it is gripping. The novel speaks of life's

writer' Susan Fletch

'Fantastically evocative and sun-drenched with a twist' *Stylist*

'We were utterly blown away by this novel. Vivid and heart-breaking in equal measure' *Novelicious*

'Haunting and full of vivid prose . . . a novel to be devoured in a couple of sittings' *Lady*

'A lovely story of a mother's love and shattered dreams' Judy Finnigan

'A stunning debut novel' *Sun*

'[A] vivid coming-of-age story' *Woman & Home*

'Beautifully nuanced' *Spectator*

'A poignant coming-of-age story of first love, desire, friendship, tragedy, grief, and self-discovery, in a stunning location' We Love This Book

'A thriller, coming-of-age story and love letter to Switzerland, all in one' *Good Housekeeping*

'The writing is so pretty you'll fall in love with the setting . . . We guarantee you'll be saving up your pennies and catching a flight to Switzerland before you're halfway through' *Heat* Magazine

'A touching coming-of-age story' *Image* Magazine

'Further proof of Emylia Hall's natural talent at story-telling, *A Heart Bent out of Shape* is a fantastic second novel. Poignant, captiving and beautifully written' The Unlikely Bookworm

'Emylia Hall creates an enchanting and vivid picture of Beth's summers in rural Hungary . . . an addictive read' *Cosmopolitan*

'Heartfelt and evocative' *Grazia*

'[An] emotive novel not to be missed' *Star* Magazine

'Hall confirms her talent for romantic but original prose' *Big Issue*

The Sea Between Us

Emylia HALL

headline
review

First published in Great Britain in 2015 by HEADLINE REVIEW
An imprint of HEADLINE PUBLISHING GROUP

First published in paperback in 2015 by Headline Review

1

Cataloguing in Publication Data is available from the British Library

ISBN 978 1 4722 1197 2

Typeset in Sabon by Avon DataSet Ltd,
Bidford-on-Avon, Warwickshire

Printed and bound in Great Britain by Clays Ltd, St Ives plc

HEADLINE PUBLISHING GROUP
An Hachette UK Company
Carmelite House
50 Victoria Embankment
London EC4Y 0DZ

www.headline.co.uk
www.hachette.co.uk

For Bobby and CJ

Live in the sunshine, swim the sea,
Drink the wild air's salubrity

Ralph Waldo Emerson

prologue

Jago, New Mexico, the present

JAGO HEARD THE HORSES BEFORE HE HEARD THE FIRE. HE WAS asleep, the sheet kicked to the foot of the bed, when something woke him. Night fell deeply here; it came down from the mountains, sweeping across the desert floor in a torrent of black. Perhaps a volley of coyote barks came with it, the rapid chattering of cicadas, but no big-city clatter of sirens and shouts, no spinning wheels or blasts of somebody else's music. It was a dark blanket that didn't lift until the pink light of dawn.

Jago's eyes snapped open and he lay still, listening. An inexplicable but quite precise sense of disquiet took over. Then a piercing whistle sounded; the warning call of a young stallion. He swung his legs over the side of the bed and moved quickly to the door. Out on the veranda his bare feet slapped against the wood. The night air was thick with heat, and a broiling wind was blowing fast. He turned his head and inhaled. Ash. Its unmistakable tang caught in the back of his throat. He scanned the skies, fear climbing in his chest, and saw a neon-tinged bank of smoke rolling in from the west. Then he heard the sounds of dry brush catching. The splintering of cacti. The relentless gobble of wildfire.

He dashed back inside and pulled on his boots, wrestled one arm into a shirt. Then he ran. There was no one to wake in the main house. Annie was at her cousin's wedding in Phoenix; at this hour she'd be asleep, her breath cocktail-sweet, her crumpled dress discarded on the floor. Pico was with his ailing father in Albuquerque. It was only Jago at the ranch. Seventeen horses, each with a name and a story, dotted across two hundred acres of pasture, and a blaze that was running on the wind. He heard their cries in fullness now, an overlapping sequence of shrill whistles, undercut by startled cries and restless hoof beats.

The only thing to do was to run towards them.

Robyn, Cornwall, *the present*

Merrin was Jago's patch long before it became hers too. Even now that he was gone, he was still everywhere. He was in the rust-brown bracken and the switchback lanes. He was at the cove she called Rockabilly, in the perfect peelers and the expanse of blue, of grey, of green, of blue again. He was in the meadow grass and the onshore gusts. And he was in her studio too.

On the tabletop, between her pots of brushes, Robyn kept a scattering of treasures, once glistening objects that were now paper-dry. Sand-dusted seashells, a handful of pebbles as smooth and round as toffees, the immaculate lightness of a cuttlebone. She would sit and work, splash paint and pencil lines, her fingers playing over these small relics, looking for the comfort of memory. It was only when she found it – the look in his water-blue eyes as he lay beside her on the beach, the slant of his smile as he cradled his mum's guitar – that she realised such glimpses weren't enough after all. Not when he was still out there somewhere, in flesh and blood, walking on ground that wasn't Merrin, talking to people who weren't her, living a life that would always be connected but was, in the end, quite separate. Then her eyes would rove to the window. She'd look and look, as though trying to see all the way across the Atlantic Ocean. She'd fix on the horizon and will it to have some feature and definition, the slightest rise of cliff, the spindliest stem of a lighthouse: something to make the shoreline seem closer, anything to make Jago seem less far away.

Spindrift

The arresting sight of offshore winds throwing
spray from cresting waves, white horses
racing into the beach.

one

Seven years earlier

THE PATH TO THE COVE WAS STEEP AND UNEVEN, PITCHING tunnel-like between rhododendrons and drapes of ivy. Robyn trod carefully, slowed by her unwieldy cargo. In the hire shop the board had looked light, a sleek blaze of blue and yellow. Now, as she lugged it along by its nose, its tail bumping behind her, she felt as though she was revealing herself as a novice before she'd even hit the water. Her wetsuit seemed to cling in all the wrong places, tight at the rear and baggy at the front, the zip catching at her chin. She was glad that she'd come on her own, and that instead of begging a lift to the tourist beach, with its sweeps of pale sand and smooth-rolling sets, she'd chosen Rockabilly as her first surf spot.

She'd discovered the cove on her second day in Cornwall, three weeks ago, and had quickly taken it for her own. It had been her parents' dream to move to the far west, not hers. As a family the Swintons were suburban by nature, landlocked and soft, but they, like so many before them, had heeded the call of the sea. Even when they'd lived on a street of neatly paved driveways and well-tended shrubbery, the walls of their sitting room had always been decorated with seascapes, not mild nursery-style friezes but turbulent oceans, vigorous slaps of paint on canvas that had unnerved and excited a small Robyn with equal measure.

Over the years, Marilyn and Simon Swinton had offered variations on the same refrain: *One day we'll buy a house on a cliff without a neighbour in sight, wake up each day tasting sea salt, go to sleep to the sound of the waves.* Robyn had always liked their neighbours. She couldn't imagine hearing the ocean's roar instead of the tinkling of next door's radio, or seeing a bare expanse of clifftop instead of the whitewashed fences that separated their gardens at neat intervals. Ben, her older brother, had left home a long time ago, and was therefore spared these Cornish plans. Robyn, thirteen years his junior, was the late child, the accident, a presence that was met with shock horror, then rueful smiles. Her place in the household was a lot like the cat's: confident in her belonging, but under no illusion that her family's life revolved solely around her. *Robyn's always been independent*, her dad was fond of saying, as though it was an accomplishment rather than a necessity.

From the house, their home now, she supposed, the path was the quickest way to the water. It took seven minutes by fleet foot, double that and more with a weighty load. The cove probably had its own name, the kind that appeared on maps or rolled from the tongues of locals, but on the day she discovered it, Robyn had called it Rockabilly. Roughly carved cliffs surrounded the water, and a jagged trail of rocks ran out at either side of the crescent-shaped cove. The last rock on the left stood tall and implausibly curved, a poser's quiff.

The first time she found herself at Rockabilly, Robyn had climbed all the way out to the granite stack. She clung to the rough face, all her fingers and toes stretching and pointing. The wind whistled, the sea swelled at her feet, and she hung on for a count of ten. Then she picked her way back, her heart bumping in her chest. It had been her own small initiation, and as she sat on the clifftop, watching the tide retreat, she'd been rewarded. A beach had appeared. It was pitted with pebbles and strewn with weed, a meagre strip compared to other places, but there was something magical about seeing a slip of sand when least expected. She watched the dark surface burn golden in the sun, then clambered down, trailing the first footprints across its unbroken sheen.

The surfing idea had come later. The Swintons had arrived in the fullness of holiday season, when the lanes were jammed with cars and the beaches were a patchwork of towels and striped windbreaks. Robyn's parents walked among the tourist crowd with the air of gentry doing their rounds about the estate, casting benevolent smiles. Robyn slipped their company, searching for people who looked as though they really lived here. At Sennen she'd spotted a trio of girl surfers. They had whip-thin waists and muscled arms, sun-freckled faces and easy laughter. She'd watched them running towards the water, their weightless boards tucked under their arms. They'd paddled into the swell, then came the moment when they'd popped up, one, two, three, catching waves in quick succession, whooping with glee. Later, she'd seen them changing by their battered car as music pealed from the open windows, stepping out of bikini bottoms, pulling on jumpers, deft and unbothered. Robyn had approached with a studied casualness, one hand fiddling with the ends of her hair. She'd asked if they were local, and they'd shaken their heads and grinned: *We wish*, they'd said. As she watched them drive away, she wondered if she would ever make Cornish friends like that, or if she'd learn to do the things they did. When the summer crowds left, before September faded and university loomed, she resolved to go to Rockabilly and try surfing for herself.

Now she staggered out from the undergrowth and took uneven steps in the sand. She let her board drop, and stood for a moment with her hands on her hips, her elbows crooked, breathing deeply. She took it all in. The water was deep blue where it met the sky. Snow-topped rollers exploded in a fizzle on the beach, leaving a lacy trail of shells in their wake. She felt a prickle of anticipation, hotly followed by a rush of nerves. She yanked at the high neck of her wetsuit. She was glad again that there was no one there to watch.

Jago saw her stumble on to the sand, the end of her board still caught in the brambles. He hadn't set out to follow her, but he was out walking Scout and he'd seen her cut across their bottom field and slip into the thicket that led to the water. Even as she struggled with her board, her stride had purpose. Jago looped the long way round to the cove. His cove. The cove that grockles never usually found. His dog followed at his heels, nose in the air, as if sensing a change in the wind.

He'd seen the girl for the first time three weeks ago, and several times after that. Maybe that was how the world divided, into the watchers and the watched. He'd been there the day she'd moved in. She'd climbed out of the car and thrown her arms in the air, yawning and stretching. Her T-shirt had ridden up, and he'd caught a brief flash of swan-pale skin. She'd trailed after her parents into the house, and he'd heard them exclaiming, delighted and giddy. He knew the place a little: it had slate floors and wide windows and a fireplace as big as a room; they were right to like it. She'd ducked her head to go inside, because the doorways were low and she was tall. *Willowy*. She was the first girl he ever saw that made sense of that word. Everything about her was long and fine; her hair was white-blond and ran past her shoulders.

Later, as the lane filled with removal vans and sofas and hat stands, and box after box was carried inside, he'd seen her face appear at an upstairs window. She'd thrown it open, taken a gulp of salt air and watched the view. He'd wished for her a glimpse of the slick head of a seal playing in the bay, or the flash of a tall ship's sail; any number of small wonders. But she seemed pleased with what she saw regardless, and he observed the slide of her smile. She left the window open and disappeared back into the house.

On the beach she wore her wetsuit back to front, the zip coursing up her middle, the fabric bunching at her belly. He bit down a grin. He watched her throw down her board and stare at the sea. He wondered then if she'd even make it to the water. The woodland path wasn't the easiest descent; that was why the cove never had too many visitors. With a surfboard, especially the giant banana of a thing that she'd kitted herself out with, it would have been particularly tricky. He sat back on his heels, wondering what she'd do next. He watched as she once more took a hold of the board, and walked down towards the water dragging it behind her, her leash unwound, trailing eight feet or more of cumbersome wake. Then she burst forward with sudden decision, and pitched down on to the board with easy grace. For all her appearances, perhaps it wasn't her first time after all; ragamuffin style on land, turning to magic in the water. Perhaps. He rolled on to his stomach and watched as she paddled out.

Robyn took a mouthful of salt water as the messy end of a wave splashed into her face. She bent her head and forged on, her teeth gritted. The zip of her wetsuit was digging in. There would be a track-mark later, cleaving her in two, her first battle scar, and a feeble one at that. Beneath her the board bobbed and skittered but she managed to find a loose rhythm, riding up over the waves, squinting into the spray. The sea stretched ahead, the sun turning the surface silver. Far away at the horizon, all looked serene and lovely, but as her board edged out level with the cove's edge, she saw the wild water hurling at the rocks. The Rockabilly quiff was her marker. She stopped paddling as she reached it, and her hands gripped the edges of her board. With effort she swung round so she was pointing back towards the beach. She kicked her legs beneath the water, and stretched out to touch the tip. Everything looked different. The cove appeared smaller, the cliffs seemed to slope gently, the tangle of woodland that ran behind looked as mild as a cottage garden. A sprightly breeze pulled at her hair.

She'd paddled further out than Jago would have guessed. He rested his chin in the palm of his hand, watching her, as behind him Scout nosed about in the grass. Jago had never surfed himself; he preferred the water's edge: fishing, beachcombing, walking his dog along the shore. He'd lost a grandad to the North Sea, his boat chewed up by rocks on a storm-lashed night. His dad, then still a small boy, had grown up fatherless and wary. Perhaps something of his dad had passed to him: an innate sense of the sea's ambivalence towards all living things except its own wild self. When too many pints of dark ale sloshed around inside him, Denny Winters grew maudlin, said that it was the unhappy fate of their family to lose the people that mattered. *We can't hold on, Jago, that's us, that's our lot, and we'd better live with it.* But Jago knew that it wasn't for lack of trying. He'd seen his dad at the hospital in Penzance, his large frame folded into a rickety chair as he hunched over the broken body of Jago's mum. His fingers were twined with hers, fixed as limpets, and he'd carried on talking, whispering and murmuring, long after all the machines had stopped.

Jago's attention was drawn back to the water as he heard the girl emit a wild cry. She'd dropped to her belly, like a strange seabird lifting on its wings. He saw her paddle furiously as the wave rushed up on her, catching her, scooping her up as though she was nothing. He realised he was holding his breath. For a moment she looked as though she might hang on, but then he saw her board disappear from under her. It sprang from the water, a fat missile popping from the surf. There seemed to be a moment of unlikely pause, the board in the air, the girl in the waves beneath, then it came crashing down and she went with it. Jago jumped up, his fingers flexing. Out on the water the board bobbed innocently, pulled this way and that by the roll of the water. The girl still hadn't surfaced. He ran.

Robyn was smacked full in the face. She felt the crash of the ocean floor. A rock grazed her elbow and she flailed, reaching for it, her legs kicking frantically. A tremendous force took hold of her and yanked her back up towards the surface. There was the briefest flash of bright light, and she gasped, her mouth gaping like a fish, then down she went again, the current dragging her, holding her under. As her arms pumped and her hair streamed, she had no sense of which way was up. She felt the slap of sand again, the crunch of pebbles between her toes, before she was spun once more. For all the disorientation, she was sharply aware of physical sensations. Her nose stung, her ears roared, her mouth was full of iron. There was fire in her lungs and a burning in her throat. She opened her eyes and saw stars. Then black. Even if there was someone to see her, she couldn't throw up a hand to wave. Even if there was someone to hear her, she had no voice to cry out with. A terrifying sense of inevitability threatened to take hold of her. She kicked, thrashed, fighting the sea's grip.

When the hands came, they were as if from nowhere. She felt the firm touch of someone's fingers, and the press of a body close to hers. At first she fought this too, then she fell limp, submitting, sure that whatever was happening now, it had to be better. Slowly, steadily, she found herself moving back towards the light.

Jago burst through the surface with Robyn in his arms. He sucked in air, stars dancing at the corner of his vision. Her board was swaying on the swell, and he moved them haltingly towards it. She'd wound herself around him, and he swam awkwardly, with just one arm, one leg. His hand slipped as he grabbed hold of the board's edge, and they dipped below the water again. He wouldn't lose her now, not when he'd fought to find her, seeing first her shadowy shape, then feeling the kick of her foot across his knee, the running of her hair between his fingers. He'd pulled her from her spin and held on, pushing back towards the surface with grim defiance. Now he spat salt and gripped the board again, his eyes stinging with tears. He lifted her from the water and laid her gently down. Her eyes stayed tight shut, but her lips were moving, one hand still clinging to him. He clambered up himself, groaning with effort, and settled on the board behind her. His body held hers in place, his head just lifted from the small of her back. His hands were shaking, the insides of his wrists marked with the print of her nails, a string of half-moons. Beneath him she was still, her cheek flat against the surface of the board, but he heard her cough, and cough again. He fell to paddling, working slowly, rhythmically, all of his muscles burning.

By the time the board's nose hit the beach, he was spent. They rocked in the shallows, all but grounded, neither one moving. She shifted first, twitching beneath him, and he rolled off, his cheeks flame-red. She coughed up a mouthful of salt water, and he picked a length of seaweed from her hair. They looked at one another properly for the first time. Her eyes were grass green, startling in their brightness. There wasn't any fear in them, nor relief, nor any of the things he might have expected to see.

In Robyn's chest her heart bumped madly, her breath still not settled. Her nose stung, and was clotted with blood. But as she stared at him, she could only marvel at how this unknown person had made himself so essential.

'You saved me,' she said, her voice a crackle. 'Without you . . .'

'You'd have been okay,' said Jago.

As the words left his lips he wanted to reel them back, to say something different; anything except the assertion that this girl, whoever she was, could survive very well without him.

two

BEFORE THE LAND RAN OUT AND THE SEA ROLLED ON, THERE was Merrin. In this small place, a one-road squiggle on a map, the earth erupted in a lush tangle of ivy trails and creeper-filled woods. Mist-strung fields dotted with fat sheep and honey-coloured cows rubbed the edges of the moorland scrubs. The sea was everywhere.

The tourist buses missed Merrin as they spun down the lanes to Land's End or the gilded beaches of Sennen and Porthcurno, as did the walkers who tramped the coastal foot-paths. When the tide was right perhaps they'd catch a glimpse of the strip of beach at Robyn's Rockabilly, but from a great height they'd see a tumult of black rocks below them, a ceaseless swirl of water, and they'd pass on. They wouldn't think to turn inland, to weave over the fields to where two houses sat, separated by a bend in the lane, a triangle of meadow, a clutch of beech trees.

The two houses were quite unalike. A straggle of outbuildings marked Hooper's House as a farm, although it was a long time since it had been worked. It had grey stone walls and a pitching roof of uneven slate, and appeared as old as the earth itself. The other was as clean and bright as a cresting wave, and beaming with windows. Its name, White Sands, was as fanciful as the ideas of the people who came and went and came again. The far west wasn't quite like the rest of Cornwall. It had a wilder edge, scattered skies and rolling mists, and on the wrong day, at the wrong time, if you were in the wrong mood, a creeping sense of desolation. Then the rain tore from blackened clouds, the land was lost in fog, the taste of salt burned on the tongue and the sea bellowed; some wondered if they'd been right to try and make a holiday last a lifetime. The occupants of Hooper's House were used to seeing new neighbours at White Sands: every two or three years a new batch came and went.

'We meant to call round when you first moved in, but our manners aren't what they used to be.'

Denny Winters stood on the doorstep and Marilyn Swinton extended a cool, delicate hand while her other played with a string of sea-glass beads. She tipped her head, smiling. Her ash-blond hair, so pertly bobbed, barely moved.

'I'm Denny,' he said, 'and this is Jago, my boy. We're your closest neighbours by, well, several country miles.'

Robyn was watching from above. She'd heard the knock at the door just as she was passing the window on the landing, and had glanced down with curiosity. As she realised who it was, the ground beneath her feet had tipped. Now, as she listened, she pushed her hand to her mouth, trying to quell her rapid breathing. She hadn't seen him since Rockabilly, three days ago, because she'd had no idea where to find him. In her crouched position she repeated his name to herself. *Jago*. It was almost foreign-sounding, soft and hard all at once. *Jay-go*.

She supposed it was Cornish but, like everything else about him, she didn't really know.

The idea of him had been following her everywhere, with a combination of gratitude and confusion. You couldn't save someone and then just shrug it off, saunter back down the beach whistling for your dog. Again and again she'd tried to piece together the exactitudes of her watery fight, but it was blurred. The one thing she was sure of was that he, Jago, had made all the difference. If she closed her eyes she could still feel his hands on her, a touch so strong that she'd known she could stop thrashing and fighting and wondering, *Is this it?* It was only when they were back at the beach that she'd seen him clearly for the first time. And she'd been convinced then that it was *it* after all. Not the end, but the beginning of something. She'd watched him walk away, stepping round the tide, leaving footprints in the sand. And now he was standing at her door.

Her parents, usually effusive in meeting new people, had been lost in themselves since moving to Merrin, and Hooper's House, with its smeared panes and mud-lashed pickup, the piles of old timber in a ramshackle yard, hadn't prompted their usual sociability. *It's probably owned by some old-timer who dresses in newspaper*, her dad had said. *I'll drop in once we're settled, but I won't say a word about being a doctor or he'll have me looking at his bunions*, and her parents had fallen about laughing while Robyn rued the fact that her neighbours didn't hold better prospects. And now here she was, her nose pushed to the window, holding her breath as she looked down on Jago. Jay-go, Jaaaay-go, not yet a friend, but more than that, far more than that. He didn't look like someone who'd saved a life three days ago. But he didn't quite look ordinary either.

Her knees were starting to stiffen, so she shifted position. Jago lifted his head, glancing in her direction, and she shrank back. She heard her mum laugh. Robyn edged closer to look again. *We'd be delighted*, Marilyn said, hitting her stride now, both charmed and charming. It was why, her dad had always said, she made the perfect doctor's wife: she was a sweetener, as he remained brisk and businesslike in the face of all bodily woes. He was retired now, his days filled with gin and tonics and watercolour brushes. The latter was a new hobby, and although he was a poor artist, Robyn's mum encouraged him, watching with a smile as he worried paint against paper. *I enjoy seeing your father doing something badly*, she liked to say. *It makes such a nice change from him winning at everything.* He'd shown Robyn one of his seascapes once. *Awful thing, isn't it?* he'd said. *Terrible*, she agreed, and he beamed happily, as if being granted permission to be bad at something was the greatest indulgence a successful man could have.

'We'd love to have you over,' she heard her mum say. 'You really must come.'

Her parents were veteran throwers of dinner parties. Out came the silver bowls of salted nuts, popping corks, salad spoons, then their affected relief when their guests had gone, slipping into a two-step in the kitchen, exchanging knowing smiles. *Poor souls, dispatched into the night when we get to stay for ever* was her dad's favourite line, its end always swallowed by her mum's low laugh. Theirs was an exquisite party of two.

She moved closer to the window to catch Denny's reply. Would they come? Cross the field with a bottle of wine tucked under an arm, arrive with wet-toed shoes and windblown hair? Jago glanced up again, and this time Robyn wasn't quick enough. She smiled. Waved casually. Spun on her heel and pounded down the stairs.

'Ah, there you are, darling. I was just talking about you.'

Her mum drew her to her side. They stood on the front step, arms around each other's waists. Jago and his father stared back.

'You're Robyn,' said Denny.

She saw Jago's lips twitch involuntarily, as though he was trying the name for himself. Robyn. With hair now dry and back to barley-blond, her nose no longer bleeding red. *Robyn.* This so-small thing, a flicker of a lip, a trying-on of her name, pleased her. She popped on her toes.

'Hello,' she said.

Jago stepped forward then, proffered his hand.

'Nice to meet you,' he said.

She waited for him to add 'properly' or 'on dry ground' or just some acknowledgement of their first encounter. But he didn't. There was, however, the slightest shimmer in his eyes, a look that was not quite impassive. It was enough to wonder if she might just give him the postcard after all, even if what she'd written no longer made sense.

Robyn kept a box of art cards, and had been adding to it since she was about thirteen years old. Some she'd found in second-hand shops and these were battered at the corners and bore smudged postmarks; others were pristine, procured in galleries and gift shops, replicas of her favourite pieces: Van Gogh's star-lit pavement café, the simple, colourful cut-outs of Matisse. She knew that somewhere she had a Roy Lichtenstein. It showed an almost-kissing couple, their eyes closed, lips parted in naked desire, as bands of water swirled between them. There was some text, written in a comic-book style: *We rose up slowly,* that was how it began. The rest of the wording didn't matter. It was all about the picture. It was the undeniable currents that ran from man to woman, the shape made by their near-enough-touching lips. It was Robyn and Jago, it was how they'd met, it was everything that had happened; or how her dreams ran, anyway. She'd plucked it from her collection and written across its back: *I don't even know your name, but I owe you my life. How do I thank you for that? With a kiss? Robyn X.* Then she'd laughed, knowing she'd never give it to him, because she didn't know where to find him, and even if she did, he'd probably think it was stupid, and then she cried, because although there were very good reasons why the card should stay in the box, she really, really wanted him to have it.

'Nice to meet you too,' she said as she took his hand.

The day after what had happened at the cove, Jago had seen Robyn sunbathing on the ridge at the top of her garden, her blanket a flash of colour in the pale grass. She was wearing a scrap of a bikini and was propped on her elbows, lost in a book. Her foot, its underside as pale and smooth as a cuttlebone, was held to the sky, and kicked languidly back and forth. He'd felt the ache of desire run all the way through him. He could have gone to her then, but he didn't.

Now he stood mutely beside his dad, watching him fall into his routine of mild flirtation.

'Will it be just the two of you?' asked Marilyn.

'Yes,' said Denny. A hesitation, then a quick grin. 'It's just us boys at Hooper's.'

Robyn glanced at Jago, but he had his head dipped, and his hands were stuffed in his pockets.

'Well, we'll look forward to it immensely, won't we, Robyn? Come at eight, and don't bring a thing, just yourselves.'

Robyn watched them walk back down the driveway, conflicting currents at work in her mind. He'd been a figment and now here he was, being swept effortlessly into her parents' circle. She wished they could have met again on their own, at Rockabilly or in the sun-bitten fields. *Jago.* She said his name, turning it on her tongue, tasting it with relish and a bristling sense of possession. *We rose up slowly*, she thought, watching them as they turned into the lane and disappeared into the green tunnels.

three

'DO YOU THINK WE DID THE RIGHT THING MOVING DOWN HERE?'

Simon was kicked back in his chair, his fingers laced behind his head in a picture of contentment. The table was strewn with wine and water glasses, and the remnants of their meal. It had been a homely roast chicken, a sauce of tomatoes and olives, bowls of salad laced with unexpected items, a slice of apricot here, a clutch of capers there. Robyn knew it for a Swinton classic, a seemingly effortless kitchen supper. Her mum poured more wine as Denny considered her dad's question.

'Depends what you're after,' he said, rubbing his chin. His face was grazed with stubble, and in the candlelight his tan was darker, his eyes a bluer blue. He was handsome in a blunt way, Robyn thought, sun-blasted, rough-hewn. Beside him, Jago was built in his image, but a softer, lighter version. No deeply stitched crow's feet, no crackle of beard; rather his lips were pink and plump as a girl's, his eyelashes long and dark. 'For my money,' Denny said, 'this place is as beautiful as it gets.'

'What's your line of work?' asked Simon.

'Wood. Carpentry.'

23

'My father loved to work with his hands,' said Marilyn dreamily. 'He used to make us the most beautiful toys when we were children. Denny, what a wonderful profession.'

'I've tried teaching Jago, but mostly it's the other way around. He's got the feel for it. A finer touch than me, I reckon. It was a good day when he left college and joined the business.'

Robyn eyed Jago again across the table, and still he refused to meet her gaze. People didn't really take on their parents' occupations, did they? Not these days. *Winters and Son*. Spelled out in block capitals on the side of a white van, one that bumped along the Cornish lanes, never crossing the Tamar. *What a waste* were the words that came to mind.

'I always thought my son would follow me into medicine,' said Simon in a wistful tone, 'but it seems the siren song of radio production was more beguiling. There we have it. As for you, Robyn, with your art history degree, what you'll end up doing is quite the mystery.'

Robyn rolled her eyes good-humouredly. It was an old joke, and she knew her part in it. 'It's a mystery to me too, if it's any consolation,' she said.

'Have your family always been in Cornwall?' asked Marilyn, turning back to Denny.

'My family?' He gave a gruff laugh. 'No, not my family. We're from all over. I've been here, let's see . . .' he counted off on his fingers, 'moved here in '76. The bone-dry summer.'

'God, I remember that year,' said Marilyn. 'In London we were crazy with the heat. A whole city trapped, unable to breathe. I swam in the Serpentine and it was as warm as a bath.'

'When did you do that?' said Simon.

'When Ben was at school, when you were at the surgery,

when I was all alone and suffocating in the tremendous *heat*,'
she said, taking his hand in hers with playful drama. 'It was
unbearable.' She turned back to Denny. 'Ben's older than
Robyn, by more years than is sensible, probably. He flew our
little nest a lifetime ago.'

'Why did you come here then, Denny?' said Robyn. 'To
Merrin, I mean.'

His name felt strange to say out loud, overly familiar. She
felt the heat of Jago's stare and wondered if 'Mr Winters' would
have been better.

'A girl, of course,' he said with a smile.

'Isn't it always?' said Simon, refilling his glass.

They laughed, the three parents.

'Rosalind lived on this peninsula her whole life. She was
born here, and she died here too.'

'Oh, I'm sorry,' Marilyn and Simon murmured, their voices
overlapping. Denny raised one shoulder, a half-shrug, a quick
shake of the head.

'They all said that life would go on, and it has, I suppose,
hasn't it, mate?' Denny looked over at Jago. It seemed as though
he might reach out a hand, or draw him into the conversation
some other way, but he appeared to change his mind.

Robyn realised that she was holding her breath. She let it
out and a cough chased behind. She quickly reached for her
water glass, her cheeks burning.

'Oh, the candles!' cried Marilyn suddenly. 'I lit heaps of
candles on the patio; they could be setting the lawn on fire for
all I know. Robyn, could you go and check on them? You can
take dessert with you. Jago, why don't you go too?'

Robyn got up readily, grateful for the exit. Across the table,
Jago matched her. They made for the door at the same time.

Outside, the garden jumped with shadows. There were candles in ruby-red glasses, flaming torches set in sticks on the lawn, and a string of Chinese lanterns lifting in the breeze. The effect fell somewhere between magical and overblown. Beside her, Robyn heard Jago exhale deeply.

'It's over the top, isn't it? Mum can't help it, she decorates everything.'

'It's nice,' said Jago quietly.

Instead of dessert she'd grabbed an almost-full bottle of wine, no glasses. She held it up. 'Want some?'

Jago had turned, his head cocked. 'You used to that sound yet?'

'What, the sea? I've come to love it. It always seems louder at night.' Then, 'Shall we go down?'

'Down where?'

'To Rocka—' She stopped herself. 'To the cove.'

'It's pretty dark.'

'Oh, there's a moon somewhere,' she said, waving her hand, attempting blitheness. 'Hey, we can take one of these things.' She wrestled one of the lawn candles from the ground, and hoisted it like a beacon. Jago took another, spinning it in his hands, the flame dancing. 'I know the way,' she said, throwing him a smile.

'I'll show you a quicker one.'

'How do you know it's not the same?'

'I saw the path you took. With your board.'

It was the first time that either had mentioned that day.

'You were watching?' said Robyn.

'Not deliberately,' said Jago quickly.

'Lucky you were, though.' She paused, but he didn't say

anything. She shrugged. 'Okay then, show me your way.'

He set off and she followed him, the Lichtenstein card burning in the back pocket of her jeans. They walked through waist-high meadow grass, damp with night-time dew. She felt something bump against her leg; it felt like the warm body of an animal, and she cried out.

'Hey, boy, how did you get out?' said Jago. He'd stopped in front of her and was crouching down. He swivelled round, and in the half-light she could see him smiling up at her.

'It's okay, it's just Scout. Scout, meet Robyn. He was supposed to be in the barn. Heard our voices, I guess.'

She reached out a cautious hand and was met with the wet brush of an enthusiastic tongue. She resisted the urge to squeal again.

'He's a good boy,' said Jago. 'He won't hurt you.'

'I know,' said Robyn quickly. 'Hey, Scout.'

'He's half-human, to be honest. His mum died when the whole litter were still really small, so we took him before you normally would.'

Jago was thirteen when his mum came home with the puppy tucked inside her coat. She'd passed him into Jago's cupped hands, and he'd bent to kiss his pink nose, instantly loving this creature that looked more guinea pig than dog. That first night they'd wrapped him in a blanket and fed him from a bottle like a baby. They'd sat up round the clock, the fire slowly dying in the grate as the thin light of morning slipped through the just-closed curtains. Jago remembered his dad creaking down the stairs in his dressing gown, his hair standing on end; him and his mum turning saucer-wide eyes on him and holding their fingers to their lips: *Shhhh, he's sleeping*. And one day Scout had returned the favour, with immaculate animal intuition. On the blackest night, five years later, he'd slunk towards Jago, laid his head against his knee and looked up at him with deep blue eyes that seemed to say, *I know, I loved her too.*

'He won't go back on his own, not now he's found us,' said Jago. 'Come on then, fella, you lead the way.'

They slipped on to the path. Neither spoke as they walked, and the sound of the sea filled the silence. Its rumble grew closer and closer, until the hiss of spray could be heard too, the noise of water exploding on to the rocks. They emerged on to the cliff, higher than the route Robyn usually took. The cove lay below them. She took a deep breath, tasting salt and cool air. It was disorientating being there by night; it felt as though the ground might tilt at any given moment, the waves hurling higher and higher until they swept the clifftop. She had the urge to grab Jago's arm, to hang on to him.

'Want to sit? Rocks right here,' he said. He climbed up, and patted a space below him. 'Ringside seat.'

Robyn handed him her torch and clambered up to join him. Scout jumped up beside her and settled down, his head on his paws.

'See, he likes you,' Jago said.

She leant back against the rock. The flames threw jagged light, and they passed the wine back and forth. Their elbows were almost touching. His foot was just a scuff away from her own. She gulped the wine and thought how his proximity was far more intoxicating. She knew that if she held a hand to her cheek, it'd be burning.

'We didn't really need the torches, did we?' she said suddenly. 'You could have done that walk blindfolded.'

'Maybe so. I've never tried it.'

'But you've come here before? At night?'

'Not for a while.'

Robyn shifted round so that she was looking at him. Behind her, the sea rolled on.

'Before, why did you pretend we hadn't met? I mean yesterday, when you and your dad came round?'

He paused, then said, 'I didn't know if you'd told anyone about what happened.'

Afterwards, Robyn had slipped back into the house unseen. In the bathroom she'd peeled off her wetsuit. She'd run a shallow bath then lain in it, surrounding herself with honey scents and soft towels. Her head had rung, and her throat rasped. Her nose had stopped bleeding, but she'd still dabbed it delicately, feeling for more long-lasting damage. Slowly she'd begun to feel tough again. Reckless. A little brave. She'd run the water deeper. In the rising steam she'd closed her eyes and made sturdy resolutions.

'Actually, you're right, I didn't tell anyone anything,' she said. 'Mum and Dad would probably have tried to stop me going again if they knew.'

'And have you?'

'Not yet,' said Robyn, 'but I will. It's not like there's much else to do round here.' He didn't take the bait, so she pushed on. 'I mean, how do you not go crazy?'

'I was born here,' said Jago.

'Okay.'

'So it's home.'

'But isn't home boring? I mean, don't you want to get out and explore? To know what it's like to be somewhere else? Even to be some*body* else?'

'Be somebody else?'

'Okay, I don't mean that, just . . . to try on other lives. I guess that's what I mean. I want to see how other people live. I want to travel the world. As soon as I'm finished with university, I'm out of here. I want to have every possible adventure, so that when I'm an old woman I can kick back in a chair and say to myself, honestly, no regrets.'

'Then just think of living here as part of your research. Cornwall, then the world.'

'You're laughing at me,' she said, wondering why she was saying so much, rushing at him with everything she'd ever thought, as though if she didn't imprint him with enough of herself he'd forget all about her.

'And you're laughing at *me*,' he replied, knowing how dull he was making himself sound, how leaden and immobile, as beside him she dashed and glittered. He realised then that he wanted to know everything about her.

'So, what, you want to stay here for ever?' she said.

'I can't imagine being anywhere else. That's reason enough for me.'

'You can't actually mean *for ever*,' she said, her voice bounding with incredulity.

'Maybe not . . .' he began.

'A-ha!'

'Because there's no such thing, is there? But for the fore-seeable future, yes . . . I want to stay here. I want to work here. I'll probably grow old here. Die here too.' His voice was quicker and more defensive than he'd intended. He tried to remedy it. 'I'll end up as one of those old seadogs with a long beard and a pipe, barnacles on my boots. I can picture that. That wouldn't be too bad.'

'Cool. Okay. At least I know,' Robyn said. 'Wine?'

He took the bottle and their fingers briefly brushed. She

heard him drink, the soft sound of his swallow and a light rasp as he ran his hand across his mouth. He passed the bottle back and she drank slowly, her lips lingering where his had been.

'Art history, then,' he said. 'What made you choose that?'

'I loved drawing and painting at school. It was a better way to spend the afternoon than messing about with equations, or sweating over Bunsen burners.'

He smiled. Even in the dark she was colourful.

'But you didn't want to go to art school?'

'Well, when I was choosing A levels, I picked history of art instead of art. I guess I thought it was more . . . academic.'

'Right,' said Jago, with a touch of disdain, 'academic.'

'I know, I know. But you try growing up with my dad around. And anyway, I don't think I'd have been good enough for art college.'

'Says who?'

'Me. Everything I've ever tried to paint has just felt . . . I don't know. Like marks on paper. Maybe this sounds stupid, but . . . it's never felt alive. I think it has to feel alive. And I think you know when that happens, and you know when it doesn't.'

Jago thought of how he felt when he worked with wood. How the rhythmic back and forth of planing, of shaping, of sanding was as much a part of him as his heartbeat. But she was probably talking about complex explosions of paint on canvas, not coffee tables.

'My dad's the classic amateur,' she went on. 'He's taken up watercolours just because he's retired and moved down here, and you know what? He loves it, because it's just a hobby to him. And it must be great to feel like that, to be able to paint and not mind how it looks, or how it makes you feel. Talk about blissful ignorance. I couldn't be like that. If I painted, it'd be because painting was the only way to say what I wanted to say.'

As Robyn talked, she was quite still, inside and out. She didn't flap her hands, or fiddle with her hair; even in the dark he could tell that much. And she didn't punctuate her sentences with ums and ahs and other uncertain fillers. Jago felt as though he could listen to her all night. He asked her, tentatively, carefully, what she would paint, if the feeling were right.

'That's the whole point,' said Robyn. 'I wouldn't know until I *knew*, you know?'

What she really wanted to say was *Love, I'd paint love*, because if you made anything from the heart, a watercolour picture or a wall of bookcases, whatever the subject, whatever the form, wasn't it always about love? But she didn't. Maybe because she didn't trust herself not to follow it with something stupid. Instead she told him how she'd spent all summer looking forward to going back to university, and now that the time had almost come she wasn't so sure. He didn't take her hint; instead he stuck to geography, said he had no idea where Warwick was and she said *Not in Warwick, well the campus isn't*, and laughed.

'It's landlocked, Jago, not your style.'

'Maybe not yours either. You looked good on the board. Before you came off. Some people can't even get the paddling bit right.'

'You think? Are you a surfer?'

'Me? No. Too dangerous . . .'

'You're not serious?'

'I'm a coward.'

'But you were amazing in the water. You were . . .'

'Scared.'

Robyn digested this. She'd been thrust into the moment; she'd felt panic, of course, as the sea churned and the waves pushed her down, but there had been no question of choice, no moment of weighing that fear and deciding to charge through it regardless. But Jago, he'd had to decide. He'd chosen danger, whereas danger had chosen her. All the times she'd thought about that moment since, she'd never once imagined him as anything but fearless. Now, in the leaping light, half moon, half flame, she watched him. And she didn't need to see his eyes to know that he was watching her back.

'God, I'm glad we left the house,' she said unguardedly. 'We could have gone all night and not even spoken properly.'

'I don't go to many dinner parties.'

'Too busy lurking on the cliffs at night?'

'That doesn't sound creepy at all. No, just . . . not much of a talker.'

'Well, you're a good listener. Letting me bang on about . . . I don't know . . . rubbish, probably. Sorry about that.'

'It's not rubbish.'

'Jago,' she said, 'can I ask you something?'

'If you want.'

'Your dad, what he said about your mum . . . When did she die? I mean, how long ago?'

'Two years. Two years this autumn. October. The twelfth.'

'I'm sorry. I can't imagine what it must be like. I'm really sorry.'

He didn't say anything back, and for a moment the quiet played out. Robyn wondered whether to break it, to ask another question about something else altogether, but she couldn't think of a single thing except how much she wished she hadn't mentioned it.

'She loved riding,' he said.

He spoke so quietly that Robyn had to lean closer to hear. Jago's hand was on his dog, his fingers stroking the lengths of his ears.

'Did she?' she said, earnestly, gratefully. 'Was she . . . good?'

'She never entered competitions or anything, she wasn't like that; she just used to ride all around here, along the cliffs, down on the beaches, up to the moor. But one day she went out and she didn't come back when she was supposed to. I was at college, Dad was working. Anyway, we got a phone call. I answered. I'd just come in. It was this old farmer who lives at St Buryan. He said . . . well, he'd found her. Actually he'd found her horse. He came into his yard, bridle, saddle, no rider, but he recognised him. Tomatillo was making a fuss, dancing about, didn't want to be caught. The farmer called us, then he took his Land Rover out, and he found her. She wasn't even that far away. Just in a field, by a fence. He thought maybe they'd jumped it. Or tried to, anyway. The ambulance came, took her to Penzance, but she'd broken her neck. There was nothing that anybody could do. She'd fallen before and been fine, but this time . . . she wasn't.'

Tomatillo. She'd seen the horse. She'd noticed him from her bedroom window, grazing the far edges of the field. A lone grey gelding who was big, rangy, flighty-looking. And sad, she thought now.

'You kept him, though,' she said. 'Tomatillo.'

'I don't know why,' said Jago. 'Dad got rid of everything else that had anything to do with her.'

He passed back the bottle, and Robyn finished what was left. Her mouth tasted berry red, inappropriately sweet.

'What does it feel like?' she asked. 'I mean, is it better than it was? Has it got better?'

34

'What does it *feel* like?'

'Sorry, that's a stupid question, I didn't . . .'

'It's not stupid. It's just . . . nobody ever asked me that. They used to say "How are you doing?" that kind of thing, "Are you okay?" but, well, those are just the things people have to say, aren't they? Because there's nothing else. Or they don't think there is, anyway. And now . . . well, round here, the people that knew her, I guess they think two years is a long time. I guess it's in the past now. That's what they probably think.'

'What about your dad?'

'Oh, my dad . . . My dad is my dad. The way he was tonight, that's him, I guess. Gets on with everyone. Pretty much always happy. That's him.'

'Is it?'

'No. But he doesn't know I know that.'

One of the torches flickered and died beside them. The other continued to burn, its light thinned and fragile. A wind came off the water and Robyn shivered.

'Shall we go back?' said Jago.

'Not if you don't want to.'

'You're right,' he said. 'I do know the way in the dark. I used to come here, just after Mum.'

Robyn turned again to the sea. She stared at the endless expanse of darkness, felt the relentless push and pull of wave upon wave. You could tell the sea anything and it'd answer you in the only way it could, stopping for nothing, stopping for no one, and there was reassurance in that.

'I think I'd have come here too,' she said.

The second candle died.

'I didn't really answer,' he said, 'when you asked me how it felt.'

35

'It was a stupid question,' she said.

He stood up, and she heard his hands moving through his hair. She stood up with him. Two slim shapes on a dark rock. She reached out her hand but he didn't see. Instead he jumped down, landing with a light thud. Scout followed, and twined about his legs.

'I haven't got the words,' he said. 'I never did have. I don't think I ever will.'

She felt his hand close around hers and she stepped down beside him. Her head spun. Her feet felt unsteady suddenly. She wondered if he was drunk too.

'Jago, thank you,' she said.

'No worries.'

Robyn held on to his hand. 'No, I mean, *thank you*. For what you did in the water.'

'It was nothing,' he said.

'It was everything.'

She could have kissed him then. It would have been so easy. A small stretch, the tips of her toes, lips meeting. She felt a bolt of desire run through her body.

'We should get back to your house,' he said. 'Shouldn't we?'

'I don't know. Should we?' she said.

'We should,' he said, moving away.

In the space where his hand had been, Robyn curled her fingers.

As their shoes squeaked across the night-wet grass of Robyn's lawn, light gleamed from all of the downstairs windows, and they could hear the bass notes of music. The driveway had a new car in it.

'Ben,' said Robyn. 'I thought he couldn't come!'

'I'll be heading, then,' said Jago. He whistled for Scout.

'But I bet your dad's still here.'

'And as long as there's wine open, you'll never get rid of him.'

They both blinked as the outside lights were flicked on suddenly and the garden glowed golden.

'Robyn Swinton, is that you lurking out there?' a voice boomed. A man followed it, taking quick steps across the grass.

'My brother . . .' began Robyn, but Jago was already turning on his heel. 'Don't you want to meet him?'

Jago hesitated. 'You get used to not talking much,' he said, 'living here.' He wanted to add, *It's one of the things I like about it*, but he knew that'd come across wrong.

'You talked tonight.'

He shrugged, a gesture that belied his own surprise at his verbosity. Even though afterwards he'd felt as though he'd lifted his shirt, exposing all of the wounds that marked his skin, it had been easy in the dark. It had been easy with Robyn.

'Please stay. I'd like you to,' she said.

Jago hesitated, the uncomplicated desire in her voice catching at something in him. Then Ben was there, engulfing her in a bear hug. By the time she'd struggled her way out of it, Jago had gone.

four

BEN STAYED FOR THE WEEKEND, AND ROBYN TOOK PLEASURE IN his presence as she always did. Her brother lived deep in the heart of London, working late and playing later. He was in his thirties, and the age gap had meant that growing up, she'd never seen him as an ungainly adolescent. She hadn't been old enough to notice his pimples or puppy fat, his uneven teenage heart. Instead he had always struck her as a shining, fully formed person, flitting in and out of her home life as brightly as a firefly and just as ungraspable. The weekends of his teenage years were spent in bands that played in garages, the nights of his twenties on stage in basement bars, and now he was a producer on a well-thought-of show, on a well-thought-of radio station. For Robyn, he was tinged with the same older-brother glamour he'd always had.

After Denny had left, Ben had moved through the Cornish house, picking things up and looking in cupboards, as though it was a holiday home. She'd followed him from room to room, stopping at the lounge window to show him what would have been the view of the sea.

'It's endlessly black,' said Ben. 'Unsettlingly so, actually. Are you saying it's all blue by day? The perfect sea view?'

'All blue,' said Robyn. 'Except when it's grey. Or greenish. Or this almost sort of soupy brown colour when there's a certain kind of storm coming.'

'Listen to you, you little mermaid,' he said, jabbing her in the ribs. 'Dad said you wanted to take up surfing.'

'I'm thinking about it,' she said carefully.

'And apparently,' his voice lowered in emphasis, 'there's even a boy next door. That guy Denny's son?'

At the mention of Jago, Robyn's body tingled with unfulfilled desire. Then she felt a kick of failure as she remembered the Lichtenstein postcard still tucked in the pocket of her jeans. She'd meant to give it to him. Or at least she'd meant to *consider* giving it to him, judging the moment and deciding there and then. But faced with Jago, she'd forgotten everything else. It was as though her mind couldn't focus on anything more than the present moment; all sensations were laced with a ripe immediacy. Her words had tumbled out, without her having any idea of where they were coming from or where they would be going next. She'd felt Jago's closeness, the heat of his eyes on her, the proximity of his foot to hers, their almost-touching knees. The way they'd passed the bottle back and forth, fingers smudging prints, the warm traces left by lips. And how he'd opened up to her, told her things she was sure he didn't share with everyone, for hadn't he said he was no kind of a talker?

'Robyn, earth to Robyn?'

'Sorry, what?'

'I was just saying that here was me thinking they'd taken you to the arse end of nowhere, with nothing and no one, and it's not like that at all. It's excitement around every corner, apparently. And to think I'd been hatching a plan to steal you away to London for the holidays. The great escape.'

'What?' cried Robyn. 'Seriously?'

'My elusive lodger finally moved out. It was just an idea.'

'But I'd have loved that! Why didn't you say anything before?'

Ben lived in a flat in Peckham where instruments were strewn about in the way that other people had soft furnishings: fat-bellied guitars occupied armchairs, a bass drum sat squat in the corner. It was a reckless, cheerful space, and one in which she could entirely imagine herself. Her coursework could be done anywhere. Or she could have ditched all that and made tea at the radio station where Ben worked, getting a first foothold on a ladder leading up and out and onwards. In a matter of moments, a whole life opened and closed before her.

'I mentioned it to Mum, just in passing, and she thought it was a bad idea,' said Ben. 'Which I suppose it is. You'd have had to put up with my miscreant mates.'

'I like your mates! Why did Mum say no? You should have said something to me first . . .'

'You only have to get through university, then you can be a slacker in the real world instead of the pretend one. The next two years will flash by, you'll see.'

'Here?' said Robyn, waving her arm at the black window. 'You think they'll flash by *here*? Marooned, every single holiday?'

She stared at the window, and her reflection stared back. The night beyond was as thick and dark as treacle. For a moment, when she and Jago had been sitting up above the water, she'd felt as though perhaps she belonged here after all.

Even if the sea wanted to swallow her, even if Jago was as likely to bolt as to stop and talk. But there was nothing quick about these things, Jago and the surf. There was too much she still didn't understand. The thought that one day she might learn their secrets was the only reason that she let her brother wrap an arm around her, and refrained from protesting when he said that London was a nice idea but it'd still be there next summer.

Along the cliff, at Hooper's House, Jago had shut the door to his room and lain down on the bed. He could hear the sea from there, a relentless wash of waves, although half the time he wondered if it was in his own head. That night he revelled in it, the dark push and pull. When he shut his eyes he still saw the flicker of their torches, and felt the heat of her presence beside him. He'd never taken a girl to the rocks, not before, and not after. It was where he'd gone the night they came home from the hospital, without her. His dad had whipped the car through the back roads, tears pooling, fast and angry. He'd slammed the brakes on in the yard and they'd spun to a stop. He'd clung to Jago and said, *I'm sorry, mate, I'm so, so sorry*, and all Jago could think was *Why aren't I crying too?* He did know why, though; when one fell, the other had to hang tight. He'd had to be strong for both of them.

When his dad had gone to bed, treading uneven whisky footsteps, skidding on tears, Jago had sat first in the dark of the kitchen, then walked out of the farmhouse and down to the cliffs. He hadn't taken a torch that night either, because there had been a giant moon, a harvest moon, close enough to touch and spilling white light. He'd found his way to the rocks and climbed on top, filling his lungs with the air, letting every feeling he had wash over him. He'd thought the tears would come then. He wanted them. Even when a sharp wind blew off the sea and he felt his eyes sting, no drops fell. *Mum*, he whispered. *Mum*, he said louder, until he was yelling: *Mum, Mum, Mum!* But the night gave nothing back, and still the tears didn't come, just the sound of the ocean's back and forth, so dark and so indifferent.

He hadn't told Robyn these things, but he might have done. The words were there, forming in his head. He had forgotten what it could be like, that feeling of someone being ready to catch anything that you threw. His dad had always swum on the surface of life, tossed questions without ever really waiting for the answers, and that was just his way. When Rosalind had died, he'd patched his sadness with sticking plasters and flimsy stitches, and it seemed to convince most people. He had appeared mended, with his broad smile and too-bright eyes. And he skimmed on, working all hours, drinking at the pub, finding the company of women, who came and went in a blaze of cheap perfume and slept-in-make-up and blown kisses at the garden gate. It was flurry and it was fury and it never fooled Jago.

That was when he started working with him: sweeping shavings, mixing varnish, eventually cutting, shaping, joining. He moved with quiet confidence, and his dad watched with something like pride as side by side they found a new rhythm of existence. Jago liked the way the wood was pliant, malleable, but strong, very, very strong. He caressed it as he worked, inhaled its scent and treasured its new forms. He helped finish a kitchen dresser on time, an embellished, showboating piece for a tourist house near St Ives. His dad banked the cheque and bought new tools, doubles, a set for Jago. *If you want*, he said, his head cocked, a passing flicker of shyness across his cheeks.

Together they worked on, father and son, and they just about stayed upright. Weekends rolled into weekdays and Jago found it was easy to forget college and the clamour of people his own age, as the barn called. Its atmosphere was cocoon-like, womb-like, and full of warm wood scents. As the number of orders grew on the board behind them, chalked there by Jago as he imposed a small measure of process on their endeavour, the two men worked with bent heads and deft gestures; quietly complicit, they talked to one another through the medium of wood. The workshop became a place of peace and stolid industry, and in its space, without ever expecting to, Jago found something of his mum.

As long as he was there, fragments of her came to him; perhaps it was the slow, repeated rhythms, the delicate touch, but his mind dwelt on her. Not in the desperate, heart-banging way of the night, or with the numbness that would coat his every movement through college – feelings he had no control over, that rendered him fearful and inert in equal measure – but with a dedicated sort of drifting, as mellow as one of the old country songs she used to always play. Rosalind had been possessed of a quiet sense of calm. She'd had a slow, soft voice and her smile tipped sideways as she weighed you up, always seeing, always knowing. That was why animals had loved her, he was sure of that. They responded to her gentle command, her solidness, her inability to lie or trick. That night on the rocks, last night, he'd recognised something in Robyn that he thought had disappeared the day his mum died. A softly spoken question that was just the one that needed to be asked, cutting straight to your heart. An understanding before you'd even given an answer.

It was a shame, then, that she wouldn't stay. She'd appeared permanent, with her family's fleet of removal vans, her parents exulting in everything Cornish, her box-fresh surfboard, but everything about her was temporary. Robyn Swinton had blown in, and she'd blow out again just as fast. He knew that much even as he'd lain with her on the beach, her breath panting, spitting seawater. He could feel it in her. She was slippery, too quick for him. She'd forget everything about that day. She'd be surfing silkily, her wetsuit the right way round, and the cove would be too small for her then. So she'd go, looking for bigger places and better people. The girl came in, the girl went out. It was only the sea that rolled on and on.

five

'IT REALLY IS THE ENDS OF THE EARTH,' SAID BEN AS HE GAZED out, his hair whipped upright by the wind.

'Two years,' said Robyn, 'and then I can go wherever I want.'

They'd rattled along the lanes, late summer sun glinting, windows down, music blaring. Cows had regarded them indolently, as blitzes of gulls and crows passed overhead, crying and cawing in black and white. Now they stood where the land ran out, the Atlantic tearing at the rocks below, the horizon darkest blue and straight as a die.

'I reckon it could go either way,' said Ben. 'You'll either run to the biggest city you can find, or you'll stay here for ever, never wanting to leave.'

'I'll want to leave,' said Robyn, 'don't you worry about that.'

She'd saved Rockabilly until last. They'd parked the car in the driveway when she'd said, 'Oh, there is one more place.' They crossed the field, and as she passed Hooper's House she waved a hand, saying in blasé tones, 'That's Denny and Jago's place,' then she took his arm and plunged him on to the jungle path.

Rockabilly had outdone itself. It was low tide and the sand glistened, straggles of seaweed and countless other treasures scattering the shore. The surf rolled and pounded. She heard Ben whistle in awe.

'No one really comes here,' said Robyn, a trace of regret in her voice. 'Hardly even locals.'

She hadn't seen Jago yet that day, which seemed unlikely given the proximity of their two houses. She'd chosen her bikini in the hope that maybe he'd spot her in it. It was new, all black, and tied at the sides with beaded string. She'd watched herself in the mirror before she'd left the house, turning from side to side, taking in the lines where her skin changed from pale gold to white. In these few weeks in Cornwall she already felt stripped and toughened. If she surfed again – *when* she surfed again – she'd grow strong all over. Quick as a fish. That was what she wanted, that was what she'd resolved. If she had to live here at the end of the earth, at least there'd be that.

'Are we going in, then?' said Ben.

She hesitated. Her stomach knotted as she watched the water, her toes curled in the sand. She glanced briefly at the clifftop, then turned to Ben. 'I thought maybe we could just sunbathe. This time.'

'Music to my ears,' said Ben, sinking into the sand, rolling up his jeans. 'It's a well-known fact that bass guitarists don't like getting wet.'

'I thought the band had broken up?'

'And got back together, and broken up again. Wives. Babies. Upwardly mobile career paths in things that aren't music.'

'I wanted to come and stay and see a gig.'

'You can. It just won't be one of *our* gigs.'

'That's what I meant,' said Robyn, and ducked as a tangled length of seaweed was flung her way.

Ben left on Sunday, the day before she was due to return to university. He waved from the window, leaning on the horn as he spun out of the driveway and into the lane. In his wake, Robyn felt listless. The house boomed with silence. Simon took his paints out, blotted watercolours, while Marilyn leafed idly through home furnishing magazines. Robyn called that she was going out, and they signalled their approval with a waved paintbrush, a fluttering of fingers. She took her board, grabbed her rucksack and went to Rockabilly.

The walk was no easier than the first time. She arrived at the beach panting, her board's tail trailing in the sand. But at least her wetsuit was on the right way round. At least she was prepared this time. The waves would sting and slap and pull her under. Her board would seek to eject her at the first possible opportunity. There would be no Jago waiting, watching, ready to run. She knew this because she'd seen their pickup turning out of the driveway, Denny at the wheel, Jago beside him, behind them a trailer piled high with timber. She was on her own, save for a pair of silken-headed terns diving for fish, and a haughty gull that watched her sideways then flew off, screeching indignantly. She felt curiously calm, and a sense of inner stillness took over.

She waded in, and as the water pushed against her, she took a deep breath. Then another, in through her nose and out through her mouth. The trick, she decided, was not to go so far out, to stay within toe-tapping distance of the bottom. She settled belly-down on her board and fell to paddling.

When it felt right, she stopped and struggled up to a sitting position. The end-of-summer sun would soon be sinking, but for now it burned golden, chased by a rippling breeze, and she bobbed on the tide, soaking it up. The surf was quieter than last time, smoother too. She watched wave after wave peel by. *There's no hurry*, she said to herself. *Just watch, find the rhythm, go when you're ready*. She counted the waves as they rolled past. Seven in a set. Lucky seven. With sudden decision, she dropped to her stomach, her hands whipping the water. 'Jago!' she yelled, in a fierce cry of ripe determination. It was the first word that came, in a sudden, unstoppable rush, just as the wave took hold of her. She tried to scrabble to her knees, but was pitched face forward into the water. She rolled and tumbled, kicking herself upright, bursting back to the surface with a gasp. A few feet away her board bobbed innocently. She began to laugh. *Jago!* A gulping, breathless laugh, not caring if the gulls broke their swirling flight to look down at the mad girl, the name of a boy falling helplessly from her lips as she was devoured by the sea.

And on it went. She fell. She got back on. She fell. She got back on. Every time she paddled into a wave she found herself crying *Jago!* Not yelled out loud, not like the first time, but a hiss of determination, a private rallying cry. She stayed out until the muscles in her arms were screaming and her throat burned with salt. Then, just as the sun was dipping towards the water, it happened. She caught one. Her bottom was thrust out, her arms were like telegraph poles caught in a gale, but she stood up for two, three seconds, before the water flew over her head and her board was hurled one way and she went the other. She swam back to the surface, her face beaming. It was her first, and it was glorious. Brief seconds turning to eternity. A world within a wave.

She decided to ride it a little longer. With a smile still at her lips, she stomped back up the beach on to the path, across the field, then instead of turning into her drive she dropped her board at the gate, and, full of the momentum of the ocean, carried on to Hooper's House. The Winterses' truck was still absent, but she moved quickly, rifling through her rucksack. Admittedly the card was a bit of a mess. She'd crossed out *I don't even know your name*, drawn a lanky arrow and written *Well, I do now!!!* except there hadn't been a lot of space so the letters were bunched together and only just legible. Thanks to the evening it'd spent in the back pocket of her jeans, the corners were bent and splitting, but otherwise it was intact. She'd put it in an envelope, *JAGO* spelled out in block capitals, and before sealing it had added a further note, one that she'd folded and folded again.

At the entrance to the yard she'd seen the Winterses' mailbox, an old American-style one, but its door had come unfastened and hung loose. The space inside looked too exposed, so instead she went to the front door, hoping for a letter box. Only there wasn't one. There was, however, the slightest gap between the bottom of the door and the step. She knelt down and slid her card through, its edges meeting a brief resistance on their otherwise smooth journey. She stood up. She pictured it lying on the mat on the other side, a bold presence in the Winterses' house.

She turned to walk away, then hesitated. She turned back. She stared at the door, her eyes widening as what she'd done sank in. She replayed the words she'd written – *Were they too much? They were too much* – and brought to mind the image

49

again, the sweep of blond hair on the girl, her provocative lips, the matinee idol looks of the guy. Would he think it ridiculous and cringe at the insinuation that they were in any way similar? Or think her twisted, that she considered his straight-faced rescue somehow arousing?

She reached for the handle, turning it, hoping that country people lived up to the stereotype and left their doors unlocked, but it wouldn't give. She might as well have handed him her heart in a box tied up with a ribbon. She grabbed her board and hurried back to the safety of her own house, glancing behind her every so often, as though white water was nipping at her heels.

six

HER UNIVERSITY WASN'T THE SAME AS WHEN SHE'D LEFT IT. TO Robyn it felt temporary now, a collection of people and buildings designed only for part-time use. Around her the Warwickshire landscape seemed flat and claustrophobic, an inert place, without any of the crash and roll and perpetual motion of the sea. Through the autumn term, amidst the Styrofoam coffees and interminable library sessions, the hot and drunken press of nights with friends in small-town clubs, her thoughts kept turning back to two things: the water, and Jago. They were perfectly entwined, each seeming to generate a combined sense of exhilaration and calm, a converse mix that was, Robyn realised, exactly right.

She'd heard nothing from him, but then she hadn't expected to, not really, not sensibly. While tucked in the back of a lecture theatre, or working her term-time job as a waitress in an imitation Italian restaurant, her mind had wandered through all the different scenarios, and she'd decided his silence was apt. Jago seemed as though he was one for watching, for waiting, dwelling on the edge of things rather than in the heaving centre. She couldn't imagine him knocking on the door of White Sands to ask her parents for her address. It made sense that he would wait until her return at Christmas.

In the meantime, she pursued the water. She went to the university pool, thinking she might perfect her stroke, practise holding her breath, but once she was there, she lost all desire. Instead she sat up in the viewing gallery, her kit balled in her lap. She watched the boys with their triangular chests and scanty pants, and the girls with their nose pegs and swim caps stalking the tiled edges of the pool. Whistles blew, stopwatches were brandished, and afterwards her skin smelt of chlorine even as a spectator. There were no boisterous gulls, or swirls of seaweed. No fragments of shell caught between your toes. No mind-bending shock at the ice-box water, nor jumping heart as you ducked beneath a wave.

The ten-week term dragged. In lectures she sat dreaming, her pen idling on the page. Once, as her tutor talked of Turner and his remarkable tricks of light, she imagined how Rockabilly would look beneath his brush: the fury and stillness, the salmon-pink dawns and the jet nights. In the margin of her page she sketched an outline of the rock stack, the quiff; she blackened the space around it until her pen cut through the paper. For the first time she truly understood why artists looked for answers in the sea.

She saved up all her tips from waitressing and bought a second-hand winter wetsuit from an advertisement glimpsed in the local paper. She tried it on in someone else's bathroom, and carried it home like a precious thing. When she went to bed at night, drifting on a tide of racketing music, her friends' gossip coming through the walls, she attempted to absent herself.

She pretended she could hear the wash of waves on a beach. If she was lucky, she glimpsed a figure with dark curled hair in her dreams, and felt the press of his hands all over again. And she thought of the card, the parted lips, the naked desire, propped on Jago's bedside table perhaps, or tucked inside the pages of a beloved book.

When she stepped from the train at Penzance there was no *Robyn!* carried on the wind. Nor was there a hand-delivered letter waiting for her at home, just a scattering of Christmas cards from old friends in the town she used to live in. She left the light on in her room all of that first evening and most of the night – a beacon in the black Merrin night – but there was no answering flicker from through the trees, no handful of pebbles scattering against the pane of her window, and no message traced on the frosted lawn when she woke up and stared out at the white and watery world.

On her first full day at home, she surfed, her new hooded wetsuit meaning she could go out on even the cold-tipped days. She ran into the water, her legs and arms pumping to drive her blood faster, her teeth chattering only a little as she paddled. She surfed again the next day, and the next, fighting the weather as well as the sea. When the board tossed her and the waves pulled her under, she learnt how to equalise, popping her ears and rising back to the surface. Very slowly, not always surely, she improved. Then came the day when she rode all the way back in to the beach, falling off as the water ran out and shouting with glee. It was just a handful of seconds of surfing, but to Robyn it felt endless. With no word, or sight, of Jago, this time it was the sea that saved her.

* * *

Back when there were new berries in the hedgerows and the lanes were scattered with hazelnuts, Marilyn had baked a batch of Christmas cakes. Now Robyn watched as she laid a delicate sprig of holly on the skating-rink-white of the icing, then stood back with her hands on her hips, a look of pride across her face.

'This one's for the chaps next door,' she said airily. 'Do you want to take it round?'

'Why for them?' then quickly, 'Okay. What, go over there now? Okay.'

Marilyn continued to cut holly sprigs from sheets of red and green icing, an amused smile playing at her lips.

Upstairs in her room, Robyn chose a jade-coloured scarf because someone had once told her it brought out the colour of her eyes. She applied a quick dash of lipstick then wiped it off, leaving its too-scarlet streak over the back of her hand. She brushed her hair again, plaiting one section then pulling loose a few strands so the effect was unstudied and folksy and the kind of thing that maybe, perhaps, Jago might like.

There was no answer at the house. She was ready to leave the cake on the doorstep and bolt when she heard a sound from the workshop. Relief and disappointment were quickly replaced by a thud of nerves. She walked across the yard slowly, her fingers twisting the ends of her hair. Just as she approached, a drill revved into loud and sustained action. She prepared to knock, then, realising it was pointless, pushed open the door.

It was a far bigger space than it appeared from the outside. Pale winter sun filtered through three immense windows revealing workbenches, piles of timber, several half-made pieces of furniture: a giant bookcase, a church-style pew, the beginnings of a table. Drifts of sawdust covered the floor, and dust motes danced in the light. She breathed in, and the warm honey smell of wood filled her senses. Despite the blast of the drill, the chaos of materials and tools, there was an intoxicating air of peace and endeavour. Jago was bent over his work in a posture of utter concentration. She took in his blue overalls, and the look of steel and serenity on his face. As the blade cut into the grain, fine shavings of wood fell at his feet like a winter blizzard. She was transfixed. Then she jumped, feeling the touch of a hand on her shoulder. Denny flashed his grin.

'Oh! Hi,' she said, 'sorry, there was no answer at the house. I . . .'

As soon as she spoke, Jago's drill stopped abruptly. Her ears rang. Her heart thudded.

'Merry Christmas, little lady,' said Denny. 'To what do we owe the pleasure?'

He dipped a mock bow and Robyn laughed loudly, masking her jitters.

'I come bearing cake. Mum made it.' Then, 'It's full of booze.'

'Then we're full of gratitude.'

He took the tin and lifted the lid. 'Stop and have a cup of coffee with us. Slice of this?'

'Okay,' she said, just as she heard the squeak of Jago's boots across the floor behind her. 'Thank you. I'd love to.'

'Hello.'

He stood beside his dad, looking exactly the same as he had at the end of the summer. He didn't appear like a person who'd spent ten weeks pining, possessed of a card and the promise of a kiss. She felt her cheeks burn. Her lips were dry.

'You're back,' he said, with an uncomplicated smile. 'How's it going?'

They kept a kettle in the corner, a jar of instant coffee and a collection of old enamel mugs, and Denny set to work. Robyn saw him pick one up and shake it vigorously, as though hurling out a spider, then wipe it on his jumper.

'Good,' she said, taking a seat on the edge of a workbench. 'You?' Her voice was studiedly casual. She pictured him opening the envelope, his eyes widening at the picture, scanning her words. How could he not react?

'Yeah, good. We've been busy, chained to the workshop, finishing orders off for Christmas. Just about caught up now. How was university?'

'Hectic,' she said, as though her days had been so full in Warwick that she'd given no thought to anything else. 'I thought I'd spend the holidays sleeping, but I can't keep away from the sea.'

'Tougher than you look, then, you are,' said Denny, reappearing with the coffee. She accepted it, grateful for something to hold and occupy her hands, and took a sip. It was awful, gritty and weak. She was handed a thick slice of cake, and took a quick bite.

'What are you working on?' she asked, looking pointedly at Denny.

'Couple of coffee tables for a hotel in Padstow,' he said. 'Piece of cake really.' He devoured most of a slice in one mouthful, and wiped his mouth with the back of his hand. 'Bloody hell, that's good. Ask your mum when she's moving in.'

'Actually, she said she was thinking of commissioning something from you,' said Robyn. 'As a sort of Christmas present to herself. If you were willing.'

'I'm willing all right,' said Denny with a wink. 'Sorry,' he reset himself, 'autopilot. Robyn, tell her that's very kind. We haven't got much in the workshop, but if her and your dad wanted to see the kind of stuff we do, then I can point them in the direction of a couple of shops in Penzance and Truro.'

'What kind of thing is she thinking of?' asked Jago.

Robyn glanced at him, her emotions scattered. Someone else might have found his impassiveness infuriating, but she was surprised to realise that it was almost a relief now, as though her unacknowledged fear of having scared him away ran deeper than her desire that he felt the same as her. She replied, grateful suddenly for the banality of the question.

'I don't know. Maybe a table. Or a bookcase.'

'I could show Robyn what we've got in the house?' said Jago, turning to his dad. 'Just for ideas.'

She held her breath and felt a flood in her chest, a burst of hope. She wished she'd worn lipstick after all.

'That's old stuff, but yeah, okay. Though Robyn, if your mum and dad are wanting a look, we'll need a week's notice to clean the place up.'

It was gloomy in the hallway, a thin light filtering from an open door down the narrow passage. Robyn followed Jago past a rack crammed with coats, kicking through a mess of discarded shoes and boots. Underfoot the flagstones were uneven, and her nose sniffed at the air like an inquisitive animal; she detected woodsmoke, and a faint tang of damp. He led her into the kitchen, a small, square space mostly eaten up by a round wooden table.

'One of Dad's,' said Jago, patting it. 'Cherry wood. It darkens with age, see? This reddish colour, it was much blonder once.'

'Smooth,' said Robyn, running her hand over the grain.

'Isn't it? Strong, too. It's a lovely wood. There's a bookcase in the sitting room, that's cherry as well.'

Robyn followed him, trying to stay steady. She glanced back, noticing the dry and cracked bar of soap on the sink, and the grey tea towel hanging on the hook by the window. The sill was a spiked garden of cacti, dusty and misshapen. The sideboard was stacked with dishes.

'This is a real beauty,' he said, pushing open the door.

In the tight space, Robyn stood beside him, shoulder to shoulder, willing the moment to last.

'You've got a bookcase, but hardly any books. What's that about?'

'Dad gave them all away.'

'Why? Don't you read?'

'Mum used to. But he cleared out a lot of stuff. The books were just sitting there getting dusty.'

'But that's what books do. You can only read one at a time.'

'Anyway, I saved the most important thing,' said Jago. 'Come upstairs.'

Jago's bedroom. It was one of the emptiest rooms Robyn had ever seen. She took in the moss-green carpet, the dark wooden bed, the desk with its squat lamp. She tried to spot the card and couldn't, but then wasn't it more like Jago to have tucked it somewhere safe? A bedside table, or a sock drawer? The one embellishment in the room was a wooden model of a boat. It filled the windowsill, a sleek dark vessel with intricate rigging and a perfectly pointed prow.

'Is this what you wanted to show me?' asked Robyn, walking to it. With her back turned, she imagined him coming up behind her, laying a kiss at the nape of her neck.

'What, that? No. I've had that since I was a kid. Dad made it.'

'But it's amazing,' she said, and she meant it. She ran a finger over the stern, tracing the letters of the name, *Wonder*.

'It's seaworthy, apparently, but I've never tested it.'

'How come?'

'I don't know. I guess I didn't want to wreck it.'

Jago was easy to imagine as a small boy, spiriting his ship upstairs, polishing its hull. Robyn knew that had it been hers, its underside would be salt-bleached, its sails sun-spotted, probably a nick in the stern. She wondered whether to tell him this, whether it would make her appear indelicate, or appealingly carefree. She turned round and saw Jago dropped to his knees, dragging something out from under his bed.

'This is what I wanted to show you,' he said, standing up, wiping his dusted hands on his jeans. He held a guitar case. It was painted all over with swirls of colour, pinks and purples and sunshine yellows. He laid it on the bed and popped back the clips, drawing out its treasure.

'Here,' he said, with reverence in his voice. 'This is it.'

It was a sea-coloured guitar. Tipped to the light it was blue, then green, inset with shimmering mother-of-pearl. The strap was made of exquisitely carved black leather, a leaping and delicate print of birds and fish. Robyn reached out her hand instinctively, ran her fingers over its smooth body, whispered, 'Wow.'

'He made this too,' Jago said. 'A long time ago. Way before the boat. Before I was even born.'

He let her take it, and she slipped the strap around her neck and held the guitar's body in her arms. She tracked her fingers up and down the fretboard, soundlessly. She noticed a line of

59

tiny letters written in brushed strokes. *Rosalind, you make my heart sing.*

'He doesn't know I've got it,' Jago said.

Robyn thought of the missing books from the shelves downstairs, the absence of anything in the house that looked like it had once belonged to a woman.

'I love it,' she said, a creak in her voice.

'I thought you would.'

'My brother was in a band for years,' said Robyn, letting her fingers trip lightly over the strings.

'Oh yeah? What sort of music?'

'Hmm. Depends who you're asking. Ben always said they were a little bit Zeppelin, a little bit the Doors.'

'Really?'

'Well, not exactly . . . If they'd pulled that off you might actually have heard of them. They were loud, anyway. Loudness was their thing.' She hesitated, then said, 'What about your mum, what kind of music did she play?'

'The quiet kind,' he said.

Soft music, Jago thought. Rosalind had drifted about the house, skirts catching at her ankles, her hair falling down her back. She'd strummed loosely, her voice falling into accompaniment, fingers darting, flexing, pointing. When he was very small, she'd sit at the end of his bed and play until he fell asleep, singing stories. Jago remembered drifting on strings, and the lift and drop of her voice. Evenings, she'd sit on the old wicker sofa under the apple tree, her music disappearing into the night, sometimes Denny beside her, rolling cigarettes and nodding in time. She sang songs of journeys and enduring love, of sunsets over undiscovered waters, and waking up happy. Sometimes her voice pitched low, with an unexpected husk to it, a throatiness that belied her pale eyes and pollen-coloured hair, and they'd look twice, then, perhaps wondering what other depths lay within this kind, contented woman who made their toast and spread their jam and shook the earth from carrots as she pulled them from the soil.

'She used to say that it sometimes felt like she must have been washed up on the coast here, drifted all the way across the sea from America. Country, the old stuff, folk music, that was her thing. Dad used to joke that she wanted to be some kind of hippy cowgirl. She used to say she sang about blue mountains and coyote cries, putting up fences and mending broken hearts.' He paused, his cheeks colouring. 'Those were her words, not mine. Bit too poetic for me.'

'Did she ever go? To America?'

'No. She didn't even have a passport. But she liked the idea of it.'

'She went there in her music,' said Robyn.

'Yeah.' He smiled, shook his head. 'That's just what she always said.'

He held his hands out for the guitar and Robyn slipped the strap back over her head. She passed it to him and he turned it over in his hands, a light caress, before placing it back in the case.

'Can you play?' she asked.

'No. I've tried, but . . . no. I'd say you could if you wanted, but I don't want Dad to hear.'

'I can't play either,' said Robyn. 'My brother's the musical one, not me.'

'You suited it,' said Jago. 'The guitar. You looked like you knew what to do.'

'Right. Unlike surfing,' she said.

'I don't know, you're getting better.'

'How do you know?'

He'd watched her once without her knowing. Tucked himself behind the rocks on the clifftop, and held his breath every time he saw her go to pop up. He saw her ride a wave in to the beach, a small, shallow thing that barely crested, but a wave nonetheless, and he'd wanted to pelt down and congratulate her, twirl her round, laughing and sea-soaked. Instead he'd hesitated, chewed the nail of his thumb and wondered what he'd say, and then it was too late, she was already disappearing up the path, heaving her board behind her.

'A hunch,' said Jago. 'Fewer bruises.'

She lifted up her elbow and showed him the inside of her arm, where a dark stain bloomed. He put out a hand and ran his fingers along the contours of colour, then, as if he'd suddenly realised what he was doing, he pulled back.

'I can't even remember how I did it,' she said, lightly. 'And look, here too.' She pushed up her jeans and balanced on one leg. She held up her knee, where a yellowing-brown patch was just visible. 'It all blurs, the bangs and the smacks. Except that first time. I remember that one.'

They stared at one another, matching looks. Jago shut the guitar case with a clap, and in the quiet of his room the sound was loud and sudden as a thunderbolt.

'I need to finish that chair I'm working on,' he said with abrupt resolution. 'It has to be in Fowey tomorrow.'

Her hand went to her hair, self-consciously, fiddling with one of the pointless plaits.

'Maybe chat to your mum about the kind of thing she wants,' he went on. 'I'm guessing it's not a boat. Or a guitar.'

Robyn had almost forgotten why they'd gone inside the

house in the first place. She nodded, attempted a smile, then tried it again with more determination.

'Thanks for showing me,' she said eventually.

As she followed him out of the room and down the stairs, she kept forming half-sentences but couldn't bring herself to try them out loud. He opened the door and cold air blew in. The fine day had turned towards an early dusk, and the farmhouse's outside light had clicked on. Jago stood on the step, haloed by light.

'Could I just use your loo?' she asked.

He looked at her quizzically.

'Sorry, desperate,' she said.

'Sure, there's one down here. Just at the back there, green door.'

'Thanks.' Then, 'You go on, I won't be two seconds. I can let myself out.'

Jago nodded. He smiled. 'If I don't see you, merry Christmas. And thank your mum for the cake.'

He closed the door, and alone in the hallway she let out her breath. It went with a judder, and she rubbed her hands together to stop them from shaking. She'd planned to fly back upstairs and have a quick look about, just on her own without the distraction of his presence. If she could only find where he'd put the card, she'd be able to work out how he felt about it, for treasured objects always lived in certain places. Before she braved the stairs and the sanctity of his room again, she went over to the door, just to make sure that he wasn't waiting outside for her after all. She opened it a crack and peeped at the empty yard, then shut it quietly. She stood on the doormat, indecision taking her suddenly. She was seized by a thought, one that had flitted into her mind earlier as she'd wondered at his even manner, and appeared again now. She felt a quick flare of perverse hope, and stepped back, kneeling down to lift the mat. It was made of a rough, brushed material and was worn and old. She struggled to shift it, for it fitted the gap exactly, butting up against the door. With a quick tug it came free and she fell back on her heels. She stared at the space it left behind. There was a layer of age-old dust, the upturned body of a dead woodlouse, and a creamy white envelope marked *JAGO*.

seven

THE SWINTONS CELEBRATED CHRISTMAS WITH VIGOUR. BANISTERS were strung with lengths of ivy, sprays of mistletoe hung in doorways, and everyone went about in a perpetual state of merriment, Marilyn humming carols, Simon whistling in accompaniment, Ben arriving from London with three bottles of port and a giant, reeking wedge of Stilton. Robyn threw herself into the scene like a method actor, only occasionally drifting to the fringes, turning the card in her hands, awash with indecision. In the end, she had to admit that it was probably a sign. She'd keep it for herself and know all of its meaning. As for the note, she ripped it into tiny pieces. Maybe she'd tell him herself one day, when the time was right.

Two days later, the afternoon before Christmas Eve, she saw Jago driving his dad's pickup, Scout skittering about in the back as they careered along the lanes. He stopped and wound down the window, asking if she wanted a lift. Robyn climbed in, neatly, carefully, after he'd leant across to sweep the detritus from the passenger seat. Only then did it strike her that he hadn't asked where she was going. She told him, wishing her destination was further, and more intriguing, than the local garage.

'Wrapping crisis,' she explained in a theatrical voice, when he eventually asked. 'We've run out of sticky tape.'

Inside the cab it smelt of diesel and sawdust. She watched his hands as they gripped the wheel, observing his inscrutable profile. In a way it was empowering for her to have kept her feelings to herself for that bit longer, and she studied him with a new sense of ease. But because it was warm in the cab, and he was so close to her, and it seemed like it would be so easy to drop her hand on his knee, or drape an arm around his shoulders, she also felt a flare of impatience, hotly followed by a rush of desire. If they'd met at university it would have been different, she was sure. There would have been a drunken night out in one of the town's clubs, his friends and her friends all egging each other on, a tune pulling even the most reluctant on to the dance floor, and she'd have caught his hand, let him twirl her, then slipped closer to him. Lips found lips easily on nights like that. Hands went to hips, breath quickened, and there they would have been, kissing in the middle of everyone, lost in a clinch, wrapped in music. But in wind-blasted, sea-struck Merrin, things were different. He was as isolated as the landscape. Even a hand-delivered card could slip through the cracks.

She sat back in the seat beside him, and joined him in watching the road, wishing they could keep driving, belt along the lanes, and on, and on, and on. Here, with the thrum of the wheels and the roar of the engine, they chatted easily, and swapped the simple details of their lives. He told her he played football for a team in a nearby town, and she found it hard to imagine: Jago changing in a room full of broad-calved men, surrounded by clouds of deodorant and ribaldry, part of a band of fast-running players. She'd always figured him for a loner. But perhaps she didn't fit his view either. She'd told him she wasn't really a joiner, but she was playing Ophelia in the university's production. She'd let Hamlet, a sleek-mannered, sandy-haired boy called Rufus, place the crown of flowers on her head as they dressed backstage. She'd worn one of her mum's white cotton dresses from the sixties, and liked the way she looked in it, wafty and undone. Rehearsals had taken her through the autumn term, and there were parties with the rest of the cast, crushed tins of beer and the spouting of monologues, thespish kisses and liberally tossed compliments. She told Jago about her wave of opening night nerves, and then how thoughts of surfing at the cove made them ebb away.

'I think about it a lot,' she said.

'The good bits or the bad bits?'

She tipped her head in consideration. 'I don't think one could exist without the other.'

'To be or not to be,' said Jago, his lips curling into a smile, 'then isn't there something about a sea of troubles?' and through her surprise she wondered if he was laughing at her, or thinking about something else entirely.

They pulled into the petrol station. Jago offered to wait for her then drop her back, but she said she liked the idea of the walk, thinking it'd make her sound hardy and accustomed. She watched him drive off, with Scout's laughing face in the rear.

On the way home, a carrier bag of sticky tape and ribbon rustling in her hand, she felt the landscape around her begin to lose its definition. The bends in the lane disappeared. She walked with her arms outstretched, footsteps faltering, as a sea mist stole everything about her. By the time she reached White Sands, her hair was damp and she gave in to shivers; it had been only the thought of Jago's truck appearing out of the gloom, its engine gunning, that had kept them at bay until then.

If he was absent from the cove at the start of the holidays, by the time Christmas had come and gone, she found him there again. He was on the rocks, a bag of kit beside him, a fishing line flung into the water. As she appeared, he waved, and she waved back, then he turned back to his rod. Instead of going over, Robyn paddled out. She had the feeling that his eyes were on her, and so she concentrated on her stroke, and the line her body made as she sat up on her board. The afternoon was cold, steely, and one of the stiller seas she'd seen. The waves were patchy and uneven, and after fifteen minutes of trying and failing, she rode messily into the beach, jumping off and kicking at the feeble splashes of white water. Feeling his eyes on her still, she threw on her old parka, and pushing off her wetsuit hood she combed her fingers through her wet hair. When she glanced up again, she saw him climbing over the rocks. He hoisted an arm and waved a pair of fish.

'I was rubbish today,' she began. 'Well, *it* was rubbish . . .'

'Hungry for mackerel?' he asked.

Afterwards, she wondered if he'd planned it, because sticks of husk-dry wood seemed easy to find. He made a fire with quick, practised strokes. The flames jumped quickly, and ash blew on their shoes. They sat beside one another, their elbows almost touching.

'Next time I'm back, this arctic water had better be a distant memory,' she said, holding her hands up to the fire.

'Spring comes late down here,' said Jago. 'Sorry.'

'Typical,' said Robyn, biting down her smile. 'Merrin. Always the last to know.'

'Why don't you surf anywhere else?'

'What?'

'This cove . . . it's not exactly Watergate Bay. Don't you want to try other spots? Or find other people to surf with? You could drive to Sennen in the time it takes you to drag your board down here.'

The truth was, surfing meant Rockabilly and Rockabilly meant surfing. It was an uncharacteristically rigid way of thinking, for in almost every other sense her eyes were always roaming to the horizon.

'I want to wait until I'm better,' she said, knowing how much she'd improved, expecting him to interject. 'No point embarrassing myself.'

'Here, hold this,' he said instead, handing her a stick with a fish. 'That's it, just above the flames. Keep it turning, watch it doesn't slip.'

'Why don't you fish somewhere else?' she said. 'Find some friends to do it with instead of sitting there all on your own?'

Jago eyed her sideways. 'Fishing's supposed to be solitary. That's what I like about it.'

'Then why are we here now?'

'This is called sharing the catch. Also customary.'

'You haven't done it before.'

'There hasn't been much of a catch before.'

'So this is my lucky day? Bad for surf, good for fish. Or . . . bad too, if you happen to be a fish.'

'I chuck them back usually.'

'Wow, you really are bored here, aren't you?'

Jago smiled at the fire.

'Get any good Christmas presents?'

'Not really,' he said. 'Usual sort of stuff. Dad's not great at gifts.'

'Give any?'

'I guess I'm not either,' he said.

The only problem with the present he'd made, and it really was the only problem, was that he knew he wouldn't be able to give it to her. It was a fin for her board, carved from cedar wood with a grain so sweet you could count its every pattern. But Christmas had come and gone, and it'd stayed hidden in a cupboard in the workshop.

'I suppose nothing happens for New Year around this place?' she asked.

'You're going to be here?'

'No,' she said. 'I'm heading back tomorrow. My friends are having a house party. I don't even really like New Year, but . . .' she flicked him a grin, 'beats being stuck on a rock, I guess.'

'Yeah, yeah.'

'Seriously, are you doing anything?'

'There'll be a party somewhere.'

'Casual.'

'Well, New Year doesn't get me that excited either.'

'Why is that, do you think? I mean, I love parties normally. I love a celebration. But there's something about it . . . It's the expectation, maybe.'

'And the inevitable disappointment.'

'Hah. Maybe I should be staying after all. We could be cynics together.' She said it glibly, but with a hint of earnestness at the last.

Jago laughed, and snatched the stick from the fire, holding up the just-charred fish in triumph. Robyn made a noise of appreciation. The New Year talk was lost.

They ate the fish with their fingers, burning their lips, spitting bones, washing it down with tea from her thermos. The wind whipped in off the water, and they hunkered closer to the fire, both pretending it was throwing enough warmth long past the point when it wasn't.

'So you're leaving tomorrow? That . . . went fast.'

'The holidays always do. Especially here.'

'You think?'

'There's never enough time to do what I want,' said Robyn.

'What didn't you do?'

'Huh? Oh . . .' she lost her nerve, waved her hand dismissively, a ragged smile at her lips, 'hang ten, ride the pipe, catch that awesome, awesome wave.'

'There's always Easter,' said Jago.

In the end dusk came early, blowing in off the sea like a darkening cloud. They admitted they should each go home, Robyn dragging her board behind her, a woollen hat pulled down over her hair, Jago taking the cliff path the long way round, shouting *See you next time, then* over his shoulder, as though they always built fires and huddled close and shared a silence that was bursting with all the things not said, and all the things not done.

eight

ROBYN'S EASTER BREAK WAS FIVE WEEKS LONG, AND PROVED time enough for her and Jago to become friends. Not the kind who talked for hours on the telephone, or whiled away afternoons at a corner table in a pub; instead, an easy acquaintance shaped by chance meetings at Rockabilly cove. Jago fished steadily, and seemingly without expression, a stoical figure perched on the rocks, his line cast for mackerel, plaice or bass. Robyn, meanwhile, cried and shouted and got bashed and hurled, was breathless, aching, sometimes afraid, and very occasionally experienced such moments of intense joy and grace that it was always, always worth it. In the spaces in between, Jago shared with her the secrets of the sea, opening his palm to reveal a glistening shell the shape of a wizard's hat, or beckoning her to a rock pool to watch a fat sea slug lick its way across the surface. Their conversations were to the tune of the sucking sea, the hiss of surf. He never made a joke about needing to save her; he simply nodded approvingly if she carried something off, or offered the tip of a smile or a shrug of a shoulder if she was spilled into the white water.

Sometimes there were fish to cook and eat; other times it was a dark bottle of cider, or some flattened sandwiches with thick crusts and woody cheese. Robyn often found herself hefting a rucksack along with her board, feeling like a character from an old-fashioned children's adventure story as she stuffed it with provisions. Merrin had that effect: the modern world was easily shrugged off. Her university friends, with their ink-stamped wrists from club nights, the girls in their glittery tops and the boys in their self-proclaimed pulling shirts, seemed a very long way away. She'd pack chocolate, a couple of plump peaches, tins of German beer snaffled from the stack in the fridge. A blanket. A box of matches. A jumper, in case the cold threatened to drive her home, and a larger spare one in case it risked doing the same to him. If she got to the cove and he wasn't there, her eyes would rove until he appeared. If he didn't come, she made up reasons on his behalf: an urgent order in the workshop, a footballing injury that kept him indoors. It was possible sometimes for several days to pass without them seeing one another, and when that happened Jago appeared nonchalant, as though their lives were never intended for tessellation. Perhaps Robyn did the same, because she never said anything about their lapses; she just gripped her board tightly and smiled, then pelted for the water, whooping as it rose to meet her.

Once, as he was fishing, she crept up behind him, a length of seaweed at the ready. She dangled it above his head, tickling his ear.

'Heard you coming a mile off,' he said, brushing it away.

She flopped down beside him on the rocks.

'I've got a cold.'

'Bad luck.'

'Didn't fancy the water today.' She sniffed. 'I thought maybe you could show me what all the fuss is about.'

'Fuss?' He turned. 'You mean you want to fish?'

'Yes.' She nodded with resolution. 'I want to fish. Today I want to be a fisherwoman.'

He got up silently and went to his pile of gear. He returned with a rod all set up, as though he'd had it there all along and was just waiting for her to ask. He crouched beside her, showing her how to thread the bait and cast the line.

'And now,' he said, 'we wait.'

'We wait,' repeated Robyn, adjusting her seat. 'Okay. I can do that.'

Spits of rain came, pockmarking the water. Robyn adjusted her hood and huddled deeper inside her coat. She sank her chin in her hand, watching the distant horizon, as the other held on to the rod. Then she jumped up.

'I've got just the thing,' she said, 'to keep the cold at bay. And make this waiting a little bit more interesting.'

Before Jago could tell her not to, she set down her rod on the rocks. It was instantly pulled into the sea, in one whipping movement, its line slicking across the granite, then gone.

'Oh my God,' cried Robyn. 'Shit, did a fish do that?'

Jago was on his feet, craning at the water.

'Where is it? It can't have gone,' she said. 'Jago?'

The waves pulled in and out, water slapping at the rocks and sending spray leaping. The rod appeared several metres out, then was yanked beneath the surface again, lost in white water. They both stared at the space where it had been.

'I am so, so sorry,' said Robyn, turning to him. 'What an amateur. *God*. I was sitting there for ages with it doing absolutely nothing. I thought I could step away for one second . . .'

He rubbed his chin. His eyes were still on the water.

'You're not thinking of going after it? Don't, please don't. I'll buy you another. Just tell me what kind it was, and I'll get you one.'

He turned to her. 'Don't worry about it,' he said. 'It was an old rod. Just a spare.'

'It looked pretty new and shiny to me.'

'Shiny, but no good. Honestly, no worries.'

He smiled at her, but his eyes still flicked to the sea, and he was loose on his feet, as if he expected it to reappear at any moment and was ready to lunge and grab it.

'Anyway, what were you getting from your bag?'

'What? Oh. I brought some brandy. There's not loads left, but I thought maybe . . .'

'Yes,' said Jago, with urgency, '*yes*.'

They stood on the rocks, swigging from the bottle, tasting the sweet burn.

'Hey, we're upgrading,' said Robyn. 'It was wine last time we shared a bottle out here. That feels like ages ago.'

'We need the hard stuff today.'

'A wake for the rod,' she said.

'Exactly.'

'Do you want to say a few words, then?'

'No, let's just drink,' he said.

'I wish there was more.'

'Anything's good.'

Later, they said goodbye in the lane. Their steps from the cove had been a little ragged. Robyn's cold had been replaced by a warm thrum in her chest, a buzz to her head.

'Jago, don't lie this time. That was a really good rod, wasn't it?'

'Nope.'

'I'm going to get you another.'

'No you're not. I was going to chuck it out anyway. You saved me the trouble.'

But she remembered how the handle had felt in her hands; it had been made of wood, the colour of dark toffee. Suddenly it became clear – it was the rod that Jago always fished with. She'd seen him with it a dozen times. She wondered if he'd made the handle himself, chosen the grain, turned it in the workshop; her hands where his had been, and she'd dropped and lost it.

Two days later she left a rod outside his front door. She'd bought it from a tackle shop in Penzance, and it was the nicest she could find. It had a wooden handle too, made of honey-coloured grain, as perfect as a chess piece. She'd be eating baked beans for the first couple of weeks back at university, begging for extra shifts at the restaurant, but at least she no longer cringed when she thought of the slap of water at the cove, and Jago standing on the rocks. She tied a ribbon to its tip and walked away, her heart singing.

The next night the Swintons had turbot for dinner. Jago had come to the door and laid it in Robyn's arms, his cheeks flushed with triumph and the fast walk from the cove. *Just a bit of lemon and black pepper*, he'd said. Robyn felt the fish's weight, her mouth agog.

'You didn't have to do that,' he said.

'I wanted to,' she said back.

He turned and headed down the drive.

'It works all right, then?' she shouted after him.

'Like a dream,' he yelled back, his face split clean in half with a grin.

It was a grey Sunday in April, and Jago was playing football. It was one of the games he'd told Robyn about, a local league, their team made up of trawlermen who came and went, a dentist, a sculptor, a farmhand in goal. Sea mist clung to the edges of the pitch and the sky was spitting rain. A small group of supporters were huddled at the touchline, hands pushed into pockets, heads dipped beneath sodden hoods. He saw her arrive, and he recognised her because of the scarf. It was the same green one that she'd worn at Christmas, and it flew behind her as she stepped lightly across the field. She held a bright umbrella, and turned it in her hands, the colours blurring like a spinning top. She'd said nothing about coming, but there she was all the same.

'Who's that?' someone said with a strip of awe in their voice, and he instantly felt a swell of ownership, followed by a duller feeling that was something like sadness.

She hadn't seen him yet. Maybe they all looked the same from a distance. Green and black shirts. Rain-slick heads. Running in loose formation and shouting over the top of one another.

It was midway through the second half, and the ball was back in play. Jago slid into a tackle and won it easily. He scrambled up and took the ball on, sending it in a looping arc to the feet of their striker, who skied it over the crossbar. Jago clapped the effort, turning again to see Robyn. She'd joined the small group on the touchline, and was in conversation with Caroline Murphy.

Caroline was a fixture at the side of the pitch. She was the sister of their right back, and if they went to the pub afterwards she was there then too, in the middle of them all, her mouth kissing a pint glass, a smudge of lipstick at its rim. She'd been two years ahead of Jago, her skirt the shortest in the school, a tiny tattoo of a butterfly just inside her wrist. They'd seen each other for a couple of months when he was at college and she was working at a gift shop in Penzance. These days she'd begun to tease him again, with a quick wink and a lopsided smile, but he preferred that to the awkward silence he'd encountered after his mum died. It was easier to ignore.

'You here for him?' Caroline asked, nodding at the running figure of Jago. She rubbed her nose with her hand and eyed Robyn suspiciously.

'We're neighbours in Merrin,' said Robyn, wondering that it was so obvious. 'I didn't believe he played so I thought I'd come along and see for myself.'

'Jago? He's one of the best we've got. You're in the big white house, are you?'

'I'm in the only other house.'

Caroline inspected a French-polished nail. She chewed busily at the quick with all the determination of a small animal.

'Bit quiet for you down here, is it? Where've you come from?'

'I didn't say that.'

'Friends, then, are you?'

'Yes. We are.'

She nodded and looked back at the pitch. 'That figures. Jago doesn't do girlfriends. Not these days.'

Robyn shifted her umbrella to the other hand and blew on her fingers. A wind ran all along the touchline, driving the rain so that it felt as if it had blown in straight off the sea. She wound her scarf more tightly and looked again to Jago. His hair was flat against his head, his curls all but gone. He had mud across the backs of his legs and the print of the ball on his chest. No matter where he ran, or how quickly the game moved, she spotted him with ease.

'What makes you say that?' she asked.

'I was his last,' Caroline said, with a smart little smile. 'His first too, I reckon, though he never said as much.'

'You went out with Jago?'

'Oh, forgot to mention that, did he? That's about right. The silent type. Even before all that with his mum.'

There was something about Caroline's tone, an all-knowing overfamiliarity, that disinclined Robyn to ask any more. Jago belonged to Rockabilly cove and the rambling hillside and wind-bitten clifftop, not to a world full of girls on touchlines with sharp eyes and polished nails.

'I liked him,' said Caroline. 'He was different from the other lads, but he was fun, y'know? Made me laugh.'

She sounded wistful, her more playful tone quite gone. Her eyes followed Jago as he chased the ball, and Robyn watched her watching him. Then she watched him too.

When the game was over, Jago found her. She'd drifted away from the small crowd, away from Caroline, and was hovering near the clubhouse.

'Hello,' he said.

She looked buffeted. The brisk wind had drawn her cheeks red, and the persistent drizzle had lent her hair an uneven wave. Her earrings were starfish, tiny and silver and studded.

'Nice day for it,' said Robyn, waggling her umbrella, gesturing for him to step beneath it. He knocked his head on the spokes, and water ran off and dripped down his back, but he stayed under it, breathing her in. Her perfume was warm and sweet, like coconuts. He was so close he could see the hazel flecks in her gem-green eyes.

'What are you doing here?' he said, in a voice that gave away how pleased he was.

'I thought I'd come and see if you could play or not.'

'Verdict?'

'Well,' she tipped her head as if studying him, 'you didn't score.'

'We rarely do.' His eyes crinkled at the sides. 'Were you bored, then?'

'I made a new friend. One of yours.'

'She likes talking, Caroline.'

'Especially about you,' Robyn said with a smile.

'So you *were* bored,' he said.

'Massively. Hey, look, do you normally go for a drink afterwards?'

'Sometimes.' He hesitated. 'You want one?'

'I would. But . . .'

'No worries.'

'No, it's just I thought maybe we could go somewhere else? I mean, unless you want to be with your teammates . . . Only I'm going back to Warwick in the week, and I thought maybe—'

'I'd like that,' said Jago, before she could finish.

They ran to the truck, heads down, splashing through the puddles. She'd felt Caroline's eyes on them as they'd left the ground, heard a few of Jago's teammates' light jeers, and felt a quick flare of triumph, one that was quelled again as she remembered that Caroline had had what Robyn hadn't. Her persistent use of the past tense where Jago was concerned wasn't just the talk of an ex-girlfriend, but someone who considered him ineffably altered. Robyn's Jago kept his mum's guitar hidden beneath his bed. He stroked his dog's ears with a gesture as practised and gentle as a mother pressing a kiss to her child's forehead. He'd pounded through the waves and saved her, before he even knew her name. Her Jago was incomparable.

A crow stalked up and down the bonnet, taking off with a clap of wings as they approached. Once they were inside, the engine took a couple of seconds to get started. The windscreen wipers squeaked back and forth.

'Where do you want to go?' he asked.

'You choose.'

'The Coake Inn?'

Robyn smiled. 'Sounds great,' she said, as though it was no big deal, as though they'd done this all before.

Jago's pub was small and dark. The floor pitched unevenly, and the beams were head-grazing low. They were the youngest people there by thirty years. Sepia photos of famous shipwrecks adorned the walls, and a row of dusty ornaments – Toby jugs and kissing figurines – sat on a shelf above the bar. It was either cosy or creepy, and Robyn couldn't decide which. She looked at Jago as he made his way from the bar, a pint in either hand. Cosy, she thought.

'One of the few places my dad doesn't come,' he said, sitting down beside her.

'Are you trying to avoid him?'

'Not him,' said Jago. 'His reputation.'

He drank from his pint, watching Robyn. She held hers with both hands, and a trace of froth lined her lips.

'It's full,' she laughed. 'I don't want to spill it. Hey, I'm glad we came here. I can't believe we haven't done this before.'

'I thought about asking you a couple of times.'

'Why didn't you?'

Jago shrugged. 'I guess I thought you'd have other plans.'

'Me? While I'm here? But you're the only person I know.'

She spoke lightly, one hand playing through her hair. Jago took hold of a beer mat and turned it between his fingers. He tapped it against the table, then tossed it down, drank quickly from his pint.

'I expect Caroline didn't hold back when she was talking about me.'

'Actually, she did.'

'But she told you we used to go out?'

'Yep.' Robyn sipped her pint, eyeing Jago over the rim.

'It was a long time ago.'

She set down her drink.

'What did you like about her?' she asked.

'Caroline?'

'Just curious.'

Jago looked thoughtful, but his mouth began to twist as if fighting a smile.

'What?' said Robyn.

'Nothing, I just . . .' He laughed. 'Okay, honestly? Hers were the first boobs I ever saw. There you go. Deep and meaningful.'

Robyn snorted. She wiped beer from her lips and laughed.

'I can't argue with that. I did notice she's, er, well endowed.'

Jago shifted forward in his chair.

'We were never really friends, though.'

'No?' She fixed him with her eyes.

'No. Not . . .'

'Like this?'

Sometimes when she was at home in bed, wrapped in Merrin darkness, she worried that the charge of their early encounters had been replaced by a platonic camaraderie. Now she felt as if the afternoon had been building to this point. That her long-pondered decision to turn up when he least expected had paid off.

Jago kicked back, as if agitated, and crossed his legs.

'I wish you'd known me before,' he said.

Robyn stared at him. His words had come out in a rush, as though he'd been saving them up, waiting for the right moment, and they'd simply boiled over.

'I was different,' he said. 'Before.'

'What do you mean, different?' she asked softly.

'I didn't worry about things going wrong, because I never thought they would.'

'But we're all like that when we're young.'

'And what, by twenty-one we're supposed to be jaded? You're not jaded. You're . . .'

He wanted to say 'how I used to be', but he didn't. Because seeing her across the table, her hair falling across her shoulders in a mess of damp waves, cat-eyes glistening, her careful smile as radiant as sun after rain, she looked about as far from how he saw himself as he could ever imagine. His sentence hung unfinished. He looked into the bottom of his pint. When he looked up again, she was still watching him.

'I guess I stood back from things for quite a while,' he said, 'and then it just became a habit. My mates started calling me Jagone.'

'Jay-Gone?'

'Yeah,' he said. 'Because I never seemed to be around.'

Robyn blurted with laughter.

'Sorry,' she said, covering her mouth. 'It's just . . . that's actually pretty funny.'

His lips twitched into the beginnings of a smile. 'Oh, you think? You going to start using it?'

'I might. You know, if I'm at the cove and you're not, I might shout for you, *Jay-Gonnnnne!* Yeah, I can see that working.'

'Just don't expect any kind of reply,' he said, and he hid his grin in his pint.

They drove home to Merrin, the rain still coming down, piercing needles followed by billowing mist. Jago had bought them each a second drink and their hands had touched briefly as he'd passed the glass to her. Her fingers had tingled afterwards, and when he wasn't looking, she'd pressed them to her lips, laughing inwardly at her own ridiculousness. Now she held those same fingers in her lap, conscious of every minute slipping past, bringing them closer to the point when they'd have to say goodbye. Again.

'The rain's not going to last,' said Jago. 'The forecast's for sun the next few days. Cold and crisp. If you were staying, you'd see some swell.'

'Don't say that,' said Robyn. She turned to look at him, but Jago was hunched over the wheel, his eyes fixed on the dusk-dimmed road. The wipers smeared the rain back and forth. She sighed, loudly, audibly, eliciting a sideways glance from him. She sighed again.

They got to White Sands all too fast. The lights were off and there was only one car in the driveway.

'Do you want to come in?' she asked, suddenly.

Jago kept his hands on the wheel; the engine juddered and coughed.

'I could make us something to eat,' she added. Then, 'My parents are out. We've got the run of the kitchen.'

His face pulled into a smile. 'I'm always hungry after a game.'

'I make the best macaroni cheese in the world. Just so you know,' she said triumphantly.

'I've never had it.'

'What? How's that even possible? Okay, so I'm about to blow your mind, Jago Winters.'

Robyn beamed, the evening taking shape before her with renewed promise. She opened the door and jumped out into the rain.

nine

HER KEY WOULDN'T TURN IN THE LOCK, AND ONE PUSH TOLD her the door was already open. As she went into the hall, Jago wiped his feet scrupulously on the mat behind her. The clock, a domineering old grandfather, chimed six o'clock as they passed it, and she heard him start. It was the first time they'd been in her house alone together. She was aware of their every move.

Two days ago she'd found an album in a record store in Penzance, and she'd wanted to play it for him. As she'd listened in the shop, her ears swamped by headphones, she'd thought of Rosalind Winters: it was the jangling chords and the deep, sweet voice, singing of cross-country road trips and losing love. Robyn had wanted to know if she'd been right to feel like that. More than anything, she'd wanted Jago to hear the music, and then watch his face shift and change. Soften. Open. But now she knew she'd keep the record tucked away, saved for another day. It wasn't the thing to draw him out.

She'd tossed her coat and scarf on the hatstand as they came in, and with her back to Jago still, she flicked a button undone on her shirt. She'd chosen her underwear with care, dressing to the tune of her fantasies, imagining him breaking away from the football game, taking her hand and pulling her beneath the line of chestnut trees that marked the fringes of the pitch. If he peeled her shirt from her shoulders, he'd find a ruby-coloured bra, and beneath her jeans she wore newly bought delicate lace knickers. Her mind unwillingly flitted to Caroline, and she pictured her full breasts emerging from an elaborate corset, and a wide-eyed Jago, an easy-smiling, quick-to-laugh Jago. She undid another button, and pushed her shoulders back to give herself a lift.

Jago followed Robyn through the hallway. As he watched the shape of her back, her cascade of hair, the flick of her narrow hips in ripped and faded jeans, something inside him turned over. He breathed deeply. She turned around and gave him a smile, and it was a smile unlike any that she'd shown him before. Her chin was tipped, and her eyes glittered with intention. He noticed that her blouse had been unbuttoned, by at least two, and he glimpsed the swell of her cleavage. He tried to smile coolly back, but he grinned wide, he couldn't help it.

They went into the kitchen.

'So what's the secret,' he began to say, 'to your—'

She came to an abrupt halt, and Jago stumbled into her back.

'Dad? What are you doing?'

The room was dark, swamped in early-evening gloom, and Simon Swinton was slumped at the table. His head was bent, and his arms encircled it, as though ducking from a savage blow.

'Dad?' she said again, and her hand reached for Jago, finding his sleeve and holding on to it.

Simon raised his head, slowly, confusedly, and she thought

87

he must be drunk and passed out at the table. An unnerving sight, an ungraceful sight, but not frightening, not worthy of the way her heart was rattling in her chest and her hand still clung to Jago's jumper. She snapped on the light switch, and father and daughter stared at one another.

'Robyn,' he began. 'I thought you were out for the evening . . .'

There was no slur to his words, and his face was drawn and pale.

'Mr Swinton, are you okay?'

Jago moved towards him, but Simon flapped his arms with sudden animation, waving him away.

'You need to find your mother, Robyn. It's your mother, not me.'

His voice was hoarse, and his words skidded on gravel. He sounded, she thought, nothing like her dad.

'What's happened? Where's Mum?'

'She's taken the car. She's gone.'

'Gone? Gone where?'

'I don't know where.'

'Dad, you're scaring me.'

'What can we do?' Jago asked levelly.

'Robyn, I'm worried she'll do something stupid,' said Simon. 'Hurt herself, to hurt me. Because I deserve it, I do deserve it. God knows I do.'

'What did you do? Dad? What's going on?'

She went to her father and shook his shoulders. This wasn't him, so it might as well not be her either. She shook him again, and his hands closed around hers and held on. He took a giant's breath, one full of the threat of tears, and sank his head.

'Stupid bloody mess,' he said. 'I made a mistake, months

ago, months and months ago, I made a mistake. And I told her. Today. I told her, and now she's gone. I'm afraid she'll do something stupid.'

Caught in their storm, no one heard the crunch of tyres and the running of the engine, nor the shuck of the door or Marilyn's soft footsteps down the hall. She appeared like an apparition. Her face was wan, her eyes red-rimmed, and when she spoke, her voice was as brittle as falling glass.

'No, dear,' she said. 'You're the only one who's done something stupid.'

She stepped past them and opened the fridge. She took out a bottle of wine and poured herself a glass with a shaking hand. Sauvignon Blanc spilled on her fingers, and she swore beneath her breath.

'Someone needs to tell me what's going on,' Robyn said. She'd attempted authority, but she sounded like a tiny girl, her voice small and trembling.

'Simon?' said Marilyn, waving her glass, high-pitched. 'Do you want to take this one?'

'I'll go,' said Jago, quietly, close to Robyn's ear, 'shall I?'

Robyn turned to him. Her face shone white with disbelief. Her eyes were brimming and seemed to say, *Stay*. But she nodded. Her lips moved, no words coming. She nodded again, more vigorously.

'No?' Marilyn went on. 'You don't? Well, that's understandable, I suppose. It is rather embarrassing for all concerned. Robyn, your father's admitted to a rather sordid little affair. There. That's . . . that's . . . it.'

Her front collapsed, and her voice went with it. She leant back against the wall, one hand held to her face, her shoulders bouncing with the force of silent tears.

Jago walked quickly from the house, but as soon as he was outside, he stopped and turned back. Light streamed from the windows, cutting across the lawn in shafts. He stood in the shadows, watching their three silhouetted shapes moving in sorry patterns. He saw Robyn come to the glass and press her face to the pane. At first he thought she was looking for him and he made to step forward, but then she reached to the side and snapped the blind down, plunging the garden into darkness.

Throughout her last day at home, Robyn listened at doorways, padded down halls with bare feet, catching raised voices. In this way she pieced together the story. Jennifer had been Simon's partner in practice, a tiny woman, she remembered, with plastic clogs on her feet, looking more lab assistant than doctor. At his retirement party her contribution to the speeches had been clipped, a nervous public speaker. At the end of the evening she had, apparently, pressed her lips to Simon's cheek and said *Very best of luck, you'll be greatly missed*, and Marilyn remembered smiling benevolently, pleased with her husband's ability to matter to people. Then, one rain-filled afternoon in Merrin, as Robyn stood at the edge of a football pitch and watched a running boy, Simon had gazed from the sitting room window and felt as though his head would split if he didn't say something.

That morning, a letter had arrived from Jennifer. It had been a harmless letter, full of *how are you?* and *how is it, the good life?* without a single allusion to what had passed between them. But there had been talk of a visit, a spontaneous drop-in *one of these days*, and Simon had read between the lines and filled them in with his own neuroses. The thought of her spinning into the driveway in a holiday hire car, crashing into his new and cherished world, had been too much. Fifteen months after he and Jennifer Elton had last seen one another, he sought out his wife, drew her hands towards him, massaging them between his own, and confessed. A conference, he said, in a nowhere town. Too many drinks. She unhappy. Him consoling. One thing. Another. For months afterwards he'd kept his secret buttoned in, more than a year of feeling only half in the room, half in his own life. On moving to Cornwall he was, in his foolery, tormented to discover that Jennifer had come too. That was before the letter. The letter just moved things along. He told Marilyn she was the only other woman in thirty-seven years, and that was true.

His wife had taken the car and driven fast towards the sea, slicking down the country lanes. Much later, Robyn would find out that her mum had made a fierce resolution that day: that she would pay him back, even the score. And it was the reassuring clarity of that intention that meant, for all the weight of sorrow, the burn of anger, that she could walk back into their home, slide off her shoes in the hallway, pour a glass of wine, and tell her husband that it wouldn't be their end.

Jago didn't see Robyn before she left. He'd spent time shaping what he might say to her, what sympathy he could offer, remembering the feeling of her hand grasping for his sleeve, and the look in her eyes when he said he should go, but in the end he missed her. He was starting up the lane towards White Sands, hoping not to see Simon or Marilyn first, when a taxi bumped out of the driveway and sped off. He saw the shape of Robyn's head in the back seat. He watched the taxi disappear around the bend, nettles in the hedgerow swaying in its wake.

Robyn had never been happier to leave Merrin. Her home

was full of strange currents. Her dad's usual ebullience was replaced by a quiet self-loathing, and much as she wanted to rage at him for his betrayal, she found she couldn't, not when her mum was so insistent that everything would be *fine, just fine*. Marilyn had broken down just that one time, and ever since had gone about cloaked in calm, her face a picture of containment. A knot of sadness had tightened in Robyn's chest and stayed there. She took it with her in the cab to Penzance, having stiffly insisted to her dad that she didn't need a lift to the station, her eyes looking to her faraway mum. She sat on the platform for an hour before her train was due, tucked in a warm coat, her toes twitching inside her trainers, desperate to be on the train, heading inland and east and a long way away.

ten

JAGO HAD BECOME RECONCILED TO HIS DAD'S WAYS. HE WAS used to the lipstick left on coffee cups, the traces of floral scents on bathroom towels, a forgotten silk scarf hanging with the raincoats in the hall. But he rarely saw the women themselves. They turned in late and left early. He'd hear the gunning of the pickup in the pale light of morning as Denny delivered them whence they came. Then there was Marilyn Swinton.

One afternoon in April, a little under a week after Robyn had left, he saw her crossing the field, the barley parting like a sea. She knocked at the door with a smart rap, a sound that meant business. Jago answered and she stepped backwards, held her hands across her chest. Her lips were painted scarlet – he'd never seen Robyn's mum in lipstick before – and her perfume was clean and bright and overpowering.

'Oh. I was looking for Denny.'

'He's in the workshop.'

'Mind if I have a word with him?'

'Do you know the way?'

'I know the way.'

There was a looseness to her voice, her intonation slightly off. The words butted against one another, when she usually spoke as precisely as an actress. He watched her pick her way across the puddles in the yard. He saw that the bottoms of her pale, billowing trousers were already sodden, the only flaw in her otherwise immaculate appearance. That and the pulsing above her eyelid as she spoke. She carried a bag in her hand and Jago heard it chink. He had a sudden vision, and his heart dropped.

'Wait!' he called. 'I got it wrong!'

Marilyn turned, her face questioning.

'He's not here, he's out . . .'

The sound of a drill pierced the air between them. Marilyn raised one eyebrow.

'That sounds like it could be him,' she said, 'doesn't it?'

Jago watched as she pushed open the workshop door, without so much as a knock, and disappeared inside. The sound of the drill stopped. He stood for a moment, listening, then turned and went to the cove.

Jago walked home to Hooper's House with slow, reluctant footsteps. He'd stayed away an hour or more. He went to let himself in, then hesitated. He spun on his heel and crossed the yard, whistling loudly. He didn't knock; instead he threw open the door. The place was deserted. He felt the tension run out of his body. He'd worried for nothing. The pieces of a dining table were stacked on his workbench and he went to them, running his hands over their unfinished surface. If there was a Denny and a Marilyn, even the most fleeting of unions, anything with Robyn would be out of the question. He turned and headed back to the house. A pale afternoon sun had split the mist, painting everything, and he turned his face to its warmth. That was when he saw her. In an upstairs window, his dad's room, the curtains were half open. A figure was there, moving as quickly as a starling, just a twitch of fabric and then the curtains were hastily drawn. Jago stopped still. This time, he couldn't be mistaken. He'd seen the smooth and uninterrupted lines of a naked Marilyn Swinton. And he was sure that she'd seen him too.

When summer came around and Robyn stepped from the train, it seemed that Simon and Marilyn had found their rhythm again. She knew she'd missed the difficult days, for she'd spoken to each of them on the telephone, huddled in the hallway of her student house, and afterwards she'd lain on her bed, crying into a pillow. Something necessary was fractured, but they'd told her they would mend it, and she wanted to believe that could be true. Marilyn had a new and loosened edge to her voice that Robyn hadn't heard before. She said that Simon had been falling over himself to prove that he was sorry, and that in his regret he was diminished, quieter, his movements around the house soft-footed. *I almost feel sorry for him*, she said, then repeated and emphasised *almost*, with a low laugh, and Robyn marvelled at her mum's apparent ability to forgive. When she spoke to her dad, he answered with relief, his speech a grateful torrent. She wanted to check him, to say that she couldn't forget what he'd done, even if her mum seemed able to, but she simply thought it instead, remaining grim, tight-lipped.

'I'm going to spend the rest of my life making up for it,' he said, in a strangled but determined voice, as if he knew exactly what she was thinking.

Robyn observed her parents' behaviour, and saw the small

signifiers of affection gradually return: a squeezed hand, a patted back, the steadfast chinking of two glasses of wine. Ben had said *Leave them to it, it's not our business*, with characteristic breeziness, but Robyn stayed shaken. Her family's harmony was broken, and everything they did now – the languorous breakfasts, the cheerful dinners, the overlapping laughter – just felt like some kind of a patch job.

There were days when Rockabilly was sullen, even in high summer. The waves tore at the beach at low tide, or poured over the rocks when the tide was high. Undeterred, Robyn took her board and let it batter her. If the rain spat, she turned her face to it, blinking it away like tears. Sometimes she'd leave her board on the beach and clamber out to the rocks, taking Jago's fishing spot. Their paths used to cross, accidentally and on purpose, yet so far this holiday they hadn't. She figured it was because of *that day*. All the good about it – the shared umbrella, the huddling in the pub, the crackle of his smile as he followed her down the hallway – was washed away by everything else that followed. Her parents bursting out of their ordinary mum and dad selves to become tempestuous creatures, startlingly real and frightening for it. No wonder Jago was avoiding her.

She'd glimpsed signs of activity at the workshop, vans being loaded and unloaded, incomings of old wood, outgoings of new furniture, and she'd heard the sounds of activity – drill blades biting timber, hammers ringing out. Denny stayed tucked away too, and Robyn thought of her old neighbours, and how their lives had intersected day in, day out. There'd been conversation over fence posts, and chats in dressing gowns while stooping to pick up milk from the doorstep. In comparison, their two houses on that wind-battered hillside seemed as separate as planets, when they should have been leaning together for comfort. She'd thought of calling round casually, picking up where they'd left off, but she couldn't quite find a way to do it.

It was almost a year to the day since they'd first met, a year since Jago had pulled her from the water, and, for Robyn, his hands had never really let go. She felt them every day: as she sat in the tiered seating of a lecture theatre, flexing her fingers, imagining them tangled with seaweed, and holding him tight; as she lay in the bath, drawing bubble shapes across her chest, ripples of desire running through her, top to toe. Instead of their shared moments since, it was that first day that she took herself back to, again and again. She didn't relive the fear of the moments before; she thought only of the afterwards: the fact of him and her. Sometimes she imagined a fiercer outcome. If more seconds had passed, if she'd swallowed more water, sunk lower and for longer, perhaps he'd have had to push his lips to hers, breathing life back in. Maybe he'd have placed his palms upon her chest and pushed and pushed again, her heart responding beat by beat. Perhaps then their fates would have been sealed. But as it was, he'd let her go.

One day in August, the water was flat as a mirror. Robyn thought of sunbathing on the rocks, but if she went to the cove she knew she'd spend all her time looking about her, like a restless sentry. The experience would be too coloured with anticipation, and an inevitable sense of rising disappointment as the sun moved round and the day wound on and there was still no Jago. She quit her house and instead trailed into the fields. Without the surf, without the hope of Jago, she realised that for the first time since she'd come to Merrin, she felt lonely.

It was then that she saw Tomatillo. The horse was standing on the horizon line, appearing like a figurine, stiff-legged and motionless against the blue sky. He always looked lonely. Robyn headed towards him. As she drew closer, the horse turned to watch her. He flicked his tail with apparent disinterest, and moved languidly off.

'Hey, what happened to misery liking company?' she said, holding out her hand. She rubbed two fingers together and clicked her tongue. 'Here, boy.'

Up close, he was big. Bigger than he'd seemed when there was a gate separating them. His eyes were liquid and morose. His muzzle twitched.

'Hello, Tomatillo,' she said. 'How are you doing? Are you lonely too? Where's your master, huh? Hiding, I reckon.'

She held out her hand again, wishing she'd brought an apple or a handful of sugar cubes. He took a step towards her and tossed his head.

'I won't hurt you, you know that, right? I just want to say hello.'

He moved closer, and she felt the heat of his breath as he nudged her hand. Then he shied away, his tail in the air, spooked by nothing.

'He's not used to strangers,' said a voice behind her.

Robyn turned. It was Jago, and he was carrying a bucket of feed. He looked so casual – as if he crossed a field and found her there every day – that instead of pleasure at the sight of him, she felt a flush of anger. He looked at the horse instead of her. Tomatillo wound his way back to them. Jago reached out an easy hand and patted his neck.

'Hey, boy, it's okay, nothing to worry about.'

'We were getting on fine, actually,' said Robyn.

'I saw you from the window. Realised I'd forgotten his breakfast.'

She put one hand on her hip, facing him with something like defiance.

'I haven't seen you since I've been back. How's that even possible, when we live so close? It's quite a feat.'

'I've been here.'

'Right. You've just been hiding.'

'I haven't been hiding.'

'You're never at the cove any more.'

'The weather's been rubbish.'

'You've never cared about the weather before.'

He set down the feed. Rubbed his hands together.

'What are you doing out here anyway?' he asked.

'Just hanging out,' said Robyn. Then, even though she hadn't thought of it until that moment, and didn't know if she really meant it, she said, 'Actually, I was thinking of riding him. Can I?'

Jago looked at her sharply. She twitched under his sudden gaze, and lost her bluster.

'I mean, it was just an idea. I felt sorry for him, out here on his own all the time. I thought it'd be . . . fun.' Her voice trailed off, and in the silence that followed, quick regret rolled in. 'Look, I can't even ride properly. Forget it.'

'You can ride him if you want,' said Jago.

'What, really?'

'I'll get some tack.'

'I was going to go bareback,' she said, thinking that if he was calling her bluff, she'd call it right back.

'No you weren't,' he said, already walking back across the field.

Tomatillo had settled down in Jago's presence, and Robyn wove her fingers through his mane. 'You need combing,' she murmured. 'You're all tangled.' The horse blew through his nostrils and she started, then laughed at herself, glad that Jago wasn't there to see. He returned in just a few minutes, a saddle and bridle draped over his arm, a hard hat in his hand.

'You're not wearing the right clothes for it,' he said, as he drew close.

She had on a pair of summer sandals, and shorts. A T-shirt that offered a glimpse of her stomach. Her hair fell about her face, and she scooped it into a ponytail, flicked a band around it.

'Yes I am,' she said. 'I'm all set.'

'You'll wear this, though,' he said, handing her the hat. She took it, turned it in her hands, then put it on without argument.

Jago fitted the saddle, slipped on Tomatillo's bridle, set the bit between the horse's velvet lips. Robyn watched him.

'I haven't been avoiding you,' he said, straightening up.

His gaze was level, and she glanced away first.

'Yes you have. You saw behind the curtain, the perfect Swintons all undone. You didn't like it, and it's fine, I don't blame you.'

Jago's hand rubbed at his hair. He looked uncomfortable.

'Honestly, I get it. No one needs to be around that if they don't have to be.'

He breathed, envying her ignorance. She didn't know, after all.

'I wanted to see you,' he said, 'to make sure you were okay, but you left too quickly.'

'Well, wouldn't you? I couldn't wait to get away.'

'I was going to call you, but . . .' He hesitated. He'd thought of asking for her number, or her address, but that would have meant talking to Simon, or Marilyn, and after what he'd seen, he couldn't bring himself to do that. And he didn't know what he would have said to her, or written; the uncomfortable knowledge of his dad and her mum clouded everything else.

'Anyway,' she said, 'it doesn't matter. I'm going away again. Italy. On Saturday. Backpacking with my friend. She got hold of some cheap plane tickets and persuaded me to go with her. I'd planned to stay here, but . . . well, there didn't seem that much point.' She tried to shake the bitter tone from her voice, but couldn't. 'We're supposedly going for the art, but more likely it'll be bars and pools and Italian boys. Knowing Ruby, anyway. Summer in Merrin's pretty much over for me. I'll be back to Warwick after that.'

'I haven't been avoiding you,' he said again.

'Yes you have. Are you going to give me a leg up, then?' Robyn jumped on the spot, reached up and laid her hands on the broad expanse of Tomatillo's back. He shifted on his feet and made a low snickering noise. 'See, he's excited, he wants a ride.'

'Robyn.' Jago touched her shoulder and she turned round. He was standing very close. She blinked.

'Yeah?'

'No one's ridden him for a long time. I don't know if it's a good idea. He might be jumpy.'

'He's not remotely jumpy, he's like a docile lamb. And he's glad of the attention, aren't you, boy?' said Robyn, rubbing his nose. 'We all like a bit of attention,' she said.

Jago looked at her. A light breeze was lifting over the hill, and her hair was pulled forward. She popped impatiently on her toes, one hand on Tomatillo, stroking his flank. Her caress was gentle, and she turned from Jago and murmured to the horse, a low stream of sweet nothings. Jago moved closer. She didn't worry, that was the thing about Robyn; she appeared to wear a cloak of invincibility. It didn't matter that the sea had nearly taken her, swallowed her in one watery mouthful: she'd gone back time and time again, dancing her rough-edged dance, spitting seawater, laughing, falling, sinking, swimming. But then he'd seen how she'd crumpled when faced with her parents' fight, and knew she was breakable after all. He hated knowing about Marilyn and Denny, but he hated the thought of her finding out even more. So he'd spent the summer dodging her, because not telling her felt like lying. He knew she was angry with him. And he knew she wanted to show him that she didn't care.

'Here, then,' he said, holding a stirrup. 'One step here, then hop up. If he starts, I've got him. Okay?'

'Okay,' she said.

She flew on to the horse's back and took up the reins, grinning victoriously.

'Do you know what to do?'

Robyn shook the reins and Tomatillo shifted on his feet, walking forward.

'We're off!' she cried.

He walked beside her. 'You need to grip with your thighs, but not too much or he'll think you want to go faster.'

'I do want to go faster!' she said, shaking the reins again.

'No you don't. Robyn, wait. Tomatillo! Hey!'

They'd skipped trotting, instead breaking straight into a canter, a long and loping stride that took Robyn across the field. She shouted with laughter. Her hat slipped, obscuring her vision; she lifted one hand to right it, then changed her mind as she slid in the saddle. She gripped the reins again, her teeth gritted. Suddenly every muscle in her body was tensed. They'd left Jago far behind, but she daren't turn to look for him. The rhythm that had felt so smooth to begin with seemed to break. Her feet began to flail in the stirrups.

'Okay, slow down,' she said. 'Maybe slow down.'

There was a hedge at the bottom of the field, a fat and overgrown thing, snarled with bramble. It loomed closer and closer, and she pulled desperately on the reins, tugged handfuls of Tomatillo's mane.

'Okay, stop now,' she cried. 'Stop!'

He was going to try and jump it, she was sure of it. No matter that it was too tall, too ragged; beneath her she felt the horse's muscles stir as though gathering, his pace quickening. She imagined him rising from the earth like a Pegasus, winged and terrific and somehow possessed, storming the hedge and blasting on towards the cliffs, the sea. She could have thrown herself from him, as you saw people escaping moving cars, rolling twice, three times on the tarmac and being safe, shaken but safe, but the ground beneath her seemed a long way down and was slipping past at too great a speed. So she held on. She squeezed her eyes shut, stars blitzing her vision.

'Robyn, you can let go.'

She opened her eyes. The light blurred, and she felt a tear track across her cheek. His hands were on her, one on the small of her back, the other gently lifting her own from Tomatillo's mane.

'I can't,' she said. 'I'm stuck.'

Her fingers were bunched and curled, hanks of grey-white

horsehair caught between them. She looked down at them as though they didn't belong to her.

Jago carefully prised each finger away. All the time he murmured, half to her, half to the horse. Then he reached under her arms and picked her up. It was a feat, really. The horse was high and Robyn didn't move towards him, but when he took hold of her he was struck again by how light she was. He lifted her down, and she stayed holding on to him. Beside her, Tomatillo's flanks were rising and falling, matched by her own panting. The horse bent his head to tear at some grass, disinterestedly.

'I thought he was going to jump,' she said quietly.

'I shouldn't have let you do it. It's my fault.'

'I should have listened to you. I was stupid. I'm sorry, I'm so sorry . . .'

'You weren't stupid. You were . . .'

Robyn looked up. Her face was burning, and her hair was damp at the nape of her neck. She blinked, blaming the bright light, the gusty wind, for teasing tears from her eyes. He stepped closer, and she saw the flecks of grey in his pale blue eyes, and the curl of his lashes, as dark as a forest.

'What was I?' she said, her voice splitting at the last.

He stared right back at her, and they matched one another, look for look. She wondered how long they could stand there, just looking at each other, neither saying a thing. She heard a roaring in her ears; it was as loud as the sea, and it unbalanced her, making her feel as if she needed to sit down, only she didn't, she stepped towards him, her hand thrown out for balance, catching at his sleeve. Her eyes went to his mouth, following the line of his lips, and she could hear the quickening rise and fall of his breathing, then he was kissing her, and she was kissing him back. It was an underwater world of a kiss, where everything is deep, and slow, and shifting with currents, and you think that if you stop you'll surely sink, so you hold on, and you hold on, and gradually you move towards the surface, together, and you're still kissing even as you rise up from the water, even as you burst into the light.

eleven

WASN'T A KISS SUPPOSED TO CHANGE THINGS? IT SEEMED incredible to Robyn that a moment that, at its occurrence, fizzed with such intensity, could fall to nothing. In the five days she'd had before she left for Italy, she'd tried to find him. And she'd tried to put herself where he could find her. She'd walk to the cove at first light, surf what she could, then stretch out in her bikini. She'd fall asleep at noon, her board and wetsuit laid out in the sand beside her like a still companion. She'd dream of being woken, a kiss dropped somewhere unexpected, the back of her knee or the inside of her ankle, but instead she just emerged feeling stiff and drowsy. On the way home she'd dawdle in the lane, giving him every chance to spot her. She knocked at Hooper's House once, but there was no answer. She could hear activity in the studio, but when she peeped in at the window, she saw only Denny, his thatch of curls falling forward as he planed a length of wood.

Their trip began in the last days of August, in the galleries of Rome, and it was the work of Caravaggio that struck her most of all. His figures leapt from the canvas with a realism that stole her breath. She found herself transfixed by the sight of an outstretched hand, thinking how it looked as though it wanted to be grasped by another, that it wouldn't be complete unless it could. She moved with quiet steps through the hush of the gallery, her body thrumming with unspent desire, her mind turning always to Jago. They moved on to Florence, to Siena, to the strung-out hilltop villages, catching slow trains and eating salami from plastic packets, drinking warm wine from plastic bottles. Ruby asked her about boys, and she hesitated. How would she describe him? In the rude Italian heat she felt a rising anger. He'd kissed her, and then nothing. Her Merrin summer was long gone, and Jago with it.

Winter came to Cornwall. It was a year when the sea took icy breaths, frost pricked the coast path, and the cries of seagulls were strangled and throaty. Simon and Marilyn had met her at Penzance station. They stood arm in arm, mended then, Robyn supposed, and part of her marvelled at that ability to consign the past, to reshape and re-form. They waved madly as they saw her, swamped her with hugs and grabbed her cases.

Christmas came and went, the cold wrapping itself around the headland. Unlike the same time last year, her board stayed in the shed. In the dead days before New Year, a handful of snowflakes fell, melting before they touched the ground. Robyn pulled on her coat and slipped out of the house, breathing in the stillness of the outside world. In the lane, she turned towards Jago's. Just inside his gateway, she stopped. Her mum was at their door. Denny was standing talking to her, leaning against the frame, his arms across his chest. Robyn was about to call out, but something made her hesitate. She stepped to one side, just obscured by the winter-tattered hedge. She listened.

'It's just a bottle of port, Denny. Take it, for God's sake.'

'Simon doesn't mind?'

'It was Simon's idea. Season's greetings from us all.'

'So he doesn't know, then?'

'Of course he doesn't know. And don't. Don't do this. We said we wouldn't talk about it.'

'I'm teasing, Marilyn. You've got to allow me that.'

'I allowed you more than that, if I remember correctly,' she said with a flicker of a smile. 'Now, no more. Just as we said.'

Robyn held her breath as Marilyn and Denny said goodbye to one another, *Happy New Year*, a neighbourly greeting that appeared to speak of nothing else. She heard her mum's footsteps moving across the yard, and bolted before she could be seen.

For the turn of the year, the Swintons drove east to spend the holiday with cousins near Cambridge. It was a last-minute invitation. Robyn had turned down her university friends so that she could be in Cornwall, and she tried, and failed, to back out of this new plan. It was a long, claustrophobic drive with Robyn plugged into headphones in the back, feeling like a surly, watchful teenager. Simon and Marilyn conversed intermittently over the burble of the radio, their accord tested only as much as anyone's by holiday traffic. New Year itself passed in a spectacle of fireworks, observed from the cousins' rear garden; there were flutes of champagne, and a whole baked salmon. Marilyn and Simon kissed beneath a spray of mistletoe, while Robyn watched them sideways.

Past midnight, just as she was climbing into bed, her mum tapped lightly at her door.

'Robyn, are you asleep?'

'Not yet.'

Marilyn slid into the room. She had dressed for dinner, just as they all had. She wore a black cocktail dress and her jewellery glinted, her heels digging into the sheepskin rug.

'Good riddance to last year,' she said, the traces of a silvery laugh beneath her breath.

'Agreed,' said Robyn, propping herself up on her pillows. 'Well said.'

Marilyn was smiling, but in the low light Robyn could see the clutch of lines across her brow, the way her eyes stayed dark. She decided to speak, to let the last of the old year go.

'You and Dad are okay, aren't you?' she asked in a quiet voice.

'Oh Robyn, of course we are. You know we are. It was a lovely Christmas, wasn't it?'

'If you weren't, would you even tell me?'

She hesitated. 'I've never wanted to burden you children with our problems.'

'Mum, I'm twenty. And what problems? Is there something else?'

Marilyn dipped her head. She tucked a stray lock of hair behind her ear, smoothing it with the tips of her fingers.

'No, darling. We're fine, really we are.' She smiled encouragingly. 'We've led a charmed life, your father and I. There has to be the odd ripple. No one can escape that.'

'I wouldn't call what Dad did a ripple,' said Robyn.

'You know, sometimes it can be for the best, something like that. In a strange way, in an upside-down way. I really have come to believe that your father and I are stronger now than we ever were before.'

Robyn shrugged at the bedclothes. She felt hot. She'd had

too much wine at dinner, and drunk the last of the midnight champagne standing in the kitchen.

'What about Denny Winters?' she said.

Marilyn's face turned ashen. She attempted a recovery, gave a barely perceptible shake of the head, offered an almost-bright smile.

'Denny?'

'Jago's dad.'

Marilyn's brow creased with confusion. She rubbed her arms with her hands, as if feeling a chill suddenly. She stayed like that, wrapped in on herself, staring at Robyn.

'I overheard you talking to him. It wasn't a usual kind of conversation.'

'When was this?' said Marilyn, very quietly.

'Two days ago.'

'I took him a bottle of port.' She gave a short, shrill laugh. 'We've always done that with neighbours, don't you remember? We always used to give one to the Wiltons. And the Jessops.'

'It seemed like more than a bottle of port to me.'

'Robyn . . .'

'I just need to know if something happened. I just need you to tell me that.'

'Your father and I—'

'This isn't about Dad.'

Marilyn moved uncertainly towards the bed. She sat down on the very edge. Robyn shifted, tucking up her legs, her fragile space invaded. She stared at her mother, her eyes burning accusation, tears threatening.

'Of course it is. Robyn, it's everything to do with your dad.'

Marilyn had taken a handkerchief from the pocket of her

dress, and she held it in her hands. It was an old, familiar thing, lace-edged and delicate, and she'd had it for as long as Robyn could remember. She smoothed it on her knee, an unnervingly repetitive gesture. When she spoke, her voice crackled at the edges, but for all its faltering rhythms, there was a surety about it that drew Robyn in and made her listen.

'No one tells you what to do,' she said, her eyes liquid, 'when you're faced with these impossible situations. Robyn, just because we seem old to you, it doesn't mean we're wise to go with it.' She pressed her fingers to her temples, and carried on. 'Your father hurt me very badly, and I didn't know what on earth to do about it. And then, suddenly, I did. I went to Denny. In a moment of utter madness, I went to Denny. All right, calculated madness, perhaps, but I had this very strong impression that if I did this one thing, this one foolish, reckless, ridiculous thing, just this one time, never to be repeated, it would somehow even things out. And you know, Robyn, it did. That's the truth of it. It really did. If your father were better equipped for coping with difficult truths, I'd tell him. Perhaps it would reassure him that everything between us really is fine, and that we're going to be all right, the pair of us. But you know what he's like . . .'

'I don't,' said Robyn. 'I don't think I know anything.'

'Robyn dear, please don't say that. You know I love your father. And you know he loves me. And you must know that we both love you, very, very much. I can't bear the thought of you hurting, of you thinking any the less of me. Please tell me you don't. Please tell me you understand.'

Marilyn looked at her so beseechingly, her face bare with such broken-heartedness, that Robyn was startled into a kind of comprehension. It was a fragile thing, when shock and hurt were mixed; it didn't take a lot to knock it askew, and replace it with something else entirely.

'I don't want to,' she said, 'but . . . I sort of do.'

'Thank you,' Marilyn whispered. She held out her hand-kerchief, a small, already damp peace offering. Robyn took it, balled it up in her hand.

'It was just once?'

'It was just once.'

'But Mum, *Denny*? How could you?'

'He's a good man, Robyn.'

'I didn't say he wasn't.'

'And he was good to me. More than anything else, I'm grateful to him.' She gave a low, sad laugh. She felt for Robyn's hand and found it. 'It's the silliest thing,' she said, 'but I feel as if we've somehow got our balance back. I feel as if Denny Winters saved our marriage.'

'What I meant,' said Robyn, 'is does Jago know?'

'No. No. I don't think so.'

'Are you sure about that?'

Marilyn squeezed her fingers. She began to speak and then tightened her lips. She shook her head.

'I couldn't say,' she said. 'But Robyn, this isn't about you and Jago, it really isn't. You mustn't let us—'

'There is no me and Jago.'

She hadn't meant to sound so desolate. Marilyn's face creased with pity.

'Oh darling,' she began, but Robyn shook her head. More than anything she wanted her mother to leave now, to let her be alone. She shuffled down in the bed, heaved the blankets pointedly around her, saying that she was tired, that it was late. Marilyn stood up, reluctantly.

'We've given you a hideous New Year, haven't we? God, I'm sorry.'

'I don't care about New Year, that doesn't matter.'

'Robyn?'

'What? Sorry . . . *yes*?'

'Can I say one last thing? If you make one resolution, it's to never give up. Because if something's worth having, it never comes easy. If I've learnt anything at all, I've learnt that.'

After she left, Robyn held her mum's handkerchief in the flat of her hand. It was damp and creased, all the way to its too-pretty edges. She pressed her nose to it briefly, breathed in the scent that was so familiar, so ineffably her mum that her eyes pricked and filled all over again. She tucked it under her pillow, and willed herself to sleep.

Denny had eschewed the pub, with its abundant tinsel, and songs around the piano, and pairs of hungry eyes marked out with extra mascara. He'd suggested to Jago that they stay at home together, and Jago had liked the idea, picturing whisky by the fire and perhaps the retelling of stories he hadn't heard in a long time. Rosalind stories. Maybe even her music, winding through the air like soft caresses. But in the end the evening had passed much like any other. Lukewarm fish and chips in vinegar-stained paper. Bottles of ale. The television flickering to itself in the corner. Denny took a pad and sketched lines for a new project, a set of garden furniture for a high-end holiday house in Porthcurno. Jago saw the way his pencil bit the paper hungrily, his face softening as he began to draw. He went to the window and stuffed his hands in his pockets. Beyond the glass, across the field, the sea crashed and rolled, the night air carrying its rough song. He looked towards White

Sands, but there were no rectangles of light, no plumes of smoke from the chimney.

'Have they gone away?' he said.

'Only for New Year, I suppose.'

'That's what I meant.'

On the television an old film was playing, jumping black-and-white images of women in furs and men in smartly tipped hats. There was dancing, the high notes of a piano.

'This film's so bad.'

'Shut it off if you want.'

'I don't know, it's noise . . .'

Denny looked up from his drawing. 'I'm not being much company. Sorry. Let's talk, then. What do you want to talk about?'

'I don't know . . .'

'What are your mates doing tonight? It's not too late, you can still join them. Write me off as a loss. Go on, I would.'

'Why? Are you suddenly wishing there was someone else here instead?'

'Someone else? Who else?'

'Anyone else. It doesn't matter with you, does it?'

'Jago . . .'

'Do you think I don't notice? Or don't care?'

'You do a pretty good impression of both, my son.'

'And why do you think that is?'

'You sound like you're going to tell me.'

'What difference would it even make? You wouldn't stop, you never have.'

'That's not true.'

'And I'd never try and make you. I understand that . . .'

'That what?'

'That this is you coping.'

There was a flicker at Denny's jaw, and Jago wanted to look away, but he didn't. He needed to see it, he needed to read his dad's face. He knew that if he didn't, the moment would be lost, and it wouldn't come again, not like this.

'It's been more than three years, and I still don't know how to be without her,' Denny said. 'That's all. That's all there is.' He shrugged. 'I can't give you more than that.'

'But why *her*, Dad?'

'Who?'

'Marilyn Swinton.'

Denny set his pencil between his teeth, bit down on it like a cigar.

'She came to me, Jago. Not the other way around. And that was months ago. Why are you bringing this up now?'

'And, what, you couldn't say no?'

'I don't suppose I could.'

'You took his port.'

'How do you even know any of this?'

'Here? In the middle of the day? Hard to miss.'

'She was a woman on a mission. You should have seen her.' He checked himself. 'Jago, her old man must have done something to really piss her off, that's all. Don't worry about it. I'm not worried about it. She's not worried about it. Forget it.'

'*Forget it?* Right. Okay.'

'Why are you bothered? This time? Her? Wait, hang on, it's not because of Robyn, is it? Does she know?'

'How should I know? I don't talk to her about it. I don't talk to her about anything any more.'

Jago drew the curtains, closing out the night, and the dark space where White Sands' lights should have been. He turned round and faced his dad. Bent back over his drawing, Denny's shoulders were stiff, his mouth a tight line.

'I'm not blaming you for anything,' said Jago.

'You'd have a right,' he said gruffly. 'Whichever way you cut it, there's some blame.'

'It's just, if Robyn knew . . . it would wreck everything. But her not knowing wrecks everything too.'

Jago and his dad stared at each other, then Denny pulled him into an embrace, one of woodsmoke and beer, sea salt and timber, and he said *Sorry*. A word that meant a lot of things, and Jago took them all.

twelve

THE DAY AFTER THE SWINTONS RETURNED FROM THE FENLANDS, Robyn went to Rockabilly. The sea was fiercely cold, and it made her skull ache, pushed the breath from her chest. When she was level with the rocks, she turned and looked back. There, after months of nothing, was Jago and his dog. She felt the swell coming, bent her head and barrelled into the wave, white water chasing her tail. It crashed over her head, as heavy as a house. She pushed back up to the surface, gasping. She grabbed her board and rode back out to do it all again.

Jago watched Robyn surf, making no pretence at doing anything else, while Scout nosed along the shore, stepping daintily over the wet sand. When she finally stomped in, he saw the fierce line to her lips, her cold cheeks burning with colour. She threw her board down on the sand and stood with her hands on her hips, her breath panting.

'You knew,' she said. 'Didn't you? That's why you've been weird. Why you've been keeping away.' She coughed. Banged at her chest. 'It's why you kissed me and then ran a mile. You knew that whole time, but you didn't say a thing.'

'I don't know what you're talking about . . .' he began.

'My mum and your dad.'

'Oh.'

'Oh? *Oh?* Like it's nothing?'

'It was nothing. Apparently.'

'Something like that is never nothing. Maybe you're used to it, your dad being your dad, but I'm not. Always a different woman, you said it yourself.'

'It wasn't like that. Your mum came to him.'

'Oh, come on. He's always creeping round, making eyes at anything that moves. My mum was feeling vulnerable and she fell for it, that's all.'

'I think your mum knows her own mind.'

'So you're an expert on my family now? You've been so superior, so distant, as if you're the only one who decides things around here. Why didn't you just talk to me?'

He stared at her. A length of seaweed was caught on her shoulder. Her hair was wet and knotted. She looked so angry, and so sad.

'Robyn, I didn't know how. I hated knowing a thing like that.'

'Or forget about talking, what about just *doing* something. Doing *anything*. What were you afraid of? That we'd be crossing a line? A line that doesn't even exist? Just because our parents don't know how to behave, it doesn't mean we have to be the grown-ups, the people walking around with all the noble restraint. Months and months, Jago, months and months, with one kiss in the middle, and then nothing.'

She picked up her board and hefted it under her arm.

'I've got a load of packing to do. I've got essays I haven't written, books I haven't read. I'm going back tomorrow. So everything that hasn't happened, and all the things that have . . . I'm forgetting them. I'm forgetting all about them.'

She started to walk up the beach, her ankle strap trailing, footprints deep in the wet sand.

'You know what,' she said, turning, 'this,' she waved her arm, 'this place, and this,' she waggled her board, 'and *you*, since I got here they're the only things that have really mattered. But I must have been kidding myself all along, because this isn't my life.'

'I should have just talked. But I didn't know how to say it.'

'What's new?' said Robyn. 'Nothing's new there.'

'I'm sorry. I shouldn't have made it about us.'

'Us? Jago, what *us*? You've had me here, week after week you've had me here, and now I'm going again. It's too late.'

'It doesn't have to be.'

Robyn stared at him, and he stared back. He realised he didn't know what to say next. 'Anyway,' he added, in a muffled voice, 'you could have done something too. It's not the eighteenth century.'

'Oh, right. Great. That's your argument.'

'I haven't got an argument. Can't we just . . .'

'Just what?'

'Can't we just start now? Start again?'

'I'm leaving tomorrow. So, what, you want to be my long-distance boyfriend? You want to come and visit alternate weekends? Phone calls, letters. Missing each other every day but knowing that when we see each other it'll be amazing. Is that what you want?'

'No.'

'But people do it. People do it all the time.'

'I don't want you to go at all.'

'But I was always going, Jago. From the minute I got here I was going again.'

'I know.'

'So . . . this is it,' she said, dropping her board again, hands outstretched. 'What do you want? I'm leaving tomorrow. What do you want?'

'What do *you* want?' said Jago. 'You don't want Merrin. Like you said, it's not your real life. It never has been for you.'

'But right now, this moment, I'm here now. This is real.'

'But it won't be for long, will it?'

She walked towards him. 'So?' she said, in a low voice. 'We don't have to make it about tomorrow, or next week, or next year. What about now? What about us *now*? If you kiss me again, if you touch me, if we do any of the things I'm pretty sure we both want, are you really going to be thinking about anything but the *moment*?' She grabbed his hands, and they were warm in her cold ones, dry to her wet. She squeezed them, and she felt him shift on his feet, take a breath. 'I mean really, Jago, are you?'

He turned his hands in hers. Ran his square-edged thumbs across her fingers.

'I don't want it to just be a moment,' he said.

'Right. So it's okay with someone like Caroline, but not with me?'

'You're different.'

A voice came from behind them, a cheerful, oblivious shout spinning across the sand.

'Hey, Robyn!'

She closed her eyes. 'Tell me that's not my brother.'

'It's . . . yes.'

'He's early. He shouldn't be here yet.'

She turned around, saw Ben emerging from the path at the foot of the beach. She snapped quickly back to Jago.

'I'm not different. I don't want to be different.'

Ben's voice cut in again before Jago could reply. He loped across the sand, shouting as he went.

'There you are! I want you to meet my girlfriend. I actually brought a girl home. God knows what I was thinking, but I did. Mum and Dad are going nuts. The wine's out, it's barely ten o'clock and the wine's out. I've left her with them, and they'll charm her to death if we don't get back there soon. Hey,' he said, as he reached them. 'Jago, isn't it? How are you doing, man? Little sister,' he clasped her shoulders, kissing her on the cheek, 'you look a sight and you're freezing. Come on. You're needed.'

'Wait,' said Robyn, wriggling away from his hold. 'I'll meet you there. Give me five minutes.'

'No chance. You'll be back in that water and you'll be hours. Come on, come now.'

'Ben, you're actually interrupting something.'

'It's okay,' said Jago. 'Robyn, I'll . . . see you later.'

'See me later? When later? Today later?'

'Oh. Sorry, guys. Ignore me,' said Ben. 'I'm going . . .'

'I'll write to you,' said Jago.

'*Write* to me?'

'Robyn,' Ben whispered theatrically, 'I'll see you back at the house.'

'No, it's all right, I'm coming. Jago's going to write to me.' She grabbed her board, roughly brushed the sand from its tip. 'I guess . . . goodbye, then. See you . . . see you sometime.'

Ben began to walk back up the beach, and Robyn followed him. Jago stood rooted. At the entrance to the path, she paused and looked back. He was in the same place. The wind was up and tore at his coat, sending his hair flying, but his feet were stuck in the sinking sand. He raised one hand to her. For a moment she thought he was calling her back, beckoning, but he was only waving, waving and turning, and then walking away in the opposite direction.

thirteen

IN WARWICK, SHE CHECKED HER MAILBOX EVERY DAY. EACH time she approached it, twisting her key in her hand, she felt hope rise inside her then fall abruptly away as she stared at its emptiness. She'd scoffed at it on the beach, a pathetic missive when what she wanted was something real. But now, holed up and hollowed out, a letter was all she could think about.

After five weeks, she broke and wrote to him. Late one night she sat in bed, a book resting on her knees, and said what she wanted to say. She didn't tame her handwriting, or measure the weight of each sentence as some might have done; instead she dashed it off, her teeth gritted.

Jago, how are you? How's Merrin? Don't tell me, I can guess. It's February so the snowdrops will be drooping, edged out by the first bursts of daffodils along the clifftops. The seawater will be kill-you-dead cold, but I miss it still. I'd be out in it if I was there, you can count on that. The seagulls won't shut up, just like always, although the crows inland will do their best to drown them out. So, that's Merrin. What of you? I thought I'd have heard from you by now. You did say you'd write, after all . . . I know I probably didn't seem that happy about it at the time, but, well, I'd just . . . offered myself to you, basically, and it felt like you were turning me down all too easily. Why is that? I want to know. Or maybe I don't want to know, but I feel like I need to. It's become important, you see. Let me try and explain. In the beginning, I felt like there was this bond between us, because of what you did for me, because of that day on the beach. You can't let the person who saves you just walk away. That's not right. And you didn't walk. You were always there, in some way or another. I want you to know that even though you think I can't wait to get out of Merrin, and maybe that bit's true, I want you to come with me. I want us to have our own adventures. I want us to be together, Jago. I don't want us to be friends, I want more than that. I've always wanted more than that. I know I'm only brave enough to say these things because I think you want them too. You told me once you were used to not talking too much, living where we live. Well, I'm making it simple for you. Just write back YES or NO. If it's YES, I'll get on the first train home. You can meet me at the station, just like in all the books and films and love songs. Did I say love? I guess I did.

   Robyn x

His reply arrived quickly.

I've thought about your letter, and everything you said,

and this is what I think . . . I know you didn't really want to move to Merrin. But I also know that since you've been here, you've found things to like about it. I know you like the sea, and I know you like to surf, even though the two together didn't seem to like you so much at first. I think it's amazing the way you've got on with that. You're a good surfer, Robyn. You've made the cove your own. Soon you'll be chasing bigger waves in better places, and so you should be. I know you'll probably never forget the first day we met. I know I won't either. You're right, there is a bond, and I don't think it'll ever be broken, it'll always be there. But I don't think you will be. And that's the kicker. My world's too small for you. So even though I thought about writing 'yes', I wasn't going to do it just to get you to come. I don't know what that makes me. Stupid, probably. But I do know that I don't want to be my dad. There's a whole other world out there, a bigger world, a brighter world probably, and you're just the girl to take it. So that's why this is 'no'.

Jago x

She stayed in Warwick for the Easter holidays. Her finals were approaching, and she hid in her student house and tried to study. She slept in a wrinkled bed, surrounded by stacks of books as high as walls, her music turned up bombastically loud. Occasionally she wondered what the waves were doing, but that was it. Merrin, clinging as it always had to the ends of the earth, appeared to drop off the edge entirely. Beyond her exams, the promise of a new world glittered, and she worked her way towards that particular light. It was, she told herself, much better to think about what could be, rather than what might have been.

In the workshop, Jago swept the shavings from his day's work. He tossed down the broom and went to the bench, pulling open a drawer. Tucked inside, way at the back, behind the rolls of sandpaper and receipt books and rusted scissors, he found the fin he'd made for her. It was one of the better pieces he'd created. He held it in the flat of his hand, watching its polished surface as though it might hold a truth. If he'd given it to her that first Christmas, perhaps there wouldn't have been a need for any kind of letter, but he'd followed his instincts then, just as he followed them now. It was important to do that, to keep to what you knew. There was enough uncertainty in life without encouraging any more, that much he'd learnt. It was better to be level. To stay steady. If great sadness still came, then at least you couldn't be accused of courting it.

'Nice piece, that.'

He turned at his dad's voice, feeling as though he'd been caught doing something he shouldn't. In his hands, the fin blazed.

'Shame to keep it hidden away.'

'It's ages old,' said Jago. 'I was going to chuck it.'

'Chuck it? Talk about a waste of good wood.'

It was whorled and the colour of coffee, polished to a high shine. On a board it'd look like a leaping dolphin, or a perfectly peeling wave. And it would work a treat, cutting the water like a hot knife through butter.

'Don't you know someone who could use a thing like that?' said Denny.

Jago glanced up quickly. 'I don't think she'd want it. Not now,' he said.

'Silly bloody sod, aren't you?'

'What? What do you know?'

'I can guess. Someone else might say you let her slip through your fingers, but I'd say you just ballsed it up. It's all the same.'

'It wasn't like that.' Then, 'She was always going to leave, Dad.'

'And what of it?'

'Well, it wouldn't have worked.'

'We're all leaving at some point.'

He looked as though he was going to say something else, but then he stopped. He reached out an uncertain hand and patted Jago on the shoulder.

Jago had never gone to his dad for advice about women. It was his mum he'd told about the girl with freckles and wonky plaits that he'd fallen in love with aged ten. She'd helped him make a Valentine's card with a pop-up ruby-red heart, lent him her calligraphy pen so he could write *Laura* in quavering letters. It was his mum he'd confided in when, at fourteen, his date for the school's Christmas disco had danced the last dance with someone else instead; she'd turned the car around and taken him all the way into Mousehole, and way past his bedtime they'd clattered down the steep and narrow streets and laughed at the blaze of Christmas lights, the humongous holly-topped pudding that marked the harbour wall, and the flashing reindeer that was bigger than Tomatillo. They'd crammed into a pub, one that smelt of pipe smoke and burning logs and sloshing beer, and they'd shared a secret plate of chips and half a glass of dark and creamy ale. And it was his mum he'd talked to when he'd had a first date with Caroline Murphy. She'd been standing in the kitchen in bare feet and a jade-green apron, stirring something on the stove, a late-night soup that smelt of fish and spice and garlic.

'You didn't wait up?' he'd said, amused, jumping to sit on the counter top, his legs swinging.

'I had the urge to make a midnight feast,' she'd said. 'Join me?'

'Where's Dad?'

She'd inclined her head towards the ceiling through which a low rumble of a snore was just detectable. Then she ladled two bowlfuls of steaming soup. Jago dipped his head to eat. It was clear and hot and bright and he spooned it quickly, his tongue burning. Four pints on an empty stomach had sent him reeling.

'So how was it?'

He'd looked up.

'Amazing. Delicious.'

'Delicious . . . Oh! Oh God, I thought you were talking about the girl. You mean the soup!'

And they'd both collapsed in laughter.

'The date was fine,' he said, recovering. 'Okay.' Then, 'The soup's better, mind.'

And they'd laughed again, rocking like lunatics, holding on to each other; Jago because he was still half drunk, and Rosalind because he was still her boy, he hadn't gone anywhere, not yet.

Jago stared down at the fin in his hand. Without a board, without water to slice through, it was just a useless object. His dad had moved his hand from his shoulder. He was making for the door. Jago took up his broom again and carried on sweeping.

'Don't ever waste something,' Denny said, turning, a ripple at his jaw. 'Not if it's beautiful. Not if it's worth something.'

fourteen

THE DAY OF HER PARTY WAS WHITE HOT. WILD FLOWERS WILTED in the hedgerows, the sand burned. Robyn woke early and went down to the cove. The waves were pulling perfectly, cresting in a burst of white water. She moved lazily, taking her time as she paddled out. When the feeling took her, she caught a wave, turning into it, driving a quick turn. She savoured the taste of the salt on her tongue, the touch of the pebble-strewn bottom between her toes.

Later, the cove would be strung with fairy lights, her brother's band straddling the rocks, their guitars throwing notes at the sky. Her friends, twenty of them, coming all the way to Merrin from Aberdeen, from Putney, from Harrogate and Brighton, would let the ebbing tide wash over their ankles as they danced and drank and sang 'Happy Birthday'. She'd made the dress code black tie; she liked the picture of penguin-suited boys clambering over the rocks, girls kicking off their heels to run barefoot. She'd thought long and hard about this invasion of her secret place, and decided it was what she wanted. Everything was changing anyway. If she moved to

London as she hoped to, she'd only be back in Merrin for odd weekends at most. Rockabilly would simply be a clutch of memories: a photograph taped to her wall, a sea-smooth pebble deep in the pocket of her coat. It had, she told herself, been too much a nowhere place, a temporary home squeezed between weeks away, and it should never have exerted such a hold over her. She blamed the sea. Its restless presence had called her from the very first day she arrived. And Jago, appearing from this landscape with his hair blown sideways, his smile pulling upwards, possessed of hands that could lift you from the water, and lips that kissed then stayed tight shut, in a line as straight and unreachable as the seaward horizon.

Her friends arrived in a flurry of sparkly dresses and strappy shoes, pristine dress shirts and puffs of cigarette smoke. They bore carrier bags that chinked and clinked with bottles. Lauren from Ely hoisted her frock to reveal the shimmer of a turquoise bikini, and Michael from Durham wore a beaten straw hat with his tuxedo. They were here for a beach party, and White Sands was everything they'd hoped for. Robyn had spent the morning lacing strings and strings of fairy lights all the way from the house to the cove. Lanterns were hung from the fingers of trees, to be lit as soon as dusk rolled in. A carnival of light that was sure to be seen from Hooper's House.

Down on the rocks, Ben and his band tuned their guitars, the last sun glinting off a single plectrum. The band had arrived that morning in a battered blue hire van. They'd reunited just for the occasion, and Robyn knew them all except for one. Ross was the drummer, with his bullet-cut red hair and his slow smile. Lucas played rhythm guitar, and was rounder than she remembered, his face a blaze of just-cut beard. The long-time lead guitarist, Richie, was now possessed of a set of twin baby girls and lived in a house in the country, but he'd sent his younger brother Eliot in his place. Eliot was, Richie had said to Ben and Ben had said to Robyn, the real deal. He had a band of his own, and they were on the up and up, only a matter of time before they were picked up by someone really big, he'd said. When Robyn was introduced to Eliot, she saw exactly what he meant, and he hadn't even played a note. He radiated self-possession, and something else, a sense of completeness. He was tall, gangly even, his arms long and knotted with muscle. His hair was dirty blond and fell into his eyes, obscuring them, until he swept it away with an unconscious flick and she saw how they were shining. His movements were cat-like, both nimble and languorous, as he skirted the lawn, and peered out towards the sea. In his skinny jeans and faded T-shirt, the toes of his boots darkened with dew, he appeared like an imposter in the landscape, an urban cowboy pitched from a basement club into her back garden. She watched him from the corner of her eye. As the others hugged and kissed her in greeting, Eliot came back over and held out his hand. She felt the calluses on his fingers, and she thought briefly of Jago.

'Welcome to Merrin,' she'd said. 'Population me.'

'Hello, Merrin,' he'd replied, with a smile as wide and open as the sky.

Jago stared at himself in the mirror. He looked like no one he knew. His jacket was stiff, tight under the arms, and the bow tie looked comedic rather than suave. They were borrowed clothes and they felt like it.

'Now that's my boy,' said Denny, coming up behind him. 'My man.'

'I look ridiculous.'

'Everybody always does. Then at a certain point in the evening, usually when you've had enough to drink, you'll realise that actually you look the business.'

'When did you last wear something like this?'

'A tuxedo? My wedding day.'

Jago pretended to take the mention lightly.

'People don't get married in black tie . . . do they?' he said.

'We did. Was the most glamorous thing we could think of.'

'Couldn't I have worn yours? It might have fitted better. Or did you . . .'

'What your mum didn't realise was that she'd have looked glamorous in an old sack. I was the one that needed the dressing.'

Jago turned back to the mirror. He twisted the bow tie, pulled at his starched collar.

'Robyn's the same,' he said. He glanced back and his dad's eyes met his with careful symmetry.

'You ever tell her that?'

'Tonight I will.'

He hadn't been invited, he hadn't heard from Robyn since his stupid, regretful letter. Then Marilyn had told him about the party, a lightly tossed mention as they'd passed in the lane, and weeks of indecision, fuelled by his dad's insistence in his idiocy, crystallised into a plan. All his reasons for saying no – and they were still there, whatever anyone said – had paled before the idea of her in a dress, surrounded by out-of-towners, at the cove he knew she called Rockabilly. Whether she stayed in Merrin or not, he knew he couldn't worry about that any more. And if it ended in heartbreak? Perhaps, just perhaps, it would be better than it never beginning at all.

'Good man,' said his dad, and they shared a smile. The moment was broken by Denny striding towards the window. He threw it open and craned out. The uneven strains of guitars tuning lifted on the air.

'What the . . . ?'

'There's a band,' began Jago. 'Her brother's . . .'

'Tomatillo's on his side,' said Denny. 'Doesn't look right . . .'

Jago joined him at the window. In the far field, just before the land ran off towards the sea, the horse was felled. His head lay in the grass, and even from that distance they could see that his legs were still, his posture not quite right.

'Wait!' shouted Jago, as Denny bolted for the stairs. He tore off his jacket, wrenched the bow tie free. 'I'm coming, boy,' he breathed. 'Hold on. Just hold on.'

The vet was in Penzance and came as soon as he could. Jago and Denny waited with Tomatillo, laid a blanket over his back. When they'd first arrived, he'd tried to get up, staggered to his feet then fell again. Now he lay still. Jago reached out his hand and stroked his soft muzzle, wiping a small burst of foam from his mouth, smearing it into the grass. Tomatillo's breath was laboured, rasping; his chest rose and fell while everything else, his usually twitching ears, his lively eyes, was unnaturally still. Down at the beach, the party had started; the cheers of strangers drifted up the hillside, music was everywhere.

'You don't like the noise, do you, boy?' Jago laid a hand on the horse's neck. Tomatillo's eyelids briefly fluttered, then closed. His chest continued to swell and drop. 'Can the vet even get through with all those cars parked in the lane?' Jago said suddenly.

'Don't worry about it,' said Denny. 'You should still go, you know. Wish Robyn happy birthday.'

Jago's hand stroked Tomatillo's coat back and forth. He would only have been a pretender in their midst anyway. The local boy in a hire-shop suit, a friend from home, not a friend she'd chosen, just one who got there first. He was made of Merrin, and that was undeniable. The rough grass, the listing hedges, the shifting sea. A sick horse lying on its side. A ghosted mother whose voice seemed to feel more distant every day. Could he even remember its exact timbre? Its rise and fall and bursts of laughter? Things were slipping from his grasp, and hope was dying too. He bent his head closer to the horse.

'I'm not going anywhere,' he said. 'Not yet.'

The vet appeared then, a wily figure in the distance, swinging a leg over the stile. Denny got up to meet him, striding across the field as Jago ran his hand the length of the horse's head. He whispered something that might have been a prayer, if he'd believed in any kind of God.

She'd never made heroes of musicians, but still she believed they were a little bit different. Her childhood memories were of Ben and his friends lolling on sofas, writing songs as easily as other people tossed a ball, throwing lyrics back and forth while someone lazily ran chords in the background. She'd watched them carrying their equipment out to a succession of broken-down cars, and even though she couldn't have been more than six or seven years old, she felt their charge, their visceral energy, as wheels spun on gravel and they drove off into the night.

The first time she saw Ben's band play she was thirteen. It was a pub in their local town, where she drank an illicit shandy and sat perched on a bar stool, her legs dangling. Once they were on stage, guitars against their chests, they stopped being familiar people. She watched with her lips apart, her eyes wide and getting wider, as they slipped from song to song, caught in their own whirl of beat and chord and vocal. They'd moved like a shoal of exotic fish, in perfect unison, a flash of colour in the pub's murky depths.

Seeing them now, years on, standing on their makeshift stage, amps balanced on rocks, seagrass bursting beneath the drum stool, she still believed in their magic. It didn't matter that their dreams of stardom were now consigned to nostalgia, or that the only songs they played these days belonged to other people. And Eliot, the newcomer, the borrowed guitarist, the real deal, shone in their midst as someone who was different again, drawing her eye back and back, despite herself.

That evening, it seemed that dusk brought with it a maudlin, reflective quality, as though someone had blurred the edges of the day, sponging the bright lines into indistinct shapes. It was July, and the night would stay away until the last. Jago would have heard the cries, surely, as her friends braved the water. And he couldn't ignore the music, lifting up and over the headland, blowing the seagrass, rattling the clifftops. She ran her hands over her hips, her dress was figure-hugging and silky, the colour of the wild roses that bloomed in the lane just down from Hooper's House. She hadn't invited him, but she thought he'd have come all the same. His absence glared, a presence all of its own.

Ruby danced past her, pulling at her arm, shaking her from her reverie.

'The band are amazing. Your brother's amazing.'

She was staring at Eliot as she spoke.

'My brother's the bassist. Are you talking about him? That's not my brother.'

'It's not? Oh, Ben, Ben's your brother. Who's that then? He looks like you. All long and blond, he looks like you.'

'That's Eliot,' said Robyn. 'And he looks nothing like me.'

She watched him, with his hair spilling into his eyes and his slender fingers picking at his strings, body swaying with the sound, and he looked up. He flicked his hair from his face and caught her eye, smiled in the middle of a verse. It was a simple thing, a smile like that, but not everybody could do it. As they played on, friends came and danced beside her, draped arms around her, pushed drinks into her hand, and she made all the right noises. She tried to stop her eyes from flitting to the coast path, to the opening at the cove's end, and even to the Rockabilly headland and the rock they'd sat on as they watched the night water and talked of far continents and Rosalind. The darkness swelled and swallowed recognisable shapes. Robyn danced slowly, her hips swaying, her arms held above her head. The sky was full of stars, constellation after constellation, bursting with so much brightness it looked as though it would fall. She closed her eyes.

'It's his heart,' the vet said. 'It's not sending enough blood to his head.'

Tomatillo had struggled up twice more, falling each time. Jago and Denny had moved with him, arms out, staggering on their feet as the horse listed. A stray hoof caught Jago's knee, and he swore, rubbing it with both hands. Tears came to his eyes and he didn't bother pushing them away. Tomatillo's nostrils flared. His coat sweated.

'It's why he keeps fainting.'

'So what can we do?' urged Jago.

Denny and the vet shared a look. 'He's shocking,' said Denny. 'A heart attack.'

Jago knelt beside him, wincing as he did so. 'It can't be. He'd just die, wouldn't he? If that was it? Drop down, and stay . . .'

'He's a tough old boy,' said Denny.

'He is,' said the vet, 'but he can't survive it. Not this.'

Jago stayed down, his hand caressing the horse. Beats carried from the beach, a frenetic sound that bounced off the clifftop. The vet's words were muffled at first. He repeated them, louder.

'A gun's often kinder,' he said. 'Or we can inject . . .'

'The gun. Put him out of his misery,' said Denny. 'If it's the only way . . .'

'Dad?' Jago appealed, his eyes wide and white by the light of the vet's lamp.

Denny squeezed his shoulder. 'I'll do it,' he said. 'He won't feel a thing. I'll be the one to help him, Jago.'

He didn't have to watch, but he did. His dad took the gun and tucked it into his shoulder. And it was done. One shot, a neat hole in Tomatillo's forehead. Right in the spot where Jago had laid his lips just before, and whispered *Bye, old boy,* then, *We love you.*

The band broke in a final flurry of flamboyant strokes and a staccato thrash of drums. Echoes boomed across the cliffs. The party crowd cheered, whistling for more. Robyn moved away, weaved through her friends. She bent to take a beer from the ice bucket stuck in the sand, and felt a light hand on her waist.

'Make it two.'

She spun round, her face bright.

'Oh, hi,' she said.

'You thought I was someone else.'

'No I didn't,' said Robyn, handing him a bottle.

He twisted off the cap and did hers at the same time, a deft move, then a chink of glass.

'Cheers. Happy birthday.'

'Thanks. Cheers.'

They drank, both turning automatically towards the sea in the way that people did by open water, as if in the hope that all that space, that freedom, would somehow open up their own lives. Robyn began to walk along the beach, away from the party, and Eliot followed her.

'I've played in some amazing places, but this definitely tops it,' he said. 'Your idea?'

'It's strange seeing the cove so full of people. I thought I'd like it, but . . . I don't know. I'm used to being here on my own. Or with Jago.'

'Boyfriend?'

'No. There's no boyfriend.'

'Surprising,' said Eliot.

'Surprising?'

'Very.'

Robyn shrugged. 'I just want to move to London now. Get away from here.'

'What's in London?'

'Everything. Isn't there?'

'Streets paved with gold, certainly, if you know where to look.'

'And do you?'

'Depends on your idea of gold. So when are you coming, then?'

'As soon as possible really.'

'Staying with your brother?'

'Maybe.'

They were walking through the shallows, Robyn barefooted, the water washing over the toes of Eliot's shoes. He didn't seem to have noticed.

'I like Ben,' he said. 'He should have stuck with the music, though. Richie's the same. These guys are acting like they're past it, and they haven't even given it a real chance.'

'He did, though. For years. All the gigs, the record company guys, all those promising noises then . . . nothing. Sometimes you've got to know when to give up.'

'Ah. I see. You're a realist.'

'People can only take so much disappointment, don't you think?'

'Disappointment is a conscious choice. No one makes you feel that way.'

'You really think that? Sounds like a bumper sticker to me.'

'You've got to keep believing,' said Eliot, 'otherwise who else will?'

'Determined, then.' Robyn nodded. 'Okay.'

'You bet I am.'

'Well, you're good at what you do, so . . .'

'You think?' His face was earnest, as though her opinion really mattered.

Robyn nodded. 'Really good. What's your band called? I'll make a note. Look out for you. Say I knew you before you were famous and all that.'

'The Fearless. We're called The Fearless.'

'I like it.'

'Look, this Jago . . . your beach buddy . . . what's the story there?'

'Just a friend who lives round here.' Robyn paused. Then she said, 'He saved me here once, right here, in fact. I was in trouble in the water, and he came and got me. Brought me back to the beach. That was how we met.'

'You're joking?' Eliot whistled. 'He saved you? No one can compete with that.'

It was an interesting turn of phrase. She glanced sideways at him. 'It was a couple of years ago now,' she said. 'A long time.'

'Okay.'

'It wasn't that big a deal. I thought it was, for a while, but . . . I guess it wasn't.'

'What was it you said? *People can only take so much disappointment?*'

'I wasn't talking about him.'

'Good,' said Eliot, and again she shot a look at him.

They'd reached the rocks that marked the cove's end. In the shadows of night they appeared like a slumbering prehistoric creature. Away from the party rabble the roar of the sea seemed louder. Robyn leant against a rock and took a swig from her beer. Eliot moved closer. It was dark, and they were almost touching.

'So there's no one special here at this party of yours? No one I should know about?'

'No,' she said quietly. Then, louder, 'No one.'

'You know that people can save each other in different ways, right? Not just the obvious ones. Like . . . if I did this . . .'

He leant in and pressed his lips close to hers. A brief kiss, so light. He kept talking, his lips brushing hers.

'This is me saving you from a loveless birthday . . .'

I don't need saving, Robyn wanted to say, but his lips were quietly insistent and she found herself falling into them. She opened her mouth and let her beer drop to the sand. Her hands pressed into his back. There was a similarity; Ruby had been right after all. Not in the brotherly way, far from that. But they fitted together. One brief kiss and that much was clear. Eliot drew back, cupping her face with both hands. He smiled.

'I told you I was determined.'

'I guess I like determined.'

'A beach, a girl, a summer's night . . . there's a song in this, you know.'

'That's an old song. It's already been written.'

'Not like this it hasn't.'

He kissed her again, and she felt the quick flick of his tongue. She closed her eyes.

'Don't stop,' she said, and he laughed, quietening her with kisses.

They walked back along the beach hand in hand. Beside her Eliot sang quietly, snatches of songs Robyn didn't know but felt she did. Now and again he turned to her, and she knew he was smiling in the dark.

'Everyone will wonder where I am,' she'd said, and he'd laid a line of kisses along her collarbone and acquiesced.

'Both host and guest of honour,' he'd said. 'I guess I can't steal you away for too long.'

'I guess not,' she'd said, a trace of reluctance creeping in.

'But later, when the party's over, when everyone's gone to bed . . . I'll find you again . . . how's that? That okay?'

'Yes,' Robyn had said, 'that's okay.'

Back in the throng, music was lifting from speakers, and her guests were strung out along the shore. Some danced, some were sitting half buried in the sand, whispering confidences, sharing bottles, the lit ends of cigarettes bobbing in the dark. Her brother threw an arm around her and she jumped.

'What have you been up to?'

'Nothing much,' she said.

'Not what Eliot said. He's smitten, Robyn, what did you do?'

'Nothing much,' she said again, but now she was doing it, smiling in the dark, because it was a good feeling to know that with just a few moments twined in each other's arms, a person could fall after all. 'What did he say?'

'That I had an amazing sister. I thought about correcting him, but I didn't want to spoil the illusion.'

'He said that?'

'He said that.'

'Aren't you supposed to be all territorial, protective?'

'I like him,' said Ben.

'I think I like him too,' said Robyn.

Jago sat high on the headland. The searing guitars and thumping drums had given way to Merrin's own music: the rattle and hiss of water on rocks, the thud of the shifting tide. On the beach below, Robyn's guests moved like shadowy animals, and he couldn't pick her out among them. A fire had been lit, and its flames jumped hungrily. He was mesmerised by it, his eyes stinging with its distant heat. He remembered another night, another fire. Precious possessions turned to ashes, his father's soot-smeared cheeks, and the clean tracks of tears running down them. So much loss.

Jago's dinner jacket was slung open, the once-white dress shirt mottled and creased. He ran both hands through his hair and sat hunched, his face pushed into his palms. Their torchlit vigil had ended. As the vet had walked back across the field, Denny had caught Jago's hand.

'It's been a long night. And you've missed Robyn's party. Why don't you go on down? Explain? She'll understand.'

'It's too late,' said Jago. 'There's no point.'

'Couldn't you use a drink? Go on. Or you'll regret it.'

'What about you?'

'Exhausted. I'm for bed.'

'You won't . . .'

'What?'

'I don't know . . . Will you be okay?'

'I'll be okay.'

'And you don't want the company?'

'Go. Go to Robyn.'

But Jago was moving slowly, weighted with sadness, and no one wanted that at a party. Instead he sat above the beach, invisible among the rocks and rough sprays of gorse. He wondered if she'd heard the sound of the shot. It had been deafening on the hillside, it still rang in his ears, but on the beach it was likely lost beneath the thrash of drums, the squeal of guitars. Even if she had heard it, she wouldn't have known what it meant. He caught a burst of laughter, and someone turned the music up again. He settled back against his rock and shut his eyes, feeling the wind blow in off the sea.

'We're done,' said her friend Phil, kissing her cheek as he passed, and Ruby, Jenna and Guy did the same. She watched as they wound their way back up the path, bound for the tented village that had sprung up in the White Sands garden. A few still lurked on the shore, swaddled in jackets and cardigans, determined to see in the white light of dawn. Ben and his band had long ago packed up their equipment; they'd have claimed the living room, be opening whisky and settling on sofas, thirty-somethings leaving the twenty-somethings to their games. Only Eliot remained.

'What do you want to do?' he asked.

'What do *you* want to do?'

'It's cold down here now,' he said. 'Go back to the house?'

'What, to bed?'

'If you want,' he said, with a wink.

'I didn't mean that,' said Robyn.

He slipped his hand into hers, leant forward and kissed her deeply. He tasted faintly of ginger, and his stubble nicked her chin. She gave a small, involuntary gasp and they broke apart, laughed at that, then kissed again. At some point they started walking up towards the house, climbing over the rocks and into the tunnel-like path. Their steps were hurried, breath becoming breathless.

'Shhhh,' said Robyn, as they sidestepped the tents on the lawn, arriving at the front door. 'No one must hear.'

Eliot nodded, and followed her inside.

fifteen

IT HAD NEVER HAPPENED TO HER BEFORE. NOT LIKE THAT. There had been a third-year student at university, Daniel, who'd lived in the opposite building and practised his saxophone by the open window. She'd called up to him once, one late night towards the end of her first year when she was feeling reckless and bold, and he'd beckoned her in. They'd kissed and kissed, and the next night they'd kissed again, and two weeks later, after more kissing, and a dinner at one of the town's better restaurants, and a back-row film at the cinema, they'd gone back to his room and had sex. It was her first time, and it wasn't as hurried, or as painful, or as world-alteringly dramatic as she'd believed it would be. Afterwards they'd lain side by side, squashed in a single bed.

'I wish the timing was better,' he'd said, curling a length of her hair around his fingertips.

'I thought the timing was pretty good,' she'd replied, grinningly flippant, because she didn't feel like she would ever love him, not this person, who was fun and kind and thoughtful and handsome in his own bear-like, stubble-chinned, brown-eyed way.

He'd moved to New York that summer and was still there, playing his saxophone for tourists. He sent her postcards every now and again, but they only ever made her sad. His lines were full of simple, heartfelt gestures but he was the wrong person. They were, she was beginning to think, always the wrong people.

Robyn woke as beside her Eliot lay sleeping. His arms were thrown up behind his head, assuming the posture of a beach-prone sunbather, his lips parted, a childlike simplicity settled upon his features. If he was made of dash on stage, angular limbs and sharp looks, in bed he was softened. She rolled on to her side and studied him for a moment longer, then fell on to her back, staring at the ceiling. Her head was fuzzy, the night's events playing back and forth like a quick-moving tide. *Okay*, she thought, breathing deeply, *okay*. She shuffled over to his side of the bed, laid a tentative arm across his chest and gently lowered her head. In his sleep he shifted and drew her closer. *Okay*, she thought, and closed her eyes, seeking to join him in his contentment, his sleep-filled peace.

The band was driving back to London after breakfast. Ben saw the last of their kit into the van, then came over to where Robyn was standing with her friends.

'Bye, not-so-little sister. You be good.'

'No goodbyes,' she laughed. 'I'm coming with you.'

'News to me.'

'I thought I might as well take advantage of the free ride. I can start scoping out jobs. Look at a few flats . . .'

'Okay. Good plan. But . . . anything prompt this sudden decision?' he said.

'Eliot asked me.'

He'd walked in on her as she was stepping into the shower. Dropped a kiss on the back of her neck and spun her round to face him.

'Come back with me to London. Let me take you on a proper date.'

'You don't think last night was a proper date?'

'I want to romance you,' he'd said. 'You're the kind of girl that should be romanced.'

'Who talks like that? No one talks like that.'

'Just say yes,' he'd said.

'Okay,' Robyn had said, 'yes. Why not? Yes.'

His eyes had lingered on her naked body and she'd pushed him away with a laugh. He'd turned and left her to her shower, a kick in his step, a whistle at his lips.

'Where will you stay?' Ben narrowed his eyes.

'With you?' she said. 'Or . . . with Eliot. Maybe.'

'Stay with me,' he said.

'Thanks,' she said. 'Maybe.'

'How long for?'

'I don't know, a day or two. Or three or four. I'm free, graduated, I've literally *nothing* to do except . . . well, all the things I have to. But let's not think about them. I'm free!'

'Take this for you?' said Eliot as he passed, nodding to the bulging rucksack that lay on its side at her feet.

'Thanks,' she said, and they shared a smile, a smile that spoke of deeper things than hefted bags and quick departures.

Her parents joined them then. They had the enthused and loosened manner of people who'd survived a youthful party,

Marilyn carrying a coffee cup into the garden, Simon in his extravagantly coloured beach shorts. He gave Robyn a brief lecture on the power of first impressions, and reminded her to polish her shoes if she was going for an interview, and make her handshake firm. Marilyn told her to have fun, to take care, to phone when she had a moment.

'Don't rush into anything,' said Simon. 'You've plenty of options, remember.'

'Yes, Robyn, don't rush into anything,' said Ben, giving her a knowing look.

'Thank you so much for the party,' said Robyn, giving them each a hug. 'And don't be too lonely without me.'

'Lonely? Hardly. We're taking that board of yours and going to your cove.'

Robyn smiled, just a beat too slow.

'Right,' said Ben, clapping his hands together. 'Let's get going, then.'

'Yeah,' said Robyn, a little thinly, then again with more vigour. 'Yes. *Yes.* It's time to get out of here.'

As the van pulled from the driveway, she leant forward. She pretended to be fiddling with her shoelace, but really she was stealing a look in the side mirror. The lane was empty. A snatch of the roof of Hooper's House was visible, a ramshackle gatepost, but nothing else. Nothing more.

Beside her, Eliot's hand found her knee and squeezed it. He turned his face to her and she thought he was looking for a kiss, but instead he put his lips to her ear and whispered, 'This is me whisking you away. Do you have any idea how happy that makes me?'

She looked at him. His eyes were the colour of hazelnuts

and shining bright. She could see all the way into him.

'Yes,' she said, 'I think I do.'

Simon answered the door, and grinned when he saw it was Jago. He was standing on the doorstep with a brown-paper-wrapped parcel in his hands.

'Morning, morning,' Simon said chirpily. 'I'm glad to see you look about as hung over as the rest of them.'

Whenever he ran into him, Mr Swinton seemed to greet Jago with excessive good humour, as if constantly seeking to show that that dark night at the kitchen table was a very long time ago.

'Hi,' Jago said, shifting on his feet. 'Is Robyn here?'

'You just missed her.'

'Oh.'

'She'll be back in a few days, I think.'

'A few days? Where's she gone?'

'To London. Hitched a ride with Ben and his cronies, cramped in that run-down van.'

'London? Why London?'

Simon waved his hand flippantly. 'Oh, flat hunting, job hunting, no doubt squired about by that bloody lead guitarist.'

A look must have crossed Jago's face, for Simon shook his head, laughing forcefully. 'Sorry. We've had a house full of young people and their gossip has been racketing off the walls ever since they got here. I'm corrupted.'

'She's missing some good surf this morning,' said Jago, stopping him. 'The best there's been all summer. That was all I came to say.'

Undertow

As each wave breaks, beneath the surface water rushes back out to sea. Beware the pull of rip currents, and other hidden forces.

sixteen

HE TOOK HER TO THE LONDON AQUARIUM. THEY HELD OUT
their fingers to the terrapins and laughed as their elderly faces
craned and snapped. They counted thirty-seven rainbow-
coloured sliver-thin fish rippling through pondweed, as fine as
the plastic kind that you held in your hand and predicted the
future. Halfway round they stopped at the café, where Eliot
bought her a hot chocolate heaped with cream and marsh-
mallows, and she felt like a child as she sucked it through a
straw. He took her hand and kissed each of her fingers.

'Stupid first date?' he said.

'I love it,' she said.

'I thought if you're ever missing the sea, now you'll know
where to come. That is, you know, if you move here.'

'You seem very keen that I do.'

'Me? I'm indifferent. Completely. Utterly. I'm . . .' he kicked
back in his chair and folded his arms across his chest, sighed,
'fooling no one.'

'It's nice,' Robyn said, 'to be wanted. It's nice.'

'Says the girl who's only ever been wanted.'

'Is that what you think? Wow, how wrong are you . . . I nearly wasn't even born, you know. My parents had an actual conversation about whether or not to keep me.'

'Come on. How would you even know a thing like that?'

Robyn paused. There was something about Eliot that made confidences easy. He's like a dog, she thought, a faithful, exuberant, tell-him-anything dog. His eyes were settled on hers, his smile willing her to go on. So she did.

'My brother told me. I don't think he meant to, I think he thought it was funny, and that I'd laugh too. I was pretty young, I didn't even really know what it meant, but I definitely didn't laugh. You've met Ben, he's quite a lot older than me, right? Mum and Dad must have thought they were done with kids, and then there's me . . . surprise! It was a shock. So they took stock, I guess. And I nearly didn't happen. But there we are, that's that, and here I am all the same.'

Behind his tumble of hair, Eliot's brow crinkled. He shook his head.

'No, hang on, don't you see? It's the opposite of what you're saying. Your parents *did* have you, *did* keep you, they actively *chose* to do both of those things, having weighed up all the alternatives. You were really wanted. Wanted more than most. Me, I just popped out. "Oh, there's another one, youngest of five, stick him over there." And then my folks moved to Australia as soon as we were all out of school. You, you were . . . considered. Chosen.'

Robyn drew out a marshmallow, let its sweetness melt on her tongue as she watched him.

'You're optimistic,' she said, 'one of those relentlessly cheerful people. Glass always, always half full. Shall we go and look at some more fish?'

He draped an arm around her shoulder as they left the café, and she leant into his side, all in one rhythmic movement that seemed practised, and maybe even perfect.

They came to the seahorses last. Robyn moved right up to the glass, and stared into the tank. Beside her she could feel Eliot twitching.

'Meet you outside?' he said. 'I'm dying for a cigarette.'

'These are my favourite. I'll be here for ages.'

'They're your favourite? I've always found them a bit . . . weird. They look sort of monstrous. And how do they get about? How do they even swim?'

'Have your smoke, and I'll bring you a leaflet so you can learn all about them.'

Robyn watched him go. He was clad in an old leather jacket and skinny jeans, an unlikely figure among the mums with pushchairs, the infants ogling fish. She liked that he'd brought her here, but was her heart leaping? Did her breath quicken when he was around? She'd spent last night with him again, and everything about it had been good. She'd liked his flat; it had reminded her of Ben's place and she'd felt immediately at home. Books and records lined the walls, guitars and amps filled the corners. It was much smarter than she'd imagined, tucked at the top of an elegant terrace in Kentish Town.

'How can a barman afford this place?' she'd asked with wonder.

'I'm not a barman, Robyn.'

'Okay, sorry, how can a struggling musician, occasional barman afford this place?'

'That's more like it, but less of the struggling, please. We're on the up and up. Actually . . . it belongs to my mum. She inherited it. And, well, why not?'

'It's a charmed life, isn't it, Eliot Turner? Beautiful houses and swooning girls.'

'I didn't see you swooning. I was the one who swooned. And it's a flat, a very small flat. A flat that has always looked pretty ordinary to me. Until today, that is. Glass of wine?'

He'd donned a sauce-splashed striped apron, and set about making dinner, pushing a glass into her hand, talking easily. Later, when they went to bed, she saw that he'd changed his sheets and lit candles and put on a record of a dusky-voiced jazz singer. A textbook seduction, maybe, but no less effective. She'd found herself not thinking of the past, or the future, the why, or the wherefore; simply him, the moment, that room, that music, the feeling inside her that had been building slowly, surely, and that now made it easier than she'd ever have imagined to fall into his kisses and sink back on to the bed. He'd told her she was beautiful. He'd kissed the insides of her wrists and the backs of her knees, run his tongue across her navel, and when they made love this time it was slower and longer, and afterwards Robyn lay awake as beside her he drifted easily to sleep. She wasn't worrying or regretting, just . . . mulling. He was making everything so easy. He'd looked into her eyes with such bare-faced truth, and held her so close, so tightly. Just because it was fast, and unexpected, didn't mean it wasn't real. She knew that. She believed in love stories as much as anyone; that wasn't the problem. The difficulty was that accepting this one meant letting go of another. And so she'd stared at the ceiling, and it was a very long time before sleep had taken her.

In their tank, the seahorses moved miraculously, swimming

quite upright, the faintest flutter of angel-like wings at their back. A pair emerged from the weeds, their tails curled, entwined. Wasn't it true that they were the only fish that mated for life? That these ancient-looking creatures with their long noses and ribbed bodies were the romantics of the ocean floor? Perhaps that was a myth, a fanciful telling, but she liked it all the same.

She turned and went outside, already knowing that she'd breathe in his smoky breath, run her hands inside his jacket, and say *Shall we go back to your place?* All enduring love had to start somewhere, and perhaps this could be it, after all.

On what should have been her last day in London, he took her to the riverside. They sat on the South Bank and watched people sauntering, posing for photographs, small children meandering among the fountains. The city slowed down here, and she slowed with it. She watched the water, and Eliot slung his arm around her shoulders, smoothed back the wind-blown tendrils of her hair, kissed the tips of her fingers.

'Stay. Live with me,' he said.

Out on the river a tourist boat moved past, tossing bloated gulls in its wake. A child on the deck threw up an arm and waved, as people do, on ships and trains and departing things. Robyn waved back, absently.

'Did you hear me? I asked if you'd move in with me. Don't go back to Cornwall.'

Eliot's face was so open that something in her ached. His eyes burned with sincerity, his lips apart with expectation.

'I know,' he said, 'I know. I never expected this, not so *soon* . . . But I really want it. I really want you.' He shook his head, swayed by his own sense of cheerful disbelief. 'It's that simple.'

'But you've known me for less than a week,' she said.

'Doesn't matter,' he said. 'When you know, you know.'

She wanted to go on watching passers-by and making idle chat. Get a couple of ice creams, steal licks from one another's cones. Go back to the flat and drink too much wine, watch a bad film, then borrow his toothbrush and throw on one of his shirts.

'You're lovely,' she said. 'And you make me . . . happy. Just purely, uncomplicatedly happy . . . That's one thing I do know.' She heard his quick intake of breath, and saw him break into an improbable smile. He took her hand and she felt his fingers close around hers. 'But,' she said, 'as much as I love the idea, I think I need to get my own place. To start with, anyway. It'd be too easy otherwise.'

'Nothing wrong with easy.'

'I just need to find my own way; then, when the time's right . . .'

'But you'll do it? You'll move here now?'

Before she could answer, he was kissing her, and she was kissing him back. On the bench, on the South Bank, as crowds drifted and passed, and somewhere close by a busker struck up a lovelorn tune. We're that couple, she thought, that couple that you sometimes see as you walk by, and you're marvelling, and you're twisting with envy, and you're full of wonder that for some, life is really like that. We're them.

seventeen

AS SOON AS SHE'D MADE HER MIND UP TO STAY, LIFE OPENED up for Robyn very quickly. Her friend Ruby had told her at her party that she'd found a flat in Angel, and there was a tiny box of a spare room, her rent suggestion similarly small. Robyn had said she was interested, but that she needed a job before she could make the leap. Now, she called her. She said if it were still available she'd love to take it.

'What, and you can move in right away?' cried a delighted Ruby.

If she telephoned her parents, she knew they could be persuaded to empty her wardrobe and drawers into a couple of cases. They'd drive to London, pleased to have a day in the city. Lunch with her and Ben. Perhaps the National Gallery. She needn't go back to Merrin at all, for even a day in Cornwall would feel like floundering backwards.

'I've already got the basics with me,' she said. 'I could move in tomorrow.'

'I have to warn you, though, it really is minuscule, more of a cupboard, some might say. Don't you want to see it before you say for sure?'

Robyn paused. 'No,' she said. 'It sounds perfect. I'm in.'

As she put down the phone, Eliot dragged her into his arms. She reeled back, laughing.

'I'll have to register with some temping agencies,' she said. 'I'm going to need a job, and fast.'

'And you'll get one, no problem,' he said.

'I don't even care what it is in the beginning. Dog walking. Phone answering. Coffee making. I just want to be here.'

They kissed with the kind of abandon that befitted a deliciously sudden decision.

That same evening, Ben called. He sounded harried, barely reacting when she said she'd decided to move in with Ruby, and that she lived in London now. His production assistant had expressed a sudden desire to travel the world, he said, and planned to leave the following week. Did she know anyone who was looking to start out in the industry?

'You're asking me?' she said.

'Yes, Robyn, I'm asking you. Have you any friends that aren't layabouts?'

'You're asking *me* if I know *anyone* who wants a job here in *London*?'

'At the station.'

'At the station that's in London.'

'What? Oh. No.'

'Come on! How perfect is this?'

'No, I don't think that's a good idea.'

'But you've suggested it before! And I did work experience with you three summers ago. Everyone said I was really good.'

'Everyone knew you were my sister.'

'Ben, I can do this. You know I can. I can take notes, make tea, push buttons at the right time . . .'

'Buttons? You wouldn't be let near any buttons.'

'Please, Ben. You can interview me. Go on, ask me anything. You know I can do this.'

'I know you can do it, Robyn, but do you *want* to do it? We have grads queuing out the door, you know.'

'Then why did you ring me?'

She heard him sigh at the end of the line.

'Ben? Benny?'

'All right,' he said. 'I'll give you a shot. Nepotism of the worst kind, but I actually think you're smarter than you let on. A trial week. If you don't screw anything up too badly, you can have an interview with the boss lady, and if she likes you, then you can stay.'

'Ben, I love you.'

'And don't you dare leave me in the lurch the minute something better comes up.'

'I wouldn't do that. Anyway, what's better? Nothing's better.'

She thanked him every way she knew how, then hung up quickly. She paused a moment. Took a breath. Balled and unballed her fists. Everything was happening very quickly.

'Was that what it sounded like?' called Eliot.

He was standing in the kitchen, pouring two glasses of wine. Robyn ran through to him, and he set down the bottle.

'Well?'

'I guess fortune really does favour the brave,' she said.

Jago was in the workshop. He wore a faded blue apron over his jeans, and a protective eye-mask was pushed up on top of his head, flattening his curls. He was bent over, intent on his work. Music filled the room, his mother's kind: guitars that rolled over plains, veranda songs, campfire melodies. He'd needed something. The sea was quiet that day, and there was no sound of surf, or the jubilant cries of a girl catching a wave. There was no whinny from the field as Tomatillo cantered its length. Jago had turned up the music and lost himself in work, the hours slipping past unnoticed. He was suddenly aware of someone in the room. He looked up, and reached for the stereo to turn it down.

'I'm not interrupting, am I?' said Marilyn, her voice loud then dropping as the music stopped abruptly.

'Nope,' said Jago. He pulled off his mask, and ran a hand through his hair. 'Hello.' He waited.

'I saw your dad in the lane. He told me about Tomatillo. I'm so sorry.'

'Thanks,' said Jago. Then, 'He was pretty old, I suppose.'

'We're going away for a couple of days,' she said. 'To London.' She spoke carefully. 'Robyn's decided to stay on, so we're taking her a few things.'

'Stay on? What, for a couple of weeks?'

'Ben needed someone at the station and so she's stepping in.'

'She's got a job?'

'Her friend was looking for a flatmate. It all just seemed to come together.'

'What friend?'

'Ruby.'

His hand went to his hair, and then stopped. 'And there's a boyfriend?' he said. 'A guitarist, or . . .'

Marilyn pushed her lips together in a not-quite-smile. Her eyes were soft.

'I don't think she planned it, Jago. Any of it.'

He fingered the mask that lay before him on the workbench. He picked it back up, pulled it over his eyes.

'It's what she wanted,' he said. 'Isn't it? This place was always too small. She said that from the beginning.'

He spoke more to himself than to Marilyn, looking about for his tools, wanting to feel the solidity of the plane in his hand, fall back into its groove.

'I was the same at her age,' she said. 'Only London would do. She'll be happy there for a bit, and then she'll be eyeing the horizon again. That's Robyn. Anyway, she wanted you to know.'

'She said that?'

Marilyn began to move towards the door. 'She said that if I saw you, I should say goodbye.'

He hesitated, pulled at his mask.

'Do you have a message for her?' she asked.

Robyn was gone, and she wasn't coming back. He thought of the party, how if he'd shaken off his sadness and gone to find her, things might be different. Now another place, another person, had taken her, and he was powerless to pull her from their grasp.

'Good luck,' he said. 'Tell her I said good luck.'

He bent his head. As she left, he turned the music back up. He saw her walk across the yard. When he was sure that she was gone, he took off his mask.

Robyn moved into Ruby's flat in Angel, her belongings filling her miniature bedroom. When she lay in bed, she felt as though she was a child hiding at the back of a wardrobe, the hems of dresses and coats brushing her face, the walls shifting ever closer. Ruby worked long hours at an advertising agency, and came creeping home exhausted, already thinking of the next day's early rise. Robyn found herself gravitating towards Eliot, who never said that he was too busy, or that he had something else on. She'd meant to be more independent, but her gaggle of university friends hadn't made the move as quickly as they'd said they would, and he was so relentlessly keen, and abundantly good company, that he was making those first London weeks feel exciting and new, but also easy.

She quickly got swept up in a new life, one that was all about paper coffee cups, and the rattling bounce of the tube ride to work, the swell of people surging from Oxford Circus station. She'd look up, see vapour trails streaking the sky, bound for far-off places, and feel a sense of innate possibility. Then she'd come back to earth and realise that she was already in the middle of it all. London was colour and riot and frenetic beauty; she slipped into the city's heart and let it pull her. Only occasionally did she feel a force in the other direction, at the glimpsed sight of a darkly curled head moving through the crowd, or the certain set of a shoulder as it turned from her. That was when she reminded herself that she'd laid herself bare and it hadn't been enough, she'd been proved all too easily resistible, and she felt the prick of that wound, and tried to ignore it. People kept moving, it was what they did; no one could be expected to stand still. But sometimes she'd shut her eyes and feel the wind lifting off the Thames, and she could imagine it was salted. Now and again the cry of a seagull would cut through the other city sounds and she'd hear it like a klaxon, twist her head to find its source, imagine messages bound to birds' feet, before she stopped herself and laughed at her own ridiculousness.

Eliot, meanwhile, swept her up just as the city did. As she followed Ben's bidding at the radio station, knowing it wasn't her vocation but enjoying it anyway, Eliot's musical wishes began to feel like hers too. He had such heart and ambition. In those first two weeks she went to two of his gigs, and she got to know each of the guys in the band. There was Simon the drummer, who was slim as a stick and with amber eyes, and Pete the singer, with a voice as sweet and rich as treacle. Ty was the bassist, and as he took her hand he shook out his dreadlocks and said, 'Eliot reckons you're half mermaid,' spinning her round so he could look for her tail.

She got to know a different version of Eliot too: before a show he was twitchy, jumping with nervous energy, gulping whisky and ginger with unsteady hands. He'd give her a kiss that was as deep as a well, then leap on to the stage, his guitar swinging at his chest. She liked the smell of him afterwards, the way his shirt stuck to the base of his back and how wired he was, his hands running over her body just as they ran over the frets and strings. Ruby made it to one gig, and Robyn loved taking her friend's arm, smiling past the doorman, saying *We're with the band*. Afterwards they drank free Jack Daniel's at the bar as Eliot and the others carried their kit to the van. *Okay, I get it*, said Ruby. *He's very cool*.

Ben seemed to like Eliot too. The three of them met for a coffee behind Denmark Street, in a dark corner of an Italian sandwich shop. Robyn watched her brother, with his slow smile and his easy talk, and realised how happy she was to have joined his world. Afterwards they looked in all the music stores, and Ben and Eliot fell to talking about Stratocasters and Gibsons, and Robyn hung back, enjoying observing their shared language. As they later went their separate ways, Eliot took

Robyn's hand and led her through the back streets, winding their way home to Kentish Town without any need for maps or Travelcards. It seemed to her that he was made of London, the city's rhythm perfectly matching his heart's pulse. With no allegiance to compass points or sides of the river, he criss-crossed and ducked and dived, at home everywhere, with anyone.

'It's how the songs come, you know,' he said. 'All these other lives. You can imagine you're anyone, because there's everyone.'

'It's the same in Merrin,' she said, surprising herself at the mention, 'the opposite but the same. When I'm surfing, every-thing else disappears. There's no one, so you can be anyone too.'

'I'll bet it feels like a world away now, though,' said Eliot, lighting a cigarette and eyeing her sideways. She looped her arm through his.

'Five worlds away,' she said.

eighteen

IT WAS A THURSDAY NIGHT, HER THIRD WEEK IN LONDON, AND she'd gone to see the band. They were playing at a tiny spot in Farringdon, a place where you had to stoop to stop your head brushing the ceiling, and the sound bounced off the walls. Robyn stood tucked beside a speaker, its vibration seeming to pass through her body. She pushed her hair out of her face, her forehead damp with sweat. A plastic glass of gin and tonic was warming up in the grip of her hand, the ice long melted. *This*, she thought, as the music roared and the crowd pushed, the complex rhythms of the city distilling and simplifying into that one beat-filled space, *this is why I came to London*.

The novelty of watching Eliot hadn't diminished. On stage he was a showman. His guitar appeared almost as if it was playing him, lurching and leaping in his hands as he fought to control it. He swayed to the left and the right, it climbed towards the ceiling and he hung on, thrashing until his fingers left blood on the strings. There were multiple Eliots, and she liked them all. She thought of the man who brought her mugs of tea in bed in the morning, with neat triangles of toast on a blue plate. Who came home with straggling bunches of park flowers wrapped in the pages of a free-sheet newspaper.

That night's crowd were lusty. Their set complete, the band kicked into a second encore. Eliot stood out front, his guitar lifting and dropping. Robyn tried to catch his eye, but he was in another place. She held her hand to her head, her attention pulled away. The room tipped and spun. It had been hot and crushing all night, but suddenly at the end the temperature had appeared to climb and climb. She was surrounded on all sides, and the crowd moved together, swaying and impenetrable. She looked round, her empty glass in her hand, but the queue for the bar was too deep. She needed water. She took deep breaths, and pushed her way to the toilets in the back, spiking her elbows and squeezing through tight spaces. As soon as she got there she rushed to the sinks. She ran cold water over the insides of her wrists, bent her face and splashed her cheeks. She'd anticipated relief but instead she felt a wave of nausea. She gagged, and slumped over the sink. She coughed. Behind her the cubicle was occupied. She coughed again, and made a cup of her hand, drank a mouthful of water, another. She closed her eyes. The music thumped through the walls, and as someone swung through the door it rose to a brief burst of raucous sound and she dipped over the sink again.

'You all right?'

A woman with razor-cut hair turned her huge eyes on her, placing a hand on her shoulder.

Robyn nodded. 'Just too hot. Drinks on an empty stomach. But . . . thanks.'

'Better out than in,' the woman said.

'I hate being sick,' admitted Robyn. 'It always feels like I'm dying.' The flush went and a girl came out of the cubicle. 'You go first,' said Robyn. 'I'm fine.'

She turned back and washed her hands with soap. The bright, brisk smell helped. As she scrubbed, the venue's stamp on the back of her hand faded. Normally she liked leaving it deliberately intact, going in to work the next day with her skin still bearing the traces of the night before. She squeezed more soap and washed her hands again. Then she took a comb from her bag and ran it through her hair, dabbed her lips with gloss.

'I'm fine,' she said again, and her pallid reflection stared back, unconvinced.

She opened the door and walked back into the wall of sound. In her stomach nausea continued to swell, and at the corners of her eyes there was a fizz of white light. She pushed through the crowd, heedless of treading toes or knocking drinks, leaving a trail of mild discontent in her wake. She fell out on to the street, gulping deep breaths, drawing in the night air; with it came the puff of traffic fumes and the spiced scents of next-door's takeaway. She bent to her knees and was sick in the gutter. She groaned, and was sick again.

Two days on, and the nausea still hadn't lifted. It wasn't relentless; it came in waves, each one reminding her that it hadn't been long since the last. She walked about London like a girl on board a slanting ship. It was then that she realised she was five days late. She took out her diary and re-counted, thinking perhaps she'd turned two pages instead of one, or lost track and muddled her numbers. She was five days late, and she was never late. She'd once heard that high states of emotion could do that to you, and leaving Merrin, bursting into London life, had sent her insides jumping, her head filled with specula-tion, anticipation and regret: a bag so mixed that it could be capable of turning anybody upside down and inside out. But then there was the sickness.

She bought the test on Great Portland Street on her lunch break. She watched the pharmacist's impassive face as she paid, expecting to see an expression of something, consolation, or encouragement maybe, but she might as well have been buying a box of tissues. She walked to work, her bag heavy with its new load. Her period was never late. She couldn't remember ever having felt sick without reason. But even as she disappeared into the toilets on the third floor, unwrapped the packaging, read over the instructions, she still thought she was doing an unnecessary thing. That was why she hadn't said anything to Ruby. And why she definitely hadn't said anything to Eliot. It was a gesture, the test, more to reassure her than anything else. They always used protection, even on the late, late nights when Eliot's breath was smoky and sweet, his movements loosened and quicker. Or when he kissed her in the kitchen, catching her unawares, his fingers teasing at her hem, her hands moving quickly to his belt. They always broke apart, split their rhythm to play it safe, Eliot dashing to the other room or pulling a condom from his back pocket. She flushed the chain, held the stick, and waited.

Back on Great Portland Street, Robyn joined the tide of homeward traffic. A pub spilled its drinkers on to the pavement, and she sidestepped the loosened ties, the rolled shirt sleeves, the spurts of laughter. She dipped inside the door. Tight groups of friends and colleagues crammed the bar, and she slipped through them, setting both elbows on the counter and catching the tender's eye. She ordered, then took a deep breath. The sounds of the bar roared in her ears. Everywhere around her was relief and bonhomie; an easy delight in the day being over and the night beginning. She was approached by an already drunken media type, his stubble artful, his T-shirt ironic.

'Don't drink alone,' he said.

'I'm not,' said Robyn, then 'Thanks,' as she took her glass from the barman and handed him a five-pound note. She turned without waiting for change and went back out on to the street. Smokers crowded the pavement and she weaved through them, avoiding the jab of their lit ends as they gesticulated wildly. She turned the corner, the quieter side of the pub, and stood with her back against the wall. The vent at her feet puffed out stale beer fumes. She blew through her nostrils. Held her glass to her lips and sipped cautiously.

'Here you are,' he said. 'You're hiding.'

Eliot found her lips and kissed her.

'I'll go to the bar. What have you got there?'

Her eyes burned, and she rubbed them fiercely.

'Just Coke,' she said.

nineteen

IN THE DAYS AND WEEKS THAT FOLLOWED HIS MUM'S DEATH, people had said to him that someone was never really gone if you kept their memory alive. They meant it well, they meant it kindly, and at the time he'd taken it with a small, grateful smile and a just-perceptible nod, but it had felt entirely wrong. His memories of his mum were not of the hazy, sun-blushed kind. They were too recent, too sharp, too much in focus, and they contrasted too cruelly with her intolerable absence. But now, four years later, he appreciated their words, and believed them to be true. If he heard a wisp of country music, he didn't flinch; instead he sought its source, opened his ears and let his mind run on unchecked. He'd make brown bread sandwiches with salted, just-pulled radishes, enjoying their rasping taste because they had been her favourite. In the spring he walked among the clifftop daffodils, and although he didn't cut their stems and bring them home, filling jam jars and milk bottles as she used to, he'd permit their jubilant blooms to give him some kind of happiness.

Robyn's absence was different. He had let her go. The only

fight he'd ever put up had been with himself, and the lesser Jago, the soft-willed Jago, had won. That was why he wouldn't go to the cove. Why he wouldn't sit atop the rocks and throw his fishing line into the water, or follow Scout along the shoreline as he rooted at low tide. Why his eyes wouldn't scan the sea looking for a darkened blond head, a flash of yellow board cutting across the waves. He had lost her, and so their shared landscapes were lost to him too. Instead he spent all his time in the workshop, volunteering to drive ever greater distances to collect timber or deliver pieces. His summer tan faded to nothing. Her parents' house, the home that had never really been hers, stood clean, and bright, and mocking.

One day, six weeks after she'd left, he saw Marilyn in the lane. She was riding a brilliant blue bicycle, with the upright stance and tightly gripped handlebars of an infrequent cyclist.

He wound down the truck's window.

'Hi,' he said, slowing to a stop. 'New bike?'

'How did you guess? I haven't ridden one in thirty years.'

'Where are you headed?'

'Into the hedge at this rate.'

Jago laughed. Sometimes he could see shades of Robyn in Marilyn Swinton. While Robyn's hair was golden, her mum's was threaded with silver, but it shared a certain quality. When the light was right it shimmered. And they both had grass-green eyes. He had made peace a long time ago with her visit to the workshop.

'What about you? We never see you these days,' she said. 'Do you hear from Robyn?'

'Robyn? No. No. Do you?'

'We might only be her parents, but she hasn't dumped us entirely yet.'

'How is she?'

'Still having a ball.'

He nodded. 'Good. That's great.'

'You should get in touch, you know. She'd love it.'

Marilyn was still astride her bicycle, but one hand rested on the side of his truck for balance. She wore a silk scarf, knotted at the neck, and had donned a swipe of lipstick for her bike's first outing. She smiled at him, and he found himself smiling back.

'Do you think?' he said.

'She left so quickly, she didn't have time to think about what she was leaving behind.'

'What do you mean?'

'Oh Jago, you know what I mean. I told you before, she never planned any of it. And she loved this place. She pretended she didn't, but she did. Everything happened at such great speed, and now she's in London, and that's wonderful and exciting, but . . . Merrin, and you, mean a lot to her.'

'There just wasn't enough to keep her here,' he said, quietly.

'Nothing's for ever. Her surfboard's in the shed. She might just be back one day.'

'Do you really think so?'

Marilyn hesitated. 'No parent likes to believe that their children have well and truly left. Your dad's lucky to have you at home.'

'I should get my own place, but . . .'

She hunted in her bag for a pen and scrap of paper. She held them up jubilantly, then scribbled out a number and an address.

'If you ever want to get in touch with her,' she said, pressing the paper into his hand. She rode off, falteringly, but only after giving him a look that seemed, that day, to be something like encouragement. He drove carefully past her, waving his hand from the window as he went.

'Go safe, Mrs Swinton,' he called.

She rang her bell in reply.

Jago had imagined Robyn so many times in her London life, caught in the city's embrace, and the thought of it had flattened him, made him feel dull and small and parochial. The glamour of her guitarist boyfriend, her media job, her first flat. Late nights, wild times. Perhaps, though, just perhaps, she did want to hear from him. Maybe even see him. An idea began to form, and it was a diverting daydream as he took the road to Penzance. The sea disappeared behind the hedges, and blue sky filled the road ahead. A steady wind was blowing offshore, and even without looking he knew the surf would be rolling evenly into the cove. It was, he had to admit, a Robyn kind of day.

Finally, she folded her hand into his. They sat across from one another, heads dipped as if in mourning.

'Talk to me,' said Eliot, his voice pushing urgency. 'Tell me what you're thinking.'

They'd walked home, eschewing too-crowded tubes and buses, the throngs of normal people living normal Friday lives. Eliot had tried to work his fingers into hers, loop an arm around her waist, but she'd resisted every time, preferring to walk in a posture of containment, her arms folded tightly across her chest. They'd passed through Farringdon, and Old Street, and everywhere there were people who looked like them, bold and bright with untroubled youth. How brief her sense of freedom had been. The city's innate sense of possibility was choked and gone. The tall buildings leered and loomed, and beyond them the strip of sky looked feeble, wan. Everywhere was a trap, and she was caught firmly in it.

She worked hard to keep her breath level. Beside her Eliot wore a dazed look. Every so often he nodded his head, as if wrapped in conversation with himself. Robyn shot him sidelong glances but mostly kept her eyes downcast, studying the old chewing gum, fag ends, uneven paving slabs. Somehow their steps took them to Eliot's house. Days ago she might have said *Let's go home*, sinking into the easy familiarity that characterised their relationship, but now she felt formal and distant, as if their bound fates had, conversely, wrought a distance between them. They had known each other for little more than a month. It had never felt like that, and suddenly it did.

She'd waited while he looked for his keys, then stepped carefully over the detritus of local newspapers and takeaway menus and followed him up the stairs, noticing the woody scent on the landing, the crooked pictures on the walls, as though she were a stranger.

Eliot lit a cigarette, then put it out again quickly. Earlier, when he'd taken a beer from the fridge, he'd said, 'Do you mind?' instead of 'Want one?' Already they'd started to behave like different people. Already their old, short, shared life was ebbing away.

'Smoke,' said Robyn. 'It doesn't matter.'

Eliot threw the pack on the sideboard. 'I want you to know,' he said, 'that whatever you decide, I'm here, and I'll support you.'

She looked up at him and shook her head, her hair falling like a curtain. She stayed behind it.

'What, you don't believe me?'

'I just can't see how it happened. I don't understand how we can be here, talking like this, in this situation. I mean, how's it even possible?'

'I guess we weren't as careful as we thought.'

'Don't say that! We haven't lost a wallet, or missed a train . . . I'm . . . God. I'm pregnant . . .' She tailed off, her eyes smarting.

'I suppose it could have been your party.'

'The first time?'

'Maybe.'

'We used protection.'

'It could've split . . .'

'But you'd have noticed. Wouldn't you? Eliot?'

'I don't know. It was dark. We were drunk. We were carried away. It's not impossible . . .'

'How could we be so stupid?' She shook her head. 'Please tell me this isn't real.'

Eliot didn't say anything. 'I'm here,' he said eventually. 'And that's real too. We're in this together, okay? Together.'

Robyn took his bottle of beer and held its cool stem against her forehead. She closed her eyes.

'I don't know what to do,' she said. 'I don't know what to do.'

Eliot stood up, taking hold of his cigarette pack again. He drew one out and held it between his lips. It bobbed as he spoke.

'There are two options, I suppose,' he said. 'Aren't there? Or three?'

'Yeah.'

'And any – any, Robyn – are good with me.'

'*Good* with you?' She set the bottle down with a clap. 'None are good. They're all bad. Very, very bad.'

They fell quiet. Eliot flicked his lighter on and off. His unlit cigarette stayed between his lips. On the street below, a passing flock of teenagers laughed and shouted. A car passed, blasting bass. Night noises.

'How can you be so calm about it?' she said, her voice querulous, her lips tight.

'I'm not calm. Not really.'

'But so measured, so sensible. How?'

'My mum had my oldest brother when she was eighteen.'

'Right. So it's normal for you.'

'Not normal, no. But it's happened, so we have to deal with it.'

'By deal with it, you mean . . .'

'No, I don't mean that. Not unless an abortion's what you want.'

'I don't want an abortion. I don't think anybody ever really *wants* an abortion.'

She knew that she was jumping on his every word, twisting it beyond its meaning. She slumped in her chair, hating the sound of her voice.

'I'm sorry. I feel sick. I feel exhausted. I feel like . . . whatever decision I make, it's going to have consequences, and either way, I don't know how I'll cope. I'm paid peanuts, and you work in a bar. And when you're not in a bar, you're rehearsing, or on stage, or dreaming of going on tour. And me, I'm free. No parents, no study, just me, doing what I want. And now . . . this. The opposite of free. I can't be a mum. I can't even think of being a mum. I'm frightened, Eliot, that's what it is. I'm really, really frightened. And I feel completely stupid.'

He crouched in front of her. He took her hands. 'I'm frightened too. But so long as we stay together, and decide this together, it'll be okay. We'll be okay. We won't just cope, we'll be great. I promise you that, whatever we do.'

'But we hardly know each other. Not really. One month. It's nothing.'

'It's not nothing. I think it's something. I think it's something pretty amazing.'

'So it doesn't matter to you?'

'This is your decision, not mine. But no, how long we've been together doesn't matter to me. Because . . . I love you.'

She exhaled, slowly, deeply.

'You're just saying that. You're lovely, but . . . you're just saying that.'

'No, I'm not just saying that. Look at me. Robyn, I love you.'

The moment was stolen as outside a siren wailed, pulling in somewhere close by, screaming to a sudden halt. It felt like it was coming for her, and she felt like she wanted it to. A desire to submit to someone else's hands, half deity, half doctor, someone with the foresight to tell her what her life would be, whichever road she took. She placed her hand on her still-flat stomach. Eliot's followed. She began to cry.

twenty

THE ATMOSPHERE IN THE CLINIC'S WAITING ROOM WAS TAUT
with private woe. Everyone there was bound by similar
circumstances, but there could be no acknowledgement of this,
except perhaps the briefest flicker of eye contact, the slightest
tightening at the corner of the mouth. Robyn sat on a hard
plastic chair, staring down at her shoes. Beside her, Eliot was
restless, drumming his knees with his fingertips. Occasionally
she glanced up at the glacial hands of the clock. People came
and went, women and girls with barely-there bumps, passing
through the swing doors, sometimes accompanied, sometimes
not. Robyn twisted her fingers together, made a steeple of her
hands and concentrated on breathing in and out, in and out.
Eliot kept on tapping four-four beats. Her name was called.
She stood up. She pushed through the doors, and they swung
shut behind her.

She was there because of the blood. There had only been a
little, but it was enough to make her phone the doctor, keeping
her voice as level as she could, and it was enough for them to

book her in for an early scan in two days' time. Until her appointment she approached each trip to the toilet with trepidation, walking about the house as though on sheets of glass. When the day came, she'd dressed formally, brushed her hair and tied it back. She'd taken time off work, endured Ben's doubting looks; despite her weeks of near-impeccable service, she was still too much his little sister, the eternal baby of the family. She'd wanted to blurt out the truth, wipe the glib expression from his face, but knew she couldn't. She'd told no one. Eliot had told no one.

Days after they'd found out, she'd woken him in the middle of the night, tugging fiercely at his shoulder. He'd bolted upright, his face pale in the dark, eyes wide with alarm.

'You know what I told you, about my mum and dad, how I'd been an accident, and they'd talked about whether to keep me?'

'Yes,' he said, his breath slowing, 'I remember.'

'I wouldn't be here,' she said, 'if they hadn't decided I should be.'

'Well, no,' he said, 'that's true.'

'So . . . I just thought of that. It woke me up, the idea of it. I thought about not being here, and I scared myself. And even though everything's crazy right now, I still want to be here. I've always wanted to be here.'

'Okay . . .' he said.

'That's all,' said Robyn. 'I just thought of it. I wanted to tell you. I know I sound ridiculous, but . . . sorry. Go back to sleep.'

'Does this mean what I think it means?'

'I don't know. Good night. I don't know. I think so.'

So they'd decided to take one road, but Robyn trod furtively, still casting glances over her shoulder, while her feet, and the tiny creature inside of her, carried her steadily forward. It was so small – at barely seven weeks it was less than the size of an apple pip – but it was already turning everything upside down. Robyn washed about on a tide of seasickness. Her mind was filled, every minute, every hour, with thoughts of this and only this. Her energy was ebbing, making the morning tube ride stifling, the claustrophobia of the lifts at the radio station verging on unbearable. She ate green vegetables and drank bottles of water and stared wistfully at bowl-like glasses of wine and hard spirits. She still didn't know if she was doing the right thing. It still didn't feel like there *was* a right thing. And then she bled.

The clinic only served women who had scares, pains, and histories of trouble, who needed attention before twelve weeks were reached. Robyn hadn't known that such a place existed. She hadn't known much about any of it. How your sense of smell could sharpen, detecting damp carpets, a neighbour's cooking, a trace of sweat on a passer-by's skin. How your breasts became sore and swollen, nipples piercing your T-shirt, the lines of your bra leaving grooves in your chest. And how the idea of sex lost its appeal, or perhaps that was just for her and Eliot. He'd told her he loved her, then they'd spent two weeks circling one another, swapping chaste kisses and homely hugs, a sudden and unfamiliar shift in their patterns. She wore a nightshirt in bed, and he kept his pants on. At night they fell asleep curled into one another, but the morning always found them on separate sides of the bed, a wash of unremarked distance between them.

The woman on reception had cut a grandmotherly figure, leafing scattily through yellow files, but her manner was brief and brisk, as though Robyn was there about a nagging tooth-ache, or a splinter in her finger. She'd given her name and taken her seat, and waited just as everyone else waited.

The scanning room was small and low-lit, equipped for one purpose only. The space was taken up by a monitor, a bed, a chair, and a rotund and smiling midwife, who stood to greet them, her voice sing-song sweet and soft with kindness. Robyn tried to smile back and realised that she couldn't. If she spoke, she knew her voice would break. Eliot took her bag from her. She did as the midwife asked, slipping off her knickers and lifting her skirt. She lay down on the bed, and closed her eyes. She winced slightly, feeling the cool gel, and the pressure inside. She bit down on her lip and waited for someone to say something.

When Robyn was a little girl, she would always stop to help the failing creatures. Any garden was filled with small tragedies, the spinning cycle of life, and perhaps young children noticed them more than most. A half-flattened worm growing dry in the middle of the path. A broken-winged bird lying beneath a bush. She laid grasses, heaped soil, lined shoeboxes with tissue paper, and whispered prayers. She'd thought that wanting something was enough to make life go on: that through the power and defiant optimism of her words, a mended butterfly would circle her head three times before taking off into the clear blue.

In that dark room, on that Wednesday morning, Robyn was told that her own small creature lived. At seven weeks, the nurse called it a baby, not a foetus or an embryo or any other distancing term. She called it *your baby*, and Robyn had never heard those words before, not like that. She lay on the hospital bed with her legs lifted and apart, and when she was asked if she wanted to look at the monitor, to watch the small blur, the barely-there shape, she hesitated, then said *no, no thank you.* Because the midwife had already said that her baby's tiny heart was beating too slowly.

'It's so early,' she'd said, in a tone imbued with sympathy. 'It's very hard to be sure of anything at this point. All we can do is wait and see. But the heartbeat does look very slow. I'm sorry.'

'What does that mean?' said Eliot, his voice lower than Robyn had ever heard it. Every nuance in that room, she read, and dreaded.

'I'm afraid it can be a sign that you'll probably miscarry . . .'

The world outside ceased to exist. In the low light, and the small space, Robyn broke into tears. Where had they come from? No place she knew. For hadn't she been ambivalent, wishing, almost, in stolen moments and unspoken words, that the decision would be taken away from her, and everything restored to normal. Her tears fell. The room closed in around them.

Miscarriage. She knew the word, but she'd never really understood it. She'd never felt its weight: the loss, the pain, the blood it carried with it. She knew it happened to women every day, for a poster in the waiting room had declared it so, as though the simple statistics should somehow make it easier to bear. But it just made it worse: to think of all the women she passed on the street, and how many of them must carry their private sadness, their extraordinary loss, while presenting an everyday face to the world.

The midwife led them to a room with a cushion-scattered sofa and potted plants. It was a room for bad news, and an atmosphere of sorrow permeated its soft furnishings and careful artwork. The walls held sorry secrets. Robyn bit down on her lip, a tissue crumpled in her fist. Eliot held her hand. They were told to come back in a week. Another scan, and see, just see. That was all they could do.

As they left the hospital, Eliot held her all the way. When they stood at zebra crossings she leant into him, her face hidden in his neck. She flicked her eyes away from passers-by, aware of her pale face, her tear-marked cheeks. Eliot wore shades, his eyes hidden, the line of his jaw clenched tightly. Together they trailed home, barely talking, with seven days to wait. Inside her was a tiny creature that was only just living, not quite dying, and there was nothing she could do to change that. She placed a hand on her non-existent belly, and she willed the heart inside to beat faster, to beat stronger. She thought of the failing creatures of her childhood, her matchboxes lined with scraps of toilet roll, her whispered prayers for broken birds. She searched her memory for one that had ever lived.

Back at home she curled on the sofa and shut her eyes. She could only count the days, the hours, until she had to go back and lie down again on that same bed and watch the nurse's face. Eliot would be beside her, his hand in hers. They would hold their breath. As an adult, Robyn had never prayed before. But she did then. She asked God, any God, to please look after this tiny creature. To make it strong. To will it to live. Let it know that so much life and love and laughter awaited, if it could only hang on. Beside her, Eliot curled his arm around her shoulders and pulled her into his chest. She breathed him in, and her tears ran.

'What will be will be,' he said, his fingers smoothing her

hair. 'Whatever happens, it's nature taking its course. It'll be for the best.'

'I know,' she said, in muffled tones, 'I know. But the thing is, the thing I've just realised, the two things . . .'

She faded, crying taking her voice.

'What, Robyn? What?'

'I want it,' she said. 'I want this baby. I don't want it to die. I want our baby more than anything in the world.'

He gently lifted her face and kissed her, salted kisses, their tears mixed.

'And the other thing,' she said, 'is that I love you. I love you too.'

twenty-one

JAGO RANG HER FROM A CALL BOX AT PADDINGTON STATION.
He'd caught the train at dawn, one of the only passengers
boarding at Penzance. The lengthy journey had sped past, the
hours slip-sliding until before he knew it he was ejected into
the hustle of the platform, tripping over suitcases, elbows
jabbing his, washed along on a tide of people who seemed to
know exactly what they were doing. He'd stayed calm for most
of the journey; it was only during the last part, where the train
had ground its way slowly between blank-faced offices, run-
down, city-smeared terraces, that he felt like a stranger in a
foreign land. He'd stared up at a high-rise, its uniformity
punctured by tattered flags, upside-down bicycles and struggling
window boxes. There was such a tangle of lives in a place
like London, so many people pushed one on top of another,
how did they not choke each other out? He wondered how
Robyn could like it there at all. There was no horizon line that
he could see, no room to stretch your wings, barely a sliver of
sky from where he sat.

Halfway along the platform he'd stopped still, letting the

train's load push past while he collected himself. He fished Robyn's address out of his pocket. He'd toyed with arriving without warning, like in all the films, but such a plan seemed too risky for real life. He imagined himself staring at the windows of an empty flat, pressing the bell, his heart jumping with expectation, only for the door to remain shut, unanswered. Or worse, a man's face appearing, the guitarist flashing a cocksure grin as he said, *She's not here right now*, then, *And you are?* So instead he called her first. He found a bank of telephones at the back of the station. The first one he tried was broken, the second had freshly chewed gum strung across the digits, so he settled on the third. He picked up the receiver with a shaking hand, and keyed in her number. It rang five times then went to the answerphone. He hesitated, hung up, then instantly wished he hadn't. He started over, dropping in all of his coins again. Her bright tones invited him to leave a message, and despite the dryness in his mouth, the weakness in his knees, he did.

'Robyn, hi, it's Jago. From Merrin. Anyway, I'm here, in London, and I thought I'd look you up. I saw your mum the other day and she mentioned . . . well . . . she said what you were up to, the job, the flat, and I realised you probably wouldn't be coming home, I mean, back to Merrin, any time soon, so I thought that seeing as I was passing I might as well drop in. On you. To say hello. And, well, to say goodbye, I suppose. Because we didn't really get to, did we? Maybe you don't know, but I came to your house the day after your party. But I'd just missed you. I wanted to talk to you, but I was too late. I'd done some thinking, and Robyn, I realised I'd been completely stupid. That letter I wrote, I got it all wrong. Anyway. I'm here now. And it'd be great to see you. There are things I want to say. Things I should have said a long time ago. I'm probably too late, but if I'm not . . . I'll do anything to make up for lost time. I still don't have a phone, so . . . I guess I'll try you again. I'm at Paddington. Okay, bye.'

He hung up, already hating the message he'd left. He'd been distracted by the buzz of the concourse around him, the deafening blast of the station announcements, and the weight of his own admission. He stared at the receiver. He wondered how long to wait before trying again. He wondered if he even had the bottle.

Two hours after he rang, Robyn listened to his message. At the sound of his familiar voice, she gasped. It might have been quieter than usual, barely audible over the clamour of background noise, but it was still Jago. Only he'd rambled on so slowly that the answerphone had cut him off partway through. Perhaps he hadn't realised, for there was no second instalment. She wondered fleetingly what had brought him to London. She wondered even more fleetingly what he'd been about to say when he mentioned coming to her house the day after the party, but that night, that world, seemed so far away now that it was impossible to spend long on the idea. She listened to the message one more time, then deleted it. Jago had to be the only person in the world not to own a mobile phone. If he'd had one, she could have sent him a text, making an apology, claiming illness, a message that was unspecific but grateful. As it was, she tossed her phone back on her bedside table and rolled over, stuffing her face into the pillows.

Eliot was in the kitchen making her a cup of tea that she'd forget to drink. Her radio was playing songs she wasn't listening to. It was Saturday; outside her window the city was crackling with weekend life, but it was just another day to get through before they went back to the clinic. Her world had shrunk, then shrunk again, and all that mattered was the life, or death, inside of her. Even if she'd known it was Jago calling, she wouldn't have picked up the phone. She couldn't have. One word from him and she knew she'd have broken into pieces before she'd even been able to explain why.

Jago finally got back on a train three hours after he'd arrived. First he'd bought a weak and overpriced coffee and sat at a metal table just off the concourse, shabby-looking pigeons scratting at his feet. He'd kept one eye and both ears on the phone in case it rang. He'd tried calling again but got only her answerphone, and he'd clicked the receiver back down before Robyn's recorded voice had finished its light entreaty. There would be no second message, he decided; the first had said it all. At the café he'd taken out the piece of paper with her address on it, looked again at his *A to Z*, wondering for the twentieth time whether he should go there anyway. In the end he'd decided not. It just wasn't meant to be. The whole trip had been ridiculous, and the fact that it had fallen through only proved it so.

Even as he'd stayed on in the confines of the station, he'd watched everyone who went by, his head raised hopefully, in case one of the many millions of people who lived in London happened to be her, just passing his way. He thought of how his palms had sweated as he'd dialled her number, how his throat had dried as he'd left his message, and how he'd rambled so incoherently, his big declaration limping in at the end as station announcements thundered in the background. He felt no relief, or triumph, at having tried to reach her. He settled into his seat on the train and slowly breathed out, the tension in his body gradually releasing. It felt good to be heading westwards again, leaving all that foolishness – the perspiring, the heart-rattling, the desperate roving eyes – behind him. If she wanted to, she'd call him in Merrin. Or write. Or even, maybe, come home.

After seven days of interminable hibernation, finding refuge only in one another, Robyn and Eliot had returned to the hospital. Their appointment was fast, and before they knew it they were back outside, their world altered inexorably all over again. They took a cab home, cocooned in the back seat, wrapped in one another.

'I can't believe it,' said Robyn, a near-hysterical edge to her voice.

'Neither can I,' said Eliot.

Their fingers were laced, their expressions matching, a dazed look that drew their mouths open, sent their eyes wide.

'I was so certain it would be bad,' said Robyn.

'I know,' said Eliot. 'Me too.'

'The way the midwife was so kind, so sympathetic, I felt sure she had bad news to give us.'

'So did I.' He shook his head.

'You know what,' said Robyn, after a while, feeling her way into each word carefully. 'You know what this means? This little baby, it really wants to be born. Don't you think? To hang on like that.'

Eliot took a deep breath and rubbed his face with both hands. His stubble made a bristling noise. As he took his hands away, his eyes swam.

'Yes,' he said. 'I do.'

'It wants us. It chose us. I never thought of it like that, but . . . it wants to be ours.'

She thought of arriving in Merrin just as the first autumn winds swept the coast, her newly rounded belly hidden under a loose-fitting dress. Her parents opening wine that she would have to refuse, surprised to see her guitarist with her, but pleased to meet him properly. *Eliot*, her dad would say, taking his hand and shaking it, *it's good to meet you*. What would she say then? Step back and link her arm through his, present themselves as a picture-book couple: *Actually, we've got some news*. Her mum's eyes would dart to her finger, looking for a diamond glint, a rash but romantic move that would startle but send them hunting for champagne. *No, not that*, she'd say, and perhaps she'd smooth her dress against her stomach, and wait for the slow dawn of comprehension on their faces, hear her mum's sharp intake of breath, her dad's unconscious growl. It was, she thought, an unreal scene.

'I've been thinking about it,' she said. 'I reckon I should tell my parents on my own. It's a lot for them to take in, and I really don't want to inflict that on you.'

Eliot looked fleetingly disappointed, and Robyn loved that about him, the fact that he was so easy to read.

'You'll thank me later, when I give you the debrief. There's bound to be tears, a bit of shouting, and that'll just be me.'

'But if I'm not there, won't they think I'm already shirking my duties?'

'I'll make sure they know you're not. I'll make sure I tell them exactly how you're being. I'll tell them that I love you, and that everything's going to be okay.'

She kissed him, sealing her words.

'What about *your* parents?'

'I'll call them. Once you've told yours. Then that bit's all done.'

'How will they take it?'

He laughed. 'They moved to the other side of the world two weeks after I turned eighteen,' he said. 'They'll take it just fine. They'll want to meet you, I'm sure they will, but they're not the kind to jump on a plane and shoot over. They'll come when it suits.'

Robyn looked somewhere between relieved and disappointed. Eliot always talked about his parents in blasé tones, and she knew only a brief history. His mum had been a teacher, psychology or sociology, she couldn't remember which, and his dad some kind of lawyer, *one who looked out for the waifs and strays*, he'd said, with a whisker of pride. They'd apparently retired early and moved to a bungalow in an inland Australian town, with a blue oblong swimming pool and a garden full of banana trees, their Joni Mitchell records and a fat orange cat called Martha. He said he hadn't seen them for two years, a length of time that Robyn couldn't fathom, but there didn't seem to be a rift. They were simply occasional visitors within his life, rather than part of every ebb and flow.

'Then I'll do a phone round of the scattered siblings. What about Ben? Will he be okay?'

'It doesn't matter,' she said. 'But yes, of course he will be. He's okay about anything and everything.'

'And that friend of yours, Jago, what about him? Will you tell him too?'

It was only then that she remembered his call. 'Jago . . .' she began, then stopped. 'I guess if he's there, I will. If he's not, I won't.'

'Okay,' said Eliot.

'I'm going to go and lie down,' she said. 'I feel sick. Again. I guess I should just get used to it.'

'Can I bring you anything?'

Robyn shook her head. Suddenly she wanted to be alone. Inside, she'd swung from joy to relief to trepidation to . . . something else. She needed to centre herself, lie back on her bed, place her hands on her midriff and think of the tiny life inside.

twenty-two

JAGO WAS SITTING AT THE KITCHEN TABLE, A STRANGE WOMAN across from him. Her skin was delicately creased at the cheek, and she kept tucking her hair behind her ears in a restless, girlish gesture. He'd made her a cup of tea and she held it reverently, smiling gratefully at him over its rim. When she'd slipped into the room earlier, wearing nothing but a pink lace nightdress, her hands had gone to her chest, fluttering like startled birds. He'd said good morning, as if it were perfectly ordinary for a scantily clad unknown woman to appear in his kitchen before the sun was up. He'd offered her a cup of tea, and busied himself making it. She'd disappeared, and returned wearing a knitted cardigan, a new composure about her.

Jago had heard his dad's truck pull out of the yard at dawn, and he'd lain in bed knowing that behind the door to his room there was someone still sleeping. He'd heard them come in the night before, muffled laughter rising through the floorboards, the chink of glasses, uneven footsteps on the stairs. He'd have found her in a pub, maybe in St Just or Penzance, and she would have fallen for his sideways smile, the way he dipped his head as he spoke, as though conspiring. His dad had always been charming, but the women he found these days didn't seem to notice the careless edge to his words. They didn't see that the shine in his eyes matched the drink in his glass, and failed to observe how his smile would drop when their backs were turned, flicking on and off as quickly as a switch. Or perhaps they did and it just didn't matter to them. Though Denny carried a reputation, it was borne quietly, and Jago had always suspected that people pitied rather than judged him. Which somehow made it all the worse.

'Does he always start work so early, your dad?' she asked, picking her way through the words carefully.

'Usually. We've a lot on at the moment. Speaking of which . . .' He stood up, rubbing his hands together as though he faced the day with eagerness.

'Of course, I'm sorry, you go on.'

'Take your time,' said Jago. 'There's more tea in the pot. Did you need a taxi, or . . . ?'

'I've got my car.'

Jago nodded, and the woman at the table held out her hand.

'I'm Lucy,' she said. 'I don't suppose you know their names normally, but I want you to know mine.'

'Oh,' he said. 'Lucy. Hi. I'm Jago.'

'I knew your mum a little, you know.'

He flinched.

'She was a lovely woman.'

She smiled as she spoke, and he saw then that her eyes were a deep hazel, almost amber. Hers was a kind face.

'How did you know her?'

'My husband ran a farm supplies shop. She'd come in now and again, for horse feed, other bits and pieces. She was always so elegant. I remember she used to wear these wonderfully shiny riding boots, immaculate they were. You'd couldn't help but notice her.'

'I think I remember it. The one just off the main road?'

'That's it.'

'Didn't it close down? I remember Mum being sad about it, saying she had to go somewhere else then, somewhere less convenient, less nice.'

'John died and it all ground to a halt, really. There were a lot of debts we didn't . . . well I didn't know about. We closed up four years ago.'

'Sorry.'

She pulled her cardigan around her. Her voice was bright, despite her words, and in her presence he felt his body begin to relax.

'Jago, I know I'm not the first person you've made a cup of tea for and pretended that it's usual for your dad to flee the house before the dawn chorus. He and I have a few things in common, you see.'

'He drinks too much.'

'Well, perhaps not that.'

'I don't really know what he cares about any more,' he said.

'He cares a great deal.'

'He wasn't always like this.'

'I know.'

'It's just . . .' He hesitated, then said, 'I don't think anyone can change him.'

'Would you mind if they tried?'

Jago thought of the empty bottles by the fireside, the wafts of strange perfume in the bathroom, the hairs trapped in the plughole, long and blond or auburn or red. He saw the botched finish on an elaborate dresser, a not quite even bookcase, the way his father had begun to pass the more delicate jobs over to him, those that required a particularly steady hand and a clear head. But more than this he thought of the way his dad ghost-walked about the house and land, and how since Tomatillo had died it had become even worse.

'I hope I see you again,' she said, before he could answer.

'I hope so too,' he said, and was surprised to find that he meant it.

At lunchtime Jago took Scout for a walk in the lane. The ground was patched with canary-yellow fallen leaves, and he stooped to pick up the spiked casing of a horse chestnut. He'd always loved autumn; it was when the tangled woods, content the rest of the year to play second fiddle to the show-boating sea, seemed to remind you of their presence. They blazed with colour, and when the ground was wet, creeping with mist and rolls of rain, they threw out their sweet, dark scent. He wondered what autumn was like in London, if you knew it was there at all, or if the city choked out the seasons altogether. Robyn had never called him back, and he'd begun to convince himself that she couldn't have got his message after all. Freed of the shame of his attempt to reach her, but burned enough to resist trying anything like it again, he'd found himself going back to his daydreams. They were safer, surer. He liked imagining her in a park, one of the big ones, putting her hands out to catch the falling leaves, turning her head to look for some sky. Or walking by the grey snake of the Thames, wishing for a cresting wave, and the sense of endless possibility that the far horizon offered and she so craved. Jago could only guess at Robyn's London, and sometimes he was kind on himself, and sometimes he wasn't.

He emerged from the woods at the back of White Sands, and straight away he heard a shout. It sounded distant, but it was unmistakably a female voice, taut and youthful. He paused, and ducked behind the hedge. It came again, followed by the slamming of a door. He pushed aside a bramble, and saw through to the Swintons' lawn.

Robyn was standing in what looked like a nightdress, her top half swallowed by an old jumper. Her feet were bare on the damp grass, and her hair blew across her face. Scout barked then, a gruff volley, and Jago saw Robyn turn at the sound. He barked again and appeared in the lane, his tongue waving like a slice of ham, tail wagging. Jago shook his head, held his finger to his lips in a pantomime display. The dog paid no heed, so Jago left his spot reluctantly, dipped fast along the lane until he was out of sight and round the corner, his breath coming fast.

Back at Hooper's House he went to the workshop. He picked up a saw and set it down again. He took up his old apron and turned it in his hands. Then he got to work, losing himself in the rhythms of sanding and polishing. An hour or so later, as long as he could bear to wait, he downed his tools and spun out of the workshop.

She was at the cove. He paused on the clifftop, the intervening months dropping away as he watched her sitting on the granite rock heap, staring out to sea. She didn't have her board with her, despite the impeccable surf rolling into the cove, but she did at least look like Robyn again. She wore jeans and a blouse, the bright tie of a bikini top at the nape of her neck. A clutch of gulls watched him watching her, then took flight noisily.

'Beautiful day, isn't it?' she said, without turning her head.

He sprang forward, heavy-footed on the turf.

'Why aren't you out on the water, then?' he said, taking a seat beside her. He felt her start at his question, and looked at her. 'How long are you back for?' he said instead.

'Maybe just today.'

'Long way to come for a day trip.'

'I got here last night.'

Beside him on the rock she sat stiffly. When the wind lifted her hair from her face he saw that her eyes were rimmed with red, her cheeks blotched. Merrin gusts could do that, draw tears from your eyes and colour your skin, but Jago had seen her like that often enough to know that this was different.

'How is everything?' he said, carefully.

She took a while to answer. Her eyes flickered, moving with the water.

'A whole lot better if I could have gone surfing today.'

'You've still got time.'

She delivered a low laugh. 'Yeah. I guess I have. So, tell me, what have I missed?'

She'd missed a white-hot September day, when the fields bristled with heat and the sea slung its spray reluctantly. It was the last day of summer, although he hadn't known it then, and the first time he'd been to the cove since she'd left. He'd dropped his clothes and swum naked, let the slow waves roll him gently this way and that, arms and legs gaping like a starfish. Unwatched, unseen, he'd drifted and thought of her. He'd stayed out until the skin on his fingers shrivelled and his chest ached and there was nothing left to do but crawl slowly back to shore.

'Tomatillo died,' he said eventually.

'No . . . When?'

'Three months ago.'

'Just after I left?'

'Just before.' A pause. 'Exactly before.'

Robyn turned to him. She took his hand and squeezed it fiercely.

'I'm sorry,' she said. 'I'm really sorry.'

'I wanted to tell you, but you'd already gone.'

'I wish you had.' A pause. 'Oh hey, about your message. I never called you back. You were in London and I missed you. I'm sorry. I'm sorry for that too.'

'It's nothing,' said Jago quickly. 'It was an afterthought. I was just . . . passing.'

'You were trying to tell me about Tomatillo and I didn't even realise,' she said. 'I'm sorry.'

He looked at her, puzzled. She'd made no reference to what he'd said, not the important things anyway: his mention of the letter, the fact that he'd got it all wrong, that the answer he'd given her had been wrong too. But she was here now. Perhaps that meant something. Perhaps it meant everything. He waited, his breath bated.

'I didn't mean to leave without saying goodbye,' she said. 'I miss it here, you know.'

'Is that why you've come back?' he said.

'What? No.' She let go of his hand and looked down, studied her fingernails. 'Not this time.'

Jago noticed her hand go to her stomach. She rubbed it idly. The sea moved in her eyes, and he realised she was crying.

'I'm like this all the time at the moment. I don't know what's up with me,' she said.

The wind took hold of her hair again. Jago wanted to catch

it, smooth it back behind her ears, then wrap his arm around her.

'I mean, I do know what's up with me.' She wiped her nose on her hand. 'I've got something to tell you,' she said, in little more than a whisper.

'So, tell me,' he said, trying to keep his own voice level.

'It's just that my parents are all over the place. It'd be better if they shouted, or said what they really thought, but they're impervious. They've honestly got nothing to say, and that's more disconcerting than a rant, or a lecture. Ben was exactly the same, and he's never stumped for words. I don't know if they're all afraid, or disappointed, or just think I'm very, very stupid . . .'

Her voice fell away. She wrapped her arms around her knees. Stared past him at the sea.

'I'm having a baby, Jago.'

A cluster of gulls erupted in a raucous chorus, their laughter bouncing off the rocks. They wheeled off into the sky, lifting and dropping on the wind. Jago watched them go.

'Jago, please, not you too. Say something.'

The gulls swept low over the water, then peeled away down the coast, yelling to one another, wings wide and sailing. They looked untouchable, as quick as the wind and just as hard to catch. He felt a hollowing inside his chest, as though the breath was blown out of him. He held on to the rock with both hands.

'Jago?'

'Congratulations?' he said.

They walked through the shallows, carrying their shoes by their laces. As the sand rushed between their toes it felt as though the earth was moving. Robyn stooped to pick up a shell, a curled mollusc, and washed the grit from its casing.

'Right now,' she said, 'it's smaller even than this.'

Jago took it from her, held it in the flat of his hand. He studied it intently.

'Twelve weeks. Just over. I'm due in the spring.'

He handed it back to her.

'Are you happy?' he asked.

'Happy?'

Jago shrugged.

'Actually, I am. Yes. I am. It's just . . . I'm getting my bearings. It's an unexpected adventure, this one, not what I ever imagined. But . . . it's exciting. Amazing. Terrifying. But . . . amazing.'

The incoming tide splashed at their calves and Jago stepped back, offering Robyn his hand. She shook her head.

'I want to swim,' she said, suddenly.

'It's had a summer's worth of sun, best time for it.'

'Do you want to come?'

'I didn't bring my kit.'

'Does that matter?'

She was already lifting her blouse. Underneath she wore a turquoise bikini, a string of beaded detailing running along each cup. As she peeled off her jeans, Jago's eyes skimmed to her still-flat stomach, then looked quickly away.

'I guess not,' he said.

'See you in there, then,' she said, and threw her bundle of clothes at the beach. She ran into the sea.

Jago pulled off his jumper, and unbuttoned his trousers. He stood in his pants, hesitating for a moment at the shoreline. Then he followed her in.

Out in the water Robyn spun round and watched him. She

took in his body as he waded. It was all angles, his chest burred and lightly tanned.

'I've missed this!' she yelled.

She had to mean the idea, for they'd never swum like this, bare-bodied, slick as eels. He felt the cloth of his pants sticking to his skin. He thought of her bikini, that was so small, negligible really. They were as close as they had ever been to naked together. He swam hard and caught up to her.

'I didn't even know how much until now, but *God*, I've missed the water.'

Her words were gulped, her breath quick. She dipped under as the swell rolled in, then pulled back to the surface, laughing as she trod water, a crazed edge to the sound. A wave had shifted her bikini, and he saw the dark swell of her nipple, peeping from the brief slip of fabric. He wanted to pretend not to notice, or throw a feather-light comment, but he was transfixed. She followed his eyes.

'Oh,' she said, 'bikini trouble.'

Before he could stop himself he was reaching out, and with a light touch he adjusted her, pulling the material back into place.

His fingers brushed her skin so fleetingly that she might have imagined it.

'You're covered,' he said.

They stared at each other for a long moment, then she turned and swam away.

For a while Jago didn't follow; instead he lifted with the waves, letting them wash over him. Robyn was moving at a fierce crawl. She grew smaller. He called her name, then again. Her head was sleek as a boy's, the blond turned water-dark, the arc of her arms throwing silver spray.

'Robyn!'

He duck-dived under, repeating the motion again and again, feeling the switch of cold currents beneath his body, the heightened swell. He found her floating on her back just beyond the tip of the cove. Her bikini was straightened but her breasts pointed in the water, her hair flowed behind her like a spread of lilies. Her stomach was pale, and just pushed the surface.

'You're too quick,' he said. His mouth tasted like salt, his lips were dry.

She rolled back on to her front, her body hidden.

'Jago, you have to tell me. Do you think I'm making a mistake?'

'I can't answer that.'

'Eliot loves me.'

'That's good, isn't it?'

'And I love him.'

'Then that's even better.'

She kept treading water, turning slowly. Her eyes glistened with seawater, making them greener than ever. A piece of weed clung to the tendrils of her hair.

'I've done my thinking, and it's okay. It's all okay. It's going to be okay. But . . . I'm sorry.'

It was her only acknowledgement of the most important contents of his message. The weight of her words, their brevity, their careful resolution, dragged him under. He swam to the bottom, letting his stomach graze the sand, opening his eyes in the dark depths. When he came back up, his chest was splitting, his head ached. In the bright light his eyes watered, the salt drawing quick tears.

'I'm going back in,' he shouted.

'I'll follow,' she said. But for once she couldn't catch him.

When she staggered to her feet he was already dressed, and walking up the beach. She pulled her own clothes on hurriedly, feeling the bite of the wind now. Her pale feet sank in the sand, and for a moment she felt as though she couldn't move, as if she were caught and held and stuck on the shore.

'Jago!' she shouted, but the wind took his name and whipped it clean away.

That was where her parents found her, as the weather turned and a dim light swallowed the cove. They crossed the beach, the water pulling at their boots, and eased her away.

'We were worried,' her dad said, folding his hand into hers.

'I was frightened you'd taken your board,' said her mum. 'I don't think that can be good, to surf, not with the baby.' She smoothed Robyn's still-wet hair.

'I was only swimming,' said Robyn.

'We saw Jago crossing the field. Was he here?'

'Yes.'

'And you're all right?'

'Yes.'

'Come on,' said Simon. 'Let's go home.'

She walked between them. For the first time in a long time, her mum and dad felt like parents again. She leant into them, allowing herself to be led, the exuberance of the water, the momentary confidence it had given her, all ebbed away.

twenty-three

THE TRAIN WHISTLED BACK TO LONDON. FROM PENZANCE TO Plymouth she sat with her face pushed to the glass, the view shifting and blurring before her. They crossed estuary waters, with tilted sailing boats and sunken mudflats. They passed forested slopes dotted with sheep, and sped through autumnal tunnels of green and gold. Robyn hung on to every scene, storing it, making it matter. Somewhere far behind was Merrin, two houses clinging to a hillside, a wave-dashed cove, and Jago Winters. The unchangeable, unshakeable Jago, who saved all his best words for the wind, and the clifftop. Only the bait he pushed on his line could know how he really felt, or the dog lead curled in his palm, or the wood he worked and polished and shaped.

Eliot made his proclamations with an open face and open heart. He was easy to love back, a man like that. Resistance would have been an unnatural thing. Jago belonged to an old life now, and inside her, a new one was beginning. She couldn't feel it yet, no kicks or thrusts or flutters, but her stomach was just slightly swelled, and she felt different. It wasn't the sickness, for that had all but ebbed away, it wasn't the brief and flashing headaches or her startling sense of smell; it was simply the undeniable knowledge that she carried a baby. The beauty of that idea caught and held her. Her parents had hung on to her tightly at the end. Her mum had said *Goodbye, little bump*. Robyn had felt the heat behind her eyes; she'd tipped her head and blinked fast, then lifted her jumper. Her mum's fingers ran across her skin, and it was like a seal, her dad looking on, a rare expression of shyness softening his face.

'You know, Robyn,' Marilyn had said, 'we all make mistakes. And sometimes they turn out not to be mistakes at all. They turn out to possibly be the best thing that ever happened to us.'

'Next time, bring Eliot,' her dad had said, his voice creaking. 'We'd like to meet him properly. We'll take you both out. The three of you out.'

And the Swintons were joined in a smile that said *This is going to be okay.*

Jago had walked home with wet hair and damp clothes. At Hooper's House he'd kicked off his sanded, mud-encrusted boots and pounded upstairs, ignoring his dad's call from the kitchen. He closed the door to his room and threw himself down on his bed. His face ached with the effort of locked-in emotion. His eyes stung. Then he began to laugh, and that was when the tears fell. He sat up, rubbed his face with both hands. Robyn was having a baby. He shook his head in disbelief.

At least three girls from his year at school had children now. One had left in the middle of the fourth year, Liane Chambers, and was seen wheeling a pushchair along the Newlyn seafront on the same morning that exams began. Another, Karenza

Cook, had married at eighteen, had a baby by nineteen and another by twenty. Her parents ran The Cormorant Inn, and she pulled pints at the bar there sometimes, while above her head the floorboards squeaked as toddler feet pounded. And Kate Matthews had, apparently, a set of flaxen-haired, blue-eyed twins, though her fisherman boyfriend was a redhead and she a brunette. But these weren't girls like Robyn. They were the daughters of young mothers themselves, girls who had always seen pushchairs and nappies and bottles in their futures, once school was done or even before. They were nothing like Robyn. And Eliot didn't sound like young father material, rolling down from London to play his guitar and pick up a girl. That Robyn should fall for someone like that made a sort of sense, but in all the versions of their story that he'd imagined, this had never featured.

Before Jago had disappeared across the field, he'd checked back and made sure that she was out. It couldn't be good for the baby if she got too cold, her fingers and toes shrivelling and pruning, her skin tingeing blue. He'd seen her standing safely at the edge of the water, her clothes thrown on. And he'd watched as Marilyn and Simon found her there, saw them huddling as a trio on the shore.

Over the weeks and months that followed, Robyn and Eliot lost themselves in one another. When she'd stepped through the door of Eliot's flat, Merrin sea salt still caught in her hair, he'd pulled her into his arms and held her very tightly. He led her to his bedroom and laid her down, kissed her along her collarbone, the inside of her thighs, flicked his tongue into her ear. He smoothed her stomach with the flat of his hand, and whispered, soothed. Robyn moved on top of him, her desire quickening, flooding, her cries matching his. Afterwards they lay entwined, the sheets kicked to the floor.

'I know this is ridiculous,' said Eliot, 'but I didn't know if you were coming back. Not until you walked through that door.'

She rolled on to her side. She pushed his straw-blond hair from his face, and felt his stubbled cheeks with the tips of her fingers, tracing a pattern.

'I didn't go anywhere,' she said. 'This is home now.'

She heard the shift in Eliot's breathing. 'Will you make it official, then? Will you move in?'

Ruby would say she'd miss her, but she wouldn't really, she was never home. Robyn's room could go back to being a wardrobe, or a box room. It would take her minutes to pack, to unstick her picture postcards, sweep the scattering of shells from the windowsill.

'Yes,' she said, realising as she said it that it was, practically, the only thing left for her and Eliot to do.

At twenty weeks they returned to the hospital, and saw a picture of their child. In a room that was just as small and dark and purposeful as the one they'd first visited, Robyn lay back, and on the screen beside her there appeared a flickering image of a baby girl.

'A little girl,' she said, trying the words, her lips curling into an unbreakable smile. Eliot took her hand and kissed her fingers. The nurse made measurements, zoomed in on a rounded belly, a moon-like head, and they both watched, hands twined, marvelling.

Afterwards they walked the corridor, heads bent over a strip of pictures; they saw the outline of a perfect foot, a wide-eyed face looming from the dark, the delicate curve of their daughter's spine.

'I can't believe it,' said Eliot.

'I know,' laughed Robyn, 'nor me,' as though the even chances of boy or girl were thrown by something miraculous, either one drawing stunned and breathless responses. 'I love her,' she said. 'I love her already.'

And she meant it. In the bathtub, Robyn talked to her. Perhaps it was the water drawing her out, as it always did, but her worries and fears fell away as she soaked, and her imagination bloomed. She lay back, her hands circling her rising belly. She thought of all the wonder that was waiting for her baby girl. She thought of her seeing sunrise, a blur of soft pink light, and then later watching sunset, all the sky on fire. She thought of her feeling sand between her toes for the first time, and kicking at a wave. She thought of the pair of them walking down a lane and together smelling a hedgerow scent so sweet that it'd stop them in their tracks, and they'd realise it was honeysuckle, threaded finely through the briars. She thought of them hearing the shouting of seagulls, and how the desire to shout back would bubble up, and it wouldn't matter because they'd have the cove to themselves, and the sea would take their voices anyway, losing them in spray.

'I've got so much to show you, my baby,' murmured Robyn, 'and it's magic and it's wonder and it's all here waiting for you.'

When Robyn craved fresh air, she hauled Eliot up to Hampstead Heath, where they walked the wild patches, beneath the sycamores and weeping willows. He always seemed glad when their feet hit the road again, when buses hissed and rumbled and people pushed and passed one another without a second glance. He took her to his favourite record shops, where he flipped through vinyl, placed headphones carefully over her ears, his face hopeful as she listened. *I want us to love the same things*, he said to her. She remembered how he was at Merrin, clad in black, picking his way along the shore. She couldn't imagine him dancing on a surfboard, or gutting a fish on the beach with a chiselled edge of stone. *We don't have to love all the same things*, she said, *just enough*.

At home, she saw how his life divided. There were the quiet spells when he was writing, plucking at the strings of his guitar, his lips moving soundlessly. She knew not to disturb him then; instead she watched him, listening for a tune to lift off, for something to sound as though she'd heard it before, because that was, he said, how you knew it was right. Then there were the loud late nights. The nights Ben had warned her about when she'd told him he was going to be an uncle – *Eliot knows what's coming, does he? Because in my very limited experience, babies and bands aren't that great a mix* – and she'd punched his arm and told him to stop worrying. He would come home exhausted, his breath alcohol-sweet and smoke-filled, dropping beside her into bed, laying kisses on her skin.

He kept up his endless stream of gigs, playing in pubs and clubs and bars, basements, rooftops and back rooms. Sometimes Robyn went along, her swelling shape not stopping her feet from moving, her hips from swirling. But as time went on she often stayed at home, swaddled in a giant cardigan and a pair of knitted socks, making elaborate stews that spat and bubbled for hours. These were her own quiet moments, her mind wandering to their tiny growing girl, and she gulped down glasses of water and chomped carrots and worked her way through bunches of bananas, wanting to give her all the goodness she could.

On gig nights Eliot would come home wired, restless beside her in bed, his fingers still twitching chord patterns, his lips remembering the best songs. *Did you eat?* she'd say. *I made a stew*, and Eliot would say something about a kebab, or a burger, and she'd drift back towards sleep, leaving him to follow her. Their day jobs filled the spaces in between, Robyn note-taking and tea-making, Eliot mixing drinks and pulling pints.

'I'm not going to take you for granted,' he said, once.

'I never thought you would.'

'I'm going to make you both so proud.'

'Eliot, you already do.'

'No, just you wait. You wait. I will. All this work, these late nights, all the times you have to put up with me not being around, it'll be worth it in the end, I promise. We need a proper label; if we get that, we'll be off. No stopping us. Robyn?'

'Yes?'

'What do you think she'll look like?'

'A little bit like me, a little bit like you.'

'We'll be okay, you know, the three of us.'

'I know. Here, quick. She's kicking.'

It was soft, but definite, a feeling like nothing on earth. She grabbed his hands and placed them on her belly.

'Did you feel it?'

He cocked his head as if listening for something. His brow crinkled.

'I missed it,' he said, mournfully.

'Stay beside me, stay right here, and next time she kicks you'll feel it. I promise.'

'Robyn, I need to leave. I'm already late.'

'Leave? What's tonight?'

'Extra rehearsal. We've got some new material we need to work through. I told you, didn't I? I'm sure I did. I'll find you in bed.'

'We'll be asleep.'

'I'll find you in your dreams, then.'

'Get out of here. God, you're soppy.'

'Too much?'

'Go, don't be late. There'll be more kicks. Plenty more. Go!'

He backed out of the door with reluctant steps. *I love you*, he mouthed.

'I love you too,' she said.

She listened to the smack of his feet on the stairs, and the slam of the front door, before the sounds of the street bore him away. Robyn hung suspended. She went into the kitchen, and filled the kettle. She bent her head against the fridge. Was it possible to live a life too quickly? To have the things that so many wanted, to love and be loved, to bring a child into the world, but too much in fast-forward? She felt her daughter kick again. In just a few months, she would never really be alone again.

As Robyn's body took on its new shape, she began to feel charged from within. In Merrin surf, on the best days, she'd experienced a sense of perfect calm and exhilaration, a marriage of two seemingly conflicting states, and that was how she began to feel in her new body. Her hand would go unconsciously to her bump, marvelling at its alien roundness, the growing life that pushed it outward. She took to getting off the bus several stops early, and walking to work, feeling the kick in her heels and the stretch in her legs and the movement of much smaller versions of these things inside of her as well. She wrapped her coat around herself protectively. She smiled at strangers, feeling as though she was possessed of the grandest secret in the world. And she began to look at things differently, with new wonder, as though she was already seeing for two.

One day she took a different route, cutting through the smart streets behind Piccadilly. This was a different London to the one she normally inhabited, no less urban but grand and discreet, a whispery stage set. She found herself on Cork Street. She walked past gallery after gallery, her eyes flicking over the pieces displayed behind the gleaming windows. She stopped in front of one. It was a river view, painted at first light. The sky was milkshake pink, the water glinted with iridescence. A blitz of starlings swept low, hundreds of specks moving as one. The churn of a boat's wake was just in view, water slopping messily towards the edge of the canvas. Robyn could almost feel the prickle of dawn at her collar, her hair lifted by a breeze, dew on her fingertips. The artist had caught so particular a moment that the picture was a dispatch. She felt a sense of familiarity, of having been there, not at that river, not with that cacophony of colour and light, but simply having looked out over water on such a morning, and sensed something remarkable. She knew why the artist had wanted to set down what he'd seen. And for the first time, she felt it too.

She arrived at work just past nine o'clock, swiping her access card, the friendly receptionist saying *Look at you, you're glowing, how long to go?* The glow carried her all the way through the morning, her mind swooping and scattered like the artist's starlings. *Little sister*, said Ben, catching her on her own, *you've got that faraway look in your eyes. Do you want to just go home and drape yourself on a sofa, or do you actually want to do some work, huh?* But he brought her a mug of decaffeinated coffee, and she knew her inattention was forgiven. On her lunch break she went to an art shop on Berwick Street. She chose a sketchpad, and a set of acrylic paints, a couple of sable brushes, one blunt as a stump, the other wispy and delicate.

That night Eliot was out with the band, and she had the flat to herself. She cleared the table and laid out her new purchases. She filled a jam jar with water, and used an old margarine tub as a paint pot. Sitting down, she twisted the cap off a tube, and squeezed. She felt her baby shift inside her, a sudden, seismic movement, as though she was swimming underwater and had flipped her whole body in one quick motion. She'd never done that before, and it was, Robyn thought, a sign – her daughter's approval of her endeavour. She picked up a brush, dipped its bristles in the water, and plunged it into the unctuous pool of Merrin blue.

twenty-four

TESS SWINTON WAS BORN ON A TUESDAY, THE FOURTEENTH day of March. The name had come to Robyn as if from nowhere, a whispering in her sleep. She liked the simplicity of it, the way it drifted at the end, both strong and gentle. Eliot had liked it too, with the apparent ease with which he approached all things. *Tess'll do nicely*, he'd said.

Tess came into the world silently, only a light slap awaking her screams, as though she'd been oblivious to the hours of torment that had preceded her arrival. Towards the end, Robyn had wailed and writhed like a far wilder creature than her newborn. The gas and air had sent her flying, buzzing above the room, the voices around her muffled and distant, the pain dulled and all awareness with it, but as long as she sucked on it she couldn't push. So they took away the precious nozzle and instead she screamed her way into every contraction, bucking on the bed, thinking that this was the end, she would surely die, that she couldn't push any harder if she tried and was fated to always have just the tip of a baby's head showing between her legs, exquisite pain streaking through her body. And then . . .

the impossible happened. Tess came, and it was over. The midwife held her baby up with jubilance, and she stared at the unbelievable sight of her, her gangly arms and legs, her skin shining purple.

Robyn lay flattened, sweat streaking her face. Her tears rolled, the instant relief shattering. Her daughter was placed on her chest, and she looked down at her with amazement. Tess's head was no bigger than a peach and just as round, just as soft-looking, as lightly burred. Robyn watched her turn, her tiny lips parting as she found her mother's breast, her suck certain from the first. She took in her spun-gold hair, her reddened skin, her gaping, busy mouth, and fell immediately, fiercely, shockingly in love. Nothing had ever felt so wholly hers.

A hand touched her shoulder and she turned her head, surprise crossing her face, for who else was there in the room in that moment? Eliot appeared wan. His eyes were round, his pupils shrunken. He opened his mouth to say something and no sound came. He shook his head.

'I couldn't do it,' he said. 'I couldn't watch. I'm sorry.'

'You weren't here?'

'I was, I was, but at the end, when you were in so much pain, I thought I'd faint, I thought . . . I had to get some air. And I missed it. I'm so, so sorry.'

Robyn curled her fingers into his, and looked again at her daughter. Tess still lay at her breast, her eyes tight shut, her sucking slowing now. Her lashes were so delicate they were barely there. Her nose a bud. Her miracle of a hand, with creases at the knuckles and nails like fragments of pearl, touched Robyn's skin.

'Nothing matters,' she breathed. 'Nothing matters except this.'

'Plenty of dads struggle,' said the midwife cheerily, 'don't you worry about that. But mum here did amazing, didn't you, love? Now will you let him hold her? Will you let her go for a second?'

Robyn nodded. She watched as Eliot took Tess, and smiled at the sight. He held her as though she were made of glass. His arms were stiff, his cheeks tight.

'Your daughter,' said Robyn. 'Our daughter.'

'I can't believe it,' he said, and there was wonder in his voice, certainly there was wonder, but there was something else too. It sounded like fear.

Robyn stayed two nights in hospital, and in those stark white corridors, beneath the too-thin bed sheets, she cradled her daughter and came to know every millimetre of her: this tiny creature who was so strange and yet so familiar, so perfect a human and yet a snuffling, burrowing animal. Tess wasn't supposed to be able to see her, not yet, but sometimes her blue-black eyes fixed on Robyn, and she truly believed that her baby saw all the way inside of her; every hope and every fear and every fibre of her love laid bare. At such moments she found herself crying helplessly and uncontrollably and immeasurably happily. *It's just the hormones*, the bustling midwives said pragmatically, handing her a box of tissues, but that made it sound involuntary and chemical and somehow diminishing, as though how Robyn felt about her daughter was by the book, no more remarkable than what the woman in the next bed was feeling, or the next. So Robyn ignored the tissues and doused her baby in salt water, kissing her skin and saying *I love you*, as though she was the only person to have ever said it. When Eliot visited, he found the pair of them huddling together.

Robyn passed him the blanketed bundle that was Tess, saying *Your daddy's here*, while trying to keep the hunger from her eyes, hiding her twitching, impatient hands beneath the covers.

In the days and weeks that followed, Robyn and Eliot were tossed about like lost souls in a raging sea. The days pitched and fell, and sometimes they wondered how they'd ever make it to shore. Their universe shrank to encompass only Tess and her rhythms: her cries for milk, her cries for sleep, her cries because she was alive in a world that was so much louder, so much fuller, so much stranger than the dark and warm cocoon she'd left. Robyn held her all the time, rocking her, cradling her, dropping kisses on her delicious head, trying to tell her that it was all right, it was okay, that this world was kindly too. When Tess slept in the day, often Robyn couldn't, her mind churned too messily, and was calmed only by gazing down at her, by marvelling at the whorl of her ear, the perfection of her lashes, the unblemished skin of her cheek. She'd take her daughter's tiny hand in hers, go fingertip to fingertip, trace her minuscule life line. *You're me*, she'd whisper.

In the beginning, Eliot would wake up with Robyn in the night, lie with her as she breastfed, blinking to keep his eyes open. By day he'd make cups of tea that went undrunk, and meals that went uneaten. He took on the harried look of every young father, wild-eyed, dark scoops beneath his eyes. He'd cancelled gigs and studio time; he didn't pick up his guitar for two weeks. More than once, Tess was inconsolable; she wouldn't stop crying no matter what they did.

'What if I play to her? "Rock-a-bye Baby"?'

'Try it,' said Robyn. 'Try anything.'

She watched him as he stood, his guitar slung low like a troubadour. She cried easily these days too, though her eruptions were silent compared to Tess's, and not solely of love as they'd been in the hospital. Perhaps the midwives and their talk of hormones had been right. She'd cry with relief in the shower as the water hit her body, knowing she had the moment to herself but it couldn't last. She'd cry as fatigue crept up on her, stealthily at first then rampant, taking her whole body in its grasp and leaving her limp, wrung out. Now the heat swam behind her eyes as soon as Eliot began to sing, his hushed and breathy voice, the naked hope that it might be he who could soothe her this one time. Eliot had held on to his wary hospital look. He rarely took Tess from Robyn. On the occasions that he did, he watched her nervously, and when her body stiffened and the crying began, he'd seek Robyn out, tapping at the shower door, poking his head into the bedroom where she was dressing, with a *Sorry, sorry, she's off again*, his face cut with an anguish that hadn't existed before Tess.

'When the bough breaks, the cradle will fall,' he sang softly, 'down will come baby, cradle and all.'

'That is the roughest lullaby ever,' whispered Robyn. 'Some comfort.'

'But look . . .'

In her arms, Tess's eyes fluttered, then stayed closed. She snuffled once, like a small animal settling itself. Her rosebud mouth parted at the lips.

'It's magic,' breathed Robyn.

Eliot continued to play; he went into 'Hush, Little Baby', and Robyn sat down carefully on the sofa, her every movement slowed. She sank back, Tess asleep in her arms. Eliot knelt beside her, down on one knee, singing and playing.

'How do you know these songs?' she whispered.

'They're not exactly complicated,' he whispered back.

'But did you learn them?'

'Yes, I learnt them.'

'For our baby?'

'For our baby. For you.'

Robyn smiled and closed her eyes. Eliot played on.

When Eliot returned to work, Robyn's mum came to stay for the week. She held Tess deftly in one arm while the other engaged in practical activities such as rinsing dishes and hanging rows of tiny clothes along the tops of radiators. Robyn looked on, her body crumpling with tiredness as she allowed herself a moment's relaxation.

'Thank you, Mum,' she said.

'It's a joy,' said Marilyn, who knew too well that no daughter truly appreciated her mother until she was one herself, 'to be here with you both. A joy.'

'I really mean thank you for . . . everything.'

'Angel, what is it? Don't cry.'

Robyn pushed her hands to her eyes. Her mum threw down her dishcloth and went to her.

'Tell me,' she said.

'I don't know,' said Robyn. 'This is my life now, and it's just so strange. I can't imagine Tess not being here, I wouldn't want it any other way, but that's strange too, isn't it?'

Days and nights were no longer distinguished. She pitched from joy to despair to joy again. Tess was dependent on her for everything, for life itself, and with that came so intense a feeling that she knew she'd never be able to explain it in ordinary old words. She looked up at her mother, her eyes blazing with it all, and Marilyn smiled, nodded.

'Nothing, absolutely nothing, can prepare you for this,' she said, smoothing her daughter's hair. 'It doesn't matter if you've wanted to be a mother for years and years, or if it happened suddenly, unexpectedly . . . It's never simple, it's never easy, but it's the greatest thing you'll ever do, I can promise you that.'

Robyn breathed deeply, in and out. She held out her arms for Tess. Pressing her close to her chest, she murmured into her warm head, 'We'll be okay, won't we? You and I?'

'Eliot does help, doesn't he?'

She looked up. 'Of course he does. He's great. He's brilliant. He even plays his guitar for her . . .' Her voice trailed. 'Sometimes I think he's a bit afraid of her, though. He doesn't hold her much. And when she cries, he's practically running for the hills. Was Dad like that?'

'Your dad's a doctor, dear, he was always used to babies. Hopeless at nappy changing, though. He left all that to me.'

Robyn rested her nose against the top of Tess's head, inhaling her scent. When her daughter was still in her arms, the peace that descended inside of her was like a drug, quick to work and instantly transforming. She closed her eyes. Everything else could slip away in such moments.

'You would say, wouldn't you, if you and Eliot were struggling?'

'We'll be okay,' said Robyn, distractedly.

'It's a terrific strain for anyone, being new parents, but for you as a couple . . .'

'A couple?' she repeated, speaking the word as though she'd never before heard it. 'We're Tess. That's what we are. There isn't a me any more, and there isn't an Eliot. We're all just Tess.'

The night before, Marilyn had put her granddaughter to

bed. Her singing had drifted through to the living room as Robyn and Eliot stood facing one another, curiously adrift without their third. Eliot had asked Robyn if she wanted a glass of wine, and she'd said no, because of the breastfeeding, because of the certain knowledge that she'd be up in the night and feel worse for it, because any moment now spent awake was a moment wasted, when her whole body screamed its fatigue and longed for bed too. Eliot had looked hurt. *Just one glass together*, he'd insisted, *and for just five minutes we can pretend to be normal again*. Robyn relented. They sat together on the sofa. She didn't know how long it was before she fell asleep on his shoulder; she couldn't have had more than a sip or two, but when she woke again to Tess's cries, the bottle was finished and Eliot was fast asleep beside her, a snore at his lips. She found herself looking at him dispassionately, as though he was any sleeping stranger. Not so very long ago they'd have devoured the bottle together, then devoured each other. She got up, and with heavy feet she'd followed the sound of the cry.

Marilyn stroked Robyn's hair, a tender gesture that felt like it belonged to a younger mother and a far smaller daughter.

'It will get easier,' she said.

'Will it? God, I hope so.'

'And when the better weather comes, you can get out and about more.'

'Yes.'

'You are seeing lots of Ben, aren't you? I've asked him to help you where he can.'

'Ben's Ben, Mum. He drops in, cuddles Tess for five seconds, then realises he's supposed to be on the other side of London in ten minutes.'

'Robyn, you're doing brilliantly. You really, really are.'

'Thanks,' she croaked, a surge of emotion taking her voice.

'I don't know if I've ever told you this, but when you were about six weeks old, you were lying in your crib, and I watched you do the most remarkable thing. You were lying on your front – they didn't tell you not to put a baby down like that, not in those days – there you were, this tiny, tiny baby, and I saw you use every ounce of your strength to haul yourself up with your little arms. You had a good look around at the world, your eyes wide as anything. Then you collapsed back down on your belly again.'

Twenty-two years of marvel were still fresh in Marilyn's voice. Robyn looked up. She smiled with her.

'I really did that?' she said.

'I couldn't believe it. I knew then what you were, Robyn, and you've never, ever changed. An adventurer, the boldest kind.'

Robyn held Tess up, and pressed her nose to hers. 'Let's both be adventurers,' she said.

twenty-five

WHEN ELIOT WAS AT WORK, OR WITH THE BAND, THE FLAT seemed to shrink around her. Days ran together, nights too, one after another, each much the same, the cycle of feeds providing the only rhythm. A breathtaking claustrophobia sent Robyn in search of wide-open spaces and the sound of lapping, fluid movement and watery scents. She walked the banks of the Thames, her daughter tucked in a sling, warm against her chest. Even though it was too tame, too built-up, and on dull days it was a sullen sight, she would still go down to the water's edge. Once she found a patch of shingle beach, a mere strip, and went and stood on it, strewn as it was with blackened pebbles and rope ends, beer bottles and a lost shoe. A lone kayaker passed her. Robyn raised her hand, waved, for there was something she recognised in his desire for movement, and when she received no acknowledgement, she understood it: he was solitary, lost in the moment, just as she had often been.

Another time, with Tess restless and crying, she walked to the boating lake in Regent's Park. She hired a rowing boat, and settled into the rhythm of strokes. Tess shifted and gurgled, snuggled deep inside the fabric. Robyn lay back on her oars. Her body had been wrenched and plied, her mind assaulted, but if she stayed quite still and trailed her hand in the silken water, she could almost imagine a sanded bottom and scattered shells beneath her feet, hear the bubble of an incoming tide. She realised that for the first time in a long time, she felt something like her old self.

By the time Tess turned two months old there were creases at her wrists and her thighs were rounded. As Robyn changed her nappy, she took her legs and jiggled them, blew raspberries on her belly.

'She's getting tubby,' she said to Eliot, with undisguised joy. 'Here, take her, feel her weight.'

Eliot cradled her carefully. Tess's head lolled and Robyn swooped in, cupped a hand beneath it, adjusted the crook of his arm. Tess began to snuffle, then cry.

'She always does that,' he said, aggrieved.

'She's a baby, she cries, that's what she does.'

'But shouldn't she cry less? As she gets older?'

Robyn shrugged. 'I don't know. I guess so. But it's the only way she can tell us anything. It's all you have, isn't it, babe?' She bent and kissed her daughter's forehead.

Eliot made to hand her back. 'Maybe she's hungry.'

'She just fed.'

'But she sounds like she's hungry.'

'Just rock her. Sing to her. She loves your lullabies.'

'She doesn't,' said Eliot. 'It only worked that one time.'

Robyn opened her arms and folded her daughter into her neck. Tess burrowed, and her crying slowed, Robyn murmuring encouragement. Eliot wandered into the kitchen, his arms loose by his sides. Robyn followed. She found him standing there, staring at the stack of unwashed dishes.

'Don't worry about those. We can do them later.'

'I wasn't. I just . . . Did you know it was going to be this hard?'

'I don't think anyone knows it's going to be this hard.'

'But you can do it,' he said. 'You can do it, and I can't.'

'Of course you can. We're both doing it. We're doing it together.'

'It doesn't feel like that,' said Eliot, his voice drawn tight.

Robyn folded an arm around his shoulders. She kissed him on the cheek. He'd been so ardent through her pregnancy, the idea of Tess bringing the two of them closer and closer together, but her arrival had undone him. Robyn found herself wishing he'd hide it better, but even when he turned his smile on them, pulled them both into an embrace, said an *I love you* that was meant for two, not just one, his eyes stayed bleary, unfocused. He had a weary set to his manner that spoke of lack of more than sleep.

'Then how does it feel?' she asked, softly.

'I don't know,' said Eliot, stiffening. 'Not like that.'

'Go out tonight,' she said, with resolution. 'Go out and have a good time. You need it.'

'But don't you need it too?'

'No,' said Robyn. 'Tess and I are fine.' Their baby was asleep, her face hidden in Robyn's neck, her legs tucked under her body. Robyn swayed on the spot, began to hum. 'Go on, honestly, it'll do you good.'

'You're just better at this than me,' he said, his voice splintering. Robyn sighed, more audibly than she'd intended. She almost said *I'm not, you're amazing*, but then stopped herself. Already it felt like her every hour was spent reassuring, placating, softening, as bound so entirely as she was to Tess. Her own self was abstracted, dim, and most of the time she felt like a faint echo of her daughter. When she lay down to sleep at night, hearing Tess's shallow breathing, as rapid as a bird's, her own breath turned to the same pace; she pursed her lips just like her baby and threw out an arm above the bedclothes. When Tess woke suddenly in the dark, with a high-pitched scream, Robyn lurched upright, her mouth agape, a wail not far from her own throat. And when Tess had finished feeding, when her head lolled drunkenly and milk dribbled from her lips, Robyn collapsed back on her pillows, similarly sated.

Just occasionally, though, her daughter seemed to her an unknowable thing, the wildest of animals over whom she had no control or influence, and even then she couldn't escape her. One time Tess screamed and screamed, her face a livid red, cheeks bursting with tears, and Robyn held her at arm's length, pleading with her, her own voice heightening in pitch until eventually sobs swallowed her words too. Then she clasped her daughter to her and collapsed in a chair. That was where Eliot found them, both fast asleep, Robyn's cheeks tear-streaked and ruddy, with Tess curled at her chest. Robyn's eyes had snapped open as she felt him standing there. She turned them on him, and he saw how red-rimmed they were, how puffy. *I hate what this baby's doing to you*, he'd whispered, as he reached for her hand. And it was the worst thing he could have said, because Robyn felt, even in the darkest moments, that Tess was the best thing about her.

'You think it hasn't been a shock for me too?' she said. 'Life changed overnight, and I didn't for a second think it'd be this hard.'

The word *hard* came out all wrong, broken and fading and

with no definition. Eliot rubbed his hands through his hair distractedly, and turned a hunted look on her. She thought she might cry. She clenched her teeth and breathed through her nose.

'But I didn't think it'd be this amazing either,' she said.

She waited for him to reply; even the most basic of platitudes would have done, or not even words, just a murmured assent, but he gave her nothing. She pressed her face to Tess, and turned away.

Somehow the weeks passed. At four months, Tess was thriving. Robyn survived. So did Eliot.

'I don't want to tempt fate,' she said, as she bounced Tess on her knee, 'but I think it's getting a little bit easier. Or maybe it's just that we're more used to it *not* being easy, don't you think?'

Eliot stretched languidly. He'd played a gig the night before and Robyn hadn't heard him come in, but she'd been aware of his sleeping form beside her as she'd shifted Tess into position on her breast, the chirruping of early-morning city birds coming through the open window.

'I don't know if I'll ever feel used to it,' he said, his voice split by a yawn.

'Come on,' she said. 'You don't mean that.'

He reached out a hand and squeezed Tess's, tried to get her attention with a whistle and a click. Her head bobbed and a string of drool fell from her lips as she looked in the other direction. Robyn laughed, mopping it with a cloth.

'Don't you ever miss your old life?' said Eliot, suddenly.

In the early days it had been almost unbearable sometimes, the glitter of nostalgia. It wasn't even the big things that had shone with allure; it was the tiny, insignificant things too. Drying her hair with a hairdryer. Taking her time over brushing her teeth. Standing in the kitchen chopping vegetables for dinner, her biggest concern wiping the sting of onion tears from her eyes. But it wasn't like that any more. Everything she worried about before felt like nothing now.

'There's no point in missing it,' she said. 'It's gone. It's a different life now.'

He was watching her, his eyes narrowed in scrutiny, and she felt self-conscious suddenly, aware that she hadn't showered yet that day, and her hair was scraped back in a lank ponytail. Earlier Tess had missed a feed and she'd leaked, leaving a dark stain across the front of her T-shirt. But her daughter was riding up and down on her knee, her small back straight, her arms thrown out in glee.

'We'll get you back to feeling like you,' he said, 'don't worry.'

She knew she'd changed, but she wasn't sure how. Sometimes she felt as if she'd become mammal-like, instinctively protective, responding only to primitive needs of hunger, warmth and sleep. The runnings of her mind were simplified, but intensified, her world revolving around a person little bigger than a decent loaf. Whatever it was, Robyn wore her motherhood like a badge of honour, because she'd clung on through those desperate first weeks, and without a scrap of knowledge or experience she'd sustained her baby, fed her, tended to her, and somehow Tess had held on too. She was proud of what she was doing, even on the days when she crawled out of bed, her head splitting with a no-sleep hangover, when she wore a sweater back to front all morning without realising, when she let herself imagine, for just a few moments, a world without Tess, and was then immeasurably relieved to find that she couldn't. She was proud. And she wished that Eliot felt it too.

'I do feel like me,' she said, prickling. 'Just . . . a different version.'

'I'd like it if the other version came back, though.'

She went for levity, punching him on the arm, but he didn't return her smile.

'What?' she said. 'What is it?'

'I miss you coming to our gigs. I miss us staying up late and getting drunk and waking up in the afternoon. I miss us staying in bed all day if we want to. And I miss us having sex. I really miss us having sex.'

'We have sex,' said Robyn.

'I can count the times.'

'We're new parents,' she said, in quick defence. 'It's always like that, right? And when we have, hasn't it been good? Hasn't it been great?'

'We're new parents, but we're a new couple too. I think . . .' His voice faded, then came back again with force. 'I think you forget that sometimes. I think we both do.'

'We've been together nearly a year. I don't know if that's *new*.'

'But how much of that was us? The two of us, without . . . without any other presence in our lives.'

Robyn stared at him. She almost said it, then. *Are you sure you still want this?* 'How much? About three weeks,' she said instead. Which, when she thought about it later, was almost the same thing.

Summer brought with it a stifling city heat. Eliot suggested the lido, teaming up with another mother from their antenatal group so Robyn could turn laps as Tess lay in someone else's safe arms. But apart from occasional coffee meets, she'd eschewed the company of other mums. Perhaps it was the fact that they looked at her as though she was a child herself, and they couldn't help their expressions as she told the story of Eliot and herself. And they talked about babies, babies, babies, and apart from her beautiful daughter, Robyn could take or leave most babies. So she mainly left them, and found her own way. Sometimes she met Ben for a coffee in Soho, watched as he played the doting uncle, hoisting Tess aloft and flying her through the air until she squealed with delight. Meanwhile she was still lured by water. Not the orderly rectangles that Eliot suggested, concrete-edged and payable by the hour, but the wildest spaces she could find. The far-flung ponds of Hampstead Heath, where she skimmed stones and chased the zigzagging path of a dragonfly at the water's edge, her baby bouncing at her chest. *Tess, it's bright blue! And green! And gold!* The towpath walks north of Regent's Park, where she greeted river-dwellers with a smile and a nod, peering past their plant pots and rickety bicycles, and once accepted a cup of ginger wine from a man with a beard and soulful eyes. *Maybe we should live on a narrowboat,* she said to Eliot once, and he laughed as if she'd suggested the moon.

'I think I might take Tess to the beach,' she said one day.

'Your mum and dad would love that.'

'I meant Brighton. Or somewhere like that. Somewhere close.'

Eliot pulled at his hair. It was long enough for a ponytail, and he scraped it back, fastened it with a band. His cheeks were drawn pale and his eyes were dull from late nights with the band and early mornings splintered by Tess's cries. But his look was less shell-shocked these days. Robyn knew that the more he cut loose, in work or play, the happier he was, so she hugged her baby to her chest and let him go.

'Your mum and dad must be wondering why we've never taken Tess to Merrin.'

'Not really. They know it's miles away, and they like coming here. Remember, they were city people once; they haven't always lived in such total isolation.'

'Then maybe I'm wondering why we've never taken Tess to Merrin. Don't you want her to see where you came from?'

'I didn't come from there.'

She did come from there. There was sand between her toes and seaweed in her hair. Without even taking to the water, her surfer's shape was returning, her waist nipped in, her arms sinewy. She didn't blink at her baby's early rising, because she'd jumped from bed in the dark to answer the call of the waves far more often than she'd languished under the covers. She liked too much salt in her food because it made everything taste like the sea. Eliot said she was the only person he'd ever met who actually submerged themselves completely in the bath, rising up and spitting water like a whale.

'But it's important to you,' he insisted. 'I think we should go.'

'Tess is only five months old. She doesn't actually know where she is, or where she isn't. We could take her to Sri Lanka, or Shangri-La, and she wouldn't bat an eye.'

'For you, not Tess.'

'If I wanted to go, I'd have gone.' She said it too quickly, and he blinked at her. She softened her voice. 'Brighton will be much more fun, just the three of us. We could go this weekend; we'd be there in an hour if we took the train.'

'Maybe I'd like to see Merrin again. I've got good memories of it.'

'I'm surprised you can remember.'

'I remember all of it,' he said.

'Then there's no need to go, is there?'

'Or is there another reason why you don't want to go home? Are you ashamed of me, or something?'

'No! Don't be crazy, Eliot, of course not. My parents think you're great, you know that.'

'Other people then, your friends down there?'

'You have been to Merrin, right? There isn't anyone else down there. I was only ever there in the holidays. I'm as much of a grockle as anyone, so no one actually Cornish would ever talk to me.'

'Apart from that guy Jago.'

'Jago and his dad. Right. They're the only other people in Merrin. Why do you think I learnt to surf? I had to give myself something to do; I'd have gone stir-crazy otherwise.'

She stood on her tiptoes and kissed him. Tess's faint cries drifted from their bedroom. Instinctively, she moved towards them.

'But think about it, will you?' he called after her. 'You and me, Tess, a weekend with your folks? I'd love it. They'd love it.'

Robyn paused at the door.

'You really want to go?'

'Yes. I really want to go.'

'Travel for hours and hours with a screaming baby, all the way to the ends of the earth and back?'

'Exactly that.'

'Go where it's probably raining, when Brighton beach is sizzling in a heatwave?'

'Sounds perfect.'

'Right. Good. I'll call Mum tonight. See if they're free this weekend.'

She disappeared into the bedroom and scooped up the wailing Tess. She sat down on the edge of her bed and lifted her top, and settled her against her chest. As Tess suckled, she breathed slowly and deeply, relaxing as her daughter's cries went and she fed contentedly. She closed her eyes.

twenty-six

SHE WOKE UP IN HER OLD BED. SHE LAY QUITE STILL, ENJOYING the rare experience of being awake before her daughter. It was early, and her room was lit with that particular Cornish light that her parents always talked about, in the way that only incomers could, with a breath of wonder, and a satisfaction at having found it for themselves. She'd expected that her mum and dad would have turned it into a brisk guest room by now, with whitewashed walls and a scattering of novels, but they'd left it just as she had. The only addition was a blue vase that normally belonged in the sitting room. It was balanced on top of a pile of books on the shelf, looking precarious. She'd taken it downstairs yesterday, told her mum she'd found it in her room and asked if it was meant to be in there. Marilyn had taken it from her with a shake of the head and held it in both hands, unsure what to do with it, finally placing it on top of the piano.

Otherwise, Robyn's room was still Robyn's room. University books were stacked on the shelves, and an unused easel stood in the corner. A roly-poly bear, a relic of her childhood, sat on a chair, a floppy sunhat hanging from the back of it. Her desk was a sea of scrap paper and Post-it notes, broken shells, and a four-fingered starfish. When she'd first taken Tess in there, it had felt strange, re-inhabiting a space that had belonged to a very different part of her life. They'd sat down on the bed together, Tess wriggling from her lap, face-planting into the bedcovers as she tried to crawl with a fierce determination that her body couldn't quite match. *This is Mummy's old room*, Robyn had said, gently adjusting her, letting her try again. Her eye had gone to the window. *Mummy's old everything*, she'd said.

Beside her now, Eliot shifted in his sleep. They should have shared the driving the day before, but he was too hung over. He'd come in late the night before that, clambering into bed murmuring apologies, the heat of a gig still about him. So it was Robyn who got them out of the tangle of the city and on to the wide-open roads that led to the west, as he'd sunk low in the passenger seat, chewing wine gums and drinking cola. Now she glanced at his sleeping form, taking in the crackle of stubble, his slack mouth. He'd wanted to shave for her parents and she'd laughed and said there was no need, so he hadn't.

Across the room, Tess slept soundlessly, in a crib her parents had bought specially. Robyn wondered how long it had been waiting in her room. They'd never pushed her to come home, but the crib gave her a small ache of sadness. A stack of baby blankets had been waiting in it too, and a long-eared white rabbit. And Tess had had one of her first good nights in the bed they'd made her. *Merrin air*, Robyn thought, although it had had the opposite effect on her. She'd taken a long time to drop off, and when she eventually did, her dreams had pushed and pulled, waking her three, four times without ever leaving her with anything more tangible than a feeling of abstract unease. Throughout, Eliot had lain stretched out, breathing deep and evenly, easy as a cat.

Robyn slipped out of bed and went over to the crib. Tess's face was turned to one side, her lips pouting. *You're beautiful*, she whispered. She left them both sleeping and padded downstairs to the kitchen.

'I knew it,' her dad said.

'What?'

'A morning surf.'

Robyn laughed. Shook her head. 'I didn't even think of that. I was awake and couldn't sleep. Thought I might as well make some coffee. What's your excuse?'

'I always get up this early.'

'No you don't.'

'Your mother's started snoring.'

'No she hasn't.'

He shrugged. 'I thought you and Tess might have been up. I didn't want to miss you.'

'Dad, we're here all weekend.'

'The light's nice on the terrace at this time of morning. I've had it re-decked. I thought we could sit out there, have a coffee.'

'Sounds great, let's do it. Although . . .'

Robyn had turned to the window. The sea was silver, the sun burning a strip of gold down its centre. A breeze would be whipping the headland, foam slapping the sand.

'I bet it's nice out there.'

'You want to take a look?'

'I think I've forgotten how. And what if Tess wakes up?'

'Eliot's here, isn't he? We're here.'

'He can't feed her, though.'

'Ah,' said her dad. Then, 'It's only five minutes to the cove. I'll come and get you if I need to. Your wetsuit's where you left it. Your board's in the shed. I went in there yesterday, took it out and gave it a wipe down. Go on. I'll listen for Tess.'

She moved quickly, as if on borrowed time. As she cut along the path, ferns slapped her legs, and drapes of ragwort caught at her ankles. She could have walked it with her eyes shut: three more twists and then the final descent, seven steps before the beach. When she burst out on to the sand, she dropped her board and her hands went to her mouth. The Rockabilly stack shone black. A troop of gulls swept low to the water. The sound of the waves pounding the beach was like the first bars of a love song. *Robyn, get a grip*, she hissed, as she drew her fingers swiftly across her eyes. She grabbed her board and ran towards the water, a whoop of joy escaping her lips. She plunged in, and paddled out, her head emptying of every possible thought except for the feeling of moving exquisitely through water.

Eliot was waiting for her on the sand. He wore a creased T-shirt, and his hair was still ruffled from sleep. Tess was in his arms, snickering quietly.

'You should have called me in sooner,' she panted.

'I was mesmerised, watching you.'

He passed their baby across, and Robyn pressed sea-salt lips to her cheek.

'Hello, my little sleepyhead, I'm so sorry I made you go hungry. I'm here now, I'm here. Eliot, can you unzip me?'

They wandered to the rocks. Robyn perched, her wetsuit

pulled down about her shoulders. The bristling breeze dotted her breasts with goose pimples. Tess hunted for her.

'Wait,' said Eliot. He licked his fingers, ran them over Robyn's nipple. 'Getting rid of the salt.'

Robyn smiled. 'So, that's surfing. That's what all the fuss is about.'

'You were amazing.'

'Not really. Pretty much a novice. But a happy one.'

'If I didn't play guitar for months on end, I'd go crazy.'

'That's different. That's your life.'

'We'll get you surfing again if that's what you want. Somewhere closer to home. Essex, are there waves in Essex?'

Robyn laughed. 'Maybe.' She twisted her head suddenly, turned towards the cliff.

'What is it?'

'Nothing. I thought I saw someone.'

'Who?'

'I don't know.'

She moved Tess to her other breast. She began to suck, then broke into high-pitched wailing.

'Oh no, babe, I'm sorry!'

Eliot licked his fingers, wiped her nipple, touched it just longer than he needed to.

'There's no one there,' he said. But he carried on watching the clifftop, just to be sure.

They saw Denny in the lane. He was hurtling past in his truck but spun to a halt at the sight of the woman in a wetsuit, her hair dark wet, a baby nestled in the crook of her arm, and the man, an urban type in stick-thin jeans and holding a surfboard so awkwardly it appeared as if it was holding him.

'Hello, beautiful,' he said, leaning out.

Denny would drive with his window down in all weathers, onshore gusts blasting his cab, throwing up his unruly hair. He grinned impishly. He looked, she thought, at least a decade younger than when she'd left.

'This is Tess,' she said, proffering her baby to the window. Tess obliged with a gooey, slack-jawed smile. Denny laughed, a deep rumble, and laid a hand on her head, as if anointing her.

'Another beauty,' he said. 'Well done.'

'And Eliot,' said Robyn, 'my boyfriend. Tess's dad.'

Eliot peered from behind the board and did his best to hold out his hand.

'Lovely part of the world,' he said.

'And this is Lucy,' said Denny.

Robyn noticed the woman beside him in the truck then. She had apple-pie cheeks and a rosy smile. It was early still, not even eight o'clock; she must have stayed at Hooper's House. The women never stayed, Jago always used to say. They upped and left by dawn, or Denny did, fleeing before the light of day could lay them bare all over again.

'We've all been wondering if we'd ever see you again,' said Denny. 'Jago's in the workshop, if you wanted to go down.'

'On a Saturday?' said Robyn, attempting levity, smoothing her hair. Tess wriggled in her arms and she bounced her up and down. 'You're a slave driver.'

'All that boy ever does is work,' said Denny. 'Go and show him this little button,' pinching Tess's chin. 'That'll make him down tools all right.'

Denny was steeped in joviality, and Robyn was happy to see it. She wondered whether Jago was too.

'I'd love to, but . . . we're just here for the weekend. I think my folks have plans to show Eliot the whole of Penwith. Land's End, the Minack, the works.'

'He's only there,' said Denny, jerking his head. 'Take you two minutes. Go now, before you get stuck with all the grockles. No offence,' he added, glancing at Eliot.

He drove off quickly, the exhaust of the old pickup roaring, and disappeared around the corner, his hand waving from the window.

'He never used to be so chatty,' said Robyn, quickly.

'It's this little one,' said Eliot. 'Everyone loves a baby. Including, apparently, your friend Jago.' When she didn't say anything, Eliot spoke for her. 'Robyn, listen, you left this place quickly, I know you did, I was there. And that must have been tough on the people you left behind. All of them.'

'I guess I could go and see him,' she said, slowly.

Eliot nodded. 'You should.'

'Do you want to come with me?'

'I'll take your board back. Put in some time with your mum and dad.'

'Thank you,' she said, and turned to walk back down the lane. She felt his hand on her shoulder.

'Wait,' he said, zipping her wetsuit. 'You're not done up.'

He dropped a kiss at the nape of her neck.

Jago looked up, greeting her evenly, as though she walked into his workshop every day with a baby in her arms. She was immediately struck by how clear he looked, how bright, and how different to all the other people she'd come to know in the past year. They wore the city etched on their faces, the late nights and long days leaving their hard traces.

'Robyn,' he said. 'Hello.'

'Hello back.'

Jago said and did all the things that everyone always said or did when they met Tess, apart from asking to hold her. When they'd run out of talk of London, and of how the surf was at the cove, she mentioned Denny, the woman by his side, and Jago's smile faltered.

'He seems happy,' he said, 'which takes some getting used to.'

'It's good, though, isn't it?'

'Yes,' said Jago. 'Yes, it's good.'

She didn't stay for more than ten or fifteen minutes, and he never quite stopped working as they talked. He moved from one end of the workshop to the other, lifting timber, throwing questions over his shoulder. He wasn't rude – he was never rude – but consciously or unconsciously he made her feel as though the world wasn't stopping for her. That even in Merrin, things carried on.

'Well, I guess I'd better get back to my folks,' she said in the end. There was reluctance in her voice, a sense of the unfulfilled, and she knew it showed. She began to walk towards the door.

'When are you leaving again?'

'We drive back tomorrow.'

He nodded, as if she were confirming something he already knew.

'I've got something for you. For Tess. I'll drop it round before you're gone.'

She couldn't imagine Jago selecting baby clothes, a pastel-coloured blanket, or a dough-bellied bear. It would be something he'd made, she was sure of it. She walked back towards him.

'Would you like to hold her?'

He looked briefly astounded. 'I don't think I've ever held a baby.'

'You're kidding?'

Jago rubbed his hands together, then held them out, as though an outfielder preparing to make his biggest catch. 'Go on, then.'

Robyn passed Tess over. She squirmed, her legs kicking, and turned her wide eyes on Jago. They stared at one another with equal amazement.

'All right?' he said, then, 'How are you?'

Tess smiled, a cock-eyed, roguish smile, and Jago laughed. 'She looks like you,' he said, hugging her to him.

'Do you think so?'

He nodded. He took hold of Tess's tiny hand, ever so lightly. 'Her fingers are perfect. Her little nails.'

'You should see her toes.'

He pressed her hand to his lips, and laid a delicate kiss in Tess's palm.

'Lucky baby,' he said.

At home, she disappeared straight into the shower, standing under the burning jets, the water as hot as she could bear. She was wrapped in a towel, her forehead dotted with perspiration, when Eliot found her. Billows of steam came from the bathroom.

'Your mum's making breakfast,' he said. Then, 'So how was that? With Jago?'

'Fine. Nice.'

She unwrapped her towel and used it to rub her hair ferociously. She stood naked, her skin pinkish from the heat.

'You look gorgeous. I'd ravish you, but everyone's waiting.'

'Give me two minutes and I'll come down.'

She made a turban of the towel, and looked around for her clothes. Eliot handed her the yellow sundress that was hanging on the back of a chair, her bra and knickers. She slipped them on. He moved closer to her, cupping her breasts with his hands.

'On second thoughts,' he said, 'maybe breakfast can wait . . .'

Since Eliot's *new couple* comments, they'd each made more of an effort with one another. Robyn had bought new underwear, a silky, slinky set that wasn't normally her style, and even when she felt blitzed with tiredness she tried not to roll away from his touch. She still didn't stay up as late as he might have wanted, or rip through bottles of Jack Daniel's with him, or stage-hang, starry-eyed, at his gigs, but at least he'd stopped comparing Robyn the mum with Robyn the non-mum.

'Come on, if we're up here too long, they'll think "no wonder she got pregnant so soon".'

'It's not my fault if I can't keep my hands off you.'

'I can hear Tess yelling,' she said, slipping his grip and making for the door.

He followed her reluctantly downstairs, her damp feet leaving faint marks in the carpet. He placed his own in them, covering her tracks.

At lunchtime they walked on the beach at Sennen. A school of beginner surfers were taking to the water, and Robyn paused to watch them, smiling at how easily tipped they were, falling like conquered chess pieces. The gulls had watched Robyn learn. The Rockabilly quiff, towering and impervious. The sand crabs, and the flies that rose in clouds from the weed-draped shore. And Jago. Often, but not always, Jago.

The others had walked on. Her parents flanked Eliot, the

criss-crossed straps of the baby carrier marking his back. She heard her dad laugh, and saw her mum place a hand on Eliot's shoulder. *My family*, she thought, and felt a sudden pang for Tess, wanting to be the one carrying her, feeling her small bulk against her chest. She kicked through the sand, and caught up to them.

Just as they reached the beach's end, clouds blew in, stealing the summer day, so they retreated to a café. Simon ordered a bottle of wine and they toasted the weekend, and Tess's first Merrin visit, as a tenacious gull edged ever closer, eyeing the open packets of crisps on their table.

'And we're very happy you could be here too, Jago,' said Marilyn.

Robyn set her glass down with a crack.

'You mean Eliot,' said Eliot.

'Mum?'

'He's Eliot, dear,' said Simon, with a pointed chuckle. 'Your son-in-law. Well, sort of son-in-law. The father of your granddaughter. Your daughter's boyfriend. Eliot.'

'Of course he is. What did I say?'

Her hand went to her throat and she fingered her beads, restlessly. They were sea glass, aquamarine and misshapen. Robyn had liked them, wanted to ask where she'd got them, but now she just shot her mum a look. Marilyn, however, was oblivious. She smiled, said *Silly, how silly*, and took another sip of wine.

'Daytime drinking,' said Simon. 'Sends us all loopy.'

As they walked back to the car, Robyn fell into step with her mum. They passed two more surfers, barefooted, slick-bodied, trotting with their boards under their arms. Robyn watched them go, turned and saw them jump down on to the beach, race towards the water.

'Mum?' she said. 'It wasn't deliberate before, was it? Calling him Jago?'

Marilyn looked confused, hurt. 'Why on earth would I do that?'

'Sorry, that was stupid. Just . . . sorry. Hey, I saw Denny's girlfriend, woman friend, whatever, earlier. She looked nice.'

'She's very nice. He deserves someone like that, actually.'

'I can't tell if Jago likes her. He always gives so little away.'

'Oh Robyn, dear, you can't mean that,' she said, with a look that was halfway between a smile and a frown. 'I think he's always been tremendously obvious in that department.'

Jago climbed to the top of the Rockabilly quiff. He sat on the sun-warmed stone and watched the waves slap lazily against the rocks far below. There was no one in the water. Merrin was a weekend place for her at best now. For her, and her tiny daughter. He thought how strange it was that he had never seen her pregnant, not after that first visit. She'd simply stayed away. He knew her parents drove to London to see her, drawing blinds across their great wide windows and reversing slowly out of the drive, but she hadn't come, not once. Was it better that she hadn't? That he hadn't seen her bursting midriff, her swollen breasts, her body shifting and morphing into something that wouldn't fit in a wetsuit, couldn't lie face down on a board; that was beautiful, quite beautiful, but belonged to someone else?

Change. It was an incomer's fantasy that nothing ever changed in their corner of Cornwall. Robyn had never thought that way. She'd known better, feeling change inside and out. She'd been sucked into the waves. And, later, she'd discovered what it was like to walk on water – no, better, to dance, brief seconds of movement so perfect, so heart-stopping, that you had to paddle right back out and try and catch it all again. Jago had known for some time that life, the good and the bad, could turn on a moment. When his mum yelled up the stairs, *See you later*, he didn't for an instant suspect that he wouldn't. That was all it took, the work of milliseconds, to change everything. And that was all it took to fall in love, too.

There was love in his house now, or something very like it. Denny was lit differently these days. He whistled in the yard, and in the workshop he offered the sort of meandering chatter that Jago had stopped even noticing was missing. Traces of Lucy were in the house too. Her rain mac hung in the hall, pink and white spots, between the waxed jackets and the navy overalls. There was a tin containing camomile tea in the kitchen cupboard, and a jar of greengage jam on a shelf in the fridge.

'Is this all right?' Denny had asked once.

'It's great,' he'd said. Then they'd shaken hands. A strange gesture, perhaps, stiff and formal, but they'd both extended their hands at exactly the same time, thumb to finger, palm to palm. A pact, perhaps. That life was changing, again, and that was okay.

Jago began to climb down from the quiff. The tide was coming in and it washed up higher now, blackening the rocks, brightening the clinging weed. It was dizzying, if you stared down for too long.

'You're a coward,' he said aloud.

The sea hissed back at him. Robyn had stood looking exactly as she used to, only she'd been holding a baby girl, the mirror of her, in her arms. He hadn't asked her how she felt, or what it was like, or whether she'd been frightened, or if she was frightened now, cradling this small, fragile life. He hadn't asked if she was happy. And he hadn't asked her whether, being back there, time hadn't fallen away after all. That in Merrin perhaps certain things *could* crystallise, that those passing milliseconds were capable of hanging suspended, and that some people, some places, some feelings, could remain just the same as when you left them.

'Coward,' he said again.

On Sunday morning, Eliot took their bags out to the car. When he came back in, he was carrying a shoebox in his hands.

'Found this on the doorstep,' he said, handing it to her. 'It's for you.'

Robyn recognised the handwriting straight away, the jagged 'R', the sharp downward stroke of the 'y'. She wanted to take it upstairs and open it alone, but Eliot was watching. Her mum and dad were watching.

'Well it's for Tess really,' she said.

'You know what it is?' he said.

'Something Jago made, I think,' said Robyn.

She untied the baler twine, took off the lid.

'Oh how wonderful!' cried Marilyn, as Robyn drew out a wooden horse. He'd laid it in a bed of straw, and she blew gently, sending dust flying, dancing in the sunlight. She held it up for them all to see.

It was about six inches tall and made of blondest wood, so pale it was almost white, and polished to a high sheen. She traced her finger over its contours, the delicate whorls, any knots falling just where it made sense that they should, at a hoof, or along the run of the mane. The tail flicked out, as though a sea wind had taken it, and the head was held high, nostrils flared slightly, as if catching a scent. One foot was just lifted. The effect was one of the promise of movement, as if at any moment the horse might fly into a run. The kind of gallop where a girl might lose her stirrups, and a boy might dash after her.

'Good lord,' said Simon, with a low whistle. 'It's exquisite.'

'It's Tomatillo,' breathed Robyn.

On the long drive back to London, she wondered how her thoughts didn't burst out of her. She felt herself swelling with them. She sat in the back beside Tess, her hand resting gently on her daughter's belly as she slept. She talked to Eliot about his next gig, the end-of-summer festival, the support slot for a much bigger act that he and his bandmates were ecstatic about and felt could be the start of something. He'd taken a phone call about it that morning, and was jumpy with excitement. As they settled into the motorway traffic, Eliot fell quiet. She leant between the seats, fiddling with the dial of the radio, looking for a song that didn't remind her of anything except the present.

The carved horse stayed on the small table beside Tess's bed, and after a week or two, or perhaps three, Robyn found she could look at it and just see it for what it was – a piece of wood, fine craftsmanship, a thoughtful gift from an old friend. After a month, she threw its box into the recycling. As she flattened and folded it, something dropped and hit her bare foot, skittered across the floor. A small, light object. She bent to retrieve it, taking it between two fingers and holding it up to the light. It was a shell. A scallop shell, with fine grooves running across it, a pinkish colour, a softer version of the setting sun. You could only tell that it was made of wood if you peered closely. Then you saw that it was a light varnish that made it shine as though it was still ocean-wet, glinting from the sand on a sun-touched beach, and that its smooth and rounded edges weren't made by endless crashing waves, but by the careful touches of a chisel, the light scrape of knife and sandpaper. She turned it between her fingers. She went back to the box again, and looked for anything, a slip of paper, a scribbled message, but there was nothing.

Robyn sat on the kitchen floor, holding her shell in the palm of her hand. She stared at it, mesmerised, as though within its shallow scoop, and between its delicate ridges, it might contain the world and all its secrets.

twenty-seven

IT BEGAN WHEN ELIOT RETURNED FROM THE FESTIVAL.

Tess was teething, racked with sobs day and night, so Robyn had stayed at home. She'd wanted to don her wellies and her cut-off denim shorts, drink cider in the sunshine and put Tess in a floppy hat, watch Eliot play to his biggest crowd yet, but her baby's teeth had other ideas. Instead she'd spent the weekend in the flat, wailing bouncing off all the walls, the echoes lasting even when Tess was exhausted into brief and patchy sleep.

Eliot came home much later than he'd said he would. Robyn had planned a celebratory dinner, but his was still in the pot and her own was half eaten, cold and melded, Tess having launched into a fit just as she'd sat down. In the end she'd gone to bed, tired of checking her phone, or waiting for a step on the stairs, and was deep asleep when she awoke with a start. She lurched up, listening for Tess's cries, sure that that was what had woken her. Instead she heard the banging of a door, followed by a *thunk*, and a string of swearing. Her first thought was that it was an intruder; her second, coming almost as quickly, was that it would wake her baby. Instantly a piercing wail rose from Tess's room. Robyn groaned and swung herself out of bed, afraid and annoyed in almost equal measure. She rushed into the living room.

'Eliot? Are you kidding?'

His guitar case lay in the middle of the carpet. He was attempting to pick up the chair he'd knocked over, but he kept missing it, each lunge accompanied by an *ohhh shit, whoops, yep, shit*. She could smell the alcohol on him from across the room. Through the wall she heard Tess yell.

'Do you know how long it took me to get her to sleep? All weekend, practically.'

He looked up at her with a glazed expression. He laughed messily. 'Ooops,' he said.

'How did you get home? You were supposed to be driving. Please God don't tell me you drove like that.'

'Lee drove. Lee drove me mad, but Lee drove me home.'

'Right. Lee. Who's Lee?'

'Old mate. Ran into a gang of them at the festival. Didn't know they were there. Didn't even know Lee was back in the country.'

Tess's shrieks changed pitch, growing choked and more desperate. Robyn pushed past him.

'Well, great that you had a happy old time, but our daughter is currently going crazy, so excuse me if I can't listen right now.'

'Don't be like that, babe. Lee said you'd be like that but I said no, not Robyn, Robyn's cool.'

'Robyn's not cool. She's knackered, and pissed off, and . . . and now talking about herself in the third person, apparently. Eliot, don't.' She shrugged off his arm as he tried to pull her into an embrace. 'I need to go to Tess.'

'It's always Tess. Tess, Tess, Tess.'

She closed the door on him and picked up her baby. Tess's cheeks were bright red and her hair stood on end. Robyn hugged her tightly to her, curling her tiny, hot hand into her own.

'Shhh,' she soothed, 'shhh, it's all right, it's okay. It's just Daddy, Daddy's home and he's going to tell us all about the festival tomorrow, yes he is. Shhh, there there, baby, there there, Tess.'

A peevish voice came through the door. 'We played what might have been our best set ever, if you want to know.'

'Of course I want to know. Only not now. Not when you're like this. Not when Tess is yelling the place down.'

There was quiet, then, on both sides.

'She's not crying any more,' he edged. 'Can I come in?'

Robyn pressed her lips to her daughter's head. The door opened very slowly. Eliot peeped in. In the pale glow of Tess's night light, he looked so comically contrite that she softened.

'Shhh, yes, okay. Just be quiet. And don't breathe your fumes all over her.'

'I missed you,' he said. He wrapped an arm around Robyn's shoulder. 'It wasn't the same without you there.'

'We wanted to be,' said Robyn. 'You know how much we wanted to be.'

'I love you so much,' he said. 'You know that, don't you? I do say it enough, don't I?'

'You do.'

Robyn laid Tess gently back down, tucking the blanket around her. She watched her, her breath held. Tess's lips were parted, her eyelashes clumped with tears, her breathing coming even. It was the peace that followed frenzy. Robyn backed away, her finger held to her lips. She took hold of Eliot's hand.

'Come on, let's go. Put you to bed as well.'

'I drank a lot, I mean a *lot*. I hadn't seen Lee for so long. Not for, like, two years. We drove all the way back to London and just talked and talked and it was great, actually, it was great.'

Robyn closed the door softly behind them.

'But all the time I was just thinking, I wish Robyn was here. I'd much rather Robyn was here. You believe that, don't you?'

'Shhh, yes, I believe it.'

He lay down on the bed in his T-shirt and jeans. His feet trailed off the end, and Robyn undid his laces, pulled his trainers from his feet. She took a cover and pulled it up around his waist. Then she slipped on to her side of the bed, and rolled over, and flicked off the light.

The next day, Eliot got home before her. She'd spent the afternoon with Tess at the river. The water had slopped thickly against the bank, soupy and uninviting, but she'd looked beyond it, towards the Albert Bridge. She loved its pomp, the ornate ironwork in candy pink and the way at night it appeared to flicker like a birthday cake; her favourite bridge, rivalled only by hoary old moss-green Hammersmith. The summer was all burned out, and autumn was coming, with fallen leaves, and puffs of white breath. They'd walked and walked, then ridden the bus home, Tess snickering at her chest, her new teeth peeping through pearly white, Robyn feeling wind-blown and happy.

'Something great's happened,' he said, catching her hands as she walked in. She laughed instinctively, caught by his dancing eyes, his bounding gait. 'Robyn, sit down, baby, sit down and let me tell you.'

'I need to change Tess, but come with me, tell me.'

'Over a dirty nappy? No, no way. Change her first – no, here, give her to me, I'll change her. Then I'm telling you. But first get the wine, it's in the fridge. I almost bought champagne, but then I thought no, not yet, don't jinx it.'

Robyn shrugged off her coat. She got two glasses and the corkscrew, went to the fridge and drew out the still-warm wine.

'Can't you give me a clue?' she called. 'Just one clue?'

'Try and guess,' he shouted back. 'Whoa, this is one smelly nappy, Tessie-Tess. Have a guess, and get that wine poured.'

She threw herself down on the sofa and drew up her knees. Took a sip. It wasn't cold enough, but it was good. Better than they usually bought.

'Someone saw you playing yesterday,' she said. 'An A&R guy. They thought you were amazing and now they want to sign you.'

Eliot walked back through, Tess wriggling in his arms.

'That would have been the champagne moment,' he said.

They chinked glasses, and he joined her on the sofa. Tess sat between them, absorbed in playing with her toes.

'So . . . ?' urged Robyn.

'So, you were half right. Someone did see us playing yesterday. And they did think we were pretty amazing. And they happen to know some people who they reckon will *also* think we're amazing. So they're going to get them to come to our next gig, these other people. And properly see us do our thing. And they think there's a really good chance that something could come of it because, this person, they really know their music. And the other people, they really, *really* know their music.'

He paused for breath, took a slug of wine. 'Well, what do you think? You're not saying anything.'

'It's good, no, it's great. It's just . . . isn't it a bit like, you know, we've heard it all before? There's always someone who knows someone. And that someone is always going to come down on one of your nights, and they never do. Or they do and then they can't stay. Or they stay and then—'

'Seriously? You're doing this?'

'Doing what?'

'Raining on my parade? Pissing on my bonfire?'

'Of course not. It's just . . . Eliot, you're not naïve. You know you've had all this before. Why so excited this time?'

'Because I trust this person. She doesn't say a thing unless she means it. And she thinks we're good. Really good. And she's connected. You don't know how much that means in this industry . . .'

'Who is she?'

'Lee Macintyre.'

'The Lee who drove you home? I thought Lee was a guy.'

'She's not.'

'And she works in music?'

'She's a journalist. She said she was freelance and I figured it was small-fry stuff still. I didn't even stop to ask, I was just blown away at seeing her again, I guess.'

'Hence the drinking,' said Robyn.

'She's been in Australia, Japan, the US. Working. Building a reputation, this amazing reputation that I didn't even know about. Only back in the UK for two weeks, and just like that, our paths cross. It feels like . . .' he rubbed his head, 'I don't know. Fate or something.'

'Then that's brilliant. That's absolutely worth toasting. I'm really, really pleased for you.' She leant across and kissed him, over Tess's head. 'I'm just very, very glad that someone else thinks you're as amazing as I do.'

They tapped glasses. Eliot took a gulp, then another.

'I need to tell you something else.'

'More excitement?'

He didn't say anything.

'Eliot?'

'We used to see each other.'

'You and Lee?'

'It was a long time ago. It feels like even longer. I didn't know she was even back in the country. We didn't stay in touch.'

'What was she, a fling?'

He ran his hand through his hair. He did that when he was nervous, or tired, and in that moment he looked both.

'You and I, we never talked about exes,' he said. 'We must be the only couple on earth who never talked about exes. And then, well it all happened so fast, didn't it? We skipped some of the things that other couples do, I guess, the things they say, because none of that felt important, did it?'

Robyn's fingers tightened around the stem of her glass. With her other hand she stroked Tess's head. Her hair was so fine, and blowaway, blond as dandelion seeds. She stroked her daughter's hair and said, 'We talked, though. We were always talking. There was plenty of opportunity to say. If it was important.'

'You never talked about anyone. Only Jago, that one time on the beach, and he wasn't an ex, was he? More of a teenage crush. The one that got away, we've all got them.'

'Right,' murmured Robyn. Then, 'Lee Macintyre, different category, then?'

Eliot nodded. 'We went out for a couple of years.'

'When?'

'God, feels like a lifetime ago. When was it? I guess . . . well, she's been abroad for ages, so I guess we must have broken up . . . what, two, three years ago?'

'Which? Two years ago, or three years ago?'

He hesitated, pushed back his hair.

'Two years ago. Maybe a bit less. Something like that.'

Robyn was silent. She worked it back.

'So when we met, you'd just broken up with your long-term girlfriend? Six months before, at the most? At the very most?'

'Four months before.'

'Four months. Eliot, that's nothing, not if it really mattered.'

'I know. I know that. But then you came along, and—'

'And everything happened very, very quickly,' finished Robyn.

'I fell in love with you straight away, Robyn. I did. You know I did. I didn't *say* it straight away, because I thought you'd think I was crazy, but I knew it. You were never a rebound thing.'

She looked down at her daughter. Took her small hand in hers. 'Rebound,' she repeated, quietly.

'Never,' he said. He lifted her chin with his finger, stared hard at her. 'Never, ever say that word.'

'You told me you loved me when we found out about Tess. That was when you said it.'

'Exactly, because at that point, I wasn't afraid of saying it any more. And it was important that you knew.'

Her voice threatened to be taken by tears. They came from nowhere, quick as a riptide. She stopped talking, she didn't want to be that girl, and Eliot pulled her towards him, Tess coming too.

'Robyn? You're okay, aren't you?'

'Of course,' she said, and she showed him a smile. The brightest she could muster.

Wind Sea

A whipping wind tears at the waves,
sending the surface choppy and confused.
Ships may topple.

twenty-eight

LEE MACINTYRE BECAME A PRESENCE IN THEIR LIVES. SHE brought people from Roaming Records to see The Fearless play, just as she said she would. They liked what they saw, and Lee and Eliot and the rest of the band celebrated afterwards with vodka, and old stories, and new talk for the future.

'How did it go?' Robyn asked, as Eliot climbed into bed later, finding her in the dark.

'About as well as it could,' he said, his tongue flicking her ear, one hand moving across her chest. 'I've got a good feeling.'

Robyn turned and met him, pushed her mouth to his, and arched her back, and they went to the place where words weren't needed.

He'd talked, because she'd asked him to. But when Robyn had said *You need to tell me about Lee Macintyre*, she'd wanted facts, not stories: the beginning, and then the end. Instead she got tales that seemed folkloric in Eliot's telling, too colourful, too important. He told her how Lee had first come to review one of their gigs, accosting him afterwards with the line *I'm*

*going to give you four stars. I'd have given you five but I'm
taking one off for self-indulgence.* She was the one who'd
knocked the multiple solos out of him, and encouraged him to
find his own style on stage. *Don't try and ape the greats*, she'd
said. *Walk your own line, Eliot, because you know you can,
and so do I.* When Robyn asked what she was like, what she
really meant was, was she pretty. He said she was their harshest
critic and their biggest fan, and, Robyn knew, that gave her a
beauty that transcended mere looks; she was part of his music.
With all of that inside of him, she thought, how could it not
have bubbled up before? How had it not overflowed into *their*
life, even accidentally? And then she understood the full stop,
the wave of silence. Eliot said that Lee Macintyre had cheated
on him. Spectacularly. Not once, not twice, but three times. At
least three. He said he'd stopped counting after that.

'How did you find out?' said Robyn, chewing her lip, her
eyes blazing with someone else's anger.

'Turned out she was a fan of a lot of musicians. That was
her thing, I guess. Get to know the bands, write about them
really well, really intimately, unravel their secrets. It was what
she did.'

'But how did you find out?'

Eliot shook his head. 'I can't even remember. I just did.'

Robyn couldn't believe that, for who could forget the
moment of uncovering such betrayal? Not her. Never her. She
took hold of Eliot's hand, and squeezed his fingers.

'I'm sorry.'

'I was embarrassed, you know? The thing was, she thought
she hadn't done anything particularly wrong. She told me she
never thought we were exclusive. She told me I could have slept
with other people too. "We should just be ourselves," she said.

Those were her words. "Not try and fit some idea of what a couple should be."'

'Wow,' said Robyn. 'What an idiot.'

'I felt like one.'

'Not you, her. *Her*. Lee sodding Macintyre. How can you bear to have her around now? Be anywhere near her, let alone sitting in a car beside her all the way back from Hampshire, and then drinking vodka until whatever time in the morning? That's the bit I don't get.'

'Because,' he said, looking right into her eyes, 'I'm so happy right now. I've got *you*. And she had a point,' he went on. 'I thought we were something, based on, I don't know, based on my idea of what I thought we should be. That wasn't her fault. That was mine. So that's how I can stand to be around her. That's why I've got no problem in letting her help us get where we want to go. She's always understood our music, and she's always thought we could be more than we are. That kind of belief doesn't come along all that often. She could be really, really helpful to us. She could make all the difference.'

Robyn met Ruby one lunchtime in a Soho coffee shop. Ruby hurried in late, her heels clattering across the tiled floor.

'Sorry, sorry, I was stuck in the world's longest meeting.'

They hugged, Robyn taking in her friend's smooth silhouette, her sleek pencil skirt and silken blouse. She wished she'd made more of an effort herself, applied a slick of mascara or at least brought a change of T-shirt. On the bus there, Tess had sneezed milk all over her shoulder, and now and again she caught the scent from its stain. She fiddled with her hair so it fell over the offending patch.

'Clients in,' said Ruby, noticing her look. 'I'm not normally this scrubbed up. And it's also why I've only got about half an hour. Boring, I know. You look great, by the way, weight's completely dropped off you. Oh, look at her, isn't she sweet? God, she's doubled in size since I last saw her.'

Between Ruby's job and Robyn's baby, they'd hardly seen one another in recent months. Their worlds turned on quite different axes, Ruby's made up of fevered pitches and client drinks and a particularly intense form of yoga. Now she sipped a smoothie through a yellow straw and eyed Robyn.

'Is it crazy? Are you okay? I'm sorry I haven't called in ages, but things have been nuts. This job,' she rolled her eyes, 'it's the hardest thing I've ever done in my life.'

'Tell me about it,' smiled Robyn.

'Oh, don't! I know, I know. I sound whiny, but the thing is, just when I think I'm getting the hang of it all, something different comes along and knocks me sideways. At least with doing what you're doing it's repetitive, right? Boring, maybe, knackering, but . . . doable?'

'Well,' began Robyn, 'sort of. But I have to make it up as I go along too. For instance, if she cries . . .'

Tess was sitting in her lap, and on cue she began to fuss. Not a full-blown cry, but a whimper, a pinking of the cheeks. Robyn bobbed her up and down.

'But you always know why,' said Ruby, 'right? If she's crying, she's hungry, or . . .'

'Or needs changing . . .'

'Exactly. That's it, the only options.'

'Or she's too hot. Or too cold. Or tired. Or just . . . trying to tell me something else entirely. Like maybe she has wind. Or she feels peaky. Or . . . no, Rubes, it's pretty much always guesswork.'

'At least you have Eliot.'

'Well, yes, but mostly it's me and Tess. If he's not at the bar then he's rehearsing, or playing, or . . . just doing band stuff.'

'Is he shirking? Don't tell me he's shirking, because I'll have words.'

'No, he's not shirking. It's just how it is.'

'I've only met him, like, four times, and two of them were after gigs and he was completely wasted. It's strange, you know, feeling like I barely know him. Love of your life. Father of your child.'

Robyn watched Ruby sort furtively through her salad, extracting slivers of onion, and wondered whether to say anything. Ruby had already told her about her latest project in some depth, a sampling campaign for a make-up brand, and related an anecdote about their boss insulting a client by asking when her non-existent baby was due. Their time was running out. Soon Ruby would be flashing back into her busy life, and it'd easily be weeks before they saw each other again.

'I'm still learning things myself,' she said.

'Baby things?'

'Eliot things.'

'That's whirlwind romances for you,' laughed Ruby, 'especially with complicated musician types. Though that's not really Eliot, is it? You always said he was more bright and breezy than dark and brooding.'

'He is,' said Robyn. 'Usually. Definitely was pre-Tess, but then a baby tests anyone, I guess . . .'

'What, this cherub? Hardly!'

'But, you know, the whole sunny demeanour thing is actually pretty deceptive, because you think you know everything there is to know, and then . . . well, then you realise maybe you don't.'

Ruby made a small noise of acknowledgement as her eyes flicked around the café. Robyn saw her wave and smile at someone in the line for takeaway coffee, a girl dressed just like Ruby, same perfect make-up, same lightness to her whole being.

'There's an ex,' said Robyn, tapping her friend's arm.

'There's always an ex.'

'But he never mentioned her, that's the thing. She was way the other side of the world, and now she's back, and they're spending time together again. For work. She's in music. She's actually being really helpful, she might even get them a record deal the rate she's going, but . . . I just wish I'd known about her. Before. I wish he'd told me about her.'

Ruby's eyes were narrowed, her focus back on Robyn. 'You don't think he has feelings for her still?'

'No. No, of course not.'

Ruby drained her drink, checked her watch. 'Exes are sent to test us,' she said. 'Mike's is a complete psychopath. She used to phone him, you know, in the middle of the night. She'd get drunk and call him and start narrating some never-ending new boyfriend problem as though he was her perpetual shoulder to cry on. I put a stop to it, though. You have to. It's the only way. Put your foot down, Robyn.'

'It's not really like that,' she said.

'You say that now . . .'

'I haven't met her yet. I might actually like her.'

'You won't. You might pretend to, but you won't.'

'If she's helping the band, if she's helping Eliot, then I am grateful to her.'

'Robyn, can I just say something? You sound like you're

trying to convince yourself. Don't be afraid to say what you really think. To Eliot, I mean. It's your relationship. It's yours to protect.'

Ruby stood up, smoothing the creases from her skirt. She'd always been territorial; Robyn remembered that from university, her pointed ownership of whichever boy she was dating. It was there in her wilful gestures, a snatched arm here, a sharp command there, and Robyn had always found it faintly amusing, her friend's heightened sense of possession. She knew Ruby probably wasn't the right person to talk to, especially when she herself didn't really know what she was trying to say, but it didn't feel like there was anyone else.

'Rubes, can I just ask you one more thing? Have you ever been cheated on?'

'Me?' She pursed her lips, nodded briskly. 'Yes. Once. Bastard.'

'And . . . can you remember the moment when you found out?'

'Er, yes, it's only seared on my brain for ever. That's not a thing you forget. Oh babe, you are worried, aren't you? You think he's lying to you.'

Robyn shook her head. 'Honestly, it's not like that. I'm just thinking about him, and when he was with her, that's all. I'm just . . . thinking too much about everything, I guess. Go on, you go, you're late already. I'll call you soon.'

They hugged each other goodbye, Ruby with a wagged finger, *Don't go taking any crap*, and Robyn watched her hurry back towards her office, her phone already pressed to her ear. She laid a hand on Tess's warm head, and was rewarded with a wide smile. The whole world fell away, just as it always did. She smoothed her daughter's flyaway hair.

'What do you reckon? Shall we stay for another coffee? No. Okay. Nor me. Home it is. Let's go the long way.'

Robyn met Lee on a Sunday afternoon, in a pub in Kentish Town. On the walk there, she and Eliot had talked brightly, but haltingly, and Robyn knew it was because they were both thinking about the meeting. *No big deal*, Eliot had said the night before, kissing the tip of her nose. *You'll probably like her, but you don't have to. You never have to.* And there was something unnerving about the last part. It implied longevity, as though Lee Macintyre was going to be around for a while yet.

'Hey, she's sweet. What's her name again?' Lee asked, bending down to Tess.

Tess was sitting in Robyn's lap, round as a ball, and Robyn wound her arms around her possessively as she studied Lee. From all Eliot's talk of her forthright ways, she'd imagined someone who was hard at the edges, but she appeared delicate as a butterfly. Her face was immaculately painted, pillar-box-red lipstick, a dash of blue behind the eyes. Her corkscrew blond curls were held loosely in place by a silk scarf. She was older than Robyn had imagined; there were light creases at the corners of her eyes, and a general wash of worldliness. Beside her, Robyn felt like a wide-eyed child.

Lee had written a piece for a music monthly on why The Fearless might just be the Next Big Thing, and it was on the table, lying open at the page. Eliot and the boys pored over it.

'This bit . . .' He laughed, then read aloud: '"Eliot Turner plays guitar as though it's his last night with a lover, and they both know it. His fingers fly like kisses up and down the neck, every stroke's a caress. Something bittersweet runs beneath his touch, angry even, giving tracks like the light acoustic 'Win Me' and 'Fighters' an angular, raw edge that threatens to break your heart if you'll only let it." Jesus. Only you could get away with that stuff, Lee.'

'It's true,' she said.

Robyn saw how Lee looked at him. Levelly. Coolly. *She really understands our music*, Eliot had said.

The afternoon rolled on, with drinks, and scattered crisp packets, and talk about bands and labels and venues Robyn had never heard of. Tess grew fractious, and weary of appeasing her, Robyn made moves to leave. Eliot jumped up to join her, despite the band's entreaties. As they said their goodbyes, Lee blew a kiss from her spot on the sofa. It was aimed at the three of them, but Eliot seemed to be the one to catch it, a smile tipping the corner of his mouth.

'Tomorrow night,' she called. 'Don't be late.'

Dark was falling outside, in that slow way it did in the city, ebbing in, flicking street lights in its wake, looming out of alleyways.

'What's tomorrow?'

'Some drinks with Lewis and Jake from Roaming Records. Lee thinks they've got some news for us.'

'Wouldn't you be going to their offices if it was serious?'

'They're not accountants,' said Eliot. 'Or estate agents. It doesn't work like that.'

'I do *know* how it works,' said Robyn. She heard the defensiveness in her voice and tried to shake it out. 'The thing is,' she said, 'I just find it very hard to look at her and not think about what she did to you, and then wonder how you can possibly be okay with it.'

'It was a lifetime ago. I'm over it, so you definitely should be.'

'You know, she didn't ask anything about me. Not one thing. I always find that weird.'

'She knows you're a new mum.'

'What's that got to do with anything? There's still a *me*, you know, there's still other things I want to do.'

'You know I didn't mean that. Just . . . it's pretty all-consuming, isn't it?'

Tess was bundled in a snowsuit and kicked from the sling at Robyn's chest. She gave a hiccuping laugh and Robyn smiled without wanting to.

'Listen,' said Eliot, encouraged, slipping his hand into hers, 'you can be, or do, anything. And you'll be brilliant at it. Tess and I will just look on, watch you in wonder.'

'And maybe someone will write about me doing it,' said Robyn, trying to shake the ice from her voice. 'Is it weird, to have her evaluate you in that way? Like she's the only one capable of interpreting what you're all about.'

'She's a journalist, that's her job.' There was a cut of irritation in his tone. 'And frankly, we're glad of it. We have to be.'

'I guess it's one way to make amends.'

'Robyn, Lee never felt like she had anything to apologise for. She's not like most people. She's . . . got her own rules. But her taking this interest in us is totally professional. Self-interested, even. Every music writer out there wants to be the one who makes the great discovery. Who champions the unknown band when no else knows their name, and then sits back and nods, says "I told you so" when they make it big. And every band is happy to have that happen.'

'So she's using you as much as you're using her.'

'Yeah, but without the cynical undertones, okay? We're mutually appreciative of each other. She could be our lucky break, and we could be hers. This is all a very good thing.'

'Okay,' Robyn said. Then, louder, 'Okay.'

They walked home side by side. At some point they stopped holding hands, but neither of them seemed to notice.

twenty-nine

'CHRISTMAS BY THE SEA?' SAID ELIOT, HIS EYEBROWS RAISED. 'I can't picture that.'

'What about when you've been to Australia? All that sunning and barbecuing and beach parties.'

'My folks are in Canberra. No beach parties. Anyway, English sea, cold and wet and grey in winter. I don't know, is that festive?'

Robyn thought of the kaleidoscope of lights in Mousehole, the harbour waters glistening with red, yellow and gold, the steep and winding streets lit like a fairy town. Cramming into a pub afterwards to drink cups of mulled wine and eat hunks of Stargazy pie on Tom Bawcock's Eve, as voices raised in carols and sea shanties steamed the windows and drowned the crackling of the fire. A walk along the cliffs on Christmas morning, the sky puffed with clouds, the sea crystal blue, a spry wind slapping your cheeks with cold. A Boxing Day surf, bursting across the silver water in a blast of colour and light, then coming back into the house and warming yourself by the early-morning fire as the house around you slowly stirred.

'Oh, you'll see,' she said.

Inside White Sands, every surface was draped with holly and ivy. Mistletoe hung in the hallway. Candles lit the windows. Ben was staying with friends in a house in Scotland, and it was the first time that a Swinton had been absent for the festivities. Robyn's parents surged around her and Tess, making up for the loss of one offspring with the arrival of another. Marilyn presented her granddaughter with a red corduroy dress and a snow-white knitted cardigan. Simon emptied bottles of wine into bowl-like glasses, then sat in front of the fire with Eliot, cracking nuts into the palms of their hands. Inside, the house glittered, while outside the sea rocked and rolled with winter storms. Rain pelted the glass. Marilyn turned up the volume on the Christmas carols. In her old room, Robyn looked across to Hooper's House. Smoke whipped from the chimney, and the roof beamed black. She imagined bundling up Tess and dashing across the yard, shaking off raindrops and stepping inside, bringing a plate of mince pies, a spray of mistletoe and holly. Instead, White Sands and Hooper's House remained quite separate.

On Christmas Eve, the night rolled in early. By four o'clock, the windows were throwing back reflections, the rain spitting down the chimney and into the fire. Simon sat with Tess on his lap, reading her a story, *The Night Before Christmas*. Eliot sat beside them, listening amiably, a glass in his hand. Robyn was at the table, drawing, a contented smile on her lips. She'd packed her sketchpads and pastels, tucking them in among Tess's things, her wrapped Christmas gifts. Since her daughter's birth there had been little time to paint or draw, but whenever the opportunity presented itself, she took it with both hands. Now she sat quietly, blurring soft blues with midnight shades until she'd made a seascape she was almost, but not quite, satisfied with. She held it up to the light.

'Where's Mum?' she asked, squinting at the lines of clifftop, the angular descent.

'Upstairs doing Christmas things,' said Simon.

'Wrapping?'

'Secret squirrel, never you mind. Take her a glass of wine, could you? She'll be in need of liquid refreshment, no doubt. Now, I think we're finished with this story. Eliot, tell me more about this deal of yours.'

Eliot sprang forward in his seat, rubbed his hands together. 'It's the start of everything, Simon,' he said.

Robyn padded into the kitchen. Roaming Records had come through, just as Lee had said they would. The contracts were signed, Eliot spitting on his palms before taking up his pen, scribbling with an exaggerated flourish, then folding Robyn into his arms and spinning her round. Later she'd heard him on the phone to Lee: *This is the best Christmas present ever. No, the best present full stop*, he'd said.

She refilled her dad and Eliot's glasses, then poured one for Marilyn. She called up to her.

'Mum, I've got you some wine. I'll leave it by the door if you're doing secret things.'

Hearing no answer she creaked up the stairs, feeling like a child again, caught by Christmas spirit.

'Mum?'

She turned on the landing and knocked at the door to her parents' room. She went to the bathroom, but the door was wide open. She checked the other rooms, and they were empty too.

'She's not there,' she called, clattering back down the stairs. Her dad looked up over the top of Tess's head. 'What?'

'Maybe she's gone out,' offered Eliot.

'Out? In this? There's nowhere to go,' said Robyn.

She saw her dad pass Tess to Eliot and stand up. He rubbed his hands together, then smoothed his hair.

'She might have gone to the garage,' he said. 'If we're low on milk, or . . . last-minute Brussels sprout emergency before everything closes tomorrow.' He went to the door, opened it. Cold air blasted in, the rain tore down. 'Her car's here,' he said. Robyn heard the tight note in his voice. She joined him at the door.

'Mum!' she yelled.

She felt her dad's hand on her shoulder. 'I'll go and have a look,' he said, squeezing it. He pulled on a jacket, and a hat. He took an umbrella from the stand in the hallway.

'Do you want me to come?' said Robyn.

'No, absolutely not. You stay here.'

He stepped outside and a gust pulled his umbrella inside out. He wrestled with it, but the wind had beaten it, the spikes were askew. He threw it back inside, swearing, and yanked his hat down.

'I'll be back soon,' he said. 'Keep an eye on the fire.'

Jago heard the knock at the door and jumped up immediately. His dad and Lucy were in Penzance, joining the queues of last-minute shoppers, clearing the shelves of brandy butter and Christmas crackers. He was wrapping gifts at the table, a beer in a glass beside him. A week ago he'd received a square brown card-backed envelope with a London postmark. Inside was a note from Robyn, just a few lines written in her lovely looping hand.

Dear Jago,

I never wrote and thanked you for the shell. I only found it much later, it was hidden in the wrapping, you see. It's so, so beautiful. I wanted to press it to my ear, to see if I could hear the Merrin sea, but it's the wrong kind of shell for that, I know. Anyway, it's perfect. Thank you. What can I offer in return? Something nowhere near as amazing, but just as true, I hope. Remember when we talked about art, that night on the rocks, just when we were getting to know each other? I told you I'd only want to draw and paint when I felt I had to, when there was something in me driving me to do it. Even as I said it, I wasn't sure I'd ever feel that way, but as it turned out, I do . . . and that thing is Tess. My body was so busy creating, I guess a little of that rubbed off on me too. Paints, pastels, pencil drawings, I just started playing around and . . . I found I couldn't stop. Anyway, when Tess was born, I had to, but now that she's sleeping better, I try and steal moments here and there, when I can. I did this picture of the cove, and I thought you might like it. I'm coming home for Christmas, but just for a couple of days. In case our paths don't cross, I wanted to send it to you. I drew it from memory, so I've probably taken some liberties. But I tried to make it exactly as it is. I tried to make it perfect.

Merry Christmas then.

Robyn x

Lucy had told him she was coming, the same day the picture arrived. *I bumped into Marilyn in the lane. They've got their daughter coming home for Christmas, she asked me to tell you,* she'd said in a chatty tone, as you might say *The weather's due to brighten up.* Then the Cornish skies had opened, and Merrin had stayed cold and soaking for days. Everybody hid indoors, and he hadn't caught so much as the briefest glimpse of her. Hearing the knock, he skidded down the passageway and threw open the door.

'Sorry to disturb,' said Simon. 'A strange question perhaps, but . . . my wife's not here, is she?'

Robyn's dad was drenched, rainwater running off his cheeks.

Jago shook his head. He turned and grabbed his raincoat and threw it on. He took the torch that was hanging on the peg, and stuffed his feet into his wellingtons.

'Where have you looked?' he said.

'I came here first.'

'Okay,' said Jago. 'Let's go.'

He'd seen her out walking before, a lone figure wandering the coast path. The first time was a chill October day, and Marilyn had looked blankly as he'd greeted her. He'd walked on, wondering if he'd done something to offend her, whether his misplaced desire was so rudely obvious within the gifts he'd made for Robyn. The second time, she'd been at the cove, the water lapping at the tops of her boots, and he'd greeted her with deliberate levity.

'Marilyn, hello,' he'd said. 'Thinking about a swim?'

'Not today,' she'd said.

They'd walked back together, and he'd found himself talking more than usual, filling the gaps. At the entrance to Hooper's House, he'd gone to leave her, but she'd caught his sleeve.

'Where are you going?' she'd said, sharply.

'I need to get on,' he'd laughed.

Marilyn had nodded, said, 'Of course you must,' and walked on up the lane.

Jago had thought about her after that. There'd been something off about her manner, though he couldn't say what. And she hadn't mentioned Robyn once: she always mentioned Robyn. Simon had come round a week later, standing stiffly at the doorstep, his arms folded at his chest. He'd explained that Marilyn had started showing signs of forgetfulness, nothing serious, nothing to worry about, but a month ago she'd gone out for her usual walk and somehow lost the path on the way back. Then the other week he'd found her standing in their own front garden at dusk, her pink slippers covered in sand and mud, a gull's feather caught in their tread. When Simon had asked her why on earth she'd gone out like that, she'd started to cry, slow, quiet tears, because she simply couldn't remember. *It's not all the time,* he'd told Jago. *I'd worry if it was all the time, and it's not. But I wanted to mention it, just in case you ever came across her.* His voice had trailed off. His brow was furrowed deeply as he spoke, his eyes darkened with the concern that he said he wasn't feeling. *Of course,* Jago had said. *No problem.* Then, *Does Robyn know?*

The wind flew off the sea, dashing rain against their faces as their torches cast a feeble beam in the all-consuming black. Jago pulled his hood down.

'Shall I head to the cove?' he said.

'Could you? I'll take the cliffs.'

Jago watched Simon stumble off into the dark, then turned quickly and jumped over the stile, striding through the sinking grass of Tomatillo's old field and on to the path. The stream, no more than a faint trickle in the summer, burst its way towards the sea. Jago pushed through it, the cold water biting through his rubber boots. It was slippery underfoot and twice he nearly lost his footing. He shone his torch left and right, looking for any sign of recent passage. The sound of the sea grew ever closer. He was used to its roar, but that night it sounded as though it was charging up and out of the cove, sweeping all before it. He stood at the entrance to the beach, water slapping, soaking his jeans.

'Marilyn!' he shouted.

It was high tide, and the strip of beach was submerged. A thin moon sent a sliver of light across the water, and slowly his eyes adjusted. The outlines of the Rockabilly stack were just visible. Slabs of granite loomed on the clifftop, like rubble at the ends of the earth. Even in brightest daylight you had to watch where you trod, but the rain had loosened everything. Any step in any direction could lead to a sudden drop. Suddenly he feared for Simon as much as for Marilyn. He shone his faint light across the cove again; seeing nothing, he slipped and slid back the way he'd come, water falling all around him.

Jago wandered for an hour or more, over the headland and into the black tunnels of lanes. Once he thought he heard Simon's call, but it was lost against the shout of the sea and the hammering of the rain. The gale tore at his collar, sending his hood flapping. His fingers were numbed with cold but he kept them out of his pockets, throwing his arms out for balance. When the clouds hid the moon, the darkness was absolute, the kind of country nightfall that could scare you if you weren't used to it, and even occasionally if you were. When he was a little boy, sometimes he'd lie in bed and hold a hand up before his face, frightening himself by the fact that he couldn't see it. He had a memory of climbing gingerly out of bed and inching towards his bedroom door, his toes curling in the carpet. His mum had had animal ears; she always woke at the slightest sound, especially if it was made by him. Before he'd reached the door she'd filled the landing with light, was scooping him up and kissing away his childish tears. That must have been fifteen years ago or more, but he remembered everything about it, how quickly she'd quelled his fear, how safe he'd felt in her arms.

He yanked his hood closer to his face. He couldn't let anything happen to Robyn's mum. He strode on through the torrents of rain, looping back over paths he'd already trodden, shouting her name until he was hoarse.

When Jago knocked at the door of White Sands, Simon answered almost instantly. He was all dried off, and warm in a knitted jumper, his cheeks shining red, from the fire and wine and good cheer. In his hand he held a bottle and a corkscrew; an apron was tied at his waist.

'Jago,' he said, weighting the name with gratitude.

He exhaled with relief. 'You found her?'

Simon glanced over his shoulder and stepped just outside the door. He closed it behind him.

'Lot of fuss over nothing in the end. She'd walked the other way, up towards the road, looking for some more holly berries, apparently.'

'And she's all right?'

'Absolutely fine. Rather wet, that's all.' He took in Jago's appearance, his blackened jeans, his slick coat, the sodden tendrils of his hair. 'Although not as wet as you. Oh Jago, have you been looking all this time?'

'It's a bad night,' he said, simply. 'I didn't like the thought of her out in it.'

'That's very good of you.' Simon looked humbled. He rubbed at his chin, as if wondering what to do or say next. 'Very good of you indeed.'

'It's fine. I'm . . . just glad she's okay.'

'I did try to find you,' he said, a tinge of embarrassment in his voice. 'For once I was wishing there was a bloody mobile signal on this peninsula.'

'No phone, anyway,' said Jago, with a wry smile.

'I feel awful for putting you out like that. Pathetic alarmist that I am. Is there anything I can do? I'd ask you in for a drink, but . . .' His voice drifted again; he glanced behind him. 'It'd be hard to explain the fact that you look half drowned.'

'So Robyn doesn't know?'

'She doesn't know.'

Jago shivered suddenly, and rubbed his hands together. 'But what do you think it is? I mean, with Marilyn. Is she okay?'

He felt Simon stiffen beside him.

'It's Christmas Eve, Jago,' he said, as if the date decreed that only staunch jollity was permitted, 'and I owe you a bottle of something warming.' His eyes went to his hand. 'Here, why not take this? It's a rather nice Merlot. Thank you for this evening, for your help, and . . . your discretion. I don't want anyone worrying needlessly, especially not Robyn.'

Simon's voice had returned to its usual fulsomeness; it was persuasive and confident and not to be argued with. Jago accepted the bottle with a brief nod of thanks. There was nothing more to say after that, but as Robyn's dad returned to his family, Jago lingered on the doorstep. The rain was abating, and after the downpour, the drizzle felt like nothing. Light burned from the window and he edged closer to it. They were all there. Marilyn in a cream-coloured cardigan, holding her granddaughter, bobbing her in her arms. Eliot by the fire, his shoes kicked off. Jago saw Simon go to his wife, lay a kiss on her head, and fold an arm around her shoulders. Robyn appeared suddenly, as though having flown in, a beautiful bird alighting on a lawn. Instinctively he drew back, then he stepped sideways, edging closer. She wore a sea-green dress. Her slender arms were bare, and pale, and as she turned, he saw the glint of a silver chain at her neck. She stood a little apart, as though she was watching her family just as Jago did. Then Eliot's head lifted and he must have said something to her, for Robyn moved to his side. She perched on the arm of his chair and wound herself into him, dropping her head close to his. Jago gave an involuntary shiver, aware, suddenly, of the wetness of his clothes, and the cold bite of the night air. He turned away, leaving them to their salvaged Christmas Eve.

thirty

BOXING DAY WAS BRIGHT AT LAST. THE SEA BEAMED BLUE AND still, the storm was all blown out. The path over the cliffs was dotted with walkers, straggling family groups and eager couples. Among them were the Swintons and Eliot, wrapped up in coats and hats and scarves. Simon had his arm linked through Marilyn's, and was laughing heartily. Eliot wore Tess at his chest, buried in a snowsuit, her legs kicking. Robyn walked by their side, her eyes on the sea.

'What are you thinking about?' said Eliot, nudging her.

'How I wanted to get a surf in, but it's flat as a mirror out there.'

'Then why don't you stay on? There's no need for you to rush back. So long as you're home in time for the party.'

On New Year's Eve the band was announcing their record deal to all their friends. They'd hired a room above a pub, and were going to play a surprise set. New songs, a new label, a new year.

'But I wanted to help you organise things.'

'There's nothing to organise. It's done. Lee's handled most of it. It's going to be one hell of a party.'

Robyn nodded, her lips tight.

'You know,' said Eliot, 'this is going to be our year. I've a feeling.'

Robyn almost said *Whose year?* But she looked at the so-level sea, watching for waves instead.

Jago was walking with Denny and Lucy, Scout bustling along beside them, nudging their ankles. He hadn't wanted to go out, but Lucy had implored him, and she was a difficult person to refuse. She radiated goodwill, and that could be infectious. She'd spent Christmas with them, and it had been the first without Rosalind where Jago had actually felt a true sense of festivity. When Denny set fire to the Christmas pudding, the blue flames had leapt a foot high and they'd all cheered. It was Jago who'd got the lucky coin, spun it in his hand then pocketed it. They'd drunk port by the fire, and burned their fingers on roasted chestnuts. Denny had told a ghost story. Jago fell asleep in an armchair and later, when he stirred, he saw Lucy and Denny dancing in the passageway, slow-waltzing across the flagstones.

'Jago, here comes Robyn,' said Lucy, pulling his arm.

In the pale winter sunshine she was iridescent. She wore a red knitted hat and mud-smeared wellington boots. Her eyes were on the water, and he watched her all the way to the point where she glanced in their direction. She saw him, and he saw her smile. He might have imagined it, but he was sure her step quickened too.

'Good morning, neighbours!' Denny hurled the greeting.

'What a wonderful day,' breezed Marilyn, 'and what a relief to be outside at last. I can't remember a wetter Christmas.'

Jago glanced at Robyn's dad, but he made no eye contact. 'Wonderful day, wonderful day,' Simon echoed.

Tess was distracted by the sight of Scout, and Eliot walked them closer, bending down to pat the dog's head. Tess held out an arm and made a high-pitched noise of pleasure. Denny and Lucy, Simon and Marilyn circled nearer.

'Oh, isn't that sweet?' cried Lucy, and Marilyn laughed with her.

'Hey, Jago,' said Robyn, quietly.

Everyone was rapt with Tess. As Eliot knelt in the damp grass, one hand on Tess, one on Scout, Jago and Robyn stood slightly to one side, unconsciously turning from the group.

'Hey,' said Jago.

'Merry Christmas.'

'To you too. How's the little one enjoying her first?'

'I think your dog might actually be her highlight. Jago, I wanted to come round before, but, well, I guess I didn't know . . .'

'It wasn't the kind of weather to be out in,' said Jago. 'Not even for five minutes.'

He was watching her for any sign of worry, and despite the smile she still wore, he thought he detected something: a tightening at the corner of her mouth, a shadow beneath her eyes. Two nights before, Simon's eyes had been black with concern, rainwater dripping from his chin as he'd stood on their doorstep, but he'd snapped back so quickly to his usual self. When Jago had got home, he hadn't been able to stop shivering. He'd set his clothes by the fire, and run a hot bath. He'd thought of Robyn in her green dress, an untroubled smile at her lips. He'd kept a secret from her before, and no good had come of it.

'How long are you down for?' he asked.

'We're due to leave tomorrow.'

'You should stay,' said Jago.

'You think?'

'Your parents miss you.'

'My parents? Right. I know.' She seemed to visibly dim before him. She glanced across at the huddled group, then back to him. 'I should be here more, I know I should.'

So she knew, after all. He nodded, feeling a rush of relief. 'I think your dad's more worried than he lets on.'

'My dad? What about?'

'Your mum.'

'What about my mum?'

He hesitated. 'It's not my place . . .' he began.

'Jago, *tell* me.'

Behind them Tess was giggling, making small noises of delight as she went nose to nose with Scout. Jago turned and saw Marilyn place a hand on Lucy's arm, smiling as she talked of the joys of grandchildren. Denny and Simon were deep into the weather, flood warnings and hailstorms. Jago turned his back on them, speaking quietly.

'It's not for me to say, but . . . Your dad doesn't think she's been herself lately, that's all. She's apparently become . . . forgetful.'

Robyn stared at him blankly.

'What do you mean, forgetful?' she said, then, 'And how do you even know this?'

'Your dad.'

'But why's he telling you?'

'Just . . . circumstance. I'm here, I suppose. And I've run into her a couple of times, and something hasn't seemed right, but . . . I don't know.'

Robyn's hands caught at her scarf. She wound it tighter, as

if armouring herself. Her face was creased with incomprehension. Jago wanted to gently take her fingers, weave them between his own and tell her that it would all be okay.

'Christmas Eve? Was that one of those times?' A faint light of understanding had appeared in Robyn's eyes. They widened with it, blazing with undue accusation. They'd walked along the path a little way, and Jago kept glancing back. Robyn grabbed at his sleeve. 'Tell me,' she urged.

'It turned out to be a false alarm. But . . . yes, your dad was worried.'

The brief fight had gone out of her, and she stood looking entirely helpless.

'Mum . . .' she began. 'She's fine, she . . . Why hasn't Dad told me any of this? Jago, he's a doctor. If he really thought there was anything wrong, he'd have said something. Wouldn't he?'

'Except . . .'

'Except *what*?'

'Sometimes,' said Jago, as carefully as he could, one hand rubbing the back of his neck uncertainly, 'I suppose, I don't know, maybe sometimes,' he sighed, 'maybe sometimes it's hard to admit the things we're most afraid of.'

He saw her face tighten, her cheeks blanching, and he hated that he'd done that to her. He sought some other words, but none were forthcoming.

'Right,' she said, her voice all stiffness. 'Thanks. Thanks for telling me.'

Robyn suggested to her parents that she stayed on, but her dad shook his head.

'No, you get back to your bright lights,' he said.

'But wouldn't you like me to?'

'We'd love you to, Robyn,' said Marilyn.

'Well then. That settles it.'

'But don't you and Eliot want to celebrate the deal?' said Simon.

'We're having a party for New Year,' said Robyn. 'That's when we're celebrating.'

'We've had you for four wonderful days. You go. Your mum and I are fine.'

'Who's going to help me serve?' Marilyn called, as she walked through to the kitchen. Eliot jumped up and went with her. Robyn caught her dad's arm.

'Dad, can I . . . I've got a question. Is everything okay with you and Mum?'

'Of course it is,' he said quickly.

'It's just, is Mum all right? Jago said something, and . . .'

She watched as her dad pushed his hands through his hair. He looked tired, and, all of a sudden, a little elderly. She noticed for the first time that his cheeks were slightly sunken, his shirt collar loose at his neck.

'Your mum's fine, Robyn,' he said.

'Don't you want to know what Jago said?'

Simon glanced towards the kitchen. He spoke in a hushed voice, one imbued with a mix of reluctance and relief. 'I know what he would have said. Though he had no place saying it. I didn't want you worrying unnecessarily. She's just been forgetful, that's all, a bit absent-minded. That's not really like your mum, she's sharp as a tack usually. But it's nothing for you to be concerned about.'

'But you were worried enough to tell Jago?'

He hesitated. 'Only because she walks about a lot, and once or twice she's had trouble finding her way back.'

'What?' cried Robyn.

Simon set his hand on her shoulder. 'That sounds far worse than it is. You know what it's like around here. The footpaths are a tangle, so much of the coastline looks the same; the mists come down and cover everything. Any one of us can wander out and lose our way. I know I damn well could.'

'But Christmas Eve you went out looking for her because you thought it'd happened again, didn't you?'

'And I was wrong. She was just in the lane, fetching holly. I sent Jago on a wild-goose chase, as I expect he told you. Gave him pneumonia, probably.'

'No, he didn't tell me that,' she said quietly.

'We're getting older, Robyn, and we all have our senior moments, some of us more than others. Most of the time your mum is fine. Perhaps in the new year we'll take her to a doctor, just for a chat.'

'But *you're* a doctor.'

He reached for a bottle of wine and began uncorking it. He held it up, pushed his glasses down to read the label.

'This'll be just the ticket with dinner,' he said, picking up a glass and filling it. She watched his careful concentration, his deft twist of the bottle to avoid any drops. He handed it to her.

'Tell me what you think,' he said. 'It should be a nice Sauvignon.'

'Dad,' she creaked, 'I . . .'

He wrapped an arm around her. 'Don't you worry, Robyn.' She pushed into his side, the years dropping away as she rested her little-girl head on his chest. 'Nothing to fret about here.'

The others came in then, carrying plates piled high with turkey leftovers.

'Dinner is served!' trilled Marilyn, with playful ceremony.

* * *

They left Merrin the next morning. The skies were clear and bright as they turned into the lane, Robyn swivelling to wave, her parents side by side outside the house, hands raised in farewell. She pressed her fingers to her eyes. Sank down a little in her seat. Eliot swerved to avoid a pheasant that was making its unhurried way into the hedge.

'Country driving,' he said, gritting his teeth. 'I won't relax until we're on the motorway.'

'That went by too quickly,' said Robyn, a mournful tone in her voice. 'Mum wanted me to stay. I should have stayed.'

'You could have done.'

She turned to Tess, reached out a hand and tickled the top of her head. 'They were on good form, weren't they? My parents?'

'They're always on good form.'

'My mum too?'

'What, another one?' He slammed the brakes on as a plump and docile-looking cock pheasant blundered its way in front of them. 'They're just *begging* to be made into a pie. Jesus, get me back to London, and fast.'

Robyn settled back into her seat, her eyes forward, resigned to the road ahead. They whipped through the lanes, the sea and Merrin dropping away behind them.

New Year's Eve. Robyn wore a black-as-night dress, one that skimmed her thighs and cupped her breasts, and was nothing like anything she'd worn since Tess arrived. She'd spent a long time in front of the mirror, running a comb through her hair, painting her lips ruby red. She spent an even longer time briefing the babysitter, a sweet girl who was a runner at the station. She edged out of the door reluctantly. Eliot waited at the bottom of the stairs, ripe with impatience.

'I can't be late to my own party,' he shouted, as she clattered down to join him.

The room above the Journey's End was full. Eliot and his bandmates had gathered on stage. Pete had talked first, a lengthy, rambling speech about where they'd come from, where they were going. He told everyone to forget the pub's name, that their journey was just beginning. He winced as he said it, already handing the microphone to Eliot as the crowd, a sea of bonhomie, groaned and laughed.

'Just a couple of special thanks, really, in addition to everything Pete said, except that bit at the end that was, I think you'll agree, atrocious.' More laughs. Whistles. 'I'd like to thank my gorgeous girlfriend Robyn for sticking with me, and for coming to our sweaty gigs even when she was pregnant with our beautiful daughter. Midnight in a basement bar in Camden was probably the last place you wanted to be.'

Robyn smiled, and tucked her hair behind her ears as people turned to look at her.

'And Lee, where's Lee?'

A hand shot up, waved, and Robyn caught the glint of silver bands on every finger. From somewhere a whoop went up.

Eliot leaned close to the microphone and dropped his voice. 'I think you need to come on up here,' he said.

Lee was on the stage in seconds, as though she was expecting to be called. Eliot threw his arm around her.

'We owe particular thanks to this woman,' he said, 'this woman and her fairy dust. She's made things happen for us. Maybe they would have happened anyway, who knows, but one thing's for sure, we're very glad we ran into you again in that field in Hampshire. Everything changed that day. Thank you.'

And he kissed her. He leant towards her cheek, but Lee got there first, and caught his lips with hers.

'Enough talk,' he shouted to the crowd. 'Let's play.'

Robyn joined in the clapping, but as everyone else watched the band settle into their positions, pick up their guitars and turn bonded smiles on one another, her eyes went to Lee. She watched her jump down from the stage and join the throng again. She was glowing, her whole face lit by Eliot's words, Eliot's kiss.

Robyn was waiting at the bar when two girls nudged their way into the throng. She realised one was Lee and quickly rearranged her features, made to say hello, but Lee hadn't seen her. She and her friend were deep in conversation, leaning against each other, half conspiratorially, half drunkenly, every spoken word a proclamation. Robyn heard Eliot's name and stiffened. *El.* It was tossed loosely, and weighted with history. She part turned from them, so as not to be noticed, so as better to listen.

'Nights like this, you know . . .' said Lee.

'I know,' said the friend.

'It's not that I wish I'd said yes to him. I just wish I hadn't said . . . no. And so massively no, so stupidly no, so totally emphatically *no.*'

She flicked her hair, and laughed, low and rueful. She leant in and took the drinks from the barman – who seemed to know exactly what they were drinking and served them before anyone else – and the two rejoined the party, leaving Robyn tossing in their wake.

They could have been talking about anything. *Said no to*

what? Robyn's mind ran on, her thoughts taking hold of her, and none of them good. However dim and unshaped, she couldn't shake them. It was like mixing paint, like tainting white. One brief touch of another colour, one accidental smudge of red, or yellow, or purple, and the white was forever altered, polluted. You could never quite get back to where you were. The night, and any remaining shine it had, was lost.

New Year fell quietly in Merrin. The good weather had held since Boxing Day, and the night was crisp and starlit. Jago had plans to go to Penzance to join some old college friends in a pub, but Denny had changed his mind at the last minute. He'd tapped at his door just as he was getting ready.

'Got a minute?'

'Course.'

'I've gone and done something,' said Denny, stepping carefully into the room. 'I've, er, asked Lucy if she'll marry me.'

Jago stopped doing up his shirt. His hands dropped to his sides.

'Dad,' he said. 'What did she say?'

'She only went and said yes.'

'But that's great! Isn't it? Great?' Jago put a hand on his shoulder. Denny hauled him into a hug.

'She makes me happy,' he said. 'That's what it is, she makes me happy.'

'You'll be excellent together.' Jago's voice was muffled, and his dad held him tightly.

'Will you celebrate with us? Tonight? I know you had plans, but . . . it'd mean a lot.'

'It's done,' said Jago. 'I'm not going anywhere.'

Denny clapped his hand to his back. 'Feels like the right

thing,' he said. 'Funny how you just know it, isn't it? You think never again, never again, and then suddenly one day everything changes. It'll happen for you too. Maybe even like that. Yes, it will.'

Jago grinned, shrugging him off, and said he'd be downstairs in a minute. He listened to the clump of his dad's footsteps on his way down, the joy in his step as the noise broke and he must have jumped, landing with both feet on the flagstones. He sat down on the edge of his bed. He heard music drift up through the floorboards, a peal of laughter. He stood up, and rubbed his face with both hands. He went over to his bedside table and picked up Robyn's picture again. *Rockabilly*. He knew every inch of that cove, he'd been going there since he was able to walk, tottering on baby legs beside his mum, but he knew he'd never be able to capture it as she had. The angle of the stack, the tumble of gorse at the cliff's edge, the sweep of the beach at low tide. The rounded rock where a clutch of gulls squatted like lazy sentries. She had it all just right. She'd used pastels, and there was a blurred quality to the scene, but every aspect was rendered distinctly. It was a picture that deserved to be hung in a gallery, mounted in a fine frame. He knew that, and he hoped she did too. He slipped it inside its envelope and placed it back on his table. For all its beauty, its accomplishment, it was hard to look at. He wondered if she'd felt even a little bit the same way as she drew it, and whether she'd made it for him, or only decided afterwards that it could be his. He thought of all the shells he'd carved, until he had one just right. The way the floor of his workshop was covered in scalloped fragments, a beachcomber's delight, until he held in his hand the perfect one, and that was for her.

thirty-one

THE FIRST DAYS OF JANUARY WERE MISERABLE. HAILSTORMS stung the streets, and when Robyn woke up her first breath was misty, her feet were blocks of ice. If she had to go out for groceries, she made the trip as quickly as possible, Tess's pushchair weighed down with spilling bags. Once they split on the stairs to the flat and she carried on up regardless, a sobbing Tess twisting in her arms, her own nerves ripping as she left a trail of rolling tins of tuna and bruised bananas behind her. More often than not she stayed at home, bundling Tess in double jumpers, curtains closed to the outside world. Only Eliot glowed. He and the band were developing new material, and the fire of good work was in him. The label was paying for studio time on the other side of London, and he dashed about at all hours. It seemed like he was always kissing Robyn and Tess goodbye, his phone in his pocket beeping with messages.

One day Ben came round, brotherly concern painted all over his face. The station was making her position redundant; he'd fought for her, he said, but there was nothing he could do except guarantee her good terms. She turned on a bright smile and made them a pot of tea, because compared to the thoughts spinning in her head, his news mattered little. He'd brought a gift for Tess, a battery-operated noisy flashing truck, and he sat with her on the floor, bashing buttons and exclaiming at the bright lights, and Robyn found herself wanting to be alone again, her and her baby and the quiet of the room, the only interruption the hissing, clanking radiators. When he eventually left, she pulled out her sketchbooks and turned the pages. Always the water. The sea. As Tess slept, she mixed paint, smudged pastels, drew strong, dark, pencil lines. She lost herself in pictures, closing her mind to just about everything except her daughter's waking cry.

After a week of moving words around in her mind, trying to fit together sentences that might make some sort of sense, she found she could put it off no longer. On the night she chose, as if in some kind of anticipation of the conflict, Eliot didn't seem his usual self. She'd made spaghetti and he twirled it on his fork, shifting it around his plate. He poured them each wine but his own glass stayed full and untouched. After dinner he sank into the sofa and cradled his guitar, letting his fingers move idly over the strings, his lips moving.

'Are you writing?' she asked.

'Playing with one or two things.'

'You seem a bit distracted.'

'Do I? I guess I am.' He was holding his guitar loosely. He set it down across his lap. 'Something's come up. We need to talk about it, but . . . I've been hesitating. I don't know why.'

Robyn stayed by the door. Inside her slippers she curled her toes, bracing herself.

'We've been offered a tour. An amazing tour.'

'What?'

'Chance of a lifetime really.'

'A tour.'

'Australia. The US. Maybe even Japan. This summer. Lee has all these contacts, she can make it happen. It'd mean three months away. Maybe more.'

'Right.'

'I've been itching to get out on the road. I didn't even know how much until this offer came up, and while I know it's not great timing, not for you and Tess . . .'

'How come you're touring when you don't have a record out? Does that even make sense?'

'To get things going. Lee knows these guys in Melbourne, Austin, Seattle, Tokyo, I mean, all *over* the place. The label are behind it, they think it's the right thing to do.'

'Right,' she said again.

'This is an incredible opportunity for us.' He was on his feet, grabbing her hands. Her fingers inside his were limp.

'For you and the band,' she said.

'And for *us*. You could come out, join us. Have you ever been to the US? To Japan? Maybe your folks would take Tess . . .'

Robyn shook his hands away. She bit her lip to stop it trembling. She felt as though if she said a word, just one more word, she'd lose all control.

'Robyn, what? I know it's a lot to think about, but it's great, right?'

She shook her head. Her hair fell in front of her face and she brushed it back fiercely. She stared at him.

'I know I should have told you the minute I walked through the door,' he said, 'but I was trying to balance it in my head. Why are you looking at me like that?'

'I need to talk to you about something too,' she said.

'About the tour?'

'And it's going to sound stupid, but it's all I've been thinking about, ever since the party . . .' She took a breath. 'What was it that you asked Lee? What did she say no to?'

'What? When?'

'I overheard her talking about you to some friend of hers. She said she'd said no to something you'd asked her, and now she really regretted it. I hate the way my mind's going, so please, just . . . Did you . . . proposition her?' Her voice had ridden up shrilly, and she hated the sound of it, but she talked on despite herself. 'All these late nights, you and her and, *supposedly*, the band . . .'

He stayed quite still. Then he shook himself, visibly. He reached for her hands again. 'I can't believe you'd think that.'

'That's not a denial, is it?'

'Of course it's a denial.'

'Then what? What was she talking about? Am I being stupid? Because I feel stupid.'

'I've never cheated on you, Robyn.'

'Because she said no . . .'

He made a strange noise, then. A growl, almost, of exasperation.

'So let me get this right. You've heard this one snatch of conversation, completely out of context, and suddenly you've written me off.'

'No, I—'

'I'd never lie to you,' he said.

His anger and earnestness, the combination of it, rattled her.

'I'm sorry,' she blustered. 'I didn't know what to think.

I still don't, I . . .' Then she stopped. Eliot had dropped her hands. He appeared to sway on the spot. Uncertainty clouded his features. 'What?' she said.

'But . . .'

'But *what*?'

'Maybe there's something I didn't say. Because I didn't see the point of it. Because it didn't matter. It *doesn't* matter.'

'Whatever it is, it matters, because we're here now, arguing, and—'

'Robyn, years ago, a lifetime ago, when I was a stupid kid who didn't know any better . . .'

'What?'

'I asked Lee to marry me.'

She plummeted.

'That's why we broke up. That was when it ended. That was her no.'

When she spoke, her voice was very small. 'You weren't a kid,' she said. 'You were twenty-five. Weren't you?'

'And I was a *completely* different person,' he said. 'Maybe at the time it was a big deal, I'm not going to pretend it wasn't, but . . . I got over it. *You* got me over it. You were this blast of fresh air, running about your Cornish beach. You took my breath away. You *know* that.'

His words fell out quickly, and it seemed as though he'd thought them over, rolled them around his head and said them into mirrors, always knowing that this day would inevitably come. She'd had no such preparation.

'You shouldn't have kept it from me . . .' she began.

'I wanted you to think I was cool,' he said, interjecting, a forced, limp grin crossing his face, 'and a guy who gets cheated on, rejected, dumped in the most spectacular fashion, there's nothing cool about that, nothing sexy either. And Lee was on the other side of the world by then. She didn't matter.'

Robyn wrapped her arms around herself, her cardigan pulling out of shape. It was cold in the room, and the chill was all about her.

'But she's in your life again now,' she said slowly, 'in a big way. Which means she's in my life too. We've talked about her, you told me why you broke up, but you left out the absolute most important part. The part that scares me a little bit.'

'*Scares* you? Don't be crazy, please don't say that.'

'What else are you hiding? What else don't I know about?'

'Nothing. There's nothing. That's it.'

'I hate that you had to go through that with her. I do. I can't imagine how completely awful it must have been. But . . . what I'm feeling right now isn't so great either.'

'I'm sorry. I truly am.'

'I don't understand how you can still be around her. I never have, but this just makes it that much more incomprehensible. I couldn't do that, Eliot. I couldn't be around someone I'd felt so strongly about, it just wouldn't work.'

'That whole drive back from Hampshire, we talked. We sorted everything out. And it felt good, it felt really, really good, and I think it was good for her too. I know it was. There's no problem. No lingering feeling, not on either side.'

He held her eye as he spoke, the emotion that had bumped through his voice replaced by a quicker, cooler conviction. She realised that she had nothing to say in reply. He drew her into an embrace.

'I never want to upset you,' he said. 'You and Tess are everything to me.'

'And you're everything to us,' she said back, mechanically.

thirty-two

HE TOLD HER EVERYTHING. THERE WAS NO RING IN A SILK-LINED box tied with a ribbon, he said. No grand plan. Just a rush of blood to the head, and the words were out. Only afterwards did he realise how ridiculous it was.

'You mean when she told you the truth about her affairs,' said Robyn.

'Not just that,' insisted Eliot. 'I was too young, she was too cynical, it was all a mistake. The whole thing.'

'Too young?' said Robyn. She looked at Tess, who was sitting on the floor surrounded by wooden blocks, her sturdy back quite upright. She'd be turning one that spring. Robyn would be twenty-three that summer. Her heart felt old.

'I want to get over it,' she said. 'I do. I just . . . wish you'd told me.'

'Babe, you keep saying the same thing. You need a break. You need to get away. Come on the tour.'

'What, with Lee?'

'Forget Lee. This is the perfect time to decide what you want to do next for work. Take three months out, travel with us. Hell, bring Tess. The three of us together.'

She thought of all the places they'd go, New York streets and Sydney Harbour, galactic Japanese cities. They'd be a family of three adventurers. The band would be ever-present, but it was the band that was making it happen. Lee was making it happen. She went back to her sketchbooks and drew the Cornish tide washing in, washing out. She didn't say yes, and she didn't say no.

They invited Simon, Marilyn and Ben for Tess's first birthday. Robyn had filled the flat with daffodils and baked a lemon cake. The day before her parents were due to arrive, her dad rang. His voice was hushed and splintered. She sat down on the edge of the sofa, biting her lip, her fingers pushing at the frayed edges of her jeans.

'Dad, what's wrong?'

'Nothing wrong as such, just . . . a development. With your mum. I just talked to Ben and I thought I should talk to you too.'

She thought of Jago on the clifftop, her dad's dismissiveness, and how, in the absence of any fact, she'd gone along with it all.

'We had her checked out,' he said. 'An old colleague of mine, he came and stayed the weekend, it was good of him, beyond the call of duty really. And then we took her to the surgery in Penzance.'

'What, because of the forgetfulness?' edged Robyn, her voice willing it to sound light, a gentle mist of absent-mindedness that could be explained away over a cup of tea.

'These last couple of months, she appears to have deteriorated a little. She'd put the kettle on and forget why she boiled it.'

'But I do things like that!'

'Or she'd ask me the same question several times without realising. It's as if there are pockets of time that just disappear. It comes and goes. *She* comes and goes. We can have a perfectly normal day and then just one thing will be out of kilter. One look she'll give, one comment she'll make. She called me Graham yesterday.' He paused, hearing her silence. 'Robyn?'

Her voice was strangled, stiff with incomprehension. 'Uncle Graham's been dead for twenty years. Are you saying she didn't *know* you?'

'There have been a few more loose threads recently, so we had her checked out. They did a physical exam, asked some questions, a few tests. The devil of it is that a diagnosis is incredibly hard. But there are some definite signs of dementia. I suppose that much is official.'

'I don't know what that is. Not really. Not what it means.'

'What it means is that all of these things I've mentioned, they gradually add up, and I'm afraid to say they're probably symptoms of Alzheimer's.'

Robyn remembered once going with a childhood friend to visit their grandfather in a home. There had been a ring of chairs in a too-hot room, elderly people with vacant stares, their lips moving soundlessly. There were sudden flashes of bad temper that drew measured responses from the nurses, and a lingering scent of instant mashed potatoes and pungent white lilies. She remembered crocheted blankets, and a television in the corner tuned to an interminable game of snooker. A lady in a dressing gown and a string of pearls had called her Camilla, waving brightly from across the room. She'd returned home that night unsettled, fearful of growing old, and her mum had phoned Laura's parents, said it hadn't been right to take a ten-year-old there.

'I thought only old people got Alzheimer's,' she said, hopelessly. In the next room, Tess started to cry, a low-level mewing that Robyn, for once, tried to ignore. 'What'll happen? Will she get worse? Oh God, she won't have to go anywhere, will she?'

'Absolutely not,' he said vehemently. 'We'll carry on just as we are. We have to expect a decline, but, well, the same could be said of any of us, couldn't it? And that could be years and years away. Everybody's case is quite, quite different. That much I do know.'

'Is that you speaking as Dad, or . . . as a doctor?'

She heard him take a shuddering sigh, and she hated that she doubted him.

'That's me speaking as someone who doesn't have a crystal ball but believes very much in positive thinking. We can all help your mum, and we can all be here for her. So we're going to come tomorrow, and we're going to celebrate Tess's birthday. And I don't want you to worry. Promise me you won't.'

Tess's wailing grew louder, but in the background at White Sands Robyn heard her mum's voice.

'Is that Mum? Can I speak to her?' she said.

'Perhaps not now, but tomorrow, we'll see you tomorrow. Tess is one! A great big girl. All right, Robyn? You're all right?'

'You will tell me if I can do anything, won't you?'

'I'll tell you.'

'What did Ben say?'

'He said much the same as you.'

'Dad?'

'Yes?'

'She's okay, isn't she? I mean, you know, in herself.'

'Your mum's okay. And we'll see you and your beautiful girl tomorrow.'

Robyn set the phone down. She stayed sitting for a while, as in the next room her daughter screamed. Then she stood up and trailed her way to her. She lifted her up and held her to her chest, very tightly. She sat down on the floor and gently rocked her until she fell back to sleep. Then she stayed that way, her legs curled beneath her, her baby in her arms. She willed time to stand still, or better still to wind back, just far enough for them all to be happy.

They came for the afternoon. Robyn had bought a kaleidoscope of balloons and hung them from every corner of the flat. The daffodils burst open, their sunshine blooms looking impossibly joyful. Tess had a brand-new toy rabbit, as big as herself, with giant floppy ears and a pink nose. Simon and Marilyn sat side by side on the sofa, Tess playing at their feet. Ben filled everyone's glasses. Robyn picked at her cake and was watchful. Eliot talked so she didn't have to.

She'd read up on Alzheimer's, and now she hunted for its signs, but all she saw was her mum. Her hair was greyer at the roots, her ash-blond highlights perhaps not as bright as usual, but that wasn't a sign. She had new bursts of lines at the corners of her eyes, the side of her mouth, but that wasn't a sign. There was a plaster on her thumb, a blue one that occasionally she fingered absently, but that wasn't a sign. Marilyn played with her granddaughter, delighted in the flowers, drank sparkling pink wine and complimented Robyn on the cake. Slowly, Robyn began to relax. At four o'clock, her dad stood up.

'We should be getting on the road,' he said.

'You're sure you won't stay?'

He shook his head. 'Another time.'

She walked with him into the hall. She took his arm, whispered, 'Dad, I can't see it.'

'It comes and goes. When she's tired . . .'

'Is that why you're leaving?'

'It's a long drive.'

'But you could have stayed.'

'I know. It's been lovely.' He kissed her on both cheeks. She embraced him.

'I was sort of dreading it,' Robyn admitted. 'I didn't know what she'd be like, but she's okay, isn't she?'

'It's been a good day,' said her dad, nodding.

The others joined them in the hall. Eliot was helping Marilyn with her coat. She leant in and kissed him, laughing as afterwards she wiped the trace of her lipstick from his stubble.

'Thank you. It's been wonderful. Now, where's my dear granddaughter?'

Tess toddled through, unsteady on her feet, her rabbit in her arms. It engulfed her, and she smiled over its head, between the ears.

'Here she is,' laughed Marilyn. 'Here's my Robyn.'

'You mean Tess,' said Ben, 'although she does look a lot like a little Robyn, you're absolutely right.' He knew, but he covered it well. He glanced up at Robyn and Simon. 'Doesn't she?'

'Who's Tess?' her mum said, brightly. 'I don't know any Tess. Simon, shall we go? It's time to go.'

It was Jago that she called. She'd never called him since being in London.

'Do you mind?' she said.

She couldn't even think where the phone was in Hooper's House. She tried to imagine him folded into a chair, still in his work clothes, his paint-flecked hand holding the receiver.

'Mind?' said Jago. 'No, I don't mind.'

His voice seemed out of place in the flat. She closed her eyes. She pretended they were down by the sea, the Rockabilly tide washing in and out. She began to talk.

'It's just so strange,' she said. 'You know what my mum's like. She's so . . . precise. But when she lapses like that, Jago, I'm frightened of her. I'm frightened of my own mum. I spoke to her later, and she was asking after Tess just like nothing had happened. She was fine again. It's like she just disappears for these brief, terrifying moments, and then she's back again.'

'I'm sorry,' said Jago. 'I'm really sorry.'

The sincerity of his so simple words pulled something inside of her. She hadn't cried with Eliot, or with Ben, and she hadn't cried as she'd talked again with her dad, but she began to cry now. She pushed her face into the sleeve of her jumper, trying to hide it, taking deep breaths as she struggled back to the surface. Jago waited, and in his quiet there was understanding, and calm. They sat for a while, phones pressed to their ears, just listening to the sound of one another's breath.

'Would you keep an eye on her?' she said at the end. 'Just, you know, when you can. If you can. I know you've been so helpful already. Dad told me about Christmas. I should have thanked you before, but I didn't know, I didn't understand.'

He didn't answer.

'Jago? Is that okay, then? Just to carry on keeping an eye?'

'I want to help. I'd do anything to help. The thing is, I'm not going to be here that much longer. What with Dad and Lucy, I figured they needed their own space.'

'You're moving out? Leaving Merrin?'

'At last. I know.'

'But where are you going?' She realised her voice was tinged with something unwanted. She shook herself. 'Jago, that's so exciting. Where are you headed?'

'America.'

'*America* America?'

'I figured it was time I saw what was across all that water.'

'But why America? I mean, where in America? What for?'

As he spoke, she made pictures in her mind, filling in the colour where he had only sketched. A red-dusted landscape in the south-west, where flat-topped mountains shone purple and the endless skies were filled with hawks. A ranch called High Desert, with running horses and strings of fences, cacti marking the edges of tracks. For all his pragmatism, and her imagined poetry, he talked about it as if it were a place he could arrive in, find his footing, even stay.

'I'll be starting at the bottom,' he said, 'the very bottom. Mending fences, outbuildings, all the manual stuff. A ranch hand, basically. The grunt jobs. But I'll have time to work on my own stuff too.'

'I thought you never wanted to leave Cornwall. Or Merrin, even. How do you know about this place?'

'I've been doing my research,' said Jago, 'and I needed a change.'

'Change is overrated,' said Robyn. 'But . . . I mean, wow. New Mexico. God. What gave you the idea? I mean, this particular idea?'

Jago laughed softly. 'Ah. Well. It was in a song. A song my mum used to sing a long time ago.'

'A song,' she repeated. A memory of Rosalind's honey voice

came to her, a memory that wasn't even hers, but it wrapped itself around her. She smiled sadly. 'I love that,' she said.

'And it just felt like the right time,' he said.

He wanted to add that now he wasn't so sure, that he'd stay if she needed him to, that he'd do any number of things if she'd only say the words, but he didn't.

'It is the right time,' she said, rubbing her sleeve once more across her eyes, and trying to sound as happy as she could. 'You seize the day, because no one ever knows what's going to happen.'

In her hand she held his seashell, and she closed her fingers tightly around it.

She told Eliot her plan, and he lifted her up and swung her round as though she weighed nothing at all. As though the heaviness she'd felt inside was shifting.

'It's perfect,' he said, his lips meeting hers.

She would go back to Merrin first, and spend some weeks with her parents. Lately, her dad's voice had turned tight with anxiety, just as her mum's was sometimes loosened, words wafting, lost on invisible slipstreams, but when she told them she would be coming to stay, with Tess, they were perfectly united, and she felt their blast of cheer through the telephone as they exulted in the anticipation of her presence. *Thank you*, her dad said afterwards, and his quiet gratitude broke her heart.

'It feels like the right thing to do,' she told Eliot. 'Then Tess and I will join you when you get to the States. We could come for a couple of weeks, or even a month. I'll book my ticket last minute and get a deal. I might even surprise you, just pitch up in the crowd one night.'

She felt footloose just saying it. The tingle of adventure ran all the way through her, from the ends of her fingers to the tips of her toes, and the fact that she'd be doing it with her daughter made her braver, and made it all the better.

Ebbing Tide

Waves rush back out to reveal the hidden ocean
floor, offering rare glimpses of deeper things.

thirty-three

ONCE ROBYN HAD CROSSED THE TAMAR, SHE ROLLED DOWN THE windows, letting the afternoon blow in. There were moorland scents of heather blossom, cow parsley in the lanes, and the sweet bite of sea air as she spun ever closer towards the blue. At the first sight of the old familiar headland, she pulled in to a gateway and climbed out of the car and stretched. She took great gulps of air, feeling her headache lift a little. She massaged her temples. Perhaps she'd just spin the car down to Sennen, walk along the beach and have a quick cup of tea at the café on the front. It was a delaying tactic, a moment of clear-sky serenity before she got to White Sands and kissed her mum and hoped that, at least for the moment of her arrival, she'd remember her name.

Glancing back inside the car, she saw that Tess was asleep still, her blond head rolled forward, her hands curled in her lap. Tess hadn't cried as Eliot had said goodbye to her, mostly because she hadn't understood. Robyn hadn't cried either. Eliot had stood in the hallway, slight in his leather jacket, his cases at his feet. *I can't wait for you to come*, he'd said. Robyn had smiled for him, squeezed his fingers. She'd already decided to let him leave the way he wanted to. In the weeks leading up to his departure, they'd argued easily and often – not fierce, fiery exchanges, remedied later with equal passion, but weary back-and-forths, every path feeling well trodden and worse for it. Eliot was often absent as he plotted the details of the tour, in a pub or a club or Lee's cavernous warehouse in Bow. Three times in two weeks Robyn's phone had bleated in the middle of the night, his message filling the screen, saying they'd lost track of time and he was staying over, but *Sweet dreams, Robyn, sweet dreams*, and a string of kisses that were invariably broken by a typo, a rogue letter interrupting their ardent flow.

So Robyn had filled his absences with paint pots and dimpled watercolour paper, rainbow pastels and Indian ink. She'd sit at the table, dipped in concentration, minutes turning to hours, afterwards wandering to bed feeling as though she'd spent the evening somewhere else, somewhere watery, the rooms around her now unfamiliar, her bed sheets strange and cool. She'd look in on the sleeping Tess then, reorientate herself by kissing the tip of her finger and pressing it lightly to her crown.

Eliot had applauded her decision to spend some time in Cornwall with her parents. *You're doing the right thing*, he'd said, echoing her own words, as Robyn bit down a childish disappointment that he'd made no attempt to persuade her otherwise. The only thing he'd pressed her for was the exact date that she planned to join them.

'But I've got your schedule. Wouldn't it be more fun if I just pitched up?'

'It doesn't work like that. I'll need to make arrangements for you being there.'

'What kind of arrangements? We don't exactly take up a lot of space.'

'Lee needs to know.'

'Why does Lee need to know?'

'She's our tour manager, Robyn, you know that. She's fine with you being there, but she does need to know when you're coming.'

Robyn's mouth dropped. '*She's* fine?'

'I don't mean it like that. But she's got a lot of experience with this. Families and tours don't always mix so well. You're different, she knows that, but I can see where she's coming from. No one else is bringing anyone.'

'No one else lives with their girlfriend and their child.'

'I do want you there, you know I do. I even wanted you to come for the whole time, but . . . I think it's right this way. Everyone's happy, you know? I get some time to be with the band, settle into our rhythm, then you come out when we hit America. Meet us in LA. I'll have missed you like crazy by then.' He circled his arms around her and kissed her neck. 'My California girl,' he said.

'Okay,' she said, slipping his grasp. 'LA, then. I'll book it. You can add me to Lee's schedule.'

The night before he left, they'd made love, Eliot moving slowly, gently, his hands tracing the contours of her body.

'How can I leave all this behind?' he'd breathed, his words hot in her ear.

'Sing that song again,' she murmured. 'The one you were playing earlier. *I'm always with you, wherever you travel*, that one.'

'You heard it?'

'I loved it.'

The uncharacteristically gentle notes of his guitar had wound their way through the flat just as she was changing Tess.

She'd stopped to listen, tiptoeing to the door. He was lying on the sofa, his instrument against his chest, his eyes tipped closed. She hadn't heard the start, but she listened until the end, feeling something that she hadn't felt in a long time.

I'm always with you, wherever you travel,
close at home or in a distant place.
Feel the strength of my arms around you,
rest assured in my warm embrace.

Should you be troubled, feeling down,
and nothing seems to fall into place,
I'm here to help you, ease off that frown,
bring a smile to brighten your face.

Our lives are busy, running around,
chasing things that hold us apart,
but I would be happy if you found
a little space for me in your heart.

Eliot had rolled on to his side.

'It's a sad song,' he'd said. 'I can't sing it now. Not on our last night. It'll tip me over.'

'It's not sad. It's lovely.' Then she'd asked the question, even though she knew the answer. 'How come I never heard you play it before?'

He'd kissed the tip of her nose. 'Because it just came to me.'

As they drifted towards sleep, she'd pressed her body against his, every inch of skin touching. *His warm embrace*, she thought, then, delightedly, jubilantly, *He wrote me a song*. But for all its beauty, she knew that when she looked into his eyes, she saw something hectic in them: the anticipation of roads travelled, stages played. He might have been sorry to leave, but he was happy to go.

You know you're making a choice, Ruby had said when she'd phoned and told her, but Robyn didn't see it like that. When she spoke to Ben, he applauded her, said in a wistful voice that she'd been right to give Eliot the space for his big moment, and, in a less wistful voice, that their parents would love having her home. It didn't really matter what anyone else said: she'd come to the realisation that life did what it wanted. Just when you thought you were in some kind of control, it would swipe you sideways without so much as a polite warning. It was rip currents and white water. Eliot and Lee would be spending three months in close company, but compared to her mum, her lovely, absent-minded, sometimes just terrifyingly absent mum, that was nothing. Going to Merrin and joining the tour later was her way of staying upright, riding it out.

Robyn had other plans too. She'd packed her sketchbooks, boxed up her tubes of paint and tins of pastels. Everything she'd drawn or painted in London had been from memory – her dreams of the wave-slapped cove, the silky feel of water pooling across her midriff as she turned on her board – and at the time that had been the beauty of it. With the prospect of an extended stay in Cornwall, she felt suddenly that her own reserves had not been enough. Memory could play tricks, all too easily come and go, important details slipping, then lost. Ultimately, it was insubstantial, and if she were to learn anything from her mum, then perhaps it would be that. The present moment, the act of seeing and recording, that was what was important. So she had packed all of her art materials, and with them a new vigour. At Sennen she took in the luminous quality of the sea-misted sky, the fast-moving rivulets that carved the sand into undulating waves, the caramel glint of a scallop shell poking through the surface, and she thought of her sketchbooks stowed in the boot of the car, their virgin pages inviting her touch. She marvelled at the fact that had it not been for the growing shape of Tess, the picture in the window of the Cork Street gallery, the impulse to simultaneously retreat inside herself and open up something new, she might never have put paint to paper.

Pulling into the drive at White Sands, she saw that her mum was kneeling in the garden, snipping roses. Marilyn got to her feet and waved. Robyn waved back, with something of a frantic note. She scrabbled to be rid of her seat belt, jumped out the car and jogged towards her.

'Was it a good journey, dear?'

'Fine, just fine,' said Robyn, throwing her arms around her. She smelt the lily perfume Marilyn always wore, and the clean, bright scent of her cashmere sweater. She pulled back and looked at her. 'How are you?'

'Very well. Now, where's my sweet Tess?'

Robyn glanced skyward. *Thank you*, she thought. Her mum's condition moved in mysterious ways, her dad had warned her as much, saying that all and any lucidity was a reason to be grateful. He'd told her that Marilyn was sometimes aware of her own forgetfulness and knew the reason for it, but sometimes she forgot that too, and she was disorientated then, dim confusion pitching across her face. The thing to do, he'd said, was to stay peaceful with her, and patient, and calm, no matter how torn up you were feeling inside. He'd told Robyn this in a voice that suggested he was taking his own advice at that very moment. She held her mum's hand and they walked back to the car.

'Your sweet Tess has been asleep for all of Cornwall, most of Devon and some of Somerset. She'll be yowling the house down later.'

'Lovely girl,' said Marilyn, lifting her carefully out of her car seat. 'She can scream all she wants. She's home now.'

Jago was leaving. He'd delayed his departure by two weeks, but now the day had almost come. He'd be able to see her before he went, to say goodbye, but little more. He managed a rueful appreciation of this fact, so perhaps America was already doing its work. He called round, Scout following at his heels, and instead of Robyn inviting him in, she suggested a walk.

'I've been back two days, and believe it or not, I haven't been to the cove yet,' she said.

It was high tide, so they sat together on the granite slabs. The sea shifted beneath them. The stack gleamed. Scout lay between them, his head on his paws, baleful eyes moving from one to the other.

'Tess loves it here, you know,' said Robyn. 'Dad's taking her all around the garden, showing her his plants. Mum's flower-arranging, just for her benefit. She saw a frog yesterday. Her first one. She tried to catch it.'

'And your mum's doing okay?'

'I think so.'

She was, and she wasn't. A lot of the time she was the Marilyn that Robyn had always known, and then sometimes she disappeared, a strange imposter in her place. A woman who turned a vacant stare on you, lost words halfway through the saying of them, casserole becoming *cass, cass, cast-off,* or

323

asked for a cup of tea when she already clutched one in her hand. Ben had visited the day before and been all bear hugs and easy smiles and pragmatism, just with the odd *You don't mean that, do you, Mum?* as though reason and good humour could coach Marilyn back to reality. Only Robyn seemed to show anything close to fear, as if just by her mum using a wrong name, or asking a strange question, her world toppled, taking everything with it.

She felt Jago shift beside her. She turned to him.

'I'm going to paint while I'm here,' she told him.

'I never thanked you for the picture you sent me at Christmas.'

'I don't think it was very good really.'

'Rubbish. You're talented.'

'You really think so?'

'I liked what you put in the letter, about that conversation we had when you said you wouldn't paint unless you had to.'

Robyn smiled. 'I've often thought of that. I meant it, you know. I meant it then, and I guess I mean it now too. Now more than ever.'

'And that was because of Tess?'

'It began with Tess, when I was pregnant with her. She was in charge, you know, even then.' She rubbed her nose. 'As soon as I started, there was no question about what I'd paint. That was a surprise. I guess I didn't even realise how far away I felt from some things. I guess I didn't realise what I missed.'

'The sea?'

'*This* sea,' said Robyn. She laughed bleakly. 'This sea that I was once in such a hurry to get away from.'

An ocean of quiet ran between them. Robyn folded her hands tightly in her lap.

'At least you can surf again,' said Jago, eventually, 'while you're here.'

'Not a lot of water for you in New Mexico. I looked on a map.'

'Did you?'

'High-altitude desert. You couldn't have picked a more different landscape. I suppose there are rivers to fish in. You won't be entirely lost.'

'I might be,' said Jago. 'I might be lost.'

'Do you even know how long you'll stay?'

'As long as they'll have me,' he said. 'Which could be six months, or a year, or . . . I don't know. We'll see.'

Robyn sighed, involuntarily. She felt him looking at her, but couldn't meet his eyes. 'You're going to miss this old boy,' she said, nudging Scout with her foot. 'He can tell you're leaving, you know. Look how sad he looks.'

'I know. I wish he could come too. But he's taken to Lucy in a big way,' said Jago. 'He'll be just fine.'

'Well, you'll have to write to us all. Let us know how you're getting on. We'll be lonely stuck here on this rock. You make up a sizeable portion of the population, you know.'

'Your head will be full of the tour, won't it? Aren't they playing in America?'

'They are,' she said. 'They're playing all over.'

'What if they come to the south-west? I could go and see them. In Albuquerque or Phoenix or . . . somewhere.'

'They're playing Austin,' said Robyn. 'I think.'

Something stopped her mentioning her own travel plans. Instead she stood up. The wind whipped her hair, and her summer dress fluttered at her knee. To Jago she looked even slighter than before. Her feet were pale in their sandals. The sea hadn't toughened her muscles, not yet; she was city slim and soft.

'I should get back,' she said.

Jago stood up too. He was on a just lower rock, and they were matched in height.

'Sorry about the timing,' he said.

'The timing?'

'Your mum. You asked me to keep an eye on her, and . . .'

'I'm back now. For a bit, anyway. It's as it should be.'

'I guess I mean that too.'

'But you're having an adventure. We all need adventures. I'll like thinking of you out there.'

'And yours worked out,' said Jago. 'Didn't it?'

'You've met Tess,' said Robyn, brushing her hair from her face, tucking it behind her ears. 'She's pretty great. I think so, anyway.'

The wind blew it out again, and Jago had to fight not to reach out for the pale blond strands, catching them and smoothing them back.

'Well, she's the best . . .' he counted on his fingers, 'fifteen-month-old I know, no doubt about it.' Then, 'So . . . I guess it's goodbye?'

It was supposed to be a question, but the wind took it, muffling the end. It came out as just five words, a statement. Robyn nodded. She leant forward and kissed him on the cheek. Not quickly, but not slowly. Just one kiss. Then she jumped down from the rocks.

'Good luck!' she shouted, against the wind. Then, 'We'll miss you.'

She waved, and disappeared over the cliffs.

thirty-four

IF THE WAVES WERE RIGHT, SHE SLIPPED OUT OF THE HOUSE AT dawn. Rockabilly glinted then, its surface throwing crystals. The gulls exulted in her arrival, wheeling, shrieking at the sky, and she'd kick off her trainers and run towards the water. She treasured the blast as the first wave hit her, the icy ache that shot through her bones and stole her breath. She'd lick her salted lips and paddle out, then sit drifting on her board in the pale light of morning, watching the sets approach. She always let the first waves roll by, counting, one, two, three, then shoot forward, arms barrelling, lifting to her feet with perfect lightness. Then came those brief, unending seconds where she rode the wave in, or swiped up its side, her body curling with the water. The tumble in the breakwater, spitting brine and laughing. Her morning surf would never amount to more than a minute of total elation. But a minute wasn't bad. A minute was pretty good.

Later in the day, she often went walking with her mum and Tess. They talked about this and that, and sometimes the wholly unexpected, Marilyn suddenly speaking of a childhood memory as though a treasure that had lain at the bottom of the ocean had surfaced with a pop. Sometimes Robyn wondered if her mother had forgotten Eliot existed, as if he'd dropped into one of her ever-shifting holes of memory and stayed there, because she rarely, if ever, mentioned him. Then one day she did. They'd driven to Porthcurno. A haze of sea spray took the edge off the day's sun, and the sand was sludgy underfoot, a retreating tide. They sank to their ankles. Tess bumbled along between them in red wellingtons, her staggering steps weighted, her laughter constant. Her humour was always infectious. Robyn smiled down at her, and saw that her mum was doing the same.

'You've done a good job with her, you and Eliot,' said Marilyn.

'There's a long way still to go. A whole life, really.'

'But you'll be okay, you'll be fine. A natural.'

'I never knew how much she'd take up,' said Robyn. 'I don't mean in time, although that too. I just mean . . . she's almost all I think about.' She laughed, shrilly. 'Sometimes I wonder if there's room for anyone else.'

Marilyn nodded. 'I've noticed you don't talk about her dad very much.'

'Have you?' She was disarmed. 'He's a long way away,' she said.

'But you do think about him, don't you?'

They waited as Tess squatted to inspect something in the sand. It was the pink half-shell of a dead crab. She worked to prise it out, lost in her endeavour.

'I do,' she said. 'But I guess it's not always straightforward.' She glanced at her mum. 'Sometimes I feel like there's still a lot we don't know about each other.'

Marilyn gave a low, sad laugh.

'Robyn, you can never know someone completely. And even when you think you do, well, they can change, believe you me. Even when we don't want to, we change. No one's very constant, in the end.' She patted down her hair, a wistful edge to her words. 'I like Eliot. He's been good to you and Tess. It could have been difficult, and yet I think he's made it as easy as he could. As have you. I think you've both compromised a great deal to make things work.'

Perhaps it was the onshore breeze, or the salted air, or her mum's perfect exactness, but Robyn felt her eyes prick. She blinked quickly.

'Sometimes I wonder if Eliot's compromised more than he's willing to admit,' she said.

Tess hoisted the crab's empty shell in triumph, emitting a squeak of pleasure. She cradled it in her arms and toddled forward, her boots sinking in the sand. Robyn stayed still, wondering if she should extract it from her daughter's grip. She spoke again, before her mum drifted.

'You know, he proposed to someone. A couple of years ago. She turned him down. Lee, she's called. She was living abroad, but now she's reappeared and just like a fairy godmother she's making everything happen for them. The deal, that was down to her contacts. And this tour, she's gone with them, for the whole three months.'

Occasionally Robyn thought of Lee standing at the side of the stage, crafting her write-ups, rolling into bars, sharing everything that Eliot experienced on the other side of the world. But the idea didn't shake her in the way it had in London. She simply felt remote from it, as though it was a film playing out on some other screen. It was only at night that such thoughts came as a choking intrusion, Lee and Eliot appearing together

329

in her dreams, her unconscious giving her no rest.

They walked forward slowly, following Tess's zigzagging path, Robyn offering sparse details of Lee and Eliot's past, and their shared present. She kept her voice light, was more dismissive than she really felt.

'But don't you mind,' asked Marilyn, with narrowed eyes, 'that she's there, and you're not?'

'It's not long until I am there.' She counted off on her fingers. 'Three weeks tomorrow and I'll be joining them in LA.'

'You didn't want to go sooner?'

'I want to be here with you.' She gave a tight laugh. 'And anyway, I'm not on Lee's bloody schedule until then.'

Her mum took her hands. Marilyn's were warm, and dry, and felt just like they had always felt.

'You mustn't stop your life for us.'

'But this *is* my life. Isn't it?'

'Robyn, are you happy?' countered Marilyn, with such matter-of-factness it was as though she'd asked if she wanted a cup of tea.

Robyn stared at her mum, but Marilyn's eyes were sharp, her gaze focused.

'I can't see beyond the summer,' she said, surprising herself with her own words. 'Some days I can't imagine being back in London. I don't know what that means.'

When they returned from their walk, Simon ushered Robyn into the kitchen. He seemed excited, and rubbed his hands together, his palms crackling as he talked.

'How are you funding this trip of yours?'

'The last of my savings. When the tour's over, I'll have to find a job.'

'But childcare's so expensive in London, isn't it?'

'Yep. More than I'd earn doing a lot of things. I'm sort of unqualified.'

'I don't know about that,' said Simon. 'I've been looking at your sketchbooks.'

'Dad, they're private . . .'

'Robyn, I'm impressed. I had no idea . . . When did you even start painting? It doesn't matter: the fact is, your work's too good to hide away. While I may be completely useless myself, I do recognise talent when I see it. God, you put me to *shame*.'

Simon had persisted with his watercolours. He'd painted the view from the White Sands garden twenty times or more. *And every time it's different*, he'd laughed as Robyn pointed this out. *Go figure*.

'Why don't you make the most of being back here? This corner of the country seems to inspire art like no other,' he said, 'and if you've got the skill, there can be money in that as well as pleasure.' He gestured at the walls of the house, every inch of which were covered with canvases bought in galleries along the coast. 'In fact, how about you sell me that latest one you've done, the one of the moors behind this place, all reds and browns and whatnot? You've caught them perfectly.'

'Dad, I don't need charity. Really, you can have the picture.'

'You're stone-cold broke, I imagine, and I'd like to support an impoverished artist. Especially a local one.'

'Very local.'

'Get it framed – nicely, mind, none of those cheap rectangles that just ruin a picture – and I'll pay you properly.'

'I might need an advance, to cover the frame . . .' said Robyn.

'It's a deal,' he said, and they shook over the kitchen table. 'But . . .'

'What's the "but"?'

'That you promise to think seriously about what I've said. You could do a lot worse than try and sell some pictures. You've got a talent for it, and your mum agrees.'

Marilyn came into the kitchen then, Tess trailing behind her, a chubby hand hanging on to her skirt.

'What do I agree with?' she asked.

'That Robyn should be doing something with her paintings.'

'I've always said she should be an artist,' said Marilyn.

Robyn looked at her. She'd never said that. But perhaps there was something in it, all the same.

She took Tess to St Ives and they ate ice cream while sitting on the sand at Porthmeor. They peered through the windows of back-street studios, and slipped into galleries. They walked around the headland, stopping to watch a group of summer-school painters who were grouped together on the sands, their easels facing out to sea. The urge to paint had surfaced of its own accord, and perhaps she just needed to see where it would take her. Tucked away in the London flat, with Eliot out and Tess asleep, her pictures had felt like a solitary occupation, a secret world of her own. Now, with her parents' encouragement and a strengthened self-belief, they seemed to become something else; they took on a new life, and so did she.

Before Robyn and Tess drove home, they walked the steep streets to the Hepworth museum. It was the end of the day and the tourists had dwindled. They strayed into the furthest reaches of the garden, found a bench beneath a giant palm. Snatches of grey slate roofs were just visible through breaks in the foliage;

here and there a blue slice of sea. She imagined waking each day and wandering into such a private oasis, crossing the lawn to the white-stone studio and bending to your work, letting the outside world, gentle as it was, slip away. It was a life that seemed so full, and yet so contained. *So peaceful*, she thought, then from nowhere the accompanying thought: *Eliot would hate it.*

Back at White Sands, she leafed through her sketchbooks again. Her mum joined her.

'I like these,' Marilyn said, indicating the early ones. They were the first seascapes she'd painted when she was in London, sometimes with a flash of green field or flame-coloured moor, each imbued with the golden light of memory. It didn't matter if it was pastels or poster paint, fine strokes or dense sweeps, she seemed to catch a sense of longing in these scenes. A benevolence towards the place. The suggestion, even, that it was treasured, and nowhere near ordinary.

'This one,' Marilyn pointed, turning to a later page, 'I like too. The most, actually. It's . . . all there. It's true.'

After Jago had left for America, she'd returned to the cove. She'd painted quickly, her eyes flicking hungrily, not wanting to miss a thing. It was Rockabilly at sundown, and it was her first time in the open air with a pad on her knee and her paints balanced in the grass beside her. The sea glowed iridescent, blurring to a distant horizon, an unseen American shore. She'd taken just one liberty, adding in two figures sitting atop the granite slabs. In the landscape they were tiny, insignificant, yet Marilyn picked them out now, and marked them with her finger. When she spoke, Robyn didn't know if she was still there with her, a mother looking at her daughter's picture, or if she had slipped somewhere distant, and abstract.

'The artist wants something they can't have,' Marilyn said, 'and making this picture is the closest they can get to it. See,' she tapped the two figures, 'see, it's all here. Everything they want is here. That's why it's perfect.'

Because of the time difference, and the band's constantly changing locations, Eliot had suggested calling just once a week, but when Robyn held Tess to the receiver, she still said *Dadadada* with delight and conviction. He talked of playing on a rooftop in Sydney, under a night sky that burned with giant stars. A hotel bar in Tokyo, where afterwards they walked through the immaculate city at white dawn, stage clothes still sticking to their backs. He said he wasn't sleeping enough, or eating enough, and was probably drinking too much, but as he talked, his joy radiated down the line. She told him she was happy that he was doing what he loved. She told him that she missed him, and he sang it back down the telephone, his words matching hers as good as perfectly.

The weeks had been passing so quickly, before she knew it she was saying, 'I'll see you the day after tomorrow. We land at four p.m.'

'I'll be there,' he said.

thirty-five

'I'M SORRY I WAS LATE,' SAID ELIOT, FOR THE FOURTH TIME.

Robyn waved his apology away. 'It's fine, I told you. We could have got a cab, we wouldn't have minded.' She tried to hide a yawn, willing the jet lag to abate. The California sunshine stung her tired eyes. Tess was crotchety. Beside her at the café table, Eliot was slumped in his chair, his hand turning hers in his lap.

'I had this image of being in Arrivals, holding up a sign, seeing you come through with all your cases, and us having this amazing reunion kiss right there in the middle of LAX.'

'Movie style,' said Robyn. 'Tell me about it.'

They were on the same street as the hotel, just one road off Sunset Boulevard. A lanky palm tree cast a scattered patch of shade, and behind them a down-at-heel mall wearily invited custom, all 99c sales and shrimp dinners. The traffic was continuous, bumper to bumper, with music thumping through windows, and everywhere a petrol smell that got inside her throat and had her glancing protectively at Tess. She'd imagined crushed-ice cocktails, rooftop lounging, a boardwalk and the stir of the ocean.

'The reality's bad traffic, and, what did you say, too much tequila the night before?' She laughed, and held a hand up to his face. 'You look different. You look knackered.'

'Thanks.'

His eyes were bleary, and his cheeks drawn white, the Australian winter sun leaving no mark. He looked like late nights, spirit-soaked and cigarette-smoked, but there was something else shining through his jaded appearance. It was happiness, Robyn decided, pure and simple.

'You've been having a ball, haven't you?'

'Better than I ever imagined.' He squeezed her hand, his eyes burning. 'Robyn, I didn't know it until I got here, but I think touring's what I really love. Japan was crazy, just ridiculous. And Oz. Then Seattle, San Francisco. Lee's put together one hell of a tour. I think that's when you realise you've really got something, you know? When you can take it anywhere and it still works. It's been exactly what we needed. For the first time I feel . . . big.'

Robyn laughed.

'I mean it, I'm serious.'

'*Big?*'

'We're not even playing to massive crowds, but just the fact that we're on the move, everything being about the next show, it feels real, it feels big.'

'It's just a weird choice of word,' said Robyn. 'Don't you mean contented?'

'Contented? No, that's way too placid. There's been nothing placid about this tour.'

'I can see that. Excited, then.'

'I'm not Tess. I'm not a two-year-old with a bowl of ice cream.'

'She's not two, Eliot.'

'Robyn, don't . . . I'm just saying that . . . I don't know. I like it. And I don't want it to stop. But,' he added hurriedly, 'I'm so glad you're both here. We've got a couple of days off now. We're going to have some fun. We thought we could drive up to Disneyland tomorrow and get some ridiculous band shots. Candy floss all over our faces on the big dipper. Ty lifting Minnie Mouse's skirts. It'll be cool. If we hit the road early tomorrow then we'll have a full day. What is it? What's up?'

'I thought maybe we'd have some time together. Just the three of us.'

'We will, we'll have plenty of time for that. You're here now.' He leant across and kissed her. Then kissed her again, deeply. She felt the fast flick of his tongue, the urgent press of his mouth. 'And I've missed this,' he said.

The hotel was a motel, a two-storey block arranged around a car park, the walkways punctuated with vending machines. Their room was on the ground floor, and when Robyn flipped the blind, the view was of plastic-packed snacks and cans of fizzy drink.

'I thought we had an apartment, or a condo, whatever they call them here.'

'Nope,' said Eliot. 'This is it.'

She sat down on the bed and the mattress pitched her to one side, the springs squealing. Eliot threw himself down beside her, and drew Tess up on to his belly. He threaded his fingers through her hair, curling the ends absent-mindedly, as Tess squirmed to get away. Robyn rolled on to her side, watching them.

'I sold a painting before I left,' she said. 'I'd like to treat us.

What about a beachfront hotel? Or a room with a slightly better view, at least?'

'We can't move now, the whole band's here. Anyway, I love these places, they're so kitsch.'

'But this one's not so much kitsch, just . . . a bit crap. And the room's the size of a shoebox; with the cot we'll barely all fit.'

'We're on a budget,' said Eliot. 'When we've made it, we'll do the whole five-star thing, but for now . . . we're a motel band.'

Robyn rubbed her face with both hands. The flight was lingering in her hair and skin. She thought about a shower, to spritz away the travel, but the jet lag was creeping deeper into her, luring her towards sleep. Outside, a motorbike revved, its sound blasting through their walls. There were more footsteps and a cacophony of passing voices. She wanted to tell Eliot about the painting. Not just the one she'd sold to her dad – his over-generous payment had felt more like a charity donation than an appropriate price tag – but the fact that through her weeks in Cornwall she'd found a new rhythm, and a purpose. She decided she'd talk about it later, when they'd settled back into each other's company. A distance ran between them, unremarked but just discernible. She moved closer to him and slung an arm across his chest. She breathed in his scent, looking for something familiar.

'So when do we get to jump on each other?' she murmured.

There was a thumping at the door and all three started simultaneously.

'The guys,' said Eliot, leaping up, leaving Tess bouncing on the bed in his wake. 'Come in,' he shouted.

They poured into the room, and Robyn scooped up Tess as she got up to greet them. Ty, Pete, Simon, dressed uniformly in black dropped-low jeans, skinny ties, smiling and kissing her, pinching Tess's cheeks. Lee came in last, leaving the door wide open behind her. She wore a purple crêpe dress that fell all the way to the floor. Her arms jangled with bangles as she air kissed Robyn, all perfume and cigarette smoke. She moved to Eliot and kissed him too. She stayed by his side.

'So what did you decide, El, are you coming?' she asked.

'Not tonight,' said Eliot. 'My girls are knackered. I'm thinking we'll just get some pizza and stay in.'

'Okay, your loss. Be ready for nine tomorrow though, yeah?' said Lee. 'Leo's with us now too. He's going to shoot some film. If you change your mind, call me. I've still got a ticket.'

Eliot shook his head and Robyn noted a look pass between them, one that spoke of prior conversations and plans already made.

'Have a good night, guys,' said Eliot as they trooped out. He closed the door behind them, turned to Robyn with a smile.

'So, pizza? Was that a good call?'

'It was. Where are they all going?'

'The Troubadour. Merlin Scott's in town, and Lee's wangled tickets.'

'Don't you love Merlin Scott?'

'I love you guys more.'

He sat down beside her on the bed. She wore shorts, and he ran his finger along her thigh.

'You're looking good. You're tanned. Your hair's even lighter.'

'It's Cornwall.'

'Cornwall suits you.'

'We could have gone with them, you know. If you wanted to.'

'I don't think Tess'd like the Troubadour.'

Eliot had put her in the travel cot and she shook the side, babbling indignantly, impatient with her prison.

'What about that ravishing you mentioned?' he said.

Tess sneezed then, a high-pitched pop, and began to cry, half-heartedly at first, then quite furiously.

'Or pizza and an early night? A bit of horrendous American cable TV?' Eliot shouted above her wail.

'Not exactly rock and roll,' said Robyn.

It was a fitful night. Tess fretted in her cot, a plaintive cough, born of in-flight air conditioning, interrupting her restless sleep. Robyn lay beside Eliot, her eyes pushed open in the dark. Beyond their room the whole of Los Angeles lay glittering – the endless ocean, the climbing hills and tears of canyon, the density of downtown, with low-lying smog and canopies of palms, the luxury, the hovels. The thought was enormous, enticing, but in the dark of the room, as the digits on the alarm clock blinked 3 a.m., her world was shrinking. She lay very still, listening to the sound of her own breath. She couldn't shake the feeling, however indistinct it was, that she was in the wrong place.

She woke to thin slivers of light coming through the still-closed blind. She stretched, and rolled over to find the bed beside her empty. She swung her legs out and peeped into Tess's cot, where she saw the shape of her still-sleeping daughter. She went to the window and pulled the blind open just a little. A line of piercing white light burst in, and she blinked rapidly. The clock said midday. A piece of paper was propped against it.

Morning (afternoon!), sleepyhead. I tried to wake you but you were out for the count, you and Tess both. I let you sleep on, figured you needed it and would thank me

340

later. Plus you didn't seem that keen on Disney – can't say I blame you, maybe it's an idiotic idea anyway. We'll be back around the end of the day, keep out of trouble until then. XXXX

Robyn went back to the window and opened the blind wide. The vending machine and the bonnets of a row of cars glinted in the noonday sun. She heard a snuffle from the cot, and turned to Tess. Her blue eyes were wide open, round as buttons. She regarded Robyn questioningly, and stretched her arms above her head in a peculiarly grown-up way.

'Morning, my baby,' Robyn said. 'Now, what do you want to do today?'

They were reunited later that evening in a Mexican restaurant, a tourist spot just off Sunset Boulevard. They sat at long tables scooping lurid guacamole, while a joyless band of mariachis kept up the music. Tess slept in her buggy, a scarf draped across her. Robyn drank an overly sugared cocktail, one hand on the pushchair, and listened to the others talk. She'd wanted to tell Eliot about the time she and Tess'd had, how they'd taken a bus to Santa Monica and watched surfers turn tricks in the water, but he was too full of the shoot to think of anything else, and she was sunburned and tired and it was taking too much effort to find a way to dodge into the band's rampant conversation.

Lee had already had the best shots printed off. They passed them around the table, wiping greasy fingers on napkins, chinking beers at every juncture. Robyn looked too, and she held on to one photograph longer than the rest. It was of Eliot and Lee sitting in a giant spinning teacup, a childish ride, made of garishly coloured plastic. They were clutching one another,

Eliot falling sideways, Lee tumbling into him. They were both laughing at the camera, and had their faces pushed together in an expression of glee. Robyn smiled, just as all the others smiled, and passed it along.

That night in bed, long after Tess was asleep, she curled into Eliot, her hands working down his body, slipping into his shorts. He murmured and rolled over, met her lips with his.

'I suddenly feel like a shower,' Robyn whispered.

'What, now?'

'I *mean* . . . do you want to join me?'

'Let's just stay here,' he said, moving on top of her, pushing his body close to hers.

'Eliot, we can't, what if Tess wakes up?'

'She won't, she's out cold.'

Robyn slid out from beneath him, slipping away from his kisses. 'We're all stuffed together in the world's smallest room. Come on, I'm showering, you are too.'

Eliot tumbled over on to his back and stayed there. He rubbed his face with both hands.

'We didn't think this through,' he said, 'the logistics of it.'

'So, we just have to be creative.'

'I've spent all day being creative. Now I just want to have sex with my girlfriend.'

'Wow,' said Robyn, 'that's romantic talk.'

She lay on her back beside him, staring at the ceiling. If she stretched, she could reach Tess's cot with her toe.

'What about the bookings in other places? Will they be proper apartments? In Vegas? Phoenix?'

'I don't know.'

'But I'll pay for us, we could get an upgrade, couldn't we? Eliot?'

'I don't want to mess with the schedule.'

'*Lee's* schedule.'

'What's that supposed to mean?'

'Nothing. It's just . . . It doesn't matter.'

'The show's tomorrow,' he said as he rolled over, his voice tight. 'I need to sleep anyway. I'm whacked.'

'Okay,' said Robyn. 'Sure. Me too. It's been a long day.'

The next night, the band played in a giant record store. Robyn stood right at the front, Tess balanced on her hip. *Just look at your daddy*, she whispered, pressing her lips to her tiny shell ear, and Tess did, a faintly startled expression on her face. The Fearless had an energy about them that seemed different to their London gigs, a wilder, sharper edge, but then when Robyn tried to remember the last time she'd seen them play, she realised she couldn't. It must have been before Tess was born. Now she watched Eliot as a stranger might. He was lit brilliantly on stage, and he looked exactly as if he belonged. His fingers danced across his strings, his lips were parted, his face a perfect balance of concentration and abandon.

Robyn felt a tap at her elbow and turned to see Lee. She wore a lanyard, unnecessarily, Robyn thought, and it lay precisely between her breasts.

'If the baby's restless, you don't have to stay for the whole set, you know,' she said. 'There's a coffee shop right outside.'

'We're fine,' said Robyn. 'We're loving it.'

Lee drifted off, and at the end she was first to the stage, falling into step with Eliot, talking rapidly, Eliot nodding and grinning, soaking up her undoubted praise. Robyn slipped to the bathroom, and when she came out, manoeuvring Tess's buggy clumsily, Lee was at the mirrors, applying lipstick. She was humming.

'I recognise that song,' said Robyn.

'My favourite,' Lee said, smacking her newly pink lips together.

'Really? Mine too.' All she had of it was the memory of Eliot's strumming the night before he left, but she'd held on to it all the same. 'Have they been playing it on the tour, then?'

She wished they'd played it that night, a secret nod to her and Tess. *I'm always with you, wherever you travel.* It would have felt like one of their first gigs, just after she'd moved to London, when she used to watch him on stage, drinking him up. *Feel the strength, of my arms around you, rest assured in my warm embrace.*

Lee gave an explosive little laugh, as though the question were a ridiculous one.

'It's an Eliot thing, not a band thing. Plus, it's ancient.'

'He just wrote it,' said Robyn. 'Before he came on tour.'

In the mirror, Lee glanced at her. She looked as if she were about to say something, then changed her mind. She pursed her lips instead, touched the corner of her mouth with her forefinger.

'Anyway, it's an acoustic ballad,' she said lightly. 'It doesn't exactly fit their set.'

Afterwards, the record store's owner wanted to take them for drinks in a basement bar two blocks away. They stood about on the pavement outside, the warm sweep of evening air all about them.

'Go,' Robyn said to Eliot. 'Enjoy it.'

'I feel bad, though,' he said.

'Don't. We're fine. It's way past Tess's bedtime, and probably mine too.'

'But will it have to be like this every night?' he said. 'Going our separate ways?'

Robyn shrugged. 'That's up to you.' She righted herself. 'You're on tour. I'd guessed what that'd be like. Go. Have fun.'

'I didn't think about this part of it,' he said. 'I wanted to share all this with you. I had this picture of us being together and—'

'But it's not like that. I don't think it'll ever be like that.'

'Don't say that,' he said, his tone quick and injured.

'Isn't it true, though? Late nights and small children just don't mix. And your job . . . involves a lot of nights.'

'Is that how you think of it, as a *job*?'

'Well isn't it?' she said, coolly.

'Robyn, it's my life.'

Lee moved in on them, a hand on each of their shoulders. Her voice was high, an uncertain note in it.

'Sorry to break things up, but the boys are getting twitchy, and if we don't get some drinks inside them, they'll combust.'

'I'll get a cab,' said Robyn, ignoring her. She kissed his cheek, briefly. 'Good night.'

'I won't be late,' said Eliot.

'Famous last words,' purred Lee, taking his elbow. Then she seemed to reset herself. She looked at Robyn with something like concern, her mouth downturned. 'Are you sure you know the way back? You'll be okay?'

Robyn threw her arm out and almost instantly a cab pulled in at the kerb. She allowed herself a small smile of satisfaction.

'We'll be fine,' she said.

thirty-six

ROBYN READ OVER THE TOUR SCHEDULE. THEY WERE DUE TO leave Los Angeles the next morning and drive up to Las Vegas. After Vegas came Phoenix, then Austin, then Denver. A line was plotted on a map, heading east, eventually winding up in New York. She traced it with her finger. She chewed her lip. Across the table Eliot was hidden behind his shades, sipping a black coffee gingerly. In the night she'd seen the digits of the alarm clock show 2 a.m., then 3, and 4. She'd woken with Tess's cries at eight o'clock, and Eliot was finally beside her then, his face pushed into the pillow, one arm curled protectively around his head. In sleep he was far away, and instead of waking him, Robyn had slipped out, taking Tess to the coffee shop across the street, soaking in early sunshine and glasses of orange juice. Eliot had found her note and joined them a couple of hours later, sloping down the pavement, his hips rolling like a big cat's, his hair still wet from the shower.

'Morning, ladies,' he'd said, kissing them both. Robyn smiled at him, her eyes hidden by sunglasses too. Over breakfast, she started talking.

'You know, you haven't asked me how Mum is.'

'Yes I have.'

'You haven't. Not once.'

Eliot had a plate of eggs and he pushed them about with his fork. He tossed it down with a clatter.

'I can't eat these,' he said. 'They taste of tequila. Everything tastes of tequila.' He ran his tongue across his teeth.

'I'm not making a big deal of it, I'm just saying.'

'Okay. I'm sorry. I forgot. I guess everything about England feels a very long way away.' He held out his hand and she laid hers in it. 'Robyn, I am sorry, I am. My mind's been pretty one-track out here. But we've been speaking every week. You've talked about your mum on the phone. What else is there to say?'

'I guess not much.' She waited, then said, 'Are you looking forward to being back in London?'

'That's not for a month. That's a lifetime away.'

'But are you looking forward to it?'

Eliot pushed his plate away and took out a pack of cigarettes. He turned them in his hand.

'Yeah. Sure. It's home. And we've a record to make.'

'Sometimes,' she said, 'I can't really imagine being back there.'

He patted his pockets for a lighter. Robyn held her coffee with both hands. Beside her, Tess laughed and blew down her straw, spurting juice.

'It's been a gradual feeling,' she said. 'It's not like it's come on suddenly. It's been a combination of different things, not least my mum.'

'It's claustrophobia, that's all. You've been cooped up at home with your folks and a baby, and . . . No, wait, I mean the other one, what's the word, when you're afraid of open spaces, freedom . . .'

'It's pretty much the opposite of that.'

'I don't follow.'

'I've been thinking about what I'm going to do, about getting a job, about whether Tess will have to go in a nursery, or . . .'

'She'll have to at some point.'

'Why? It doesn't have to be like that.'

'Then don't. Be a stay-at-home mum, if that's what you really want.'

'What I want is to do something for myself too. I look at you out here, all of you, and you've got such purpose. Even Lee.' She glanced at him quickly, but with his shades on, his look was impossible to read. 'You're doing what you really love,' she said, 'and that's pretty amazing to see.'

'You'll work out what that is for you. You know you will,' he said airily.

'That's the thing. I think I already have. I want to paint.'

'Paint?'

'I want to give it a proper shot. Just like you've done. I want to work really hard at something and see if it can take me somewhere.'

'Robyn, babe, no offence but I've been making music for years. I got my first guitar when I was seven years old. I've only ever wanted to be a musician.'

'So maybe I've come to my dream a little later. But maybe it's always been in me, just waiting for the right moment to come out.' He was looking at her blankly, so she said, 'I just never talked to that many people about it, that's all.'

'I like those seascapes you've been doing, they're pretty good,' edged Eliot, 'but . . .'

'They've got better, Eliot, they really have. Just these last two months in Merrin, I've been working differently. I've been outside, painting from life, and for the first time I've got a proper feel for what I want to do. I'm not just looking, I'm *seeing*. In fact—'

'So what are you thinking?' said Eliot, his brow furrowed, his tone still sceptical. 'Art school? St Martin's or somewhere?'

She glanced at Tess, who was busily chewing the end of her straw, engrossed in the task, a tiny line of indentations marking the plastic. She slowly exhaled.

'I think I just need to do it,' she said. 'To paint, and find my own way. I want fresh air, and I want the sea. I want to soak it all up, and I want Tess to be with me and have those things too. I want her to grow up running wild, somewhere beautiful. I think . . . I guess what I'm trying to say is that I can't imagine doing any of that in London.'

'I can't move.'

'I know that. I'd never ask you to.'

'Then what are you saying?' His voice was raised, his tone jumpy. 'There was a time, not so long ago, when you were desperate to be in London. You loved everything about it. You left Cornwall overnight with me, mad to get away.'

'And then came Tess.'

They both turned to look at their daughter. Robyn felt her eyes burning, and she took off her sunglasses, rubbed them fiercely. Eliot reached out and gently stroked the top of Tess's head. The gesture tore at her heart.

'A lot of things have changed in the last two years. You know they have,' she said quietly, trying to keep the quaver out of her voice. 'Eliot, we got together so quickly. Everything moved so fast.'

'I liked it moving fast,' said Eliot. 'I still do.'

'But that's the thing,' said Robyn. 'I don't think we are moving fast any more. I think we're . . . stuck.'

Eliot shifted in his chair. He pulled at a loose thumbnail. The scratting noise irritated her, made her want to grab his hand away. He shook his head.

'How long have you been feeling like this?' he said.

'How long have you?' said Robyn.

Eliot took off his sunglasses. She was surprised to see that despite his slouch, his impassive face, his eyes were wet with tears.

'Okay. It was tough in the beginning, when Tess first came. But then I thought things got better. Between us, I mean.'

'I think,' said Robyn, 'we just got used to them not being that great.'

He let out a long, slow breath.

'I wanted us to work,' he said, 'so much.'

In the burn of mid-morning sunshine they both sat quite still, as if with one slight move everything would fall apart. Around them in the café all carried on as before: the bored-looking waitress cleared tables, a couple of teenagers sat twined in kisses, an old man in a panama hat mumbled into his coffee cup. Passing cars blasted music. Palm trees cast their shaded shapes. Tess grabbed her straw with both hands and stabbed the air with it, proclaiming joyously, looking from one parent to the other.

'So did I,' said Robyn.

They followed the sound of the sea. Tess sat in the back seat of the hire car, holding on to her own feet, gurgling and laughing obliviously. As soon as they hit the beach road, Robyn drove

350

with the air conditioning off and the windows wound down. Her hair whipped about her face, and her hands were tight on the wheel. She kept her eyes on the road ahead, following its loops and turns, as beside her the ocean spun away, glittering, endless, and full of hope.

Eliot had mentioned Lee only at the last. As they'd parted in the motel car park, he said her name in a strangled voice. That was when she saw it, and knew. Whatever he was feeling, he was smashed into a hundred pieces. Everything she'd noticed about him that first night in Merrin, his glimmer, his sparkle, was, in that moment, shattered and gone.

'Please don't,' she had said. 'There's no need.'

'There is,' said Eliot. 'I didn't want there to be, but . . . there is.'

'I really don't want to know.'

'Nothing's happened exactly,' he said, 'I wouldn't do that to you, but . . .'

As the highway looped past sanded beaches and wound into the blue-topped mountains, she knew this much to be true: Lee had reappeared because, really, she'd never gone away. Some people were like that. They were part of who you were, and it didn't matter if they stayed away for years, or if they were on the other side of the world, sooner or later they always came back, simply because there was nowhere else for them to go. Even if you folded them into your work, or wrote them into a song, thinking that that was enough. She didn't want to know where it was that Lee had bared her heart, or Eliot had caught her by the hands, stared into her eyes and said, *I know, me too.* Perhaps in a way it was just the world righting itself. Lee had hurt him, but then perhaps he'd hurt her too, by moving on, by taking his heartbreak to Robyn and disguising it as something else, perhaps even believing that it was this new and precious other thing. She did trust that Eliot had loved her. And she believed that he meant everything he'd said when they talked about the baby, the sudden, unasked-for, almost lost, then deeply cherished baby. *I would be happy if you found a little space for me in your heart.* Lee was wrong when she'd said the song was ancient, because that suggested it was history, and it wasn't, not even close.

As the road pitched them into Santa Barbara, all red tiles and sprays of palm, she knew she had to stop. She pulled into the car park of an ocean-front hotel and sank her head on to the steering wheel, her hands shaking. She tried to think what she would say to Tess. It didn't matter that she wouldn't fully grasp it, because simply telling Tess anything was like telling herself. She clambered into the back of the car, settling herself beside her daughter. Tess had fallen asleep, her tiny lips just apart, a lock of hair falling across her forehead.

'Oh baby girl,' she murmured. 'I hope one day you understand. I hope you know I'm sorry.'

The hotel on the seafront was too expensive, so they slipped into the back streets, and found a pistachio-coloured motel with candy-pink shutters. Then Robyn took them to the first beach she could find. They wandered along the wharf hand in hand. Tess squatted to inspect a blue bottle top, a scuffed pebble, Robyn letting her meander as slowly as she wanted. They stayed out for hours. When she looked back, night was falling, and as the sun dipped, she saw the startling white facades that lit up the shoreline turn to dusky pink, the sea washed a darker shade of blue. Behind, the hills rolled purple, and innumerable lights clicked on and on and on.

'Bedtime in Santa Barbara,' she said out loud, thinking of all the families tucking up in their houses, the fathers running baths for babies, the mothers clearing dinner plates, the kisses, the stories, the promises that the next day would be just as fine as the last. She picked Tess up and cradled her tightly, then set her on her hip. Her legs dangled, and she pushed a sleepy head into Robyn's neck.

'This is us on our own,' Robyn murmured. 'It's not so bad, is it? We can do this, can't we? You and me?'

She was grateful for her daughter's quick and easy slumber, for her voice, she knew, lacked conviction. Her throat was tight, and she drew deep, shuddering breaths. The view before her blurred, the colours spilling into one another like a watercolour painting.

thirty-seven

PENZANCE STATION. WHISKERY PALM TREES WERE BUFFETED BY unseasonal gusts, and the sky was leaden with the prospect of an August downpour. Robyn's parents were waiting for her on the platform, their hands aloft in greeting as she stepped from the train. Her mum helped with Tess's buggy, her dad shouldered her rucksack, both chatting brightly all the while, but Robyn saw the concern that shaded each of their faces. Neither mentioned Eliot. She'd phoned them from the airport before flying home, and again from the London flat as she'd sat surrounded by the vestiges of an old life: scattered record sleeves on the carpet, a broken-stringed guitar, her soup-splashed apron folded over the back of a chair. She'd spoken clearly, crisply, her voice only faltering when she talked about Tess.

'We're so sorry it had to happen this way,' Marilyn had said, 'but you've no idea how happy we'll be to have you home.'

Her dad had taken the phone then. He said, 'She means that, your mum. And she's exactly right.'

As she'd left the flat, Robyn had turned and glanced back up at the windows, half expecting to see the quick wave of a hand, or her own face looking back; a different version of herself.

They'd spent two weeks driving up and down the California coast, their days made of fierce sunshine and white sand and crescents of watermelon. At Big Sur they'd stopped to watch the passing plunge of a school of dolphins, and Robyn had drawn them afterwards, their cartoon smiles, and given Tess the picture to crumple in her hand. At Point Lobos they'd taken to the trails, seeing the water go from parrot green to true blue, the sides of the cliffs bristling with vivid vegetation: cypress trees and live oak, patchworks of orange monkey-flowers. Sets of perfect peeling waves rolled by again and again, and Robyn had watched with hungry eyes, following the surfers as they loped towards the water, spinning their moves with effortless grace. She filled a sketchpad with colour and light, and Tess went about with a blueberry-stained smile.

She'd called Eliot from a payphone in Carmel, her coins clicking rapidly through, her fingers twining the cable. She'd asked him how the shows were going, and he'd talked quickly, buoyantly, then checked himself abruptly, as if suddenly remembering there were reasons for sadness. Robyn had told him about Tess: the seashells she'd gathered, her newly browned toes, the taste she'd developed for syrup-lashed pancakes.

'And you?' said Eliot. 'How are you?'

A pause. Robyn heard a woman's voice in the background, distinct against the rising sounds of a bar heading towards night.

'I'm okay,' she'd said. 'I'm good.'

And she *was* good. It was only sometimes that she felt a

blast of pain so acute that she'd have to stop mid-step, her hand going to her chest. She didn't know if it was loneliness, or fear, or simple sorrow, but whenever it stole in and took her, she had to fight it off with deep, gasping breaths, or a fierce embrace of her daughter, or a wash of plain old tears into the cup of her hand.

Back in her room at White Sands, Robyn found the letter. Her mum had placed it on her bedside table, beside a bouquet of heavy-headed peonies, and the two together felt like *Welcome Home*. She'd thought of Jago in California. It was right at the end of their trip and they were in Santa Cruz. Amongst the boardwalk's fairground attractions they'd found an old-style carousel, with its fleet of perfectly carved wooden horses. Every one was prancing, caught in postures of movement and speed. Tess had strained at Robyn's hand, her own wooden horse thousands of miles away, beside a cot in a flat that she'd no longer sleep in. The two of them had stood and watched the horses flying by, each enraptured by what they saw. And Robyn's mind had begun to turn in an old, familiar direction.

She sat down on the very edge of her bed, and tore open the letter.

Dear Robyn,

I'm here. It's hot and it's dusty and I can't hear the sea at night, but I'm getting used to all of these things. I've been here two months, and it feels like longer. It feels, funnily enough, like home now.

I'm sorry it's taken me this long to write. I guess I've been trying to work out what to say. Maybe you're wondering what I'm going on about, thinking nothing needs to be said because it's all so long ago anyway, but . . . there's something about this place, the big skies, the open country, the fact that it's very, very far away . . . so here I am, eventually finding the words, even if they're not particularly good or clever ones. Sorry for that.

I know that as you read this (I'm hoping it's been forwarded from White Sands) you'll have left Merrin and be back in London with your family, back in your 'real life'. Just like you said once. Well, perhaps Merrin isn't real life for me any more either. And you know what, I'd never have come to think that way if it wasn't for you leaving, and the whole place suddenly seeming less than it was before. I thought that feeling would fade with time, but it didn't. So, whatever this letter is, most of all it's a thank you, because if it weren't for you, I'd never have come to this corner of America; maybe I wouldn't have crossed the sea at all. It was the place Mum dreamt of, and she feels closer here somehow – I never expected that. And you? Maybe you feel a little bit further away.

I did love you, you know. I never said it, but I always did. I had my chance, several of them probably, and I never took it, and then it was too late. I reckon that means it was never really meant to be. This probably all feels like ancient history to you, but not to me. Because here's the thing: I reckon most people can be easily forgotten. Or if not forgotten, put somewhere until we're ready to take them out again. I've known just two who've refused to stay put, who are always with me, probably because they're . . . not. Mum, and you, Robyn. Don't feel strange about that. I mean it in a good way. The best way, really.

Anyway, don't feel like you need to reply. I just wanted to write the words that have been swimming around my head for a while now. Out here they feel easier to catch. Everything feels easier, really.

Hope your days in Merrin gave you the inspiration to paint. I'll see your name in lights one day, I know it. And I'll tell people that we were friends. That we still are, I hope.

Jago

PS I hope your mum's doing okay. Kiss Tess.

She read it through twice more, lingering on some lines, tracing over them with her finger. The truthfulness was startling, diminished only fractionally by its past tense. She slipped it back into its envelope, and set it neatly on the table, beside the flowers. Then she lay down on her bed, because she knew what would come next. Tess was downstairs. She could hear her dad singing her a nonsense song, the shriek of her easy laughter, and Marilyn's delighted voice rising behind. There was no risk of anyone charging in. Robyn was alone. Robyn was alone, alone, alone.

She screwed her eyes shut, tears already bursting through her lashes. She opened them again, and salt water streamed down her cheeks. This wasn't the usual kind of crying, she knew that much. This was the deluge that had often threatened but had never quite broken. She heard herself gasping, and the sound was so involuntary that for a moment it appeared to come from someone else. She drew breath, as desperate as a struggling swimmer, fighting to stay above the surface, and her chest ached. This time there was nobody to save her. There were no hands reaching from the water, no shape of a body folding itself around her own. All the bravery she'd felt in California, under that too-bright sun, fell quite away. She thought of Eliot, and she thought of Jago, and everything she'd ever felt for either of them grew tangled, and indistinguishable, and just as lost.

thirty-eight

TESS TOOK TO MERRIN. ITS WILDNESS MADE HER STEPS GROW bolder, until she could run along the sand and pelt across the White Sands garden, quick and joyful as a kite. Her hair curled past her ears and tangled in the wind; her round toddler cheeks grew ruddy. She stared into rock pools, entranced, her finger tracing shapes on the surface, once squealing in delight as a crab burst from the surface and scuttled past her toes. She learnt the words *Grandpop* and *Nanny*. *Gull*. *Beachy*. *Surf-surf*. After Eliot returned from the tour, she said *Daddy* into the telephone most weeks. *We live by the sea!* Robyn heard her exclaim to him once. She was too little to follow it with *When will you visit?* Instead she cried sometimes at bedtime, murmuring *Dadadada* into the belly of her rabbit, quickly switching to *Mummy Mummy Mummy* as Robyn bent to enfold her in her arms.

Robyn found her own solace in surfing, and the phosphorescent light of Rockabilly in the early morning. Each time, the cleansing, head-emptying effects of the water lasted her a little longer on the land too. When she burst back in the door, her dad had a pot of tea waiting, and her mum's arms were full of Tess. Still in her wetsuit, her hair tangled and wet, she bent to give her daughter a salty kiss, beginning to feel as though she was, at last, in the right place.

'You and Tess will be staying on, won't you?' her dad said to her one day, catching her arm as she walked through the kitchen. 'I mean, we've presumed it, but it struck me that perhaps we shouldn't have. I realised I never actually asked.'

'Don't be ridiculous, Simon,' said Marilyn, overhearing. 'This is Tess's home.'

Robyn and Simon swapped a look.

'Mum's right,' said Robyn, emphatically. 'This *is* home.'

She found a job at a busy café in Penzance. She served scones and cream to passing visitors, and grew to know the regulars by name and by order. She'd come home with aching calves, fingers that smelt of coffee grains, and a pocket full of small-change tips. Sometimes, in the afternoon lull, as she was polishing cutlery or wiping down tables, she'd stare out of the wide windows and her mind would drift. She'd think of red buses and basement bars, the jump and jive of the city, and Eliot's fast fingers and deep kisses as he rolled in from a gig, breathing words of love and lust. It was a life that already felt like a long time ago, and brief at that, but she'd still find her eyes pooling at such moments, and feel a pull in her chest. She'd drop a fork to the floor with a clatter. The swipe of her cloth would catch a salt-shaker and send it tipping. She always thought of Tess, then. Wanted to hold her closely, feeling the hot press of her small cheek against her own, and say *I'm sorry, I'm sorry it couldn't be done.*

On the café days, her mum watched Tess, and her dad watched her mum, a triangular arrangement that seemed to work for everyone. Tess never started if Marilyn groped for the right word, or cast a troubled look when she switched her stare to somewhere in the middle distance. She would just climb up her grandmother's leg, or present her with a palm full of treasures: crumpled sycamore leaves, or the broken corner of a shell. Often their heads were bent together conspiratorially, whispering and laughing.

More than once Robyn found her dad fallen in on himself, sunken at the kitchen table or staring at the boiled kettle, a teaspoon loose in his hand. She'd give him a fierce hug then throw him a joke, something silly that Tess had said or done, and watch as he turned back into her father. *Thank you*, he'd say. If she'd lost her respect for him once, observing the way he was with her mother restored it: his relentless dedication and boundless patience. Unconditional love was theirs again too.

Ruby visited for a night from London, in a rare break from the grip of city life. They stayed together in a smart hotel on the north coast and drank too many cocktails in the bar. They were having fun, but then Robyn started crying, her lips sticky from her Manhattan, the mascara she hardly ever wore any more streaked across her cheeks.

'I feel weird being out at night and leaving Tess,' she said, her face pushed into her friend's shoulder. 'It feels so, so strange.'

'Is that all?' coaxed Ruby.

Robyn heaved a breath, gulped at her cocktail. 'And I don't want her to grow up and hate me for the choices I've made. I can't bear the thought of her asking me one day why we're not a family any more, and my reasons not seeming like they're good enough.'

'Robyn, Robyn,' Ruby said, regarding her friend with the

kind of fondness that sent tears tipping, 'Tess can't even *talk* properly yet. And by the time she can, by the time it matters, you'll have worked out exactly what to say. And then you'll realise that she knows it all already, because she'd never doubt you. You're an amazing mum. And Eliot will always be her dad. Doesn't he coo down the phone to her all the time? And isn't the door always open for him to see her, whenever he wants? You've taken nothing away, and you've given her so, so much.'

Robyn blew her nose. She kept her face turned away from the line of locals who eyed them from the bar.

'She's the love of my life, Ruby.'

'Yes,' said Ruby, 'yes, she is. But she shouldn't be the only one. And one day she won't be.'

In a moment of impulse, she sent an email to a local artist called Peter Brent. She'd seen his work in St Ives and admired its luminosity, his magician's way with brush and canvas. She received an unexpectedly generous reply, and after the tentative exchange of more mails, and a wild proposal from Robyn that left her chewing her nails as she waited for his response, he agreed to let her spend two days on the north coast with him. He showed her his *plein-air* work spots, an old shack tucked beside a crumpled section of cliff, a white-stone cove at the end of a minuscule valley. She watched him paint, setting her own easel beside his. He worked quickly, almost violently, his strokes capturing the movement of the ever-shifting water, the wheeling gulls and fast-blown ferns. In his hands a picture was anything but static, his landscapes pulsing with a deep energy that she would never have associated with his insular, softly spoken manner. Together they drank tea from a faded thermos and shared flattened ham sandwiches. They scarcely swapped words, the quiet proving companionable enough for both. At first she was tentative in his presence, feeling too much the novice, without training or true craft, and the marks she made were slow and hesitant, her paint already drying before she'd decided on the next stroke.

'Loosen up,' he told her, jiggling his shoulders, turning his wrists, in a burst of animation that made her blurt with laughter. 'Paint what you feel, as well as what you see.'

And so she did, and that was when she realised she'd brought the brave colours of California home with her after all. The purple skies above Santa Barbara, the pink and pistachio and lemon-yellow villas, the turtle-green water and sticky bursts of orange flowers emerging from red rocks – her road-trip palette found its way into the Penwith landscape. She painted a clutch of blue-trunked trees, a slice of mauve where the last of the day's sun hit the water, a powder-pink path winding between chalky rocks. The use of unexpected colour, not dazzling kaleidoscopes, just dashes here and there, made her bolder, and her strokes grew deft. The paint on her brush made her smile, her heart climbing as she swept a line of cadmium yellow across the horizon line, or mixed the perfect shade of violet to track across a sky. She caught Peter Brent watching her approvingly. He told her she was good. He said it in a matter-of-fact, almost off-hand manner, as though he was simply reaffirming a previously uttered sentiment. *Good*. Coming from him, good was great.

When the water at the cove was mirror-like, or a wash of uneven chop, when the skies shone true blue or glowered like gun-metal, she headed to Rockabilly regardless, an easel under her arm. She'd pat down the seagrass and set out her painting board, arrange her tubes of acrylic, her spread of brushes. Knowing her parents were with Tess gave her the licence to take her time, and the hours could be swallowed that way. She worked methodically, but with something of Peter Brent's rapidity, her daughter always somewhere on her mind. She narrowed her eyes and squinted, watching a view just as she'd watch for a wave from her board, waiting for the right moment to sweep her brush and ride out the line. Her paintings were full of commitment, clean and bright and bold. She'd stomp home, her face lit with the satisfaction of work, her daughter hurling herself at her legs as she walked back in the door.

She began by asking if she could display a couple of pictures in the Penzance café. She hung them nervously, apologetically almost, in unobtrusive corner spots. A woman she hadn't seen before came in one quiet afternoon. She wore a scarf the colour of a Californian sunset, and ordered jasmine tea. Robyn noticed her peering at her paintings, her head tipped, eyes narrowed in appraisal. As she settled her bill, she asked after the artist, and Robyn wiped her hands on her apron, smiled a different kind of smile.

'Actually, it's me.'

'Is it? Really? Well I'll tell you one thing. They shouldn't be on the wall in here.'

Her face fell. She'd expected indifference, but never the sting of criticism. She was only glad there were no other customers around to hear. Before she could hunt for a dignified reply, the woman went on.

'Don't get me wrong, this is a perfectly nice café, but your paintings are, frankly, far too good for it. I'm Mary. Mary Dodds. I run the Rock Gallery.' She extended her hand, and

Robyn shook it, her eyes widening. 'Have you got a couple of minutes?'

'Of course, I . . .'

'I see a lot of work – believe you me, there's no shortage of skilled artists out there. Some of it's accomplished, technically impressive even. But occasionally I come across someone whose work has a special quality, a uniqueness, their signature in every mark they make. Now that's what gets me excited.'

Mary turned to look at Robyn's paintings again. She spoke over her shoulder. 'It's also pretty rare to find someone who can handle such vivid colours, such flamboyant brushstrokes, without getting into deep water . . . excuse the pun. It's obvious you've got a strong emotional commitment to your subject matter. You know it intimately, don't you?'

'I fell in love here,' said Robyn, finding her voice at last, 'with the place, I mean, and—'

'People do,' Mary said, turning back to her, her smile knowing. 'It's wild, and it's wonderful, and down here on the right day, it still feels like a secret. But few can truly capture that. You know, galleries along this coast are chock-a-block with striking artwork, but to be honest, a lot of it's superficial. An artist hits on a formula that sells, then off they go, churning out a succession of – with respect – clones. It's almost as if they've made one enormous painting then cut it up into lots of smaller ones. *West Coast Morning Tide* is just like it says on the tin, anywhere on the west coast, any tide, any morning. There's a market for that, of course there is, but it's not for me. But this . . .' she fluttered her fingers in the direction of her pictures, '*this* is genuine. This is for me. Robyn, I don't think you've any idea how good your work really is. And that's where I come in. That's where I'd *like* to come in, if you'll let me.'

She handed her a business card, a bright white oblong with *The Rock Gallery* in clean, unadorned type. Robyn held it lightly, reverently, and, still stunned, agreed to go by after her shift.

The gallery was three streets back from the harbourside, tucked away on a narrow cut-through, which was maybe why she'd missed it when she'd toured the town before.

'No, we're new,' said Mary, draping a light arm around her shoulders as she steered her towards the walls. 'And that's what I'm looking for in my artists too. Newness.'

Inside, the floor was polished boards, the walls stark white. Every picture popped. The price markers were discreet, the sums significant. Mary wanted to know more about Robyn, asking who she'd trained with, how she painted, and if she had many more finished pieces. It was only after she left and was bumping along the lanes back to Merrin, speeding so as to get there for bath time, that Robyn really took in all her words, and what they might mean for her.

As she changed Tess that night, folding her nappy, bending down to kiss her dough-white belly, she whispered, *Baby, something exciting happened today*, but Tess responded with a disconsolate howl, having recently decided that having to get ready for bed was the worst thing in the world. As her daughter screwed up her face with anger, fast tears rolling from her eyes, Robyn took a deep breath and broke into undeterred song.

Eliot telephoned later, when Tess had quietened and gone sweetly to sleep. In their short conversation, she almost told him, then stopped herself.

She put everything in a letter to Jago, and added it to the small pile of all the others she hadn't sent. At the very bottom lay his own, a letter that was definitely finished, full of past tenses and separate futures. She didn't know how to reply to a letter like that, and so she waited for the words to come – her own, or his next ones. She wanted to tell him how happy she was that he'd found his place out there, but a letter that didn't also contain the news of her separation felt like a betrayal; of whom, she wasn't sure. And so she waited. She surfed when she could, she painted with an ever-heightened vigour, she still swirled leaf patterns in frothed coffee in Penzance, and she filled her world with Tess, her mum and her dad. If she ever felt as though her life was moving backwards, all she had to do was look at her daughter, or pick up a brush, and realise that was far from true.

Autumn became winter became the first throes of spring. Marilyn slipped on a patch of ice in the driveway, and came home from the hospital with her wrist encased in a plaster cast. Robyn painted tiny blue flowers on the plaster from top to bottom. *Forget-me-nots?* said her dad, one eyebrow raised. Robyn shrugged. *Stupid*, she said, *I know*. He kissed her on the top of the head, in the very same way that she kissed Tess.

Her paintings were now out of the café corner and into Mary's Rock Gallery. When she sold her first, a study of Rockabilly at first light, she and Mary chinked glasses of champagne, the fizz of triumph tasting sweet on her tongue. *First of many*, Mary said, with a glittering smile, and Robyn felt a rush of affection for this woman who'd believed in her. She sent an email to Peter Brent, thanking him again for those two days, and the difference they'd made. He wrote back, kindly and measured, and Robyn felt that particular ripple of pleasure that came with professional gratitude, of someone believing in your ability. Mary went on to talk about a London friend who was also interested in her work. He had a gallery in Marylebone, and had invited her for a visit.

She took the train from Penzance to Paddington, staring from the window all the way. She'd swapped her sand-scuffed trainers for leather boots that went tip-tap along the pavements. She wore a smart red coat. She met her brother first, and Ben kissed her on both cheeks, not his usual style at all, and said, *I'm so unbelievably proud of you, little sister.* Later, when she shook Marcus Broughton's hand and said her name, *Robyn Swinton*, so clearly, so brightly, she remembered how she was in the café with Mary that first day, and realised how something fundamental had changed again. She liked his gallery very much, and without hesitation he said that he'd love to represent her. She left him having said yes, unequivocally, and she cut through the Marylebone streets walking on air just as on the best days at Rockabilly she still walked on water.

She met Eliot in an old-style café off Piccadilly, where the waiters looked like bell boys, with ragged epaulettes and unpolished buttons. They poured each other tea from steel pots. It was the first time they'd seen each other since Los Angeles. She'd expected a tumult of emotion, had been nervous as she sat awaiting his arrival, smoothing her skirt and fiddling with her necklace, but instead she felt the simple enjoyment that came with meeting an old friend. She said it was good to see him, and he said it back, each meaning exactly what they said, and each about as much.

Before they went their separate ways, Eliot took out his wallet and gave her a cheque.

'It's not a lot,' he said, 'but I want to help. They'll get bigger, I promise.'

'You really don't need to,' she said. 'I'm doing okay.'

'I need to,' he said. 'Please let me.'

She'd brought with her a pack of photographs of Tess, and she gave them to him now. Tess in wellingtons and a yellow raincoat, charging along the headland. Tess with a chocolate-smudged mouth, laughing in a blaze of sweetness. Tess curled asleep on the sofa, her cheeks puffed out, her lips parted in an unconscious smile. The photographs had caught her beautifully, but they didn't carry the scent of her, like just-made fudge, or the feel of her hot, tiny hands gripping your own, or the sound of her laugh, a peal that was so guilelessly joyful it made your heart twang. Beside the real Tess, the pictures felt like nothing, and Robyn wanted to apologise, to say that next time she'd bring her with her. Eliot looked at each one slowly, a smile at his lips.

'Do you think she'll forgive me one day?' he said, looking up suddenly.

'Forgive you? What do you mean?'

'For not being there enough.'

'You can be there as much as you want, you know that.'

'I mean before. When we were still together. I wanted to be, I just . . .' His voice wandered; he scratched the side of his head idly.

'Eliot,' said Robyn, 'you're her dad. There's nothing to forgive.'

She didn't ask about Lee. She didn't need to. He had the air of someone who was exactly where they should be, who'd found the thing they didn't even know they'd been missing.

On a damp April day, when the hedgerows were flecked with harebells and the air hung thick and salty, she was walking with Tess in the lane and they saw Denny.

'We're finally going,' he said.

'What, to America? To visit?'

'To Somerset. An inland village with a duck pond. We've found this two up two down that needs a ton of work but Lucy thinks is as pretty as a picture.'

'You're moving?'

'It's time,' he said.

Robyn shook her head. 'Everything's changing.'

'And you the artist. I heard about your pictures doing so well.'

'It's not much yet,' she said, 'but one day it could be.'

'And we've already been,' said Denny, 'to America. We got back last week.'

Robyn hadn't noticed that Hooper's House had lain quiet. She'd started looking the other way.

'Quite a set-up he's got out there,' he said. 'Course, they work him hard, but he likes it. His hands are more calloused than mine. Got a few bruises from a brush with a bull. Skin burned brown.'

'And he likes it?' asked Robyn.

'He's doing what he's always loved,' said Denny. 'They've got him labouring on the ranch, but he's working the wood too. Fences. Stables. Making some more of those horses like the one he did for Tess. Selling them through some fancy gallery in Santa Fe, by all accounts. It's another world, Robyn.'

She smiled. She wanted him to keep talking. She wanted to hear everything, and then she'd go home and finally write her letter back. She had so much to say to him, and at last she knew how she'd begin.

'I never told him about you,' he said, 'being back here again. Lucy thought we should have, but we didn't.'

Denny laid a hand on her shoulder. His nails were chipped, and round like moons.

'He's had enough time to think about missed chances,' he said. 'And the way we saw it is that he'd have missed his chance to be out there doing what he needed to do. If he knew that you and Tess were on your own . . .'

'I haven't told him either,' she began to say, 'not yet,' but Denny cut in.

'See? That's because you know it too. You're a good friend, Robyn, you always have been. You know more than anyone that at some point you've got to shake off the past. Give yourself a chance for something new. And Jago, how he is out there, everything he's got going for him, well, I've never known him so happy. It's a miracle to see, and long may it last.'

She watched him cross the yard back to Hooper's House. Soon there'd be a *For Sale* sign marking the hedgerow. In a week's time, Tess would turn two. And Jago had never been so happy.

Spring Tide

When high tide is at its highest and low tide is at its lowest. The sun, the moon and the earth are perfectly aligned.

thirty-nine

IT WAS MARILYN WHO SAW THE FIRE FIRST.

'You need to watch this,' she said.

Robyn was working at the sitting room table, her back to the television. She glanced over her shoulder. The screen showed the juddering view from a chopper, a rolling forest whipped with smoke and jumping with flames. It was a fire somewhere far, far away. The cameras swooped in closer, over the tops of haggard pine trees, the bald and ashen stretches of fire-licked land. They were prehistoric scenes, dead and desperate. She heard the words *wildfire, heat wave, devastation*. Her mum leant closer to the television, her hands balled into loose fists. Outside their window a summer rainstorm pooled in the gutters, the sea beyond shifting restlessly; it was a distant cry from burning bush. Robyn turned back to her work.

'That's where he is!' Marilyn cried.

Robyn made a small noise of acknowledgement. It was the best way, she'd found, to let such things wash over her. The week before, Marilyn had stared at Simon and said, *Who are you and why are you in my daughter's house?* Before that, she'd been listening to an afternoon play on the radio, a murder mystery, and she'd said, *This is Denny talking, come and listen.* It had been more than three years since her mum's diagnosis, and her deterioration hadn't been as rapid as Robyn had feared. Sometimes she wondered if perhaps they might all just carry on, years rolling by, Marilyn washing in and out on erratic tides of absentness but well in herself, often happy enough, still finding pleasure in things, certainly. That she'd be able to pick Tess out of not just her primary school photo, but one day her secondary one too. Late night searches on the internet had told her it didn't really work like that, but it didn't stop Robyn hoping. Nothing could stop that.

'Jago's place,' said her mum. 'Robyn, come and look.'

She mixed fresh paint. Splashed it loosely, drew her brush across the page. She was just playing, sketching, which was why she was working inside at her parents' table rather than in her own studio. She'd been back in Merrin for three years now, and had carved out her own life – a treasured workspace for herself, Tess running happy riot in the local pre-school – yet still the mention of his name pulled at something inside of her. He had never come back. And she had never written.

'Hang on a second,' she said, her voice tightening. 'Let me just finish this.'

She blurred two lines of blue with a streak of silver. It was sun on early-morning water. She squinted, eyeing the colours.

Then the moment – the one that happened in certain films, or in cold-waking nightmares, or sometimes to other people but never you – the moment when you realised that one of the many calamities that occurred up and down the world each and every day, reassuring only in their remoteness, their separation from your own life, was, despite being five thousand miles away, closer to home than you ever thought possible. *North of Santa Fe, New Mexico. The High Desert Ranch.*

In her haste to hear, she missed the specific detail, but this much she knew: people were injured and in hospital. Someone had died. Two young stallions were trapped in a ring of fire, and a blazing eagle had fallen from the sky. Robyn knelt in front of the television, but the newscaster had moved on. Now there were images of disgruntled workers, a strike, a politician filling the screen, chewing his words. She struggled up and went over to her laptop. She tapped in the words she was afraid of, and clicked through report after report. A video clip showed a burly bank of smoke, shot from someone's back garden in Santa Fe; an awed voice – a dad whose children were tucked indoors, and who watched wide-eyed from the window – talked about the force of the fire. How they could taste the ash fifty miles away. A low chuckle, said he'd need a beer to clear his mouth, then a sallow sigh. Then finally a local news report, and buried within it, among the names of people and places she didn't know, was this: *Jago Winters, 27, airlifted to hospital in Santa Fe*. There was no picture; no snap showing his curling hair, his wide mouth, the tiny mole on his left ear lobe, his sea-blue eyes so full of stories, only some of which he told. But Robyn saw him just like she always saw him. Perfectly clear, distinctly unreachable.

'Mummy, what's wrong?'

Tess was standing in the doorway. She was balanced on one foot, her head tipped to the side. Robyn held out her arms and Tess went to her, burrowing into her chest. Robyn squeezed her tightly. She smelt of strawberry shampoo, a clean, bright smell; a world away from smoke and ash and wildfire. Robyn cupped her daughter's face in her hands. She was only four years old but an old soul, the kind who exclaimed on windy days, *Oh dear, it's blowy!* or ate a piece of cake with her eyes closed, and said, *It's perfection.* Now her almond eyes were wide, concerned, sensing all of Robyn's fear.

'You should go,' said Marilyn. 'You should go to Jago.'

She turned. Her mum was staring out of the rain-streaked window, a distant sort of pose, but her voice was clear, and definite. As Marilyn spoke, her fingers played with her string of beads, knotting and twisting, knotting and twisting.

'Go, get on a plane, find him, be there for him.'

'I don't think I—'

'Denny probably left a forwarding address, but of course I've lost it. I don't know a telephone number. I doubt your dad does either. There's no other way. You have to go. Robyn?'

She shook her head. 'Mum, I can't just—'

'We don't talk much, not about my illness, and I prefer it that way. But let me just say this. While I still can. All I have is the moment. *This* moment. The past, the past is . . . not altogether reliable . . . which is possibly an understatement, but there you have it. And the future . . . well, I don't know about the future; who really does? But now, this moment, Robyn, this minute, I'm here. I'm all here. Aren't I? And when that's how you have to live, well, you seize it, don't you? You cherish it. A nice cup of tea. A splendid view. My granddaughter laughing because she's . . . because everything's wonderful and funny and delightful and fearless, and . . . I'm so enormously proud because she's like that because of you.'

Robyn stayed as still as she could, as if too sudden a movement would startle her mum back to abstraction. She felt a heat rise behind her eyes, and she pressed her lips together tightly.

'What I'm saying, what I want to tell you, is that I have to live in the present, and, in a different sort of a way, you used to be like that too. And I think you've lost that a little bit. Oh, how you're looking at me! Did I say something wrong? I don't know. Robyn, you've been back with us for . . . now then, how long is it? A long time . . .'

'Three years.'

'Then don't you think it's time?'

'Time for what?'

'To go. To be with him. Your boy. Jago.'

Robyn wove her fingers through Tess's. Her daughter was wide-eyed as she watched them both.

'He saved me once, you know,' Robyn said, her voice not quite steady. She'd set down her paintbrush, but now she picked it up again. She smoothed its bristles, the yellow acrylic marking her fingertips. 'It was just after we first moved here. I was trying to surf and it all went wrong and he was there. He pulled me from the sea. I never told you and Dad about it. I was afraid you'd stop me surfing, but also I wanted to keep it for myself, something that was just me and this boy . . . this boy whose name I didn't even know.'

She stopped talking. Her mum would be gone again soon, she knew. But Marilyn's words, spoken so slowly, so deliberately, as if she were checking each one before she sent it out, shone like beacons in the fog, like fire-bright torches on a black-sea night. Marilyn was already looking past her, her gaze searching the distance. Robyn pressed her hands to her face, smudging her cheeks with paint, trying not to fall apart as she thought of Jago caught in a fire thousands of miles away, and how her mum, in that moment, knew exactly what to say and how to say it.

forty

IN THE ROSE LIGHT OF DAWN THEY LANDED IN ALBUQUERQUE. Throughout the flight Tess had curled in her seat like a kitten, her mouth open as she slept, a bedtime flush across her cheeks. Robyn had ignored the blinking screen of movies, the crumpled magazines, and tray after tray of plastic food. Instead she'd sat with her arm pulled protectively around her daughter, her mind travelling. A zipping slideshow of images had stopped all chance of sleep. She saw herself sitting cross-legged in the sand, behind the jumping flames of a campfire, as he turned a fish on a stick, licking his fingers one by one. She saw him lifting her from the slick back of a runaway horse and kissing the fear from her lips in a way that could have, should have, lasted for ever. She flinched as Tess murmured in her sleep beside her, and Robyn found her fingers and squeezed them. She took a sip of water and closed her eyes again. Perhaps it was a mistake to have come. In the muted confines of the cabin, the sense of urgency she'd felt in Merrin was already dissipating, replaced by a low-lying worry, the simple need of knowing that he was okay. Their lives, hers and Jago's, ran separately. Apart from a few perfect moments when they'd seemed as bound as two people ever could be, their years had stretched in different directions, their absences more defining than their presences. Maybe she had no right to board a plane, to cross the sea and skim the earth and land in his life, but in the moment, spurred on by Marilyn's delicate insistence, it had felt like the only thing to do.

After sixteen hours of travel, she and Tess picked their way down the plane's steps. It was early morning but her forehead already prickled in the heat. She licked her dry lips, imagining the taste of ash on the dead air. Her eyes were saucer-like through lack of sleep.

'Before we hit the road, I need more coffee,' she said as they walked towards the hangar. 'And how about we get you a muffin the size of your head? When in Rome . . .'

'Are we in Rome?'

'No, we're not in Rome, it's just something people say. We're in Albuquerque. Don't ask me how to spell it . . .'

'Mummy, you sound funny.'

Robyn rubbed her face with both hands. She felt sick suddenly. 'I wasn't very clever on the plane. I stayed awake the whole time.'

'But you said we had to sleep.'

'I know I did. You're the smart one, you know that, don't you?'

'Is it bedtime again now, then?'

'I wanted us to drive straight up to the ranch. It's about three hours from here, I think.'

She patted her cheeks with her hands in an attempt to rouse herself. She used to berate Eliot for driving when he was tired, but then again, it was never just fatigue with him. It was always a hangover too, ears buzzing with tinnitus, the night before pervading the morning after. She could remember such things

381

with flattened emotion now, as a fact of his life rather than a jagged piece of her own.

She clapped her hands with resolution. 'Right. Let's pick up the car, get out on the road, then the first diner we find, we'll stop and have a proper rest. Okay?'

'Can I have American fries?'

'You can have American fries. And I'll have a nap.'

They parked their car between two trucks with silver-trimmed cabs and giant wheels. Robyn had rolled the seats back, and the remnants of their meal lay scattered on the dashboard: the paper burger wrappings, ketchup-smeared cartons, limp scatterings of salad. Tess shut her eyes and opened them again.

'I'll keep watch,' she said.

'Keep watch for what? It's safe here, Tess.'

They'd drawn stares as they'd walked into the diner. They'd ordered their food so very Englishly, with clipped vowels and Robyn saying chips instead of fries. The truck drivers hunched at the counter, one with a string-thin beard, another with a stomach bursting through his shirt like a bowling ball, had turned their eyes on them. Tess hadn't reacted. It was Robyn who'd smiled defiantly, gathered their bags of food and taken them back to the hire car.

'I mean the fire,' Tess said. 'In case it gets us too.'

An hour later, an hour of sleep that was interrupted only by the departing roar of one truck and the arriving bellow of a motorcycle, they were on the road again and headed north towards Santa Fe. The pink morning light had turned to vivid blue skies, dotted with powder-puff clouds. On a different day, Robyn would have filled a sketchbook. She fiddled with the radio's dial, skipping through sermons, advertisements, silver-stringed rock. She settled on a country station, hearing the songs of rough-voiced cowboys, their honeyed lyrics. *Rosalind music*, she thought, and even though she'd never known Jago's mum, she felt the connection, saw it as a sign, and gripped the steering wheel a little tighter. She glanced back at her daughter, taking in her whorls of sunlit hair, her vagabond smile. Tess held a rumpled map spread across her knees, one finger pretending to trace their progress. Robyn felt a burst of love, the best and least complicated kind there was. Then she went back to staring at the mountain-marked horizon, foot on the accelerator, as the other kind of love, the knotted, messy kind, burned inside her.

They drew closer, following a road called the Turquoise Trail, Tess expressing disappointment that the road wasn't paved in bird-breast blue. Robyn marvelled at the sun-scorched plains, the spindly undergrowth, the sense of deeply engrained dryness everywhere. It couldn't be further from Merrin, even if the landscape seemed intent on playing tricks on her. The road ahead shimmered with a mirage so believable she felt as though she was driving them headlong into the sea. *Nothing between us and America*, Jago had once said as they sat atop the granite rock, a rare wistful note creeping into his voice. It'd been a scintillating thought at one time, that a place could be so far and yet so near, waves rolling back and forth between two distant points. That was part of why she loved water: for its transience, its ability to reshape and re-form and keep moving, no matter what else.

'Tess, what have I told you about Jago?' she asked, looking at her daughter in the mirror. Tess's nose was pressed to the window, watching this new world slide by.

'Why aren't there any sheep anywhere?'

'There's horses where we're going . . . and they're much more exciting, don't you think?'

'Curly hair, used to live by us, and good at making things out of wood,' she said, counting off on her fingers as she talked.

Their tyres hummed in the dust, country music jangled on the radio, heat burned through the windscreen. Robyn glanced again in the mirror. Tess had folded her hands in her lap. Kicked off her sandals, her bare feet crossed. They were Robyn's feet; she had the same squared-off toes and high arches.

'He held you when you were a tiny baby, you know. He tickled your toes.'

Tess squealed with laughter. 'I hate my toes being tickled.'

'He tried to teach me how to fish once, but I wasn't very good.'

'Did he really save you from the sea? Like you said to Nanny?'

'Yes,' she said. 'I really believe he did.'

The bars of a love song fell into her head then, quietening the radio. Eliot's song. Not hers after all, and yet. At some point in the last years, the song had changed for her. It no longer made her sad, or bitter; instead it felt like comfort, and hope. Sometimes she'd find herself humming it unconsciously. *I'm always with you, wherever you travel.*

'And now we're saving him,' said Tess.

In panicked moments, she'd imagined him with blackened fingertips, loosely wound bandages, a crackling voice. A flat-roofed brownstone hospital, with pickups parked out front, but inside the same sharp scent and unsettling feeling of hospitals all over. She went to the ranch first because she didn't know what else to do. She took the wrong turning off the highway, bumping her way down a gritted track and executing a U-turn in amongst some sun-bleached cacti. Finally she saw the sign, *High Desert*, carved from iron in an embellishment of horses and riders. There were no *Warning – do not enter* notices, no camera crews or soot-swept fields. But the space out front was full of vehicles, seven or eight of them, chrome shining in the afternoon sun. She found a space by the fence, and sat for a moment, the engine ticking over. She climbed out of the car and stretched in the way that people do after long journeys, holding her hands to the sky, standing on her tiptoes. She opened the passenger door and Tess came tumbling out.

'Are we here? Is this it?'

'Yes, baby. I think it probably is.'

They scuffed their way across the red dust yard. Was there the scent of ash? Perhaps the faintest trace, but the wind had died to nothing. She paused, suddenly aware of the far-off hum of voices, and tinkling notes of music. She squinted at the farmhouse. It was built in adobe style, its bald face offering up no clue to what lay behind. A row of animal skulls was mounted on the wall; they were bone-white and startling in the bright light. She saw Tess staring at them, her lips quivering, and took her hand. Together they stepped between wooden columns to find the doorway. She knocked, then stepped back in sudden diffidence, for the sound of it was far more confident than she felt. She waited four beats, five, but no one came. She knocked again. Then she tried the door.

It opened straight into a wide room, full of light and colour but empty of people. Then she saw the horse. It was grazing on the windowsill, toffee-coloured, exquisitely carved, unmistakably Jago. She felt perspiration prick at the palms of her hands, and her heart bumped in her chest. She charged urgently across the room, Tess behind her. On finding another door, she threw it open, and there they all were. Twenty or so people, gathered at the far end of a parched lawn. There was a fluttering plastic gazebo, and the sizzle and scent of a barbecue. A beer keg stood in the shade of a pompom-headed lilac tree.

With the kind of reason known only to small children, Tess chose that moment to burst into sudden, uncharacteristically noisy tears. Robyn scooped her up, murmuring words of comfort. Tess grabbed a fistful of her hair and pulled at it fiercely, while pushing her hot face into her mum's neck. Willing her daughter to quieten, for their entrance to be altogether less conspicuous, Robyn set her against her hip and walked towards the crowd. There was an obvious air of celebration, a stark contrast to anything she'd expected. Her eyes searched the figures on the lawn, no longer sure what she was looking for.

A man stepped forward then, breaking from the throng. He was swinging an empty jug in his hand, and when he looked up and saw them, he dropped it. It fell to the ground with a dull thunk, spilling lime quarters in the grass. He pushed his hand quickly through his hair, then broke into a smile, a smile so broad, so dazzling, and lit with so much incredulity that she gave a shout of laughter at the sight of it. He was, Robyn saw, entirely intact, no sign of any kind of wound. It was only when she moved closer that she realised something was wrong. The traces of his smile still lingered, but she saw then that his eyes were burning with a pain that was so unmistakable, so *pointed*, that instead of any other greeting all she could say was his name. She posed it as a question, as though she wasn't sure if it was really him, or as if something terrible had happened after all.

forty-one

THEY STOOD TOGETHER IN THE KITCHEN, THE EXPANSE OF TILED
floor spinning out between them. Tess was alone at the table,
blowing bubbles into a glass of cola and kicking her legs with
quick-resumed contentment. Robyn watched as Jago filled the
jug with water, breaking cubes of ice and sending them in with
a clatter, a splash. It was a room full of noises, and none of
them speech.

'Please say something,' she said.

He picked up the jug, then set it down again, with a force
that sent liquid spilling all over the counter top.

'Limes,' he said. 'I forgot the limes.'

He looked like the Jago she knew, but there was an agitation
to him that had never been there before. His voice had a taut,
terse edge.

'Jago, please,' she said. 'Talk to me. Because I'm beginning
to feel like all of this was a really bad idea.'

'All of what?' he said, his head snapping upward.

'Me being here.'

He stared at her. Then he shook his head, his curls falling

as they'd always fallen. He pulled his mouth into a sorry smile. Suddenly she wanted to cry. Not loudly and briefly and publicly, as had Tess, but instead to take herself away to an unpeopled corner of this cavernous house, and turn her face to the wall.

'I just can't really believe it,' he said. 'That's all.'

'I know. I probably should have called, or written, or . . . something. I can't believe it's been three years. Not now that I'm here, and you're just the same. You're . . . Oh God, I'm just so relieved you're not hurt. I really thought . . .'

'Jago!'

A young woman appeared in the doorway, singing his name. She wore a rippling satin dress in vivid scarlet, a shade that almost matched her hair.

'Where's that water? My mom's just about dyin' of thirst out there. Oh!' She saw Robyn and stopped. Flashed a brilliant smile. 'Hi. Sorry for bargin' in here. I'm Annie.'

She trod across the floor, light on her bare feet, holding out her hand. Robyn introduced herself, and her name sounded so flat and boyish that she said it again, with a better attempt at brightness.

'From England? No way! I can't believe you came, that's amazing.'

She leant in and hugged her tightly, and Robyn caught a sweet vanilla scent. Annie's cascade of hair tickled her neck. She pulled away, still beaming, as if she were waiting for Robyn to say something.

'I saw the news,' said Robyn. 'And . . . I had to come.'

'Okay, Jay, so you're forgiven for the delay on the water,' laughed Annie. 'You guys go on catching up.' She took the jug and headed for the door, but not before landing his cheek with

388

a fast kiss. An act that was, dismayingly, full of the confidence of unrivalled possession.

In the bathroom, Robyn stood by a sink edged with turquoise tiles, the intricate Navajo patterns swimming before her eyes. She set both taps running, and splashed water across her face. Staring at her pale reflection, she noticed the dark scoops beneath her eyes, the lankness of her hair. She suddenly felt a long way from home. *It's the jet lag*, she reasoned as she crumpled before herself, the jet lag and the shock that he was fine after all, that he didn't need her, and that he wasn't, or so it seemed, even a little bit glad to see her. She buried her face in a soft towel, its smell vaguely familiar, only baulking when she realised it bore the same sweet vanilla scent that lingered on her skin from Annie's vigorous hug. *Annie.* She set the towel back on the rail, and glanced once more in the mirror, practising a smile. But there was no conviction in it, not even a grim amusement at her own naivety, her foolishness in imagining that she could swing back into his life, and find it just as she'd left it.

When she came out, he was waiting for her, loitering in the hall, his hands loose by his sides. She stopped abruptly, her face too slow to adjust. She saw him register her creased brow, her downward mouth, and reddened.

'Sorry. I felt light-headed suddenly. The jet lag . . .'

'Are you all right?'

'Where's Tess?'

'Playing with Slingshot.'

'What?'

Jago waved his hand and gave half a laugh. 'The dog. The dog's called Slingshot. And he's a softie, so no worries. They're in the kitchen. Robyn . . .'

'I'm sorry I never wrote.'

'What?'

'It doesn't mean I wasn't thinking about you. Because I was.'

He coughed, and it was a rattler. The only betrayal, perhaps, of his fight. His hand made a fist and he knocked his chest, and coughed again.

'Tell me about the fire,' she said. Then, 'Please.'

There was a low-benched seat in the hallway, and Robyn sat down. Jago hesitated, then perched on the end, his legs kicked out before him.

'I still can't believe you came,' he said. Then, 'What do you want to know?'

'Whatever you want to tell.'

Running like wildfire. He'd known the phrase, had probably even used it himself, and now he knew its truth. The flames had devoured the landscape, suffocating the sky with billows of grey, the smoke wringing tears from his eyes, settling in his skin. And it had roared, louder than any storming sea. Was it strange that he'd thought of Merrin at that moment? Perhaps not, for fire had once raged there too. The week after Rosalind had died, on an autumn-dry night, Denny had lit a bonfire. The wind had caught hold of the smoke, blowing it out over the black water. Clouds of ash had followed, flying south-westerly, sprinkling the waves with memories of paperback novels, black and white photographs, embroidered scarves and fringed leather boots. Everything that was hers had gone, everything that his dad had grabbed and dragged with whisky-shaking hands, a fit of madness that he'd stand by, defiantly, his regret never uttered, for the loss of objects was nothing, nothing at all, compared to the loss of her life. Jago had stood watching, open-mouthed, his eyes pouring. He'd only stepped in when Denny had taken her guitar by its neck and made to hurl it. He'd entreated his dad to keep it, said it was too beautiful a thing to ruin, that one day he might want to hold it again. The last had never happened, but Jago had kept it hidden in case it one day did. Yes, he knew fire, he knew what it could do, how people could scream their sorrow at its burning heart. The ranch fire had raged and Jago had seen the rearing horses, dancing on fear. He'd run towards them, his own dread not pushing him away but pulling him closer, until the heat jumped all around him, swallowing him up.

'It was a close call,' he said. 'If I shut my eyes now, I can still feel the heat. I can still hear the flames. I thought I was stuck.'

'But you reached the horses?'

'Not all of them.' His ferocious cough came again, swallowing the sad words.

'But you made it. You're okay. And that's . . . that's worth celebrating. That's worth a party. Who are all these people? Your friends out here?'

'Yes.'

'And Annie, she's . . . your girlfriend?'

'Yes.'

'I guess if I'd written, I'd have known these things.'

She offered him a rueful smile, but he didn't return it. He dipped his head, took to studying the palm of his hand, fingering the edges of a callus. He'd always had workman's hands, but now his whole body had a hardened look to it. His shoulders seemed squarer than before. His forearms were taut with muscle, his wrist marked with a tangle of leather bracelets, an uncharacteristically decorative touch. The high desert had thrown three summers of heat and sent his skin a dark honey brown. She saw that for the first time ever the ridges of his cheeks were marked with faint freckles. As she watched him, she felt a sudden flip of desire, a rush of feeling that was startling in its familiarity. Suddenly the gaps between them, the years, the people, the places, fell away. She reached out a hand, and he took it, as if instinctively. He ran his finger across the pale side of her wrist, a touch so brief, so light that later she'd wonder if she'd imagined it. Then he let her go.

'I never expected a reply,' he said, looking at her. 'I wrote because I wanted to. I came out here, and I realised I had some things to say. New things, and, well, old things too. My way of saying goodbye, I guess.'

'Old things,' repeated Robyn. She leant back on the seat, set her head against the cool wall. What a peculiar feeling it was, to know that despite all appearances of being there in the present, to someone else you were firmly in the past. That was the kind of time travel that could split a person, that could leave them cleaved in two. 'It's ridiculous, really,' she said. 'I thought I was being some kind of hero, turning up from nowhere. Doing for you what you did for me. But . . . you're fine.'

'Airlifted. Lucky escape.'

'I don't mean that. I imagined you broken, in a hospital, a long way from home, but . . .' Her voice wandered. 'This is home, isn't it?'

'Near enough.'

'And Annie? You've got an Annie. Tell me about her.'

'When I moved here, she was one of the first people I met.'

'She's not the girl next door, is she?'

'No, she's not.' It was his turn to smile ruefully. 'Robyn, the fire scared her. She's not an impetuous person, not normally, but I guess it jolted her.'

'Sometimes we need that. We need a scare, to remind us how we really feel.'

'A bolt from the blue,' murmured Jago.

'It's so easy to just roll along with someone. With Eliot, it took us being apart for me to know that, actually, we were better that way. Happier.'

He bucked forward in his seat. 'You're not together any more?'

'No.' She hesitated, then said, 'Tess and I live in Merrin now.'

He laughed, a sudden bark, a rip of incredulity running through it. 'You live in *Merrin*?'

'I always loved it, deep down. You know that.' She glanced at him, thrown, suddenly, by the look on his face. 'I went for Mum and Dad – well, for Mum, really,' she said, 'but I ended up staying for me. And for Tess.'

'How long? How long have you been back?'

'About three years.'

'So I left and you . . . stayed. All this time, you've been there.'

'Yes.' She attempted lightness. 'I didn't plan it that way. Far from it.'

'How can I have not known that?'

Robyn let his question hang. There were so many ways to answer, but looking at him now, watching the hurt she'd seen in his eyes when she first appeared blaze again across his face, none of them seemed right.

A motley tennis ball bounced into the corridor, energetically pursued by Tess and the dog, Slingshot. They brought with them the sound of quick feet on tiles, child and animal, and the bubble of Tess's laughter. Robyn spun her head, startled by the intrusion. She stared at her daughter with faint surprise, as though she'd forgotten her presence, or expected her to be tiny and immobile again, the Tess that Jago had last seen.

'I'm sorry,' she began. 'I wanted to tell you . . .'

'Don't.'

He was on his feet, grabbing the ball, holding it aloft as Tess popped on her toes and Slingshot barked. He hurled it through the rooms, and they gave chase, delighted. Quiet returned. Jago stayed standing.

'Why not? Jago, it's why I came.'

'You need to stop talking,' he said. 'Please. Just shut up.'

Anger quickened inside her. 'I come five thousand miles, and you're telling me to shut up?'

'Three years. Three years of you being there and me being here.'

'I know. I'm sorry. But I needed that. *You* needed that. Your dad said you were happy. I wanted you to be happy. *I* wanted to be happy too, and I needed time to get there.'

'Happy? Well, you got that right. This is my engagement party, Robyn. Annie proposed. I said yes. We're getting married.'

She stared at him. He stared back.

'Congratulations?' she said eventually, in a voice as limp and sorry as a punctured balloon.

The rest of the day passed, time rolling on regardless, and Robyn did her best impression of rolling with it. In a determined show of valour, she fell into the party's embraces. It had a wholesome, neighbourhood atmosphere, with paper-cut pennants strung between the trees, meadow flowers drooping in jam jars, children and old people, here and there a dog in the shade. It was not the kind of party for raging or tears; there were no strange currents to ride out, or dark corners to huddle in. She accepted a glass of champagne from a woman who looked like she could be Annie's grandmother, and drank it quickly, the bubbles catching at the back of her throat and making her eyes sting. She was introduced as 'an old friend from back home', and instead of it investing her with a sense of ownership, or history, to Robyn it served only to remind her that she belonged in neither the present time nor place.

She was passed a plate loaded with vibrant salads and extravagantly large cuts of meat, but despite her hollow stomach, the diner stop feeling like hours and hours ago, she couldn't take more than a few small bites. She tried to stay at the fringes of the group, but circles kept breaking and re-forming, and in the end she met everyone: a neighbouring rancher called Erwin, who talked like a silver screen cowboy; a middle-aged woman called something like Kerry, or Cherry, who teetered on a pair of implausibly high heels and kept saying *We're so glad you could make it, sweetie*, as if her presence had been no kind of surprise. A pack of girls, friends of Annie's from high school, with lacquered lips and easy laughs, tried to draw embarrassing stories of Jago's boyhood from her, as though she and Jago were one-time frequenters of paddling pools, or had once lain sprawled in tree houses reading comics. It was dizzying – the desert heat, the bright champagne, the whirl of chatter – and Robyn stayed hidden behind her shades, now and again wiping her brow with the tips of her fingers, trying to get through the next minute, then the next, then the next.

Tess had eventually tired of Slingshot and had fallen in with a pack of other children, charging the length of the lawn and shrieking with glee. Robyn watched her daughter with longing, wishing she was weepy and shy still, so she could weave her fingers through hers, whispering assurances, feeling useful and needed, and possessed of an existence that made sense. Jago seemed to disappear for a time, and even when he was back he came and went, came and went, never staying in one place for very long. Carefully and quietly, she watched him too. She saw the warmth and affection that people had for him, the way they clapped his shoulder, chinked bottles, said words that drew slow smiles from him, a low laugh. She heard him offer names like Pico, and Cassie, and Buck, and they didn't sound foreign on his tongue, but as plain as Simon, or Marilyn, or Lucy might have sounded once. More than once she heard a new lilt in his voice, an unconscious drawl. Kiss an American girl for long enough and maybe that was what happened.

Annie. Her red dress was always at the edges of Robyn's vision, a swish of scarlet. Her laugh exploded high above everybody else's. She heard her call him – *Jay, come over here!* – and she thought how loose and easy it sounded. How untroubled. She knew she had to say congratulations, but when she practised it, alone for a moment as she stooped to replace Tess's discarded shoe, lost in the rambunctious game of chase, the word felt over-long and ostentatious, and as she attempted all of its syllables she felt ripples of discomfort spreading up and down her body. Perhaps *congrats* was better, but it seemed too blithe and off-hand and she knew she couldn't carry it off with the ease it required.

'I'm so happy for you both,' she said eventually, spoken in a rush, catching Annie's elbow as she shot past with a tray of drinks.

'Hey, thank you. Thank you so much. That means a lot, it really does.'

Annie's smile was wide, and it ran all the way to her eyes. The daughter of a rancher, Jago had said; she was born in the saddle, still rode in the cattle drives, jumped cacti out in the desert on a russet mare called Flashdance. And she had a voice like a songbird, playing with a local bluegrass band. That was how they'd met, after a gig in a bar, when he was just arrived and homesick and lonely and wondering if he was crazy after all to cross all that sea. It was Robyn who'd filled in this colour, pressing him for details, for Jago had offered only an outline. And it was Robyn who thought of Rosalind as he talked of Annie and horses and music, and how, perhaps, in this girl he was going to marry, he'd found the shape of her.

Annie offered her a drink from the tray, a sweet lime cocktail in a sugar-tipped glass. Robyn already felt woozy, and a headache was pushing at her temples, but she took one anyway, and drank it thirstily.

'I can't get used to this heat,' she said, between gulps.

'Never lived anywhere else and neither can I.' Then, 'You know, I thought I'd lost him in the fire.'

'I know. He said.'

'He tell you it was me who proposed?'

'He did.'

'Course,' she continued brightly, 'do it like that and you never know if he'd have got there on his own. We never talked about marriage. But we talked about forever, so, I guess, same thing, right?'

'Jago doesn't do anything he doesn't believe in,' said Robyn.

'You two go back a long way?'

'Feels like forever.' She corrected herself. 'Seven years. Something like that. All the big things that have happened to me, he was there for, in one way or another.'

'That's nice, to have a friend like that. You've gotta miss him.'

Robyn raised her glass to her lips but it was already empty. She took a mouthful of half-melted ice, wondering what words she could possibly use in reply.

'Where are you staying tonight?' Annie asked.

'Here.'

At Jago's voice, Robyn turned.

'If you want,' he said.

'Really?' said Robyn. 'Are you sure? Because we can get a hotel, or a motel, I saw some places on the drive up . . .'

'They're dives. Tess'll get bed bugs.'

'Well in that case . . .'

'Coffee like engine oil. If you're even lucky.'

'So we're better off here?'

'Just,' said Jago, with a half-smile.

Beside him, Annie smiled too. Only this time Robyn noticed that it stopped at her lips. Her eyes had turned flat brown, and watchful.

By sunset, the party had wound down. The last neighbours had gone on their way, bumping their pickups down the track, clouds of dust in their wake. They were driving home to places miles away, flat-topped houses dotted across the desert, or tucked against the wooded mountains' rise. Robyn watched as Jago and Annie stood side by side on the veranda's edge, waving off their friends, looking as neat together as a bride and groom atop a wedding cake. She was standing at the window of the room that Jago had given her. When Annie turned to him for a kiss, Robyn stayed watching. She saw the way his arms reached around her shoulders, drawing her close, and how Annie's fire-coloured hair was taken by a lick of breeze and blew about his face.

She hadn't meant to slip away, hadn't meant to be a watcher at windows. She'd gone looking for Tess, and found her slumped in sleep, in the middle of the double bed. Her cheeks were pink from the day's sun, and her still-dusty feet were kicked wide. Looking at her daughter, she'd felt a surge of fatigue, a desire to give up, to stop pretending, and collapse alongside her. Then she'd heard the departing vehicles, the cries and hollers and well wishes, and had been pulled to the window. Now, turning, leaving Jago and Annie to each other's embrace, she submitted. She sank on to the bed, her body curving around the shape that Tess made, exhaustion swallowing her up. As she rode towards sleep, her thoughts were pulled on restless currents. She hadn't said thank you, or good night, or anything else that a house guest might. She hadn't said any of the things she'd meant to say.

When she woke later, her neck stiff, her arm tingling with pins and needles, the room was dark as desert night and the bedspread beneath her cheek was wet through. Beside her, Tess murmured something in her sleep. Then she said it again, a small, anxious voice in the dark.

'Mummy, who was that crying?'

It took Robyn a long moment to realise that the tears had been hers.

forty-two

'WHERE DID YOU GO LAST NIGHT?'

Robyn hesitated in the doorway of the kitchen. At empty dawn she'd woken with a thumping hangover, an ache in her chest, and a desire for instant and unobserved flight. She'd slipped to the car, looking at it longingly, jangling the keys in her pocket, then delved into the boot and pulled out her bag. Back in her room, she'd showered, combed her hair, and pulled on fresh clothes, while Tess sprawled on the bedclothes, watching cartoons on Robyn's phone. A fierce need for coffee had sent her out of their safe quarters to seek it out.

She'd half expected to find Annie marking her territory in the kitchen, sizzling bacon and pancake batter, an old shirt of Jago's loose around her slim frame, but instead there was only him. He was sitting at the table, the pages of a newspaper spread out before him. He lifted his head. His eyes were clear, and sharp, and questioning.

'Last night,' he said again. 'You disappeared.'

'I just crashed out,' said Robyn. 'I didn't mean to. The jet lag, all those cocktails . . .'

She slid into the chair opposite him.

'Where's Annie?'

'Out running.'

Robyn waited for more, but it didn't come. She studied him, taking in his sun-blasted forehead, the fine lines at the edges of his eyes, the pale scar that ran the length of his thumb. She couldn't tell what he thought about Annie running, whether he liked the idea of her long legs crossing the desert, her red hair whipped back in a ponytail, her sharp elbows pumping. She couldn't tell what he thought about anything.

'Coffee?' he asked, with sudden and quick enthusiasm.

'Please,' said Robyn.

He jumped up. Soon the kitchen's quiet was filled with the rustling of filter papers, the tapping of a spoon against the pot, the gurgle and spit of the machine.

'Have you set a date?' she asked.

'What was that?'

'A date. For the wedding. Have you set one?'

He clattered two mugs together. Kicked the door of the fridge shut with the sole of his bare foot.

'No. Not yet.'

Robyn examined a nail, worrying at the loose edge of it. 'How come?' she asked.

'Annie said she's always dreamt of a winter wedding up in Taos. Sleighs and fire pits. Guests on skis. I don't know.'

'Will your dad and Lucy come out?'

'I should think so.' He waited a beat. 'Tell me about Merrin. Tell me what I've missed.'

So she did. She told him how last week her mum had made a cake, one of her once-celebrated sponge cakes, and iced its top with shaving foam. She'd found her in the kitchen, her face flushed with concentration as she created perfect frosted swirls, and how she couldn't find the words to tell her that it was wrong, all wrong. She told him how her pictures were selling, in Cornish galleries and London too, and she was making not just a living but a life from her art; how when she painted, settled in her usual spot at Rockabilly, tumult turned to peace. She told him how she still surfed their cove, it would always be her favourite spot, but she'd taken to going to Sennen now too, to Porthmeor and Godrevy and sometimes even up the coast to Fistral. She told him how Tess went on a bodyboard, just in the shallows, and how she screamed with laughter as spray splashed her face and she was dumped on the beach, and how in her yellow wetsuit with her wet-through curls she looked like a water-winged cherub, a mini surfer girl who she couldn't believe was hers.

'I wanted to give her this life,' said Robyn. 'I wanted her to feel sand between her toes, and grow up knowing the names of all the flowers in the hedgerows. Whenever I worry about how things have turned out, I just think of the look on her face as she charges towards the water, and I know I did the right thing. She's got a pack of friends at the local pre-school, proper little Cornish kids; she's already getting a trace of the accent. She said the other day that she was going to live in a lighthouse and marry a boy called Arthur.'

'I bet your mum and dad love it, having you back.'

'They love being with their granddaughter, that's for sure. It's like I've given them something, you know? They thought I'd wrecked my life at first – they never quite said it, but I knew – and now, well, now Tess is everything to them. To all of us. In fact sometimes it feels like she's the thing that holds us together. She's this bundle of infinite joy, of optimism.' She felt a quick heat rising behind her eyes. She rubbed them fiercely, and forced a laugh. 'Apart from when she's being a crazy four-year-old, of course. Refusing to wear clothes. Crying at everything, at nothing. Pounding into my room at five in the morning, jumping on the bed . . .'

'You're a good mum,' he said gently.

'Me?' She laughed shrilly. 'How could you know? Here I am, dragging Tess halfway across the world, just because . . .'

'Because what?' he said.

She took a deep breath, resisting the temptation to push her fingers in her ears, to equalise, just like she did in the surf when white water crashed over her head.

'Hooper's House,' she said instead, 'I need to tell you about Hooper's House,' because she didn't know how far Annie ran, or how quickly, and if she said any more then she knew she'd cry, and she didn't want to be that person, the crying girl in the kitchen, for Annie to walk in and find.

'What about it? Still packed with grockles? I gave Dad such a ribbing for selling it to a holiday company.'

'Ah. Well, not exactly. Although . . . sort of. You might think so.' She felt shy suddenly, but it was safer territory, so she forged on. 'I want to be close to Mum and Dad, but we do need our own space. I spoke to the guy who owns it now, and amazingly he's happy renting it to me instead.'

She waited for his reaction. When he eventually smiled, some kind of new light flooded in. She smiled back. She wished they could just sit across from one another, smiling back and forth, letting everything else fade into the distance.

'But how can you afford it?' he said. 'Those tourists must be paying top dollar through the summer.'

'Well, my pictures are selling. Which never strikes me as

anything less than amazing. Plus . . . I'm getting it for a good price. The landlord likes my work. I said I'd give him a couple of smaller paintings for his other cottages, and it sealed the deal. You don't mind? If you did, I'd back out, it's not too late.'

'I don't mind,' said Jago, then, 'I like it. Dad and Lucy would like it too.'

'I thought I'd make your workshop into a studio. The light's too good to waste in there. It'll be great. It'll feel . . . permanent.'

'So you're really staying?'

She nodded. Held his eye. He whistled.

'I'd never have seen that coming.'

'Don't you ever miss it?' she said. 'Even the smallest bit?'

'Did you miss it when you were in London?' he shot back.

'Every day. You know I did. I told you.'

'I remember you saying you missed the sea. The freedom. I know you missed the surfing.'

'It was never just those things.'

Jago had always been a still person, with looks that nudged impenetrable, smiles slow if they came at all. Now, beneath his tan, his cheeks bloomed red. He looked like a child who'd just been given something wonderful, then swiftly had it taken away. He raked a hand through curls that'd grown longer, looser. She felt her throat tighten.

'So I was thinking Tess and I would take a road trip,' she said, studying her hands. 'Head on to the old Route 66, see if we can get to California. We've got a flight home in two weeks' time.'

'Two weeks?'

'I had to pick something,' said Robyn. 'I didn't really know.'

'And you're not going to stick around here?'

'I think maybe . . . not.'

Jago spun his coffee cup between his fingers.

'Robyn, what do you want? Why did you come?'

'I told you.'

'No you didn't. Not really.'

'I owed you one. I thought you were hurt, and I wanted to be here for you, your hour, your need . . .'

'And you thought that was *now*?'

His coffee slipped from his grip and spread in a pool across the table. He wiped it with his sleeve, the material of his shirt soaked dark.

'You always do this,' he said. 'You pitch up, do exactly what you want to do, and go again. You don't think about what it means for anyone else.'

His words rushed out, bumping against one another. His drop of reserve was strangely intoxicating. It didn't matter that the words stung, that they didn't even seem true. They were real. They were present.

'I thought you'd be glad to see me,' she said, holding his eye, not caring any more if Annie walked in. 'After the things you wrote.'

'I wrote them a long time ago. And I was writing about a time even before that.'

'Maybe some things don't change as much as we think they do. Maybe they're always there, even if we ignore them for a while, even if other things seem to replace them.'

'I'm happy here,' he said.

'I know you are.'

'I want to carry on being happy here.'

'Jago, you will.'

'Easy for you to say.'

'Actually, it's not.'

They both turned at the click of the door opening. There was the sound of running shoes being kicked off, the pad of feet coming down the hall.

'The problem is, Robyn,' he said, his eyes on fire, his voice low, 'all this time I thought you were living one life, but you weren't. You were living ours. You were living our life, and I didn't even know it.'

Robyn and Tess were gone by lunchtime. Before they left, she walked with Jago to the edge of an ashen landscape, saw the ground falling away to a canyon. *Do you want to see where the fire burned?* Jago had asked, and she'd said, *Yes, yes, I do*, as though a contemplation of the aftermath was all that was left. Annie gave them the space to do that; she'd taken Tess's hand and said she'd show her how to plait a ribbon through a pony's mane. Robyn, twisting with gratitude, and guilt, and envy, had thanked her.

The fire had left a lunar landscape in its wake. They both stared, taking in the destruction. Robyn glanced sideways as Jago gazed ahead, his hands thrust in his pockets. He had an aura of calm as he stood contemplating the place that could have taken his life.

'When the worst happens,' he said, 'maybe some people are spurred on to do the things they've never done before; maybe they take whatever's thrown at them and throw something right back. But that's never been me. After Mum, I just ploughed on. Eyes down. I didn't look beyond Merrin, I didn't want to. And then you came, and I didn't know what to do with that. Everything changed. But I knew you wouldn't stay. I knew that wasn't *you*, even if, for a little while, you thought it was. Even if now . . .' His voice trailed off.

'I wanted it to be, even back then. You were the one who turned me down, if you remember.'

'Self-preservation. I knew you'd have grown bored.'

'We were so young. What did we know about anything?' she said.

'I knew you mattered too much. I knew that you mattered too much for anything less than everything.'

Robyn took a sharp breath. The dead air still carried a hint of smoke, and she felt it catch at the back of her throat.

'And so did you,' she said. 'I wanted to tell you about being back in Merrin, but I had to figure some other things out first. I was suddenly a single mum. I didn't want Tess to lose her dad, but I knew we weren't right together. You've no idea how that felt, making that decision, taking her away from this funny little family we'd made. And then there's Mum, and me so afraid that one day she'll disappear inside herself and never come back again. With all of that, there just . . . wasn't much of me left. And in the middle of it all you wrote and told me that leaving was the best thing you ever did. You seemed so happy. Your dad said so too.'

'I was. I am.'

'Three years sounds like a long time, but it hasn't been, not for me. It's gone in the blink of an eye.'

'And then you travelled five thousand miles. You came here from nowhere.'

'It didn't feel like nowhere. Jago, I didn't want to lose you,' she said suddenly, with a grim laugh. 'That was why I came. I saw the fire, and I realised just how much I didn't want to lose you. I didn't think for a moment that someone else had the same idea. A much better idea, really. Annie . . . she's lovely. She's . . .' Robyn drifted. She dug her nails into the palm of her hand. 'I should have told you before that I was back. It's that simple, isn't it? I did write to you, you know. I just never felt like I was saying the right thing, so I never finished a single letter; all those useless words just stacked up, unsaid and unread. My one consolation was that I knew you were happy.'

Jago scuffed his boots at the ground, their toes gone pale with ash. His hands were sunk all the way to the depths of his pockets.

'This place didn't always feel like home. And then, one day, it did,' he said.

'When you met Annie.'

'You always do that. You believe your own stories, whether you want to or not.'

'Well tell me, then. Tell me how it is. Because when I look at you out here, you seem the picture of contentment. And then . . . you say something, or you give me a look, or you just seem so *angry* with me, and suddenly you don't seem like a man who's got it all. You actually seem like you're missing something.'

Jago looked at her once, twice. His head dipped again, as if in quiet consultation with himself.

'Once, I'd have done anything to have you turn up at my door,' he said.

'Apart from telling me that that was how you felt.'

'I tried that. I came to London. I called you and I told you exactly how I felt about you.'

'When? When did you do that?'

'See? You can't even remember.'

'Not that message you left? When I was just pregnant with Tess, and . . . Wait, you didn't say anything about you and me.'

'I did. But you never once acknowledged it.'

Robyn's face creased with confusion.

'Then the next time I saw you,' he carried on, 'you were telling me you were having a baby.'

'That didn't have to stop you.'

'That's not fair.'

'No, it's not. But . . . it's true.'

'And this is true too: you said you didn't want to lose me, but we lost each other a long time ago, didn't we?' said Jago. 'No fire, no drama, just two people moving in different directions, and now . . .'

'That message you're talking about, Jago, it was cut off. I never heard the end of it. If you told me how you really felt, I've never known it. The bit I heard was just . . . chat. And I thought I was losing Tess. I was barely pregnant, it was such early days, and I thought I was losing her, and then you called and . . .'

'You never heard it?' His mouth dropped, his face turned boyish suddenly, disbelief washing over him. Then he shook his head. 'I didn't know that about Tess. I'm sorry.'

'How could you have?'

'You nearly lost her?'

Robyn nodded. 'But . . . she hung on.'

Jago blinked. Covered his mouth with his hand as he coughed. It was one more thing he hadn't known about her, one more part of her life that he hadn't been there for. It didn't matter that his place on the outside was of his own making, that it was, probably, rightful: it still hurt. He started to walk away. Three, four paces, then he stopped, and turned around. His arms hung limply by his sides, his fingers curling into loose fists. When he spoke, his words came softly, but precisely, as though he was remembering lines that he'd rehearsed.

'It takes a great act of will to love someone when you're getting nothing back. But I think it takes an even greater will to know when to let that same person go.'

Robyn took a breath, and the ashen air tasted like the end of things. Her throat stung as she spoke.

'I think Annie's really terrific.'

'Terrific? That's a word people use just before they add "but",' said Jago.

'Is it? You know, I've never actually said it before. *Terrific.* I guess I don't know what word to use. I guess . . . I don't really know how to talk about you and Annie. And maybe you don't either, not when I'm around. But you don't need to spare my feelings, really you don't.'

Jago had crossed the dirt and was back by her side. His trail of scuffed footsteps remained. She stared at the shape of them, temporarily mesmerised.

'I'm sorry about you and Eliot,' he said, quietly.

'Thanks. That means . . . a lot.'

'How did you know? That it wasn't right?' he asked. She felt the brief fluttering of hope. He rubbed his neck, and she thought of the way his hair brushed against his collar, the skin beneath burned brown from living outside in the glare and the heat. She thought of Annie's lips laying a trail of kisses at his nape, tasting the salt of a day's work. Just as quickly, hope went again. 'Because of a dozen small things, and, in the end, one big one,' she said.

'You never really loved him,' he said, in a voice that told her he wanted to believe it; had, perhaps, believed it all along.

'I did love him.' Then, 'But I loved him because of Tess. And that wasn't enough, not for either of us, not for any of us, actually.'

Jago thought of Robyn's barely rounded stomach as she'd dipped under the waves at Rockabilly. How even then he'd wished that that tiny being, bigger than a grain of sand, smaller than a shell, belonged to him. Was his to care for, to nurture, to break his world apart and then make it right, better than right. If there had been any love at all, however it came, he'd have taken it. For him, it would have been enough. Once.

'You should get back to her,' he said. 'She'll be wondering where you are.'

'Annie too.'

She reached for his hand, and after a moment's hesitation, he gave it to her.

'Before we go – and we are going to go, we've probably stayed too long already – let me just say this. It was Mum who told me I should come. And don't say that she doesn't know her mind, because sometimes, just sometimes, she still does. Jago, she told me to live in the present, and she was right, because memory's slippery, it's not to be trusted: we can turn people into things they're not, or pretend that things have stopped mattering. We can do all that ourselves, or something else can come along, something unexpected and wicked and cruel, and do it for us. I don't want you to be a memory. I don't want my feelings for you to be memories. I want you to be the present. I want you to always be the present. In your letter, the one I'll always wish that I'd answered when I first got it, you told me that you loved me once. Well, the hopeless thing is that I loved you too. And the really hopeless thing is that I still do. I know it's useless, I'm about three years, five thousand miles and one marriage proposal too late, but . . . I just had to tell you that.'

She squeezed his hand, feeling the rough edges of his fingers, the warmth of his palm, the very solidity of him. Then carefully, deliberately, she let him go.

Robyn drove slowly down the track, the windows down, the stifling air unmoving. The engine ticked and chinked, the wheels crunched. In the rear seat Tess sat cradling a horse. It was dark wood, polished until it shone like treacle. Jago had produced it as they stood on the veranda, saying their goodbyes. He'd knelt before Tess and given it to her shyly, and Robyn had had to look away. She knew that when they got home her daughter would place it beside the other he'd made her. Tess was neat like that. She treasured small objects, found wonder in the spaces between.

Robyn tightened her hands on the wheel. They'd parted formally, in the end. A brief embrace, a kiss on each cheek. Their walk home from the fire's ruin had been brisk, the air taut with remnants of conversation, her *I love you*, his shell-shocked silence, then just two words: *I'm sorry*. When it came to leaving there was, it seemed to Robyn, nothing more to say.

Her brief look inside his workshop had told her where she really belonged these days. She'd slipped in there just as she was carrying her bag to the car. It was a cavernous barn, and Jago's space was tucked in one corner of it. There was a workbench, a pair of tattered gloves, his tools hanging neatly. On the wall behind, he'd taped a few pictures. There was a photograph of his mum standing in the garden of Hooper's House, back when its borders were full of sweet peas and snapdragons and sunshine-headed daisies. She had long hair, and longer skirts, and her fingers were caressing the neck of her guitar. Her smile was Jago's. Next to it was Tomatillo, a picture of him at full gallop, his mane streaming as he pelted down the field towards the sea. And her picture. Her pastel-smudged drawing of Rockabilly. She remembered making it, pouring everything she had into it, as she hunched over the kitchen table in Eliot's flat. Jago had made a wall of the things he'd left behind, the people and the places that were quite gone.

She reached into her pocket. She'd kept the Lichtenstein card for seven years. At university she'd pinned it to the wall in her room. In London she'd carried it in the back pages of her diary. Back in Merrin, she'd kept it in her bedroom drawer. She peeled a fragment of tape from the bottom corner of Tomatillo's photograph and stuck the postcard to the wall, beside her sun-faded Rockabilly picture, below the laughing Rosalind. *So long*, she'd murmured. Then, *It's time to go*.

Now she looked in her mirror one last time, and saw Jago standing on his own, his hand raised in farewell. She leant on the horn in bright reply. They rounded the corner, and when she looked again he was, of course, gone.

'How about we see some American sea, Tess?' she said. 'Big waves. The Pacific Ocean. We went before when you were small. It was just you and me then too.'

'Will we be able to see all the way home?'

'Wrong direction,' said Robyn, 'wrong coast. But it'll be an adventure. And when we get home, we'll have lots to tell Nanny and Grandpop about.'

'Will Jago be there?'

'At home?'

'At the American seaside.'

How could she say yes? That every time she caught the scent of salted air, he was there. Every time she looked out on an expanse of blue, saw white-topped cresting waves, he was there. When she curled her toes in damp sand, bent to pluck a shell from the shallows, ran towards the water with her board under her arm, he was always, always there.

'No,' she said. 'Jago lives here now.'

When she glanced back, she saw that Tess had nodded asleep. Her rose lips pouted, she clutched her wooden horse close. She was perfectly at peace. Robyn blinked, stared down the dirt road ahead. It was a long drive to California. It was a long way to the water.

forty-three

FROM THE STUDIO SHE COULD HEAR THE SLAP OF SEA, AND THE
rustling of the wind in the sycamore trees. Outside, the autumn
sky was sheet-metal grey, scudded with ominous clouds.

Hooper's House felt like hers now. Tess's room had been
the first to be readied, followed by her studio. In Denny and
Jago's old workshop she'd cleaned the windows, swept away
the remnants of sawdust from the cracked frames, and all the
light had flooded in. She'd set up her easels, and filled the
shelves with paint pots and glasses stuffed full of brushes. Gone
were the holidaymakers' badminton rackets and inflatable lilos;
it had begun to feel like a place of endeavour again. At the back
of a cupboard she'd found Denny's old paint-smeared radio.
She'd plugged it in, and let it play wherever it'd left off. Country
music, old tales and lost hearts, had drifted across the workshop.
Robyn had mixed paint and splashed it at the canvas, letting
everything wash over her, feeling a sense of purpose, and peace.

Tess was with her grandparents. Yesterday, in a burst of
October sunlight, Marilyn had taken her all the way around
the garden, teaching her the names of plants. Simon had

followed behind, and later, in a voice that creaked with wonder, he said that Marilyn had remembered every single one, and afterwards so had Tess. Like this, days were made of the smallest miracles. Today they were going to a riding stable. Tess had returned from America talking not about Jago, to Robyn's relief, but of horses. Simon had found out where the nearest stables were, and the three of them were paying the ponies a visit, bearing carrot ends and a bag of fallen apples. Robyn had stayed behind. She'd risen early, as she always did, but the waves had been uneven that morning, swilling into the cove without shape or direction, so she'd gone to the studio instead.

She had a solo exhibition to prepare for, her biggest yet. She was showing fifteen pieces, among them a sequence of four giant pictures showing Rockabilly through the seasons. She'd spent the last year working from a space just below the stack. Sun-hatted, jumper-swaddled, rubber-booted, she'd sketched and inked and painted in all weathers, filling sketchbook after sketchbook, each page timed and dated. It had been almost impossible to choose how to depict each season on just one canvas, for Merrin weather turned on a dime, and she wanted to say it all, and show it all. *But that's the beauty of painting*, Peter Brent had said. *You're never done until you want to be. There's always the next picture, and it's the next picture that will always be your best.* That morning, after four hours of stooping over her work, she was ready for a break. She would go in the water after all.

She set her brushes in a glass of white spirit, and made for the door, unbuttoning her painting shirt as she went. She'd paddle out regardless, and ride what there was. Duck under the water and plunge deep towards the bottom. Tess wouldn't be home until three o'clock, and it made her smile to know that when next she saw her she'd be bursting with new stories, her cheeks pink from Nanny and Grandpop's kisses. She crossed the yard in her jeans and vest, and, once inside, undressed quickly in the hallway, before running barefoot, naked, up the stairs to her room. Her bikini was on in moments, her wetsuit after that. She peered in the mirror and saw a fleck of paint on her cheek. She scratched at it with her nail, then gave up. Her skin was still tanned from California, the winds of Merrin adding their own mark. She pounded back down the stairs, Eliot's song at her lips. *I'm always with you.* It felt like hers in that way that all good songs did, now more than ever, against all odds. A song for anybody who'd ever mattered, and who mattered still.

In the porch she grabbed her board, and swung out into the yard. She paused, thinking she heard voices drifting down from White Sands, then carried on, into the field, over the stile and along the path. She brushed through nettles without caring, caught a blackberry bramble with the back of her hand, jumped over a swell of mud. There had been a lot of rain recently, gushing from the hills, running off at the foot of the cliffs. As she arrived at the beach, she kicked off her trainers and darted across the sand. The sea hissed and grumbled in dubious welcome. She splashed into the first waves, laughing at the cold as she always did, planting herself on her board and stroking her way out. It was a bad day for surfing. Movement was uneven, sets spilling into the cove with neither shape nor intent. Robyn bobbed on her board, kicking her legs, watching the sea behind her. Sometimes you could still be surprised, the perfect wave appearing when you least expected it. She waited. Patiently. Hopefully. She gave it fifteen minutes, then rode in on little more than a rolling tide. She jumped off into the shallows and stood with her board, contemplating paddling out again. One more time. One more try. But her hands were pink with cold. Her cheeks smarted with goose pimples. There was nothing good to be had.

She was reluctantly making her way up the beach, dragging her board like a lazy beginner, when she thought she heard her name. She looked up. A clutch of gulls rose from the rocks at the foot of Rockabilly, shrieking complaint. Behind her a bigger wave hit the beach and drew pebbles back with it, rattling over the sand. There was always sound and movement at the sea, a sense of unending rhythm; inland you could believe the world was grinding to a halt, but not here. Everything was changing, all of the time, and it was a gift for a person, that feeling of motion. Sometimes Robyn pictured herself old and alone and living by the sea, and because of the last, she never minded the first two. Tess grown up and moved away, and Robyn angular and wrinkled, blitzing into ice-cold water with her board under her arm. Sun spots on her hands. Eyes ever on the horizon. She wondered if that was how her mum felt, on the days when she was lost in abstraction. So long as she sat at the window of White Sands and watched the water, memory would come washing back, piece by piece, flotsam and jetsam, pebbles on a beach. Nothing stayed still or stuck for long. Such interior travels each of us made. She knew her dad felt this way. He liked to stride along the clifftop, one hand stopping his hat from being snatched by the wind, taking great gulps of salted air as he went. When he returned to the house the sea was still in him, and it kept him moving as he cooked a meal, as he read to Marilyn, as he changed the sheets on their bed. It kept them all moving, and it brought them each back to one another. The tide goes in, the tide goes out. Everything and nothing changes.

As she reached the cliffs, she glanced up again. The gulls were gone, wheeling above the waves now, lifting on the wind, leaving bald rocks in their place. She plunged on to the path, eventually emerging at the bottom of the Winterses' old field. It belonged to a St Just farmer now, a small addition to his already handsome spread. He couldn't know that an old grey horse used to roam there, died there too, on a night when electric guitars screamed at the sky and drumbeats swallowed the sound of a gun. He couldn't know that a boy and a girl had once walked through the meadow grass one late August evening, not yet friends, not quite. It was dotted with sheep now. There was an upturned feed trough and a string of incongruous orange electric fencing.

Returning to Hooper's House, she passed her studio. Unsatisfied with her surf, she was eager to get back to work, to ignore the rain-smeared view from the window and mix her colours. A pink-trunked tree. A purple coast path. Splash an orange cloud clear across the sky. She quickened her step. First a hot shower, next the kettle on, then into her painted world. But she saw the door was ajar, and stopped abruptly. Ordinarily she'd imagine it was her dad, or her mum, or even Tess, slipping cheekily between her easels, waving stolen paintbrushes. But not today. She dropped her board against the fence and walked towards the door, starting as it pushed open and a dog bounded out. He jumped up, planting his paws on her legs, his mouth laughing as it always had. She let her fingers run the lengths of his ears, turning her hand so he could lick the salt from it, but she stayed quiet. She kept walking.

As she stepped inside, she saw him right away. He had his back to her and was looking at one of her paintings. It was a picture she'd finished just last week, and she'd kept it turned out facing the room, its canvas vista appearing like another window in the wall. It was a Merrin view, just as they all were, but this time there were people too, and she hardly ever painted people. There were two versions of the same girl, one bigger, one much smaller, and they held hands as they walked towards the sea. The smaller girl was waving, and in the opposite corner, at the top of a stack of rocks painted brown against the sea, was a man. He was waving back, with both arms, a giant semaphore signal, a jump of triumph. He was tiny in the picture, the three figures all were really, but they seemed to leap from the canvas. Perhaps it was because in that wild spot, where landscape trumped everything with its audacious colours and bold lines, you didn't expect to see the details of the people too. But Robyn had spent the longest on them.

Scout streaked in behind her, his feet skidding on the slate floor. Jago turned at the sound. He didn't even say hello. He simply nodded, as though agreeing with something that she'd just told him, or affirming something he'd already thought.

'What are they saying?' he asked, jerking his thumb towards the picture.

'I don't think they're saying anything.'

'But their mouths are open.'

'They're happy, I guess. You know, no one was supposed to see that painting.'

There could be any number of explanations, she thought. Annie could be waiting in the lane, picking the first blackberries, marvelling at the green tunnels, the wetness of everything, the smell of soil and salt. It could be the briefest visit and then off again, back to flat skies and red dust and coyote calls at night. But he was looking at her differently now. He was running a hand through his hair and turning a smile, and on that grey, rain-lashed day, without any of the lamps on in the studio, he cast a light all of his own. Scout's damp nose pushed at her hand, her hair dripped on the floor, a gust of wind took the door and banged it on its hinges. She stayed quite still.

'They are happy,' he said. 'You're right.'

He'd meant to tell her everything. How after she and Tess had left, he'd gone back to the scene of the fire, as one who's lost something retraces their steps, desperately trying to find it again. How it was there, on the edge of all that destruction, that he realised he was afraid, and that he'd always been afraid, because right from the beginning she'd had his heart, and he'd never felt like that, not ever. And she had gone away, maybe because he hadn't said any of the right things, or maybe just because life was like that, but she went. Then one day she came back, and she was even more amazing than before, because this time there were two of her. And that made everything worse, because he found he loved them both then, and he knew he had no right to feel that way. So it became his turn. He went all the way across the sea, just about as far as he could go, but she followed him, and was everywhere that he was. In the woods, in the desert, in the mountains. And then one day she really was there, standing on the lawn in the heat of the afternoon, holding her daughter in her arms and saying his name. And he was scared all over again. That was why he let her leave, and why he let her think that he was happy without her. Fear.

Back at the site of the fire he'd smelt the ash, closed his eyes, and seen the lick of flames once more. When he'd opened them again, he knew what he had to do. He'd tried to explain it to Annie, that maybe love without fear wasn't really love at all, it was affection, or companionship, and she'd slipped the ring from her finger and held it out to him, with a not-quite-steady hand. With ice in her voice and pools in her eyes, she'd said she deserved more than that, and so did he. That maybe deep down she'd always known he'd go back to where he really belonged. She just didn't know that it was to a girl called Robyn.

He stepped towards her, and she stepped towards him. They were inches, just inches, apart. She could see the faint graze of stubble at his jaw, the ink drops of his pupils. Closer still. Their lips almost, but not quite, touching. Outside the window the sea kept on singing, for somewhere in the world a distant storm was blowing, wave after wave rolling to shore. In Merrin, Robyn and Jago stood poised at the very edge of the shoreline. Then they ran all the way in.

Acknowledgements

Thank you to my agent Rowan Lawton – your boundless enthusiasm, encouragement and all-round nous is loved and appreciated. Thank you to my editor Leah Woodburn, the best accessory to darling killing that any author could wish for. I count my lucky stars to be working with you, and am so grateful for all of your wit and wisdom. Thank you to Vicky Palmer, Amy Perkins, Yeti Lambregts and all the team at Headline; you continue to rock my working world.

Thank you to Kate Haines and Robin Etherington, my truly valued early readers. This is our third novel together, and I owe you both so much for braving first draft stormy waters, time and time again.

Thank you to the Hall family, my mum, dad and sister, for reading the novel before it was really fit for it, and giving me such love and support along the writing road. I hope you find something of our far western adventures, past and present, within these pages. Thank you to the Etheringtons for all your kind words and book championing.

Thank you to Gary Egerton, my most rad surf consultant, for checking that I wasn't hanging five when it should have been ten, and for sharing your love of the sea with me. Thank you to Jeff and Mary Dodds who gave so generously in the

CLIC Sargent Get In Character Auction – I was thrilled to name the proprietor of the Rock Gallery after you, Mary.

Thank you to my clever dad, Alwyn Hall, for the use of his music and lyrics with the song *I'm Always With You*. Who'd have thought, back when we were in Mallorca, that the song you were strumming would one day appear in my story. Thank you to Kate Haines, Ed Wallis, and Jim Wallis for creating such a beautiful version of my dad's song, and to Gary Egerton and John McLaren for making such a beautiful film to go with it. There's nothing lovelier for a solitary writer than collaborating with friends old and new, and you're each so generous with your talents, thank you, thank you.

On 6 February 2014 Calvin Jack Etherington was born, four and a half weeks early, and exactly ten days before I was due to turn in my first draft. See, my little son – you've ruled the roost from day one. Much of this novel was written while I was carrying you, and we shared Cornish adventures together even then – swimming in September seas on Porthmeor, on wintry retreat at The Old Coastguard in Mousehole – and rewritten once you were here (when I realised my description of childbirth and early weeks of parenthood didn't even touch the sides). I think it's a better book because of you. Calvin, everything is better because of you. If I gave you this book to hold you'd only chew it, but make no mistake, it's yours.

And, finally, thank you to my beloved husband Robin Etherington. It is no exaggeration to say that I couldn't have written it without you – our 50/50 parenting makes me a very happy writer and a very happy wife. You continue to surprise and amaze me, as a husband, a father, a writer, a red-pen-wielding early reader. Thank you, as always, for everything.

The Sea Between Us

Bonus Material

Adventures in the Wild West

The Inspiration of Art

Reading Group Questions

Adventures in the Wild West: The Inspiration of Cornwall

I went to Cornwall for the first time when I was five years old. There was something about Penwith that captured my imagination even as that tiny girl; it was wilder than we were used to, and about as westerly as you could go. We stayed in a farmhouse near Marazion, and certain details stand out gembright in my memory. We ate goose eggs for breakfast, each as big as the noon-day sun. My sister and I ran naked on deserted sandy beaches, the springtime ocean nipping at our heels. We drove to Land's End looking for a sunset, but it rained and rained and we fell asleep in the back seat of the car in our pajamas. In later years I returned to Cornwall several times – exploring the Tate in St Ives with my sister, to a surf festival in Newquay where my husband's band was playing – but it wasn't until I started work on *The Sea Between Us* that I truly fell in love with the Far West, and came to know it well enough to write about it.

Spending time in the locations of my novels is an important part of the process for me. In April 2013, as I was just beginning to feel my way into the story, we stayed for a week in a cottage near St Buryan. It was tucked at the end of a farm track, the perfect hideaway, and an ideal base from which to explore the area. We drove to St Just, the most westerly town in England, then walked through the Cot Valley to a cove with rocks as round and smooth as hens' eggs. We followed the coast path to Lamorna in the mizzle, the cliff-top bursting with daffodils. We wandered the back streets of St Ives, peeping in artists' studios, kicking through the sand on Porthmeor. We bought fish in the harbour town of Newlyn, fat scallops and pale lengths of turbot, and walked all the way along the front to Penzance. We marveled at the Minack and paddled at Porthcurno. Ate crab sandwiches in Mousehole. Ran along the beach at Sennen, watching the surfers as they bobbed and ripped. I came home to Bristol with sea salt in my hair and sand between my toes, and was ready to transport myself to Cornwall all over again – this time from my desk. Throughout the novel's writing I kept going back to Penwith – two family holidays in St Ives, a solo writing retreat in Mousehole – and each time it was harder than ever to leave. *The Sea Between Us* was my only solace. That's the beauty of writing – you inhabit a world of your own making, and it's yours to return to whenever you want. And it's the joy of reading too.

While both Merrin and Rockabilly are fictitious, they're inspired by some very real places. Here are the places behind my settings . . .

Merrin

Even when the idea for my novel was still in its infancy, the place where Robyn and Jago would live was fixed firmly in my mind. Two houses perched side by side on a remote hillside, the sea falling away before them. While Merrin is less than a hamlet, it's born of bigger places like Lamorna and Sennen. Its geography is a microcosm of the Penwith landscape – fields, woodland, steep cliff drops, and over the hill, the moors.

The path to Rockabilly

A footpath that runs through the Boskenna estate, ending up at St Loy Cove (too rocky to be Rockabilly) inspires the path that Robyn takes with her surfboard in the very beginning of the novel. It cuts through a wooded valley, and there's a stream that pelts down to the sea; it's a walk that's lush and creeper-filled and makes the moment when you emerge on to the beach all the more startling – the shining simplicity of the ocean before you, the bright light after the shaded descent.

Rockabilly

Rockabilly is a dream of a hidden cove, but it's inspired by two real places. One is Pedn Vounder in Penwith. Reached by a footpath from Treen, you get to the beach by scaling the cliff, searching for handholds and footholds in the rocks as you go. The beach, when finally jumped down upon, is glorious. It's bigger than Rockabilly, but has the same air of adventure and magic about it. On that blustery, bright spring day we laid the first footprints in the sand, and, despite it being in all the guidebooks, we felt as though we'd discovered Pedn Vounder for ourselves. The other cove that led to Rockabilly isn't in Cornwall at all, but my own patch of Devon. Back in 2009 we were walking the South West Coast Path from Prawle Point. It was a weekday in November and there were few people around, but we came across a young surfer sitting with his board, his feet dangling over the edge of the cliff. We stopped and talked, and we must have said something right because he pointed down, far beyond the rocks, and told us about the strip of beach that appeared at low tide, and how the waves were perfect as they rolled into the tiny cove. It was, he said, his secret spot. A hidden cove, a surfer, a local boy – years later Rockabilly, Robyn and Jago were born of the memory of that moment.

The Inspiration of Art

The Sea Between Us is your second novel to feature art and artists (*The Book of Summers* was the first). Where does the fascination come from?

I grew up in a creative household – my dad is an excellent painter and was an art teacher for all his working life, my mum has always made beautifully intricate patchwork quilts, my sister is a university lecturer in art education, and my husband's family is full of artists too. It's a world I know and love. I used to do a lot of drawing and painting, and for a while – before writing became my focus – I made (and occasionally exhibited, and *very* occasionally sold!) elaborate collages. Sometimes I fantasize about an alternative existence as an artist – when you're occupied entirely by words, there's something quite tantalizing about working in a medium that requires none at all.

433

Cornwall has long held an attraction for artists; why do you think this is?

There's such a strong tradition of art in Cornwall, particularly in the far west where *The Sea Between Us* is set. Artistic communities have flourished from the late nineteenth century all the way up to the present day, and there's so much for art lovers to discover; the painters of The Newlyn School, the landmark buildings of the historic Porthmeor Studios and the Tate in St Ives, plus all the thriving contemporary galleries and art societies up and down the coast. There's a certain magnetism among creative types – they soon find one another – but part of the attraction of Cornwall is also, I think, its remoteness, the sense of being at the ends of the earth, the drama of the ever-changing landscape, the force of nature, and everywhere the *light*. The same stretch of sea can look completely different from minute to minute, let alone day to day, making it an intoxicating subject for a painter. In *The Sea Between Us* Robyn is, eventually, drawn to landscape painting, and in this sense there's definitely an element of wish fulfillment on my behalf – I'd love to spend my days trying to paint the sea.

Were there any particular artists or paintings that inspired you while writing the novel?

The celebrated Penwith-based artist Kurt Jackson is one of my favourite painters – when it comes to seascapes, he's a magician. I have several of his books and often used his pictures as reference points when I was back at my desk in Bristol, away from the sea, but still wanting to feel all of its energy. When I describe the kind of work that Robyn does, I was inspired by

David Hockney, particularly his Yorkshire landscapes. He uses colour to such striking effect, and I liked the synchronicity of the California influence on Robyn's art too.

Your writing has been described as 'artistic' (by American review site, Book Reporter) – would you agree?

For me, it's the perfect compliment. I'm drawn to lyrical, descriptive writing, as a reader as well as a writer. And I certainly find it easier to create a picture using words, rather than a brush. With paint, there's no delete button!

Reading Group
Questions

What effect did the drama of the novel's prologue have on your subsequent reading of the book?

When we first encounter Merrin, Robyn finds it a bleak and lonely place. How does her view change throughout the course of the novel?

Robyn is often the more proactive of she and Jago. Did you find this approach to life and relationships refreshing or frustrating?

How did you feel about Jago as a 'watcher'? How did you feel his character grew and developed over the course of the novel?

Did you anticipate Robyn's 'unexpected adventure' in the story? Do you think it draws her further apart or ultimately closer to Jago?

Cornwall is a setting that holds great allure for writers and artists. What do you think it is about the place that is so inspiring?

How did you feel motherhood influenced Robyn as a character?

How do parental relationships impact the novel?

How did you feel the contrasting locations of Cornwall, London and America influenced your reading of the novel?

What do you feel is the importance of the characters' creative pursuits in the novel; to what extent do you feel they influence their futures?

Did you anticipate the ending? What do you imagine will happen once Robyn and Jago have 'run all the way in'?

The Book of Summers

EMYLIA HALL

Beth Lowe has been sent a parcel.

Inside is a letter informing her that Marika, her long-estranged mother, has died. There is also a scrapbook Beth has never seen before. Entitled The Book of Summers, it's stuffed with photographs and mementos compiled by her mother to record the seven glorious childhood summers Beth spent in rural Hungary. It was a time when she trod the tightrope between separated parents and two very different countries. And it was a time that came to the most brutal of ends the year Beth turned sixteen.

Since then, Beth hasn't allowed herself to think about those years of her childhood. But the arrival of The Book of Summers brings the past tumbling back into the present; as vivid, painful and vital as ever.

978 0 7553 9085 4

headline
review

A Heart Bent Out of Shape

EMYLIA HALL

Life for Hadley has so far been uneventful, with no great love affairs, no searing losses. But then she decides to spend a year studying in the glittering Swiss city of Lausanne, a place that feels alive with promise. It's here that she has a passionate romance with a man who's out of bounds, and meets Kristina, forming the strongest of friendships. Yet, one night, tragedy strikes unexpectedly, and what was supposed to be a carefree adventure becomes a darker journey of self-discovery.

'A novel that glints with passion' *Marie Claire*

'Highly evocative and a joy to read' *Sunday Express*

978 0 7553 9089 2

headline
review